Praise for #1 bestselling author Lee Child and his Reacher series

"If you're a thriller fan and you're not reading the Reacher series, you're not a thriller fan."
—*Chicago Tribune*

"The indomitable Reacher burns up the pages of every book in Child's series."
—*USA Today*

"If there were such a thing as a writer-magician, Lee Child would be the face above the cloak."
—Associated Press

"Lee Child [is] the current poster-boy of American crime fiction."
—*Los Angeles Times*

"Jack Reacher is a tough guy's tough guy."
—*Santa Monica Mirror*

"Jack Reacher is one of the best thriller characters at work today."
—*Newsweek*

"Reacher is Marlowe's literary descendant, and a 21st-century knight—only tougher."
—Minneapolis *Star-Tribune*

"Child has long been one of the best contemporary thriller writers."
—*The Daily Beast*

"That this Reacher is so effortlessly larger than life is evidence of how intense the overall series has become."

—Janet Maslin, *The New York Times*

"No one kicks butt as entertainingly as Reacher."

—*Kirkus Reviews*

NEVER GO BACK

"Lee Child's bodacious action hero, Jack Reacher, has already tramped through seventeen novels and three e-book singles. But his latest, *Never Go Back,* may be the best desert island reading in the series. It's exceptionally well plotted. And full of wild surprises. And wise about Reacher's peculiar nature. And positively Bunyanesque in its admiring contributions to Reacher lore. . . . A breathless cross-country spree . . . featur[ing] some of the best, wiliest writing Mr. Child has ever done."

—Janet Maslin, *The New York Times*

"The title notwithstanding, you'll definitely want to go back to the Jack Reacher series, which is still conjuring thrills after eighteen novels."

—*Entertainment Weekly*

"For the pure pleasure of uncomplicated, nonstop action, no one touches Reacher."

—*Kirkus Reviews* (starred review)

"Child never, ever slips. He keeps the action cranking better than anyone, but, best of all, he keeps us guessing about Reacher. . . . Brilliant."
—*Booklist* (starred review)

"One of the best [entries] in the series."
—*Publishers Weekly* (starred review)

A WANTED MAN

"A solid addition to the canon . . . Each of his books is meticulously plotted and magically propulsive."
—*The Boston Globe*

"Feverishly thrilling . . . the pure giddy rush we get reading undiluted Reacher, straight from Child's fertile imagination. . . . With Child, you can always count on furious action—and a damned good time."
—*The Miami Herald*

"Seductive writing and irresistible plot twists keep Child's books from feeling like they were written on autopilot, and the latest is subtle and nuanced. Another constant appeal is Reacher's moral code."
—*Newsweek*

THE AFFAIR

"The novel fans have been waiting for."
—*USA Today*

"As usual, plenty of eggs get broken in spectacular style on the way to making a Reacher omelet. Child's mastery of high-octane plotting remains remarkable, as does his ability to inject what, in other hands, might have been cartoon characters with all the sinews that power human beings."

—*Booklist* (starred review)

"He is the best in the business and this only solidifies that truth."

—*RT Book Reviews*

"Exciting and suspenseful, with deceit and cover-ups, violence, and sex, this is another great entry in Child's compelling series. Reacher's many fans can only hope there will be many more. Highly recommended for anyone who likes intelligent, well-written, tense thrillers."

—*Library Journal* (starred review)

WORTH DYING FOR

"At times here, he channels Hemingway, which makes a certain sense, since Reacher is nothing if not a chiseled Hemingway hero without the self-pity. He still channels the tough-guy prose as well as anybody alive. . . . This series is as good as pop fiction gets."

—*The Miami Herald*

NOTHING TO LOSE

"Electrifying . . . utterly addictive . . . dazzles. Not for nothing has the cover art of his recent books depicted a bull's-eye."

—*The New York Times*

"Explosive and nearly impossible to put down."

—*People*, "Sizzling Summer Reads"

"Child's hard-boiled meal ticket shows no signs of drying up anytime soon. Thank goodness."

—*Entertainment Weekly* (A-)

BAD LUCK AND TROUBLE

"Electrifying . . . A top-tier Reacher book."

—Janet Maslin, *The New York Times*

"As always, the action is intense, the pace unrelenting, and the violence unforgiving. Child remains the reigning master at combining breakneck yet brilliantly constructed plotting with characters who continually surprise us with their depth."

—*Booklist* (starred review)

"Perhaps there are action-lit writers more recognizable than Child, but the bet is that none of them will turn in a tighter-plotted, richer-peopled, faster-paced page-turner this year."

—*Kirkus Reviews* (starred review)

THE HARD WAY

"The best thriller writer of the moment."
—*The New York Times*

"Jack Reacher, the tough-minded hero of a series of best-selling noir thrillers, has all the elements that have made this genre so popular among men for decades. He travels the country dispensing his own form of justice, often violently and without remorse. . . . Reacher is doing something surprising: winning the hearts of many women readers."
—*The Wall Street Journal*

ONE SHOT

"Ranks in the first tier . . . Before it's all, vividly, over, one feels confident that Reacher—smart, rootless, and brave—will not only get his man but make him suffer."
—*The New Yorker*

By Lee Child

Lee Child

Dell New York

Never Go Back

A JACK REACHER NOVEL

2014 Dell Mass Market Edition

Copyright © 2013 by Lee Child
Excerpt of *Personal* copyright © 2014 by Lee Child
"High Heat" copyright © 2013 by Lee Child

Published in the United States by Dell, an imprint of
Random House, a division of Random House LLC,
a Penguin Random House Company, New York.

DELL and the HOUSE colophon are registered trademarks
of Random House LLC.

Originally published in hardcover in the United States by
Delacorte Press, an imprint of Random House,
a division of Random House LLC, in 2013.

This book contains an excerpt from the forthcoming book
Personal by Lee Child. This excerpt has been set
for this edition only and may not reflect the final content
of the forthcoming edition.

ISBN 978-0-440-24632-9
eBook ISBN 978-0-440-33937-3

Cover design: Carlos Beltrán
Cover image: Tom Hallman

Printed in the United States of America

www.bantamdell.com

9 8 7 6 5 4 3 2 1

Dell mass market edition: April 2014

For my readers,
with my grateful thanks.

NEVER GO BACK

Chapter 1

Eventually they put Reacher in a car and drove him to a motel a mile away, where the night clerk gave him a room, which had all the features Reacher expected, because he had seen such rooms a thousand times before. There was a raucous through-the-wall heater, which would be too noisy to sleep with, which would save the owner money on electricity. There were low-watt bulbs in all the fixtures, likewise. There was a low-pile carpet that after cleaning would dry in hours, so the room could rent again the same day. Not that the carpet would be cleaned often. It was dark and patterned and ideal for concealing stains. As was the bedspread. No doubt the shower would be weak and strangled, and the towels thin, and the soap small, and the shampoo cheap. The furniture was made of wood, all dark and bruised, and the television set was small and old, and the curtains were gray with grime.

All as expected. Nothing he hadn't seen a thousand times before.

2 | LEE CHILD

But still dismal.

So before even putting the key in his pocket he turned around and went back out to the lot. The air was cold, and a little damp. The middle of the evening, in the middle of winter, in the northeastern corner of Virginia. The lazy Potomac was not far away. Beyond it in the east, D.C.'s glow lit up the clouds. The nation's capital, where all kinds of things were going on.

The car that had let him out was already driving away. Reacher watched its tail lights grow faint in the mist. After a moment they disappeared completely, and the world went quiet and still. Just for a minute. Then another car showed up, brisk and confident, like it knew where it was going. It turned into the lot. It was a plain sedan, dark in color. Almost certainly a government vehicle. It aimed for the motel office, but its headlight beams swung across Reacher's immobile form, and it changed direction, and came straight at him.

Visitors. Purpose unknown, but the news would be either good or bad.

The car stopped parallel with the building, as far in front of Reacher as his room was behind him, leaving him alone in the center of a space the size of a boxing ring. Two men got out of the car. Despite the chill they were dressed in T-shirts, tight and white, above the kind of athletic pants sprinters peel off seconds before a race. Both men looked more than six feet and two hundred pounds. Smaller than Reacher, but not by much. Both were military. That was clear. Reacher could tell by their haircuts. No civilian barber would be as pragmatic or brutal. The market wouldn't allow it.

The guy from the passenger side tracked around the hood and formed up with the driver. The two of them stood there, side by side. Both wore sneakers on their feet, big and white and shapeless. Neither had been in the Middle East recently. No sunburn, no squint lines, no stress and strain in their eyes. Both were young, somewhere south of thirty. Technically Reacher was old enough to be their father. They were NCOs, he thought. Specialists, probably, not sergeants. They didn't look like sergeants. Not wise enough. The opposite, in fact. They had dull, blank faces.

The guy from the passenger side said, "Are you Jack Reacher?"

Reacher said, "Who's asking?"

"We are."

"And who are you?"

"We're your legal advisors."

Which they weren't, obviously. Reacher knew that. Army lawyers don't travel in pairs and breathe through their mouths. They were something else. Bad news, not good. In which case immediate action was always the best bet. Easy enough to mime sudden comprehension and an eager approach and a hand raised in welcome, and easy enough to let the eager approach become unstoppable momentum, and to turn the raised hand into a scything blow, elbow into the left-hand guy's face, hard and downward, followed by a stamp of the right foot, as if killing an imaginary cockroach had been the whole point of the manic exercise, whereupon the bounce off the stamp would set up the same elbow backhand into the right-hand guy's throat, one, two, three, smack, stamp, smack, game over.

Easy enough. And always the safest approach. Reacher's mantra was: *Get your retaliation in first.* Especially when outnumbered two-to-one against guys with youth and energy on their side.

But. He wasn't sure. Not completely. Not yet. And he couldn't afford a mistake of that nature. Not then. Not under the circumstances. He was inhibited. He let the moment pass.

He said, "So what's your legal advice?"

"Conduct unbecoming," the guy said. "You brought the unit into disrepute. A court martial would hurt us all. So you should get the hell out of town, right now. And you should never come back again."

"No one mentioned a court martial."

"Not yet. But they will. So don't stick around for it."

"I'm under orders."

"They couldn't find you before. They won't find you now. The army doesn't use skip tracers. And no skip tracer could find you anyway. Not the way you seem to live."

Reacher said nothing.

The guy said, "So that's our legal advice."

Reacher said, "Noted."

"You need to do more than note it."

"Do I?"

"Because we're offering an incentive."

"What kind?"

"Every night we find you still here, we're going to kick your ass."

"Are you?"

"Starting tonight. So you'll get the right general idea about what to do."

Reacher said, "You ever bought an electrical appliance?"

"What's that got to do with anything?"

"I saw one once, in a store. It had a yellow label on the back. It said if you messed with it you ran the risk of death or serious injury."

"So?"

"Pretend I've got the same kind of label."

"We're not worried about you, old man."

Old man. For no good reason Reacher saw an image of his father in his mind. Somewhere sunny. Okinawa, possibly. Stan Reacher, born in Laconia, New Hampshire, a Marine captain serving in Japan, with a wife and two teenage sons. Reacher and his brother had called him *the old man,* and he had seemed old, even though at that point he must have been ten years younger than Reacher was that night.

"Turn around," Reacher said. "Go back wherever you came from. You're in over your heads."

"Not how we see it."

"I used to do this for a living," Reacher said. "But you know that, right?"

No response.

"I know all the moves," Reacher said. "I invented some of them."

No reply.

Reacher still had his key in his hand. Rule of thumb: don't attack a guy who just came through a door that locks. A bunch is better, but even a single key makes a pretty good weapon. Socket the head against the palm, poke the shaft out between the index and middle fingers, and you've got a fairly decent knuckle-duster.

But. They were just dumb kids. No need to get all bent out of shape. No need for torn flesh and broken bones.

Reacher put his key in his pocket.

Their sneakers meant they had no plans to kick him. No one kicks things with soft white athletic shoes. No point. Unless they were aiming to deliver blows with their feet merely for the points value alone. Like one of those martial arts fetishes with a name like something off a Chinese food menu. Tae Kwon Do, and so on. All very well at the Olympic Games, but hopeless on the street. Lifting your leg like a dog at a hydrant was just begging to get beat. Begging to get tipped over and kicked into unconsciousness.

Did these guys even know that? Were they looking at his own feet? Reacher was wearing a pair of heavy boots. Comfortable, and durable. He had bought them in South Dakota. He planned to keep on wearing them all winter long.

He said, "I'm going inside now."

No response.

He said, "Goodnight."

No response.

Reacher half turned and half stepped back, toward his door, a fluid quarter circle, shoulders and all, and like he knew they would the two guys moved toward him, faster than he was moving, off-script and involuntary, ready to grab him.

Reacher kept it going long enough to let their momentum establish, and then he whipped back through the reverse quarter circle toward them, by which time he was moving just as fast as they were, two hundred and fifty pounds about to collide head-on with four hundred, and he kept on twisting and threw a long left hook at the left-hand guy. It caught him as designed, hard on the ear, and the guy's head snapped sideways and bounced off his partner's shoulder, by which time Reacher was already throwing a right-hand uppercut under the partner's chin. It hit like a how-to diagram and the guy's head went up and back the same way his buddy's had bounced around, and almost in the same second. Like they were puppets, and the puppeteer had sneezed.

Both of them stayed on their feet. The left-hand guy was wobbling around like a man on a ship, and the right-hand guy was stumbling backward. The left-hand guy was all unstable and up on his heels and his center mass was open and unprotected. Reacher popped a clubbing right into his solar plexus, hard enough to drive the breath out of him, soft enough not to cause lasting neurological damage. The guy folded up and crouched and hugged his knees. Reacher stepped past him and went after the right-hand guy, who saw him coming and swung a feeble right of his own. Reacher clouted it aside with his left forearm and repeated the clubbing right to the solar plexus.

The guy folded in half, just the same.

After that it was easy enough to nudge them around until they were facing in the right direction, and then to use the flat of his boot sole to shove them toward their car, first one, and then the other. They hit head-on, pretty hard, and they went down flat. They left shallow dents in the door panels. They lay there, gasping, still conscious.

A dented car to explain, and headaches in the morning. That was all. Merciful, under the circumstances. Benevolent. Considerate. Soft, even.

Old man.

Old enough to be their father.

By that point Reacher had been in Virginia less than three hours.

Chapter 2

Reacher had finally made it, all the way from the snows of South Dakota. But not quickly. He had gotten hung up in Nebraska, twice, and then onward progress had been just as slow. Missouri had been a long wait and then a silver Ford, driven east by a bony man who talked all the way from Kansas City to Columbia, and who then fell silent. Illinois was a fast black Porsche, which Reacher guessed was stolen, and then it was two men with knives at a rest stop. They had wanted money, and Reacher guessed they were still in the hospital. Indiana was two days going nowhere, and then a dented blue Cadillac, driven slowly by a dignified old gentleman in a bow tie the same blue as his car. Ohio was four days in a small town, and then a red crew-cab Silverado, with a young married couple and their dog, driving all day in search of work. Which in Reacher's opinion was a possibility for two of them. The dog would not find easy employment. It was likely to remain forever on the debit side of the ledger. It was a big useless mutt, pale in color, about four years old, trusting and friendly. And it had hair to spare, even though it was the middle of winter. Reacher ended up covered in a fine golden down.

Then came an illogical loop north and east into Pennsylvania, but it was the only ride Reacher could get. He spent a day near Pittsburgh, and another near York, and then a black guy about twenty years old drove him to Baltimore, Maryland, in a white Buick about thirty years old. Slow progress, overall.

But from Baltimore it was easy. Baltimore sat astride I-95, and D.C. was the next stop south, and the part of Virginia Reacher was aiming for was more or less inside the D.C. bubble, not much farther west of Arlington Cemetery than the White House was east. Reacher made the trip from Baltimore on a bus, and got out in D.C. at the depot behind Union Station, and walked through the city, on K Street to Washington Circle, and then 23rd Street to the Lincoln Memorial, and then over the bridge to the cemetery. There was a bus stop outside the gates. A local service, mostly for the gardeners. Reacher's general destination was a place called Rock Creek, one of many spots in the region with the same name, because there were rocks and creeks everywhere, and settlers had been both isolated from one another and equally descriptive in their naming habits. No doubt back in the days of mud and knee britches and wigs it had been a pretty little colonial village, but later it had become just another crossroads in a hundred square miles of expensive houses and cheap office parks. Reacher watched out the bus window, and noted the familiar sights, and catalogued the new additions, and waited.

His specific destination was a sturdy building put up about sixty years before by the nearby Department of Defense, for some long-forgotten original purpose. About forty years after that the military police had bid on it, in error, as it turned out. Some officer was thinking of a different Rock Creek. But he got the building anyway. It sat empty for a spell, and then it was given to the newly-formed 110th MP Special Unit as its HQ.

It was the closest thing to a home base Reacher had ever had.

The bus let him out two blocks away, on a corner, at the bottom of a long hill he had walked many times. The road coming down toward him was a three-lane, with cracked concrete sidewalks and mature trees in pits. The HQ building was ahead on the left, in a broad lot behind a high stone wall. Only its roof was visible, made of gray slate, with moss growing on its northern hip.

There was a driveway entrance off the three-lane, which came through the high stone wall between two brick pillars, which in Reacher's time had been purely decorative, with no gates hung off them. But gates had been installed since then. They were heavy steel items with steel wheels which ran in radiused tracks butchered into the old blacktop. Security, in theory, but not in practice, because the gates were standing open. Inside them, just beyond the end of their swing, was a sentry hutch, which was also new. It was occupied by a private first class wearing the new Army Combat

Uniform, which Reacher thought looked like pajamas, all patterned and baggy. Late afternoon was turning into early evening, and the light was fading.

Reacher stopped at the sentry hutch and the private gave him an inquiring look and Reacher said, "I'm here to visit with your CO."

The guy said, "You mean Major Turner?"

Reacher said, "How many COs do you have?"

"Just one, sir."

"First name Susan?"

"Yes, sir. That's correct. Major Susan Turner, sir."

"That's the one I want."

"What name shall I give?"

"Reacher."

"What's the nature of your business?"

"Personal."

"Wait one, sir." The guy picked up a phone and called ahead. *A Mr. Reacher to see Major Turner.* The call went on much longer than Reacher expected. At one point the guy covered the mouthpiece with his palm and asked, "Are you the same Reacher that was CO here once? Major Jack Reacher?"

"Yes," Reacher said.

"And you spoke to Major Turner from somewhere in South Dakota?"

"Yes," Reacher said.

The guy repeated the two affirmative answers into the phone, and listened some more. Then he hung up and said, "Sir, please go ahead." He started to give directions, and then he stopped, and said, "I guess you know the way."

"I guess I do," Reacher said. He walked on, and ten

paces later he heard a grinding noise, and he stopped and glanced back.

The gates were closing behind him.

The building ahead of him was classic 1950s DoD architecture. Long and low, two stories, brick, stone, slate, green metal window frames, green tubular handrails at the steps up to the doors. The 1950s had been a golden age for the DoD. Budgets had been immense. Army, Navy, Air Force, Marines, the military had gotten whatever it wanted. And more. There were cars parked in the lot. Some were army sedans, plain and dark and well-used. Some were POVs, personally-owned vehicles, brighter in color but generally older. There was a lone Humvee, dark green and black, huge and menacing next to a small red two-seater. Reacher wondered if the two-seater was Susan Turner's. He figured it could be. On the phone she had sounded like a woman who might drive such a thing.

He went up the short flight of stone steps to the door. Same steps, same door, but repainted since his time. More than once, probably. The army had a lot of paint, and was always happy to use it. Inside the door the place looked more or less the same as it always had. There was a lobby, with a stone staircase to the second floor on the right, and a reception desk on the left. Then the lobby narrowed to a corridor that ran the length of the building, with offices left and right. The office doors were half glazed with reeded glass. The lights were on in the corridor. It was winter, and the building had always been dark.

There was a woman at the reception desk, in the same ACU pajamas as the guy at the gate, but with a sergeant's stripes on the tab in the center of her chest. Like an aiming point, Reacher thought. Up, up, up, fire. He much preferred the old woodland-pattern battledress uniform. The woman was black, and didn't look happy to see him. She was agitated about something.

He said, "Jack Reacher for Major Turner."

The woman stopped and started a couple of times, as if she had plenty she wanted to say, but in the end all she managed was, "You better head on up to her office. You know where it is?"

Reacher nodded. He knew where it was. It had been his office once. He said, "Thank you, sergeant."

He went up the stairs. Same worn stone, same metal handrail. He had been up those stairs a thousand times. They folded around once and came out directly above the center of the lobby at the end of the long second-floor corridor. The lights were on in the corridor. The same linoleum was on the floor. The office doors to the left and right had the same reeded glass as the first-floor doors.

His office was third on the left.

No, Susan Turner's was.

He made sure his shirt was tucked and he brushed his hair with his fingers. He had no idea what he was going to say. He had liked her voice on the phone. That was all. He had sensed an interesting person behind it. He wanted to meet that person. Simple as that. He took two steps and stopped. She was going to think he was crazy.

But, nothing ventured, nothing gained. He shrugged to himself and moved on again. Third on the left. The door was the same as it always had been, but painted. Solid below, glass above, the reeded pattern splitting the dull view through into distorted vertical slices. There was a corporate-style nameplate on the wall near the handle: *Maj. S. R. Turner, Commanding Officer.* That was new. In Reacher's day his name had been stenciled on the wood, below the glass, with even more economy: *Maj. Reacher, CO.*

He knocked.

He heard a vague vocal sound inside. It might have been *Enter.* So he took a breath and opened the door and stepped inside.

He had been expecting changes. But there weren't many. The linoleum on the floor was the same, polished to a subtle sheen and a murky color. The desk was the same, steel like a battleship, painted but worn back to shiny metal here and there, still dented where he had slammed some guy's head into it, back at the end of his command. The chairs were the same, both behind the desk and in front of it, utilitarian midcentury items that might have sold for a lot of money in some hipster store in New York or San Francisco. The file cabinets were the same. The light fixture was the same, a contoured white glass bowl hung off three little chains.

The differences were mostly predictable and driven by the march of time. There were three console telephones on the desk, where before there had been one old rotary-dial item, heavy and black. There were two computers, one a desktop and one a laptop, where before there had been an in-tray and an out-tray and a lot of paper. The map on the wall was new and up to date, and the light fixture was burning green and sickly, with a modern bulb, all fluorescent and energy saving. Progress, even at the Department of the Army.

Only two things in the office were unexpected and unpredictable.

First, the person behind the desk was not a major, but a lieutenant colonel.

And second, he wasn't a woman, but a man.

Chapter 3

The man behind the desk was wearing the same ACU pajamas as everyone else, but they looked worse on him than most. Like fancy dress. Like a Halloween party. Not because he was particularly out of shape, but because he looked serious and managerial and desk-bound. As if his weapon of choice would be a propelling pencil, not an M16. He was wearing steel eyeglasses and had steel-gray hair cut and combed like a schoolboy's. His tapes and his tags confirmed he was indeed a lieutenant colonel in the United States Army, and that his name was Morgan.

Reacher said, "I'm sorry, colonel. I was looking for Major Turner."

The guy named Morgan said, "Sit down, Mr. Reacher."

Command presence was a rare and valuable thing, much prized by the military. And the guy named Morgan had plenty of it. Like his hair and his glasses, his voice was steel. No bullshit, no bluster, no bullying.

Just a brisk assumption that all reasonable men would do exactly what he told them, because there would be no real practical alternative.

Reacher sat down in the visitor chair nearer the window. It had springy bent-tube legs, and it gave and bounced a little under his weight. He remembered the feeling. He had sat in it before, for one reason or another.

Morgan said, "Please tell me exactly why you're here."

And at that point Reacher thought he was about to get a death message. Susan Turner was dead. Afghanistan, possibly. Or a car wreck.

He said, "Where is Major Turner?"

Morgan said, "Not here."

"Where, then?"

"We might get to that. But first I need to understand your interest."

"In what?"

"In Major Turner."

"I have no interest in Major Turner."

"Yet you asked for her by name at the gate."

"It's a personal matter."

"As in?"

Reacher said, "I talked to her on the phone. She sounded interesting. I thought I might drop by and ask her out to dinner. The field manual doesn't prohibit her from saying yes."

"Or no, as the case may be."

"Indeed."

Morgan asked, "What did you talk about on the phone?"

"This and that."

"What exactly?"

"It was a private conversation, colonel. And I don't know who you are."

"I'm commander of the 110th Special Unit."

"Not Major Turner?"

"Not anymore."

"I thought this was a major's job. Not a light colonel's."

"This is a temporary command. I'm a trouble-shooter. I get sent in to clean up the mess."

"And there's a mess here? Is that what you're saying?"

Morgan ignored the question. He asked, "Did you specifically arrange to meet with Major Turner?"

"Not specifically," Reacher said.

"Did she request your presence here?"

"Not specifically," Reacher said again.

"Yes or no?"

"Neither. I think it was just a vague intention on both our parts. If I happened to be in the area. That kind of a thing."

"And yet here you are, in the area. Why?"

"Why not? I have to be somewhere."

"Are you saying you came all the way from South Dakota on the basis of a vague intention?"

Reacher said, "I liked her voice. You got a problem with that?"

"You're unemployed, is that correct?"

"Currently."

"Since when?"

"Since I left the army."

"That's disgraceful."

Reacher asked, "Where is Major Turner?"

Morgan said, "This interview is not about Major Turner."

"Then what's it about?"

"This interview is about you."

"Me?"

"Completely unrelated to Major Turner. But she pulled your file. Perhaps she was curious about you. There was a flag on your file. It should have triggered when she pulled it. Which would have saved us some time. Unfortunately the flag malfunctioned and didn't trigger until she returned it. But better late than never. Because here you are."

"What are you talking about?"

"Did you know a man named Juan Rodriguez?"

"No. Who is he?"

"At one time he was of interest to the 110th. Now he's dead. Do you know a woman named Candice Dayton?"

"No. Is she dead too?"

"Ms. Dayton is still alive, happily. Or not happily, as it turns out. You sure you don't remember her?"

"What's this all about?"

"You're in trouble, Reacher."

"For what?"

"The Secretary of the Army has been given medical evidence showing Mr. Rodriguez died as a direct result of a beating he suffered sixteen years ago. Given there's no statute of limitations in such cases, he was technically a homicide victim."

"You saying one of my people did that? Sixteen years ago?"

"No, that's not what I'm saying."

"That's good. So what's making Ms. Dayton unhappy?"

"That's not my topic. Someone else will talk to you about that."

"They'll have to be quick. I won't be sticking around for long. Not if Major Turner isn't here. I don't remember any other real attractions in the neighborhood."

"You will be sticking around," Morgan said. "You and I are due a long and interesting conversation."

"About what?"

"The evidence shows it was you who beat on Mr. Rodriguez sixteen years ago."

"Bullshit."

"You'll be provided with a lawyer. If it's bullshit, I'm sure he'll say so."

"I mean, bullshit, you and I are not going to have any kind of a long conversation. Or a lawyer. I'm a civilian, and you're an asshole wearing pajamas."

"So you're not offering voluntary cooperation?"

"You got that right."

"In which case, are you familiar with Title 10 of the United States Code?"

Reacher said, "Parts of it, obviously."

"Then you may know that one particular part of it tells us when a man of your rank leaves the army, he doesn't become a civilian. Not immediately, and not entirely. He becomes a reservist. He has no duties, but he remains subject to recall."

"But for how many years?" Reacher said.

"You had a security clearance."

"I remember it well."

"Do you remember the papers you had to sign to get it?"

"Vaguely," Reacher said. He remembered a bunch of guys in a room, all grown up and serious. Lawyers, and notaries, and seals and stamps and pens.

Morgan said, "There was a lot of fine print. Naturally. If you're going to know the government's secrets, the government is going to want some control over you. Before, during, and after."

"How long after?"

"Most of that stuff stays secret for sixty years."

"That's ridiculous."

"Don't worry," Morgan said. "The fine print didn't say you stay a reservist for sixty years."

"That's good."

"It said worse than that. It said indefinitely. But as it happens the Supreme Court already screwed us on that. It mandated we respect the standard three bottom-line restrictions common to all cases in Title 10."

"Which are?"

"To be successfully recalled, you have to be in good health, under the age of fifty-five years, and trainable."

Reacher said nothing.

Morgan asked, "How's your health?"

"Pretty good."

"How old are you?"

"I'm a long way from fifty-five."

"Are you trainable?"

"I doubt it."

"Me too. But that's an empirical determination we make on the job."

"Are you serious?"

"Completely," Morgan said. "Jack Reacher, as of this moment on this day, you are formally recalled to military service."

Reacher said nothing.

"You're back in the army, major," Morgan said. "And your ass is mine."

Chapter 4

There was no big ceremony. No processing-in, or reprocessing. Just Morgan's words, and then the room darkened a little as a guy in the corridor took up station in front of the door and blocked the light coming through the reeded glass panel. Reacher saw him, all sliced up vertically, a tall, broad-shouldered sentry, standing easy, facing away.

Morgan said, "I'm required to tell you there's an appeals procedure. You'll be given full access to it. You'll be given a lawyer."

Reacher said, "I'll be given?"

"It's a matter of simple logic. You'll be trying to appeal your way out. Which implies you're starting out in. Which means you'll get what the army chooses to give you. But I imagine we'll be reasonable."

"I don't remember any Juan Rodriguez."

"You'll be given a lawyer for that, too."

"What's supposed to have happened to the guy?"

"You tell me," Morgan said.

"I can't. I don't remember him."

"You left him with a brain injury. It caught up with him eventually."

"Who was he?"

"Denial won't work forever."

"I'm not denying anything. I'm telling you I don't remember the guy."

"That's a discussion you can have with your lawyer."

"And who is Candice Dayton?"

"Likewise. But a different lawyer."

"Why different?"

"Different type of case."

"Am I under arrest?"

"No," Morgan said. "Not yet. The prosecutors will make that decision in their own good time. But until then you're under orders, as of two minutes ago. You'll retain your former rank, for the time being. Administratively you're assigned to this unit, and your orders are to treat this building as your duty station and appear here every morning before 08:00 hours. You are not to leave the area. The area is defined as a five-mile radius of this desk. You'll be quartered in a place of the army's choosing."

Reacher said nothing.

Morgan said, "Are there any questions, major?"

"Will I be required to wear a uniform?"

"Not at this stage."

"That's a relief."

"This is not a joke, Reacher. The potential downside here is considerable. For you personally, I mean. The worst case would be life in Leavenworth, for a homicide conviction. But more likely ten years for manslaughter, given the sixteen-year gap. And the best case is not very attractive either, given that we would have to look at the original crime. I would plan on conduct unbecoming, at the minimum, with a new discharge, this time without honor. But your lawyer will run it down for you."

"When?"

"The relevant department has already been notified."

There were no cells in the old building. No secure facilities. There never had been. Just offices. Reacher was left where he was, in the visitor chair, not looked at, not spoken to, completely ignored. The sentry stood easy on the other side of the door. Morgan started tapping and typing and scrolling on the laptop computer. Reacher searched his memory for Juan Rodriguez. Sixteen years ago he had been twelve months into his command of the 110th. Early days. The name Rodriguez sounded Hispanic. Reacher had known many Hispanic people, both inside the service and out. He remembered hitting people on occasion, inside the service and out, some of them Hispanic, but none of them named Rodriguez. And if Rodriguez had been of interest to the 110th, Reacher would have remembered the name, surely. Especially from so early, when every case was significant. The 110th had been an experimental venture. Every move was watched. Every result was evaluated. Every misstep had an autopsy.

He asked, "What was the alleged context?"

No answer from Morgan. The guy just kept on tapping and typing and scrolling. So Reacher searched his memory for a woman named Candice Dayton. Again, he had known many women, both inside the service and out. Candice was a fairly common name. As was Dayton, comparatively. But the two names together meant nothing special to him. Neither did the diminutive, Candy. Candy Dayton? Candice Dayton? Nothing. Not that he remembered everything. No one remembered everything.

He asked, "Was Candice Dayton connected to Juan Rodriguez in some way?"

Morgan looked up, as if surprised to see he had a visitor sitting in his office. As if he had forgotten. He didn't answer the question. He just picked up one of his complicated telephones and ordered a car. He told Reacher to go wait with the sergeant downstairs.

Two miles away, the man who only three people in the world knew as Romeo took out his cell, and dialed the man only two people in the world knew as Juliet, and said, "He's been recalled to service. Colonel Morgan just put it in the computer."

Juliet said, "So what happens next?"

"Too early to tell."

"Will he run?"

"A sane man would."

"Where are they putting him?"

"Their usual motel, I expect."

* * *

The sergeant at the desk downstairs didn't say anything. She was as tongue-tied as before. Reacher leaned on the wall and passed the time in silence. Ten minutes later a private first class came in from the cold and saluted and asked Reacher to follow him. Formal, and polite. Innocent until proven guilty, Reacher guessed, at least in some people's eyes. Out in the lot there was a worn army sedan with its motor running. A young lieutenant was stumping around next to it, awkward and embarrassed. He held open the rear door and Reacher got in the back. The lieutenant took the front passenger seat and the private drove. A mile later they arrived at a motel, a run-down swaybacked old heap in a dark lot on a suburban evening–quiet three-lane road. The lieutenant signed a paper, and the night clerk gave Reacher a key, and the private drove the lieutenant away.

And then the second car arrived, with the guys in the T-shirts and the athletic pants.

Chapter 5

There were no pockets in the athletic pants, and none in the T-shirts, either. And neither man was wearing dog tags. No ID at all. Their car was clean, too. Nothing in it, except the usual army document package stowed neatly in the glove compartment. No weapons, no personal property, no hidden wallets, no scraps of paper, no gas receipts. The license plate was a standard government registration. Nothing abnormal about the car at all, except the two new dents in the doors.

The left-hand guy was blocking the driver's door. Reacher dragged him six feet along the blacktop. He offered no resistance. Life was not a television show. Hit a guy hard enough in the side of the head, and he didn't spring back up ready to carry on the fight. He stayed down for an hour or more, all sick and dizzy and disoriented. A lesson learned long ago: the human brain was much more sensitive to side-to-side displacement than front-to-back. An evolutionary quirk, presumably, like most things.

Reacher opened the driver's door and climbed inside the car. The motor was stopped, but the key was still in. Reacher racked the seat back and started the engine. He sat still for a long spell and stared ahead through the windshield. *They couldn't find you before. They won't find you now. The army doesn't use skip tracers. And no skip tracer could find you anyway. Not the way you seem to live.*

He adjusted the mirror. He put his foot on the brake and fumbled the lever into gear. *Conduct unbecoming, at the minimum, with a new discharge, this time without honor.*

He took his foot off the brake and drove away.

He drove straight back to the old HQ building, and parked fifty yards from it on the three-lane road. The car was warm, and he kept the motor running to keep it warm. He watched through the windshield and saw no activity ahead. No coming or going. In his day the 110th had worked around the clock, seven days a week, and he saw no reason why anything would have changed. The enlisted night watch would be in for the duration, and a night duty officer would be in place, and the other officers would go off duty as soon as their work was done, whenever that might be. Normally. But not on that particular night. Not during a mess or a crisis, and definitely not with a troubleshooter in the house. No one would leave before Morgan. Basic army politics.

* * *

Morgan left an hour later. Reacher saw him quite clearly. A plain sedan came out through the gate and turned onto the three-lane and drove straight past where Reacher was parked. In the darkness Reacher saw a flash of Morgan at the wheel, in his ACU pajamas and his eyeglasses, his hair still neatly combed, looking straight ahead, both hands on the wheel, like someone's great aunt on the way to the store. Reacher watched in the mirror and saw his tail lights disappear over the hill.

He waited.

And sure enough, within the next quarter hour there was a regular exodus. Five more cars came out, two of them turning left, three of them turning right, four of them driven solo, one of them with three people aboard. All the cars were dewed over with night mist, and all of them were trailing cold white exhaust. They disappeared into the distance, left and right, and their exhaust drifted away, and the world went quiet again.

Reacher waited ten more minutes, just in case. But nothing more happened. Fifty yards away the old building looked settled and silent. The night watch, in a world of its own. Reacher put his car in gear and rolled slowly down the hill and turned in at the gate. A new sentry was on duty in the hutch. A young guy, blank and stoic. Reacher stopped and buzzed his window down and the kid said, "Sir?"

Reacher gave his name and said, "I'm reporting to my duty station as ordered."

"Sir?" the guy said again.

"Am I on your list?"

The guy checked.

"Yes, sir," he said. "Major Reacher. But for tomorrow morning."

"I was ordered to report before 08:00 hours."

"Yes, sir. I see that. But it's 23:00 hours now, sir. In the evening."

"Which is before 08:00 in the morning. As ordered."

The guy didn't speak.

Reacher said, "It's a simple matter of chronology. I'm keen to get to work, therefore a little early."

No answer.

"You could check with Colonel Morgan, if you like. I'm sure he's back at his billet by now."

No answer.

"Or you could check with your duty sergeant."

"Yes, sir," the kid said. "I'll do that instead."

He made the call, and listened for a second, and put the phone down and said, "Sir, the sergeant requests that you stop by the desk."

"I'll be sure to do that, soldier," Reacher said. He drove on, and parked next to the little red two-seater, which was still there, exactly where it had been before. He got out and locked up and walked through the cold to the door. The lobby felt quiet and still. A night and day difference, literally. But the same sergeant was at the reception desk. Finishing her work, before going off duty. She was on a high stool, typing on a keyboard. Updating the day's log, presumably.

Record keeping was a big deal, all over the military. She stopped and looked up.

Reacher asked her, "Are you putting this visit in the official record?"

She said, "What visit? And I told the private at the gate not to, either."

Not tongue tied anymore. Not with the interloper Morgan out of the house. She looked young, but infinitely capable, like sergeants the world over. The tape over her right breast said her name was Leach.

She said, "I know who you are."

Reacher said, "Have we met?"

"No, sir, but you're a famous name here. You were this unit's first commander."

"Do you know why I'm back?"

"Yes, sir. We were told."

"What was the general reaction?"

"Mixed."

"What's your personal reaction?"

"I'm sure there's a good explanation. And sixteen years is a long time. Which makes it political, probably. Which is usually bullshit. And even if it isn't, I'm sure the guy deserved it. Or worse."

Reacher said nothing.

Leach said, "I thought about warning you, when you first came in. Best thing for you would have been just to run for it. So I really wanted to turn you around and get you out of here. But I was under orders not to. I'm sorry."

Reacher asked her, "Where is Major Turner?"

Leach said, "Long story."

"How does it go?"

"She deployed to Afghanistan."

"When?"

"The middle of the day, yesterday."

"Why?"

"We have people there. There was an issue."

"What kind of an issue?"

"I don't know."

"And?"

"She never arrived."

"You know that for sure?"

"No question."

"So where is she instead?"

"No one knows."

"When did Colonel Morgan get here?"

"Within hours of Major Turner leaving."

"How many hours?"

"About two."

"Did he give a reason for being here?"

"The implication was Major Turner had been re-lieved of her command."

"Nothing specific?"

"Nothing at all."

"Was she screwing up?"

Leach didn't answer.

Reacher said, "You may speak freely, sergeant."

"No, sir, she wasn't screwing up. She was doing a really good job."

"So that's all you've got? Implications and disap-pearances?"

"So far."

"No gossip?" Reacher asked. Sergeants were al-ways part of a network. Always had been, always would be. Like rumor mills. Like uniformed versions of tabloid newspapers.

Leach said, "I heard one little thing."

"Which was?"

"It might be nothing."

"But?"

"And it might not be connected."

"But?"

"Someone told me the guardhouse at Fort Dyer has a new prisoner."

Chapter 6

Fort Dyer was an army base very close to the Pentagon. But Leach told Reacher that eight years after he mustered out a cost-cutting exercise had merged it with the Marine Corps' nearby Helsington House. The newly enlarged establishment had been given the logical if clumsy name of Joint Base Dyer-Helsington House. In Reacher's day both Dyer and Helsington House had been very high-status places in their own right, staffed mostly by senior and very important people. With the result that the Dyer PX had looked more like Saks Fifth Avenue than a Wal-Mart. And he had heard the Marines' store was even better. Therefore the new blended version was likely to be no lower on the social totem pole. Therefore its cells were likely to house only high-status prisoners. No drunken brawlers or petty thieves there. An MP major with a problem would be a typical tenant. Therefore Leach's rumor might be right. The Dyer guardhouse was located north and west of the Pentagon. Diagonally across the cemetery. Less than five miles from the 110th's HQ. Much less.

"The army and the jarheads in the same place?" Reacher said. "How's that working out for them?"

"Politicians will do anything to save a buck," Leach said.

"Can you call ahead for me?"

"You going there? Now?"

"I have nothing better to do at the moment."

"Do you have a vehicle?"

"Temporarily," Reacher said.

The night was quiet and dark and suburban, and the drive to Dyer took less than ten minutes. Getting into the Joint Base itself took much longer. The merger had happened less than four years after 9/11, and whatever cost-cutting money had been saved hadn't been saved on security. The main gate was on the south side of the complex, and it was impressive. There were concrete dragons' teeth everywhere, funneling traffic through a narrowing lane blocked by three consecutive guard shacks. Reacher was in battered civilian clothes and had no military ID. No ID at all, in fact, except a worn and creased U.S. passport that was already long expired. But he was in a government car, which created a good first impression. And the military had computers, and he showed up as on active service as of the middle of that evening. And the army had sergeants, and Leach had lit up the favor network with a blizzard of calls. And Dyer had a Criminal Investigation office, and to Reacher's mild surprise there were still guys around who knew guys who knew guys who remembered his name. The upshot was that just forty-five minutes after stopping at the first barrier he was face to face with an MP captain in the guard-house front office.

The captain was a serious dark guy of about thirty, and his ACU nametape said his name was Weiss. He looked honest and decent and reasonably friendly, so Reacher said, "This is just a personal matter, captain. Not even remotely official. And I'm probably a little toxic right now, so you should proceed with extreme caution. You should keep this visit off the record. Or refuse to talk to me altogether."

Weiss said, "Toxic how?"

"Looks like something I did sixteen years ago has come back to bite me in the ass."

"What did you do?"

"I don't remember. No doubt someone will remind me soon enough."

"The computer says you were just recalled."

"Correct."

"I never heard of that before."

"Me neither."

"Doesn't sound good. Like someone really wanted you back in the jurisdiction."

Reacher nodded. "That's how I took it. Like I was being extradited out of civilian life. To face the music. But it was a much simpler procedure. There was no kind of a hearing."

"You think they're serious?"

"Feels that way at the moment."

"What do you need from me?"

"I'm looking for Major Susan Turner of the 110th MP."

"Why?"

"Like I said, it's personal."

"Connected with your problem?"

"No. Not in any way."

"But you were with the 110th, right?"

"A long time before Major Turner got anywhere near it."

"So you're not subverting testimony or coaching a witness?"

"Absolutely not. This is a different matter entirely."

"Are you a friend of hers?"

"I was hoping that might be a future development. Or not, depending on what I think of her when I meet her."

"You haven't met her yet?"

"Is she here?"

Weiss said, "In a cell. Since yesterday afternoon."

"What's the charge?"

"She took a bribe."

"From who?"

"I don't know."

"For what?"

"I don't know."

"How much of a bribe?"

"I'm just a jailer," Weiss said. "You know how it is. They don't give me chapter and verse."

"Can I see her?"

"Visiting hours are over."

"How many guests have you got tonight?"

"Just her."

"So you're not busy. And we're off the record, right? So no one will know."

Weiss opened up a green three-ring binder. Notes, procedures, standing orders, some of them printed, some of them handwritten. He said, "She seems to have been expecting you. She passed on a request through her lawyer. She mentioned you by name."

"What's the request?"

"It's more of an instruction, really."

"Saying what?"

"She doesn't want to see you."

Reacher said nothing.

Weiss looked down at the three-ring binder and said, "Quote, per the accused's explicit request, under no circumstances is Major Jack Reacher, U.S. Army, Retired, former commander of the 110th MP, to be granted visitation privileges."

Chapter 7

Getting out of the Joint Base was only marginally quicker than getting in. Each of the three guard shacks checked ID and conducted a trunk search, to make sure Reacher was who he said he was, and hadn't stolen anything. Then after clearing the last of the barriers he threaded his way along the same route the local bus had taken. But he stopped early, and pulled in at the curb. There were plenty of highway ramps all around. There was I-395, spearing south and west. There was the George Washington Memorial Parkway, heading north and west. There was I-66, heading due west. There was I-395 going east, if he wanted it. All of them quiet and flowing fast. There was a big country out there. There was I-95, all the way up and down the eastern seaboard, and the West Coast, five days away, and the vast interior, empty and lonely.

They couldn't find you before. They won't find you now.

A new discharge, this time without honor.
She doesn't want to see you.

Reacher moved off the curb and drove back to the motel.

The two guys with the T-shirts were gone. Evidently they had gotten up and staggered off somewhere. Reacher left their car on the curb two hundred yards away. He left the key in the ignition and the doors unlocked. Either it would be stolen by a couple of punks, or the two guys would come back to get it. He really didn't care which.

He walked the last of the distance and let himself into his dismal room. He had been right. The shower was weak and strangled, and the towels were thin, and the soap was small, and the shampoo was cheap. But he cleaned up as well as he could, and then he went to bed. The mattress felt like a sack stuffed with balled-up plastic, and the sheets felt damp with disuse. But he fell asleep just fine. He set the alarm in his head for seven, and he breathed in, and he breathed out, and that was it.

Romeo dialed Juliet again and said, "He just tried to make contact with Turner over at Dyer. And failed, of course."

Juliet said, "Our boys must have missed him at the motel."

"Nothing to worry about."

"I hope not."

"Goodnight."

"Yes, you, too."

Reacher didn't make it to seven o'clock. He was woken at six, by a brisk tap at the door. It sounded businesslike. Not threatening. *Tap, tap, tappity tap.* Six o'clock in the morning, and someone was already cheerful. He slid out of bed and hauled his pants out from under the mattress and put them on. The air in the room was sharp with cold. He could see his breath. The heater had been off all night.

He padded barefoot across the sticky carpet and opened the door. A gloved hand that had been ready to tap again was pulled back quickly. The hand was attached to an arm, which was attached to a body, which was in a Class A army uniform, with JAG Corps insignia all over it. A lawyer.

A woman lawyer.

According to the plate on the right side of her tunic her name was Sullivan. She was wearing the uniform like a business suit. She had a briefcase in her non-tapping hand. She didn't say anything. She wasn't particularly short, but her eye line was level with Reacher's shirtless chest, where there was an old .38 bullet wound, which seemed to preoccupy her.

Reacher said, "Yes?"

Her car was behind her, a dark green domestic sedan. The sky was still black.

She said, "Major Reacher?"

She was in her mid-thirties, Reacher guessed, a major herself, with short dark hair and eyes that were neither warm nor cold. He said, "How can I help you?"

"It's supposed to be the other way around."

"You've been assigned to represent me?"

"For my sins."

"For the recall appeal or the Juan Rodriguez thing or the Candice Dayton thing?"

"Forget the recall appeal. You'll get five minutes in front of a panel about a month from now, but you won't win. That never happens."

"So Rodriguez or Dayton?"

"Rodriguez," Sullivan said. "We need to get right to it." But she didn't move. Her gaze traced its way downward, to his waist, where there was another scar, by that point more than a quarter century old, a big ugly white starfish overlaid by crude stitches, cut through by a knife wound, which was much more recent, but still old.

"I know," he said. "Aesthetically I'm a mess. But come in anyway."

She said, "No, I think I'll wait in the car. We'll talk over breakfast."

"Where?"

"There's a diner two blocks away."

"You paying?"

"For myself. Not for you."

"Two blocks away? You could have brought coffee."

"Could have, but didn't."

"Some big help you're going to be. Give me eleven minutes."

"Eleven?"

"That's how long it takes me to get ready in the morning."

"Most people would say ten."

"Then either they're faster than me or imprecise." He closed the door on her and padded back to the bed and took his pants off again. They looked OK. Laying them out under the mattress was as close as he ever got to ironing. He walked on to the bathroom and set the shower running. He cleaned his teeth and climbed under the weak lukewarm stream and used what was left of the soap and shampoo. He dried himself with damp towels and dressed and stepped out to the lot. Eleven minutes, dead on. He was a creature of habit.

Major Sullivan had turned her car around. It was a Ford, the same model as the silver item that had driven him across Missouri many days before. He opened the passenger door and climbed in. Sullivan sat up straight and put the car in gear and eased out of the lot, slow and cautious. Her uniform skirt was at her knees. She was wearing dark nylons and plain black lace-up shoes.

Reacher asked, "What's your name?"

Sullivan said, "You can read, I presume."

"First name, I mean."

"Does it matter? You're going to call me Major Sullivan." She said it in a way that was neither friendly nor unfriendly. Nor unexpected. A personal relationship was not on the agenda. Army defense lawyers were diligent, intelligent, and professional, but they were on nobody's side but the army's.

The diner was indeed two blocks away, but the blocks were long. A left, and then a right, and then a ragged strip mall, on the shoulder of another three-lane road. The mall featured a hardware store, and a no-name pharmacy, and a picture framing shop, and a gun store, and a walk-in dentist. The diner stood alone at the end of the strip, in its own lot. It was a white stucco affair with the kind of inside decor that made Reacher bet the owner was Greek and there would be a million items on the menu. Which made it a restaurant, in his opinion, not a diner. Diners were lean, mean, stripped-down places, as ruthless as combat rifles.

They took a booth in a side wing, and a waitress brought coffee before being asked, which raised Reacher's opinion of the place a little. The menu was a multi-page laminated thing almost as big as the tabletop. Reacher saw pancakes and eggs on page two, and he investigated no further.

Sullivan said, "I'm recommending a plea bargain. They'll ask for five years and we'll offer one and settle on two. You can do that. Two years won't kill you."

Reacher said, "Who was Candice Dayton?"

"Not my case. Someone else will talk to you about that."

"And who was Juan Rodriguez exactly?"

"Someone you hit in the head who died from his injuries."

"I don't remember him."

"That's not the best thing to say in a case like this. It makes it sound like you hit so many people in the head that you can't distinguish one from the other. It might prompt further inquiries. Someone might be tempted to draw up a list. And from what I hear it might be a very long list. The 110th was pretty much a rogue operation back then."

"And what is it now?"

"A little better, perhaps. But far from outstanding."

"That's your opinion?"

"That's my experience."

"Do you know anything about Susan Turner's situation?"

"I know her lawyer."

"And?"

"She took a bribe."

"Do we know that for sure?"

"There's enough electronic data to float a battleship. She opened a bank account in the Cayman Islands at ten o'clock in the morning the day before yesterday, and at eleven o'clock a hundred thousand dollars showed up in it, and then she was arrested at twelve o'clock, more or less red-handed. Seems fairly open and shut to me. And fairly typical of the 110th."

"Sounds like you don't love my old unit, overall. Which might be a problem. Because I'm entitled to a competent defense. Sixth Amendment, and so on. Do you think you're the right person for the job?"

"I'm what they're giving you, so get used to it."

"I should see the evidence against me, at least. Don't you think? Isn't there something in the Sixth Amendment about that, too?"

"You didn't do much paperwork sixteen years ago."

"We did some."

"I know," Sullivan said. "I've seen what there is of it. Among other things you did daily summaries. I have one that shows you heading out for an interview with Mr. Rodriguez. Then I have a document from a county hospital ER showing his admission later the same day, for a head injury, among other things."

"And that's it? Where's the connection? He could have fallen down the stairs after I left. He could have been hit by a truck."

"The ER doctors thought he had been."

"That's a weak case," Reacher said. "In fact it's not really a case at all. I don't remember anything about it."

"Yet you remember some stairs that Mr. Rodriguez might have fallen down, after your interview."

"Speculation," Reacher said. "Hypothesis. Figure of speech. Same as the truck. They've got nothing."

"They have an affidavit," Sullivan said. "Sworn out by Mr. Rodriguez himself, some time later. He names you as his attacker."

Chapter 8

Sullivan hauled her briefcase up on the booth's vinyl bench. She took out a thick file and she laid it on the table. She said, "Happy reading."

Which it wasn't, of course. It was a long and sordid record of a long and sordid investigation into a long and sordid crime. The root cause was Operation Desert Shield, all the way back in late 1990, which was the build-up phase before Operation Desert Storm, which was the Gulf War the first time around, after Saddam Hussein of Iraq invaded his neighbor, the independent state of Kuwait. Half a million men and women from the free world had gathered over six long months, getting ready to kick Saddam's ass, which in the end had taken all of one hundred hours. Then the half-million men and women had gone home again.

The materiel wind-down had been the problem. Armies need a lot of stuff. Six months to build it up, six months to break it down. And the build-up had received a lot more in the way of care and attention than the wind-down. The wind-down had been piece-meal and messy. Dozens of nationalities had been in-volved. Long story short, lots of stuff had gone missing. Which was embarrassing. But the books had to be balanced. So some of the missing stuff was writ-ten off as destroyed, and some as damaged, and some as merely lost, and the books were closed.

Until certain items started showing up on the streets of America's cities.

Sullivan asked, "You remember it yet?"

"Yes," Reacher said. He remembered it very well. It was the kind of crime the 110th had been created to fight. Man-portable military weapons don't end up on the streets by accident. They're filched and diverted and stolen and sold. By persons unknown, but by per-sons in certain distinct categories. In logistics compa-nies, mostly. Guys who have to move tens of thousands of tons a week with hazy bills of lading can always find ways of making a ton or two disappear, here and there, for fun and profit. Or a hundred tons. The 110th had been tasked to find out who and how and where and when. The unit was new, with its name to make, and it had gone at it hard. Reacher had spent hundreds of hours on it, and his team had spent many times more.

He said, "But I still don't remember any Juan Ro-driguez."

Sullivan said, "Flip to the end of the file."

Which Reacher did, where he found he remem-bered Juan Rodriguez pretty well.

Just not as Juan Rodriguez.

* * *

The 110th had gotten a solid tip about a gangbanger in South Central LA, who went by the street name of Dog, which was alleged to be a contraction of Big Dog, because the guy was supposedly sizeable both in terms of status and physique. The DEA wasn't interested in him, because he wasn't part of the drug wars. But the tip said like neutrals everywhere he was making a fortune selling black market weapons to both sides at once. The tip said he was the go-to guy. The tip said he was angling to unload eleven crates of army SAWs. SAWs were not metal things with little teeth, good for cutting wood. SAWs were Squad Automatic Weapons, which were fearsome fully-automatic machine guns, with fearsome capacities and fearsome capabilities.

Reacher had gone to South Central LA and walked the hot dusty streets and asked the right kind of questions in the right kind of places. In that environment he was unmistakably army, so he had posed as a disaffected grunt with interesting stuff for sale. Grenades, launchers, armor-piercing ammunition in vast quantities, Beretta handguns. People were naturally cautious, but ultimately the pose worked. Two days later he was face to face with the Dog, who turned out to be big indeed, mostly side to side. The guy could have weighed four hundred pounds.

The last sheet in the file was the affidavit, which was headed *Evidentiary Statement of Juan Rodriguez, a.k.a. Big Dog, a.k.a. Dog.* Reacher's name was all over it, as well as a long list of injuries, including a broken skull and broken ribs and tissue damage and contusions. It was signed at the bottom, by Rodriguez himself, and witnessed, by a lawyer on Ventura Boulevard in Studio City, Los Angeles, and notarized, by someone else entirely.

Sullivan said, "Remember him now?"

"He was lying in this affidavit," Reacher said. "I never laid a finger on him."

"Really?"

"Why would I? I wasn't interested in *him*. I wanted his source, that's all. I wanted the guy he was buying from. I wanted a name."

"You weren't worried about SAWs on the streets of LA?"

"That was the LAPD's problem, not mine."

"Did you get the name?"

"Yes."

"How?"

"I asked, he answered."

"Just like that?"

"More or less."

"What does that mean?"

"I was a good interrogator. I made him think I knew more than I did. He wasn't very smart. I'm surprised he even had a brain to injure."

"So how do you explain the hospital report?"

"Do I have to? A guy like that, he knows all kinds of unsavory characters. Maybe he ripped someone off the day before. He wasn't operating in a very civilized environment."

"So that's your defense? Some other dude did it?"

"If I'd done it he wouldn't have made it to the hospital. He was a useless tub of lard."

"I can't go to the prosecutor with *some other dude did it*. I can't say the proof is you would have actually killed him, rather than merely mortally injuring him."

"You'll have to."

"No, I won't have to. You need to listen up, Reacher. You need to take this seriously. I can get you a deal, but you have to get out in front of it. You have to own it and show some contrition."

"I don't believe this."

"I'm giving you my best advice."

"Can I get a new lawyer?"

"No," Sullivan said. "You can't."

They ate the rest of their breakfasts in silence. Reacher wanted to move to another table, but he didn't, because he thought it would look petty. They split the check and paid and went out to the car, where Sullivan said, "I have somewhere else to go. You can walk from here. Or take the bus."

She got in her car and drove away. Reacher was left on his own, in the restaurant lot. The three-lane in front of him was part of the local bus route. There was a bench stop thirty yards to his left. There were two people waiting. Two men. Mexicans, both of them much thinner than the Big Dog. Honest civilians, probably, heading for yard work in the cemetery, or janitor jobs in Alexandria, or in D.C. itself.

There was another bus stop fifty yards to his right. Another bench. On the near side of the street, not the far. Heading north, not south. Heading out, not in. To McLean, and then Reston, maybe. And then to Leesburg, probably, and possibly all the way to Winchester. Where there would be more buses waiting, bigger buses, which would labor through the Appalachians, into West Virginia, and Ohio, and Indiana. And onward. And away.

They couldn't find you before. They won't find you now.

A new discharge, this time without honor.

She doesn't want to see you.

Reacher waited. The air was cold. The traffic was steady. Cars and trucks. All makes, all models, all colors. Then far to his left he saw a bus. Heading north, not south. Heading out, not in. The bench was fifty yards to his right. He waited. The bus was a big van, really, converted. Local, not long distance. A municipal service, with a subsidized fare. It was snorting and snuffling its way toward him, slowly.

He let it go. It passed him by and continued on its way, oblivious.

He walked back to the 110th HQ. Two miles in total, thirty minutes exactly. He passed his motel. The car with the dents in the doors was gone from the curb. Reclaimed, or stolen.

He got to the old stone building at five minutes to eight in the morning, and he met another lawyer, who told him who Candice Dayton was, and why she was unhappy.

Chapter 9

The sentry Reacher had met the afternoon before was back in his hutch. The day watch. He nodded Reacher through the gate, and Reacher walked onward to the short flight of steps and the freshly painted door. The Humvee was still in the lot. As was the small red two-seater. The car with the dents in the doors was not.

There was a new sergeant at the desk in the lobby. The night watch, presumably, finishing up. This one was male, white, and a little more reserved than Leach had been in the end. Not explicitly hostile, but quiet and slightly censorious, like a milder version of the guys in the T-shirts from the night before: *You brought the unit into disrepute.* He said, "Colonel Morgan requires you to report to 207 immediately."

Reacher said, "Immediately what?"

The guy said, "Immediately, sir."

"Thank you, sergeant," Reacher said. Room 207 was upstairs, fourth on the left, next to his own room.

Or next to Susan Turner's, or Morgan's, now. Back in the day 207 had been Karla Dixon's office, his number cruncher. His financial specialist. She had busted open plenty of tough things. Ninety-nine times out of a hundred, crimes come down to love, hate, or money, and unlike what it says in the bible, the greatest of these is money. Dixon had been worth her modest weight in gold, and Reacher had fond memories of room 207.

He used the stairs and walked the corridor and passed his old office. The nameplate was still on the wall: *Maj. S. R. Turner, Commanding Officer.* He heard Captain Weiss' voice in his head, and Major Sullivan's: *She took a bribe.* Maybe there was an innocent explanation. Maybe a distant uncle had died and left stock in a uranium mine. Maybe it was a foreign mine, hence the offshore status. Australian, perhaps. There was uranium in Australia. And gold, and coal, and iron ore. Or somewhere in Africa. He wished Karla Dixon was there. She could have taken one look at the paperwork, and seen the truth in an instant.

He didn't knock at 207's door. No reason to. Apart from Morgan he was likely to be the highest rank in the building. And rank was rank, even in his peculiar circumstances. So he went straight in.

The room was empty. And it was no longer an office. It had been converted to a conference room of some kind. There was no desk, but there was a big round table and six chairs. There was a black spider-shaped thing in the center of the table, presumably a speakerphone for group discussions with remote parties. There was a credenza against one wall, presumably for in-meeting coffee and sandwiches. The lightshade was the same glass bowl. There was an economy bulb in it, turned on already, glowing weak and sickly.

Reacher stepped over to the window and looked out. Not much to see. The lot was narrower on that side of the building. No parking. Just a big trash container, and a random pile of obsolete furniture, desk chairs and file cabinets. The chair upholstery looked swollen with damp, and the file cabinets were rusty. Then came the stone wall, and over it was a decent view east, all the way to the cemetery and the river. The Washington Monument was visible in the far distance, the same color as the mist. A watery sun was behind it, low in the sky.

The door opened behind him and Reacher turned around, expecting Morgan. But it wasn't Morgan. It was déjà vu all over again. A neat Class A uniform, with JAG Corps insignia on it. A woman lawyer. Her nameplate said Edmonds. She looked a little like Sullivan. Dark, trim, very professional, wearing a skirt and nylons and plain black shoes. But she was younger than Sullivan. And junior in rank. She was only a captain. She had a cheaper briefcase.

She said, "Major Reacher?"

He said, "Good morning, captain."

She said, "I'm Tracy Edmonds. I'm working with HRC."

Which was the Human Resources Command, which back in the days of plain English had been the Personnel Command. Which at first made Reacher think she was there to take him through the paperwork. Pay, bank details, the whole nine yards. But then he realized they wouldn't have sent a lawyer for that kind of thing. A company clerk could do that stuff perfectly well. So she was there about the Candice Dayton thing, probably. But she was junior, and she had given up her first name unasked, and she had an open look on her face, all friendly and concerned, which might mean the Candice Dayton thing wasn't as serious as the Big Dog problem.

He asked, "Do you know anything about Susan Turner's situation?"

She said, "Who?"

"You just walked past her office."

She said, "Only what I've heard."

"Which is what?"

"She took a bribe."

"For what?"

"I think that's confidential."

"It can't be. She's confined prior to trial. Therefore there must be probable cause in the record. Or have we abandoned civilized jurisprudence while I've been away?"

"They say she took a day to pass on crucial information. No one understood why. Now they do."

"What information?"

"She arrested an infantry captain from Fort Hood. An espionage case, allegedly. The captain gave up the name of his foreign civilian contact. Major Turner sat on it for twenty-four hours, and the contact used the time to get away."

"When was this exactly?"

"About four weeks ago."

"But she wasn't arrested until the day before yesterday."

"That's when the foreign contact paid her. Which was evidence they had to wait for. Without it the delay could have been explained as incompetence, not criminality."

"Has the pre-trial confinement been appealed?"

"I don't think so."

"Who's her lawyer?"

"Colonel Moorcroft. Out of Charlottesville."

"You mean the JAG school?"

Edmonds nodded. "He teaches criminal defense."

"Is he commuting from there to here?"

"No, I believe he's in the Dyer VOQ."

Which were the Visiting Officers' Quarters, at Fort Dyer. Or, now, Joint Base Dyer-Helsington House. Not the Ritz exactly, but not too far from it, and no doubt a whole lot better than a crappy motel on a three-lane a mile from Rock Creek.

Edmonds pulled out a chair for him, and then one for herself, and she sat down at the conference table. She said, "Candice Dayton."

Reacher sat down, and said, "I don't know who Candice Dayton is. Or was."

"Denial is not a smart way to go, I'm afraid, major. It never works."

"I can't pretend to remember someone if I don't."

"It creates a bad impression. It reinforces a negative stereotype. Both things will go against you in the end."

"Who was she?"

Edmonds lifted her briefcase onto the table and

opened it up. She took out a file. She said, "You were posted to Korea several times, is that correct?"

"Many times."

"Including at one time a short spell working with the 55th MP."

"If you say so."

"I do say so. It's all here in black and white. It was very late in your career. Almost the last thing you did. You were at Camp Red Cloud. Which is between Seoul and the demilitarized zone."

"I know where it is."

"Candice Dayton was an American citizen, and at that time she was temporarily a resident in Seoul."

"A civilian?"

"Yes. You remember her now?"

"No."

"You had a brief affair."

"Who did?"

"You and Ms. Dayton, of course."

"I don't remember her."

"Are you married?"

"No."

"Have you ever been?"

"No."

"Have you had many sexual liaisons in your life?"

"That's a very personal question."

"I'm your lawyer. Have you?"

"As many as possible, generally. I like women. I guess it's a biological thing."

"So many there may be some you don't remember?"

"There were some I try to forget."

"Does that category include Ms. Dayton?"

"No. If I was trying to forget her, that would mean I remember her. Right? And I don't."

"Are there others you don't remember?"

"How would I tell?"

"You see, this is what I meant about reinforcing a stereotype. It won't help you in court."

"What court?"

"Candice Dayton left Seoul pretty soon after you did, and she went home to Los Angeles, which is where she was from. She was happy to be back. She got a job, and she did quite well for a number of years. She had a daughter early on, who thrived and then did well in school. She got promoted at work, and she bought a bigger house. All the good stuff. But then the economy went bad, and she lost her job, and then she lost her house. As of right now, she and her daughter are living in her car, and she's looking for financial assistance, from anywhere she's entitled to get it."

"And?"

"She got pregnant in Korea, major. Her daughter is yours."

Chapter 10

Edmonds paged through the file, walking delicate fingers from sheet to sheet. She said, "Army policy is to take no proactive steps. We don't send out search parties. We merely make a note against the father's name. Usually nothing happens. But if the father comes to us, as you did, then we're obliged to act. So we're going to have to give your current status and location to the court in Los Angeles."

She found the page she was looking for. She pulled it out from among all the others. She slid it across the conference table. She said, "Obviously, as your lawyer, I would strongly recommend a paternity test. You'll have to pay for it, but it would be most unwise to proceed to a final settlement without one."

Reacher picked up the sheet of paper. It was a crisp new photocopy of an affidavit. Just like the Big Dog's. Signatures, and lawyers, and seals, and stamps, all done in a law office in North Hollywood, apparently. His name was all over it. Dates were given for his deployment with the 55th. Dates and times and social activities were recorded. Candice Dayton must have kept a comprehensive diary. The baby's date of birth was noted. It was exactly nine months after the midpoint of his time at Red Cloud. The baby's name was Samantha. Sam for short, presumably. She was now fourteen years old. Nearly fifteen.

Edmonds slid a second sheet across. It was a crisp new photocopy of a birth certificate. She said, "She didn't put your name on it. I think originally she was happy to go it alone. But now she's fallen on hard times."

Reacher said nothing.

Edmonds said, "I don't know your current financial situation, obviously. But you're looking at a little more than three years of child support. Plus college, possibly. I imagine the court will contact you in about a month, and you can work it out with them."

Reacher said, "I don't remember her."

"Probably best not to say that too often. These things are fundamentally adversarial in nature, and you should avoid extra resentment on Ms. Dayton's part, if you can. In fact it might be a smart move to contact her proactively. As soon as possible. To show willingness, I mean."

Edmonds took back the affidavit, and she took back the birth certificate. She slotted them back into the file, each in its allotted place. She put the file back in her briefcase and closed it. She said, "As you know, major, the Uniform Code of Military Justice still lists adultery as a criminal offense. Especially for those with security clearances. Because the risk of compromise is generally seen as significant. Especially where a civilian is involved. But I think if you're seen to be acting reasonably with Ms. Dayton, then I can get the prosecutor to let that aspect slide. Especially if you were to approach Ms. Dayton proactively, with an offer. As I said. Right away, perhaps. I think that would be well received. By the prosecutor, I mean."

Reacher said nothing.

Edmonds said, "It was a long time ago, after all. And no harm to national security has been apparent. Unless your other issue interferes. The thing with Mr. Rodriguez, I mean. They might want to hit you with everything they can find, in which case I really won't be able to help you."

Reacher said nothing.

Edmonds stood up from the table and said, "I'll keep in touch, major. Let me know if there's anything you need."

She left the room and closed the door behind her. Reacher heard her heels on the linoleum in the corridor, and then he heard nothing at all.

Fatherhood was up there as one of the most commonplace male experiences in all of human history. But to Reacher it had always seemed unlikely. Just purely theoretical. Like winning the Nobel Prize, or playing in the World Series, or being able to sing. Possible in principle, but always likely to pass him by. A destination for other people, but not for him. He had known fathers, starting with his own, and his grandfathers, and his childhood friends' fathers, and then some of his own friends, as they got married and started to raise families. Being a father seemed both straightforward and infinitely complex. Easy enough on the surface. Underneath, simply too immense to worry about. So generally it seemed to come out as a day-to-day thing. Hope for the best, one foot in front of the other. His own father had always seemed in charge. But looking back, it was clear he was just making it up as he went along.

Samantha Dayton.

Sam.

Fourteen years old.

Reacher got no more time to think about her. Not right then. Because the door opened and Morgan walked in, still in his ACU fatigues, still wearing his spectacles, still all groomed and fussy and squared away. He said, "You're dismissed for the day, major. Be back here before 0800 tomorrow."

Punishment by boredom. Nothing to do all day. Not an unusual tactic. Reacher didn't respond. He just sat and stared into the distance. Bad manners or minor insubordination couldn't make his situation any worse. Not at that point. But in turn Morgan just stood there too, dumb as a rock, holding the door, so eventually Reacher had to get up from the table and file out of the room. He took it slow in the corridor until he heard Morgan shut himself back in his own office.

Then he stopped and turned around.

He walked back to the far end of the corridor and

checked the office on the left. Room 209. Calvin Franz's office, back at the beginning. A good friend, now dead. Reacher opened the door and stuck his head in and saw two men he didn't recognize. NCOs, but not the two from the motel the night before. Not the two in the T-shirts. They were at back-to-back desks, working hard on computers. They looked up at him.

"Carry on," he said.

He stepped back out and tried the opposite door. Room 210, once David O'Donnell's billet. O'Donnell was still alive, as far as Reacher knew. A private detective, in D.C., he had heard. Not far away. He stuck his head in the room and saw a woman at a desk. She was in ACU fatigues. A lieutenant. She looked up.

"Excuse me," he said.

Room 208 had been Tony Swan's office. Another good friend, also now dead. Reacher opened the door and checked. No one there, but it was a one-person billet, and that one person was a woman. There was a female officer's hat on the window sill, and a tiny wristwatch unlatched and upside down on the desk.

He had seen 207. Once Karla Dixon's domain, now no one's. The conference room. Dixon was still alive, as far as he knew. In New York, the last time he had heard. She was a forensic accountant, which meant she was very busy.

Room 206 had been Frances Neagley's office. Directly opposite his own, because she had done most of his work for him. The best sergeant he ever had. Still alive and prospering, he thought, in Chicago. He stuck his head in and saw the lieutenant who had dumped him at the motel the night before. In the first car, driven by the private first class. The guy was at the desk, on the phone. He looked up. Reacher shook his head and backed out of the room.

Room 204 had been Stan Lowrey's office. A hard man, and a good investigator. He had gone early, the only one of the original unit smart enough to get out unscathed. He had moved to Montana, to raise sheep and churn butter. No one knew why. He had been the only black man in a thousand square miles, and he had no farming experience. But people said he had been happy. Then he had been hit by a truck. His office was occupied by a captain in Class A uniform. A short guy, on his way to testify. No other reason for the fancy duds. Reacher said, "Excuse me," and headed out again.

Room 203 had been an evidence locker, and still was, and 201 had been a file room, and still was, and 202 had been the company clerk's quarters, and still was. The guy was in there, a sergeant, relatively old and gray, probably fighting involuntary separation on an annual basis. Reacher nodded a greeting to him and backed out and went downstairs.

The sour-faced night guy had gone and Leach had taken his place at the reception desk. Behind her the corridor led back to the first-floor offices, 101 through 110. Reacher checked them all. Rooms 109 and 110 had been Jorge Sanchez's and Manuel Orozco's offices, and were now occupied by similar guys from a newer generation. Rooms 101 through 108 held people of no particular interest, except for 103, which was the duty officer's station. There was a captain in there.

He was a good looking guy in his late twenties. His desk was twice the normal size, all covered over with telephones and scratch pads and message forms and an untidy legal pad, with its many used pages folded loosely back like an immense bouffant hairdo from the 1950s. The face-up page was covered with angry black doodles. There were shaded boxes and machines and escape-proof spiral mazes. Clearly the guy spent a lot of time on the phone, some of it on hold, some of it waiting, most of it bored. When he spoke it was with a Southern accent that Reacher recognized immediately. He had talked to the guy from South Dakota, more than once. The guy had routed his calls to Susan Turner.

Reacher asked him, "Do you have other personnel deployed around here?"

The guy shook his head. "This is it. What you see is what you get. We have people elsewhere in the States and overseas, but no one else in this military district."

"How many in Afghanistan?"

"Two."

"Doing what?"

"I can't give you the details."

"Hazardous duty?"

"Is there another kind? In Afghanistan?"

Something in his voice.

Reacher asked, "Are they OK?"

"They missed their scheduled radio check yesterday."

"Is that unusual?"

"Never happened before."

"Do you know what their mission is?"

"I can't tell you."

"I'm not asking you to tell me. I'm asking whether you know. In other words, how secret is it?"

The guy paused a beat and said, "No, I don't know what their mission is. All I know is they're out there in the back of beyond, and all we're getting is silence."

Reacher said, "Thank you, captain." He headed back to the reception desk, where he asked Leach for a pool car. She hesitated, and he said, "I'm dismissed for the day. Colonel Morgan didn't say I had to sit in the corner. An omission, possibly, but I'm entitled to interpret my orders in the best possible light."

Leach asked, "Where do you want to go?"

"Fort Dyer," Reacher said. "I want to talk to Colonel Moorcroft."

"Major Turner's lawyer?"

Reacher nodded. "And Dyer is definitely less than five miles away. You won't be aiding or abetting a serious crime."

Leach paused a beat and then opened a drawer and took out a grubby key. She said, "It's an old blue Chevy sedan. I need it back here before the end of the day. I can't let you have it overnight."

"Whose is the red sports car outside?"

Leach said, "That's Major Turner's ride."

"Do you know the guys in Afghanistan?"

Leach nodded. "They're friends of mine."

"Are they good?"

"They're the best."

Chapter 11

There were three Chevrolet sedans in the HQ lot, and two were old, but only one was old and blue. It was dirty and all beat up and saggy, and it had about a million city miles on the clock. But it started up fine, and it idled OK. Which it needed to, because the daytime traffic was slow. Lots of lights, lots of queues, lots of jammed lanes. But getting into Dyer itself was quicker than the first time. The main gate guards were relatively welcoming. Reacher figured Leach must have called ahead again. Which meant she was turning into a minor ally. Which Reacher was happy about. A sergeant on your side made the world go round, smooth and easy. Whereas a sergeant who took against you could kill you dead.

He parked the car and went inside, where it got slower again. A woman at a desk called around and was unable to locate Moorcroft anywhere. Not in the VOQ, not in the legal offices, not in the guardhouse, and not in the cells. Which left only one place to look.

Reacher moved on, deeper into the complex, until he saw a sign with an arrow: *Officers Club.* It was late for breakfast, but late breakfasts were a natural habitat for senior rear-echelon staffers. Especially senior rear-echelon staffers who were also academic pointy-heads on short-term visits.

The OC dining room turned out to be a pleasant, bland space, low, wide, and long, recently refurbished, probably by the same guy who did the dining rooms in mid-price chain hotels. There was plenty of blond wood and mid-green fabric. Plenty of angled dividers, and therefore plenty of separate little seating areas. There was carpet on the floor. There were venetian blinds on the windows, cracked open about halfway. For no good reason Reacher remembered a joke his old colleague Manuel Orozco liked to tell: *How do you make a venetian blind? You poke his eyes out.* And then: *How do you make a Swiss roll? You push him down an Alp.* Whereupon David O'Donnell would start pointing out that Swiss rolls weren't really Swiss. More likely British. Nineteenth century. Like a Victoria sponge, but assembled differently. O'Donnell was the kind of pedant that made Reacher look normal.

Reacher moved on. Most of the little seating areas were empty, but Moorcroft was in one of them. He was a short, rotund, middle-aged man with an amiable expression, in a Class A uniform, with his name big and obvious on the flap of his right breast pocket. He was eating toast, at a big isolated table for four.

And face to face at the table with him was Major Sullivan, Reacher's lawyer for the Big Dog. Sullivan wasn't eating. She had already had breakfast, with

Reacher, in the Greek establishment. She was cradling a cup of coffee, nothing more, and talking, and listening, in what looked like a very deferential manner, like majors often converse with colonels, or students with teachers.

Reacher stepped into the intimate little area and pulled out a chair and sat down at the table between them. He said, "Do you mind if I join you?"

Moorcroft asked, "Who are you?"

Sullivan said, "This is Major Reacher. My client. The one I was telling you about."

Nothing in her voice.

Moorcroft looked at Reacher and said, "If you have things to discuss, I'm sure Major Sullivan would be happy to schedule an appointment at a more appropriate time."

"It's you I want to talk to," Reacher said.

"Me? About what?"

"Susan Turner."

"Do you have an interest?"

"Why has her pre-trial confinement not been appealed?"

"You must state a legitimate interest before we can consider specifics."

"Any citizen has a legitimate interest in the correct application of due process against any other citizen."

"You think my approach has so far been incorrect?"

"I'll be better able to make that determination after you answer my question."

"Major Turner is facing a serious charge."

"But pre-trial confinement is not supposed to be punitive. It's supposed to be no more rigorous than is required to ensure the accused's presence at trial. That's what the regulation says."

"Are you a lawyer? Your name doesn't ring a bell."

"I was an MP. Actually, I *am* an MP, I suppose. All over again. Therefore I know plenty about the law."

"Really? In the same way a plumber understands the science behind fluid mechanics and thermodynamics?"

"Don't flatter yourself, colonel. It's not brain surgery."

"So enlighten me, by all means."

"Major Turner's situation doesn't require confinement. She's a commissioned officer in the United States Army. She's not going to run."

"Is that a personal guarantee?"

"Almost. She's the commander of the 110th MP. As was I. I wouldn't have run. She won't, either."

"There are elements of treason here."

"Here, maybe, but not in the real world. No one is thinking treason. Or they wouldn't have brought her here to Dyer. She'd be in the Caribbean by now."

"Nevertheless, it's not a speeding ticket."

"She won't run."

"Again, is that a personal guarantee?"

"It's a considered assessment."

"Do you even know her?"

"Not really."

"So butt out, major."

"Why did she instruct you to prevent me from visiting?"

"She didn't, technically. That instruction was passed on by the duty lawyer. At some unspecified time in the late afternoon. Therefore the restriction was already in place before I took over her case, which was the next morning. Which was yesterday."

"I want you to ask her to reconsider."

Moorcroft didn't answer. Sullivan leaned into the conversation and looked at Reacher and said, "Captain Edmonds told me she'd met with you. About the Candice Dayton matter. She said she advised you to take proactive steps. Have you yet?"

Reacher said, "I'll get to it."

"It should be your first priority. Nuances count, in a thing like this."

"I'll get to it," Reacher said again.

"This is your daughter we're talking about here. She's living in a car. That's more important than a theoretical worry about Major Turner's human rights."

"The kid is nearly fifteen years old in Los Angeles. No doubt she's slept in cars before. And if she's my kid she can take a day or two more of it."

Moorcroft said, "I think Major Sullivan and Captain Edmonds are trying to make the point you might not have a day or two more. Depending on what the prosecutors decide to do about the Rodriguez issue, I mean. I imagine they're rubbing their hands with glee. Because it's a perfect storm. Clear evidence, plus a disastrous PR angle."

"The clear evidence is clear bullshit."

Moorcroft smiled, practiced and indulgent. "You're not the first defendant ever to say that, you know."

"The guy is dead. But I'm supposed to be able to confront the witnesses against me. So how is this even legal?"

"It's an unfortunate anomaly. The affidavit speaks from beyond the grave. It is what it is. It can't be cross-examined."

Reacher looked at Sullivan. She was his lawyer, after all. She said, "The colonel is right. I told you, I can get you a deal. You should take it."

And then she left. She drained her cup, and stood up, and said goodbye, and walked away. Reacher watched her go, and then he turned back to Moorcroft.

He asked, "Are you going to appeal Major Turner's confinement?"

"Yes," Moorcroft said. "As a matter of fact I am. I'm going to ask for confinement to the D.C. military district, and I expect to be successful. She'll be out and about before long."

"When will you start the process?"

"I'll put in the paperwork as soon as you let me finish my breakfast."

"When will you get a decision?"

"By the middle of the day, I should think."

"That's good."

"Good or bad, it's really none of your business, major."

Moorcroft chased toast crumbs around his plate for a minute more. Then he stood up in turn and said, "Good day, major," and strolled out of the room. He waddled a little as he walked. Much more academic than military. But not a bad guy. Reacher felt his heart was in the right place.

Samantha Dayton.
Sam.
Fourteen years old.
I'll get to it.

Reacher walked all the way north through the complex and stopped in at the guardhouse, where a different captain was in charge. Not Weiss, from the night before. The day guy was an aquiline black man about seven feet tall, but slender as a pencil, folded into a desk chair that was far too small for him. Reacher asked to visit with Susan Turner, and the guy consulted the green three-ring binder, and he refused the request.

Nothing ventured, nothing gained.

So Reacher walked back to where the old blue Chevy was parked, and he drove it back to the 110th HQ, and he left it where he had found it. He went inside and gave the key to Leach. She was agitated again. Nervous, stressed, and uptight. Not terrible, but visible. Reacher said, "What?"

Leach said, "Colonel Morgan's not here."

"You say that like it's a bad thing."

"We need him."

"I can't imagine what for."

"He's the CO."

"No, Major Turner is your CO."

"And she's not here either."

"What happened?"

"Our guys in Afghanistan missed their second radio check. It's forty-eight hours since we heard from them. And therefore we need to do something. But Morgan's not here."

Reacher nodded. "He's probably having a new poker fitted. Up his ass. It's probably a lengthy procedure."

He moved on, into the ground-floor corridor, to the second office on the left. Room 103. The duty officer's station. The guy was in there, behind his huge desk, handsome, Southern, and worried. His doodles were bleaker than ever. Reacher asked him, "Didn't Morgan tell you where he was going?"

"Pentagon," the guy said. "For a meeting."

"Is that all he said?"

"No details."

"Have you called?"

"Of course I have. But it's a big place. They can't find him anywhere."

"Does he have a cell phone?"

"Switched off."

"How long has he been gone?"

"Nearly an hour."

"What would you want him to do?"

"Authorize a request for a search party, of course. Every minute counts now. And we have lots of people over there. The 1st Infantry Division. And Special Forces. And helicopters, and drones, and satellites, and all kinds of aerial surveillance."

"But you don't even know where your guys are supposed to be, or what they're supposed to be doing."

The duty officer nodded and jabbed his thumb at the ceiling. At the upstairs offices. He said, "The mission is in Major Turner's computer. Which is now Colonel Morgan's computer. Which is password-protected."

"Do the radio checks go into Bagram?"

The guy nodded again. "Most of them are routine data. Bagram sends us the transcript. But if there's anything urgent, then they're patched through to us, right here in this office. On a secure phone line."

"What was it the last time they transmitted? Routine, or urgent?"

"Routine."

"OK," Reacher said. "Call Bagram and get an estimate of their range, from that last time."

"Will Bagram even know their range?"

"Those radio guys can usually tell. By the sound, and the signal strength. By a gut feeling, sometimes. It's their job. Ask for their best guess, to the nearest five miles."

The guy picked up a phone, and Reacher walked back to Leach at the reception desk in the lobby. He said, "Get on the line for the next ten minutes and hit up everyone you know at the Pentagon. Full court press, to locate Morgan."

Leach picked up her phone.

Reacher waited.

Ten minutes later Leach had nothing. Not altogether surprising. The Pentagon had more than seventeen miles of corridors and nearly four million square feet of office space, all occupied by more than thirty thousand people on any given workday. Trying to find a random individual was like trying to find a needle in the world's most secretive haystack. Reacher walked back to 103 and the duty officer said, "The Bagram radio room figures our guys were about two hundred and twenty miles out. Maybe two hundred and thirty."

"That's a start," Reacher said.

"Not really. We don't know what direction."

"If in doubt, take a wild-ass guess. That was always my operating principle."

"Afghanistan is a big country."

"I know it is," Reacher said. "And it's unpleasant all over, from what I hear. But where is it worst?"

"The mountains. The border with Pakistan. Pashtun tribal areas. The northeast, basically. No one's idea of fun."

Reacher nodded. "Which is the kind of place the 110th gets sent. So get on the horn to the base commander and ask him to order up an air search, starting two hundred and twenty-five miles northeast of Bagram."

"That could be completely the wrong direction."

"Like I said, it's a wild-ass guess. You got something better?"

"They won't do it anyway. Not on my say-so. A thing like this would need a major or better."

"So take Morgan's name in vain."

"Can't do it."

Reacher listened. All quiet. No one coming. The duty officer waited, his hand curled into a fist, halfway between his lap and his phone.

You're back in the army, major.

You'll retain your former rank.

You're assigned to this unit.

"Use my name," Reacher said.

Chapter 12

The duty officer made the call, and then the military machine took over, distant and invisible and industrious, on the other side of the world, nine time zones and nearly eight thousand miles away, planning, briefing, readying, arming, and fueling. The old stone building in Rock Creek went quiet.

Reacher asked, "How many other people do you have in the field?"

The duty officer said, "Globally? Fourteen."

"Nearest?"

"Right now, Fort Hood in Texas. Cleaning up after Major Turner's thing down there."

"How many in hazardous situations?"

"That's a moving target, isn't it? Eight or ten, maybe."

"Has Morgan gone AWOL before?"

"This is only his third day."

"What was Major Turner like as a commander?"

"She was fairly new. She only had a few weeks."

"First impression?"

"Excellent."

"Is this Afghanistan thing hers, or did she inherit it?"

"It's hers," the duty officer said. "It's the second thing she did when she got here, after Fort Hood."

Reacher had never been to Bagram, or anywhere else in Afghanistan, but he knew how it would work. Some things never change. No one liked sitting around doing nothing, and no one liked their own people in trouble. Especially not in the tribal areas, which were brutal and primitive in ways too drastic to contemplate. So the search mission would be undertaken very willingly. But it would carry significant danger. Combat air support would be needed, and overwhelming air-to-ground firepower would be required. Lots of moving parts. Therefore mission planning would take some time. Two hours minimum, Reacher figured, to get all the ducks in a row. Then two hours of flight time. There would be no early resolution.

Reacher spent some of the wait time walking. Back to his motel, and past it, and then left and right on the long blocks to the ragged strip mall ahead of the Greek restaurant, which he ignored, because he wasn't hungry. He ignored the picture framing shop, because he had no pictures in need of framing, and he ignored the gun shop, because he didn't want to buy a gun, and he ignored the walk-in dentist, because his teeth felt fine. He stopped in at the hardware store, and bought a pair of dark khaki canvas work pants, and a blue canvas work shirt, and a brown field coat padded with some kind of trademarked miracle insulation layer. Then he stopped in at the no-name pharmacy and bought dollar socks and boxers and two white T-shirts, which he figured he would wear one on top of the other, under the work shirt, because the T-shirt fabric looked thin, and the weather showed no signs of warming up. He added a three-pack of disposable razors, the smallest available, and an aerosol can of shaving foam, the smallest available, and two packs of gum, and a plastic comb.

He carried his purchases back to the motel, two long blocks, and he let himself into his room. It had been serviced in his absence. The bed had been made and the meager bathroom supplies had been replaced. Fresh towels, dry but still thin, and new wrapped soap, still small, and a new tiny bottle of shampoo, still chemically identical to dishwashing liquid. He stripped in the chill and crammed his old clothes in the trash buckets, half in the bathroom and half in the bedroom, because the buckets were small, and then he shaved very carefully, and then he took his second shower of the day.

He started the heater under the window in the bedroom and dried himself with a hand towel in its hot raucous blast, to save the larger towel for a future occasion. He dressed in his new clothes and put his old boots back on and combed his hair. He checked the result in the bathroom mirror and was satisfied with what he saw. He was at least clean and tidy, which was about as good as it ever got.

She'll be out and about before long.

* * *

Reacher walked back to the 110th HQ. His four upper-body layers plus the miracle insulation did their job. He stayed warm enough. The HQ gates were open. The day guy was in the sentry hutch. Morgan's car was back in the lot. The plain sedan. Reacher had seen it the night before, with Morgan himself at the wheel, all prim and upright. Reacher detoured across toward it and laid his palm on the hood. Which was warm. Almost hot. Morgan had just gotten back.

Which explained Leach's state of mind. She was silent and uptight at the reception desk in the lobby. Behind her the duty officer was inert in the ground-floor corridor, all pale in the face, just standing there. Reacher didn't wait to be told. He turned and headed up the old stone stairs. Third office on the left. He knocked and entered. Morgan was at the desk, thin lipped and furious, practically quivering with rage.

Reacher said, "Good of you to drop by, colonel."

Morgan said, "What you just did will cost the Pentagon more than thirty million dollars."

"Money well spent."

"It will be a court martial all its own."

"Possibly," Reacher said. "But yours, not mine. I don't know where you've served before, colonel, but this isn't amateur hour anymore. Not here. Not with this unit. You had two men you knew to be in danger, and you absented yourself for two whole hours. You left no word about where you were going, and your phone was switched off. That's completely unacceptable."

"Those men are in no danger. They're poking around with some trivial inquiry."

"They missed two consecutive radio checks."

"Probably goofing off, like the rest of this damn unit."

"In Afghanistan? Doing what? Hitting the bars and the clubs? Checking out the whorehouses? Spending the day at the beach? Get real, you idiot. Radio silence out of Afghanistan is automatically bad news."

"It was my decision."

"You wouldn't recognize a decision if it ran up and bit you in the ass."

"Don't speak to me like that."

"Or what?"

Morgan said nothing.

Reacher asked, "Did you cancel the search?"

Morgan didn't answer.

Reacher said, "And you haven't told me we're looking in the wrong place, either. Therefore I was right. Those guys are lost on the border in the tribal areas. You should have done this twenty-four hours ago. They're in real trouble."

"You had no right to interfere."

"I'm back in the army, I'm assigned to this unit, and I hold the rank of major. Therefore I wasn't interfering. I was doing my job, and I was doing it properly. Like I always used to. You should pay some attention and pick up some pointers, colonel. You've got maybe a dozen people in the field, exposed and vulnerable, and you should be thinking about nothing else, all day and all night. You should leave a precise contact number at all times, and you should have your cell switched on, and you should be prepared to answer it, no matter what else you're doing."

Morgan said, "Have you finished?"

"I've barely even started."

"You understand you're under my command?"

Reacher nodded. "Life is full of anomalies."

"Then listen up, major. Your orders have changed. From now on you are confined to your quarters. Go straight back to your motel and stay there until you hear from me again. Do not leave your room at any time for any reason. Do not attempt to communicate with anyone from this unit."

Reacher said nothing.

Morgan said, "You are dismissed, major."

The duty officer was still in the ground-floor corridor. Leach was still behind the reception desk. Reacher came down the stairs and shrugged at them both. Part apologetic, part rueful, partly the universal military gesture: *same old shit.* Then he headed out the door and down the stone steps to the cold midday air. The sky was clearing. There was some bright blue up there.

Reacher walked the rest of the hill and turned on the three-lane. A bus passed him by. Heading out, not in. Onward, and away. He walked on, down a slight dip, up a slight rise. He saw the motel ahead of him, on the right, maybe a hundred yards distant.

He stopped.

The car with the dented doors was in the motel lot.

Chapter 13

The car was easily recognizable, even at a distance. Make, model, shape, color, the slight deformation in the driver's side sheet metal. It was alone in the lot, level with where Reacher guessed his room must be. He moved three paces forward, on a diagonal to the edge of the sidewalk, to improve his angle, and he saw four men coming out his door.

Two of them were as easily identifiable as the car. They were the guys from the night before. One hundred percent certain. Shape, size, coloring. The other two men were new. Nothing special about the first of them. Tall, young, dumb. As bad as his two pals.

The fourth man was different.

He looked a little older than the others, and he was a little bigger than the others, which made him close to Reacher's own size. Six-four, maybe, and two-forty. But all muscle. Huge thighs, small waist, huge chest, like an hourglass, like a cartoon drawing. Plus big knotted shoulders, and arms propped away from his sides by the sheer bulk of his pectorals and his triceps. Like a world champion male gymnast, except more than twice the size.

But it was his head that was truly extraordinary. It was shaved, and it looked like it had been welded together from flat steel plates. Small eyes, and heavy brows, and sharp cheekbones, and tiny, gristly ears, like pasta shapes. He was straight-backed and powerful. Slavic, somehow. Like a poster boy out of an old Red Army recruiting advertisement. Like the ideal of Soviet manhood. He should have been holding a banner, one-handed, high and proud, his eyes fixed mistily on a golden future.

The four men shuffled out and closed the door behind them. Reacher walked on, ninety yards away, then eighty. An Olympic sprinter could have closed the gap in about eight seconds, but Reacher was no kind of a sprinter, Olympic or otherwise. The four men stepped over to their car. Reacher walked on. The four men opened their doors and folded themselves inside, two in the back, two in the front. Reacher walked on. Seventy yards. Sixty. The car moved through the lot, and stopped nose-on to the three-lane, waiting for a gap in the traffic, waiting to turn. Reacher wanted it to turn toward him. *Turn left,* he thought. *Please.*

But the car turned right, and joined the traffic stream, and drove away into the distance, and was lost to sight.

A minute later Reacher was at his door, unlocking it again, opening it up, and stepping inside. Nothing was disturbed. Nothing was torn up or tipped over or trashed. Therefore there had been no detailed search. Just a cursory poke around, looking for a first impression.

Which was what?

There was a wet tub, and a wet towel, and some old clothes stuffed in the trash cans, and some abandoned toiletries near the sink. Like he had just upped and quit. Which they had told him to, after all. *You should get the hell out of town, right now. Every night we find you still here, we're going to kick your ass.*

Maybe they thought he had heeded their warnings.

Or maybe not.

He left the room again and walked up to the motel office. The clerk was a squirrelly guy about forty, all bad skin and jutting bone, perched up on a high stool behind the counter. Reacher said, "You let four guys into my room."

The clerk sucked his teeth and nodded.

Reacher said, "Army?"

The guy nodded again.

"Did you see ID?"

"Didn't need to. They had the look."

"You do a lot of business with the army?"

"Enough."

"To never ask questions?"

"You got it, chief. I'm sweetness and light all the way, with the army. Because a man's got to eat. They do anything wrong?"

"Not a thing," Reacher said. "Did you hear any names?"

"Only yours."

Reacher said nothing.

"Anything else I can do for you?" the guy asked.

"I could use a fresh towel," Reacher said. "And more soap, I guess. And more shampoo. And you could empty my trash."

"Whatever you want," the guy said. "I'm sweetness and light all the way, with the army."

Reacher walked back to his room. There was no chair. Which was not a breach of the Geneva Conventions, but confinement to quarters was going to be irksome for a large and restless man. Plus it was only a motel, with no room service. And no dining room, and no greasy spoon cafe across the street, either. And no telephone, and therefore no delivery. So Reacher locked up again and walked away, to the Greek place two blocks distant. Technically a grievous breach of his orders, but win or lose, trivialities weren't going to count for much, either one way or the other.

He saw nothing on the walk, except another municipal bus, heading out, and a garbage truck, on its rounds. At the restaurant the hostess gave him a table on the other side of the room from his breakfast billet, and he got a different waitress. He ordered coffee, and a cheeseburger, and a slice of pie, and he enjoyed it all. He saw nothing on the walk back except another bus heading out, and another garbage truck on its rounds. He was back in his room less than an hour after leaving it. The squirrelly guy had been in with a new towel, and new soap, and new shampoo. The trash cans were empty. The room was as good as it was going to get. He lay down on the bed and crossed his ankles and put his hands behind his head and thought about taking a nap.

But he didn't get one. Within about a minute of his head hitting the pillow, three warrant officers from the 75th MP showed up to arrest him.

Chapter 14

They came in a car, and they were driving it fast. Reacher heard it on the road, and he heard it thump up into the lot, and he heard it slew around and jam to a stop outside. He heard three doors open, a ragged sequence of three separate sounds, all contained in the same second, and he heard three pairs of boots hit the ground, which meant three guys, not four, which meant they were not the guys from the car with the dented doors. There was a pause, with one set of footsteps receding fast, which he guessed was someone running around to cover the rear, which was a waste of time, because there was no bathroom window, but they didn't know that, and better safe than sorry. Which told him he was dealing with a competent crew.

He uncrossed his ankles and unlaced his hands from behind his head and sat up on the bed. He swiveled around and put his feet on the floor. Right on cue the hammering started on the door. Nothing like

Major Sullivan's polite little *tap, tap, tappity tap* from six o'clock in the morning. This was a full-on furious *boom, boom, boom,* by big strong guys trained to make a paralyzing first impression. Not his own favorite method. He had always felt self-conscious, making a lot of noise.

The guys outside stopped banging long enough to shout something a couple of times. *Open up, open up,* Reacher guessed. Then they started banging again. Reacher stood up and walked to the door. He thumped on it from the inside, just as hard and just as loud. The commotion stopped on the outside. Reacher smiled. No one expects a door to talk back.

He opened up and saw two guys in army combat uniform. One had a sidearm drawn, and the other had a shotgun. Which was pretty damn serious, for a suburban Virginia afternoon. Behind them their car had three doors hanging open. Its motor was running.

Reacher said, "What?"

The guy on the hinge side of the door was in charge. Safest spot, for the senior guy. He said, "Sir, you're to come with us."

"Says who?"

"Says me."

"Unit?"

"75th MP."

"Acting for who?"

"You'll find out."

The name on the guy's uniform tape was Espin. He was about the size of a flyweight boxer, dark haired, hard and muscled, with a flattened nose. He looked like an OK type of guy. In general Reacher liked warrant officers. Not as much as sergeants, but more than most commissioned officers.

He asked, "Is this an arrest?"

"Do you want it to be?" Espin said. "If so, keep talking."

"Make your mind up, soldier. It's one thing or the other."

"I prefer voluntary cooperation."

"Dream on."

"Then yes, you're under arrest."

"What's your name?"

"Espin."

"First name?"

"Why?"

"I want to remember it as long as I live."

"Is that a threat?"

"What's your name?"

"Pete," the guy said.

"Got it," Reacher said. "Pete Espin. Where are we going?"

"Fort Dyer," Pete Espin said.

"Why?"

"Someone wants to talk to you."

The third guy came back from behind the building. Junior to Espin, but only technically. All three of them looked like veterans. Seen it all, done it all. Espin said, "We're going to search you first."

"Be my guest," Reacher said. He held his arms out wide. He had nothing to hide. He had nothing in his pockets except his passport, his ATM card, his toothbrush, some cash money, some gum, and his motel key. Which was all quickly confirmed. Whereupon the guy with the shotgun motioned him over to the car. To the back seat on the passenger side. Which was the safest spot to carry a bad guy in a four-place vehicle without a security screen. Smallest chance of him interfering with the driver. The guy who had checked for a bathroom window got in the driver's seat. Espin got in next to Reacher. The guy with the shotgun closed Reacher's door on him and then climbed in the front passenger seat. All set, nice and easy and professional. A good crew.

It was too late for lunch and too early for rush hour, so the roads were clear and the drive was quick, on a different route than the one Reacher had used before, through a tangle of streets to Dyer's northern entrance, which seemed much less used than the main gate to the south. But it was no less secure. Getting in took the same amount of time. Dragons' teeth, barriers, and check, check, check, three separate times. Then they drove a looping back way around and fetched up at the rear door of the guardhouse. Reacher was ushered out of the car, and in through the door, to a guy behind it. Not exactly a prison guard. More like a clerk or an administrator. He was unarmed, like most prison staff, and he had keys on his belt. He was in a small square lobby, with locked quarantine doors to the left and the right.

Reacher was led through the door on the left and onward to an interview room. Which had no windows. Just four blank walls, and a table bolted to the floor, with two chairs on one side and one on the other. The room had not been designed by the dining room guy. That was clear. There was no blond wood or carpet. Just scuffed white paint on cinder block, and a cracked concrete floor, and a fluorescent bulb in a wire cage on the ceiling.

A Dyer guy Reacher hadn't seen before came in with a clear plastic zip bag and took away all the stuff from his pockets. Reacher sat down on the solo side of the table. He figured that was his designated position. Espin sat down opposite him. Everyone else left. Espin said nothing. No questions, no pleasantries, no bullshit to pass the time.

Reacher said, "Who wants to talk to me?"

Espin said, "He's on his way."

"He?"

"Some Polish name."

"Who is he?"

"You'll see."

Which Reacher did, about twenty minutes later. The door opened, and a man in a suit came in. The man was on the early side of middle age, with short dark hair showing some gray, and a pale, pouchy face showing some fatigue, and a hard compact body showing some time in the gym. The suit was black, not cheap, but worn and shiny in places, and it had a badge holder flipped open and hooked in the top breast pocket. The badge was Metro PD. Which was D.C.'s local police department.

A civilian.

The guy sat down next to Espin and said, "I'm Detective Podolski."

"Good to know," Reacher said.

"I need some answers."

"To what kind of questions?"

"I think you know."

"I don't."

"Questions about a felony assault."

"How old this time? Twenty years? A hundred? Something that happened during the Civil War?"

"Tell me about your morning."

"What morning?"

"This morning. Today."

"I got up, and then I spoke to a lawyer, and then I spoke to another lawyer, and then I spoke to another lawyer. This morning was wall to wall lawyers, basically."

"Their names?"

"Sullivan, Edmonds, and Moorcroft."

"And Moorcroft would be Colonel Moorcroft, of your JAG school in Charlottesville, but temporarily working out of this base?"

"Not my JAG school," Reacher said. "But yes, that's the guy."

"And where did you speak with him?"

"Right here, on this base. In the OC dining room."

"And when did you speak with him?"

"This morning. Like I said."

"What time specifically?"

"Does a private conversation between two army officers on an army base fall into your jurisdiction, detective?"

"This one does," Podolski said. "Believe me. When did you speak with him?"

"His breakfast time," Reacher said. "Which was later than mine. I would say the conversation began at twenty-three minutes past nine."

"That's certainly specific."

"You asked me to be specific."

Podolski said, "What was the conversation with Colonel Moorcroft about?"

"A legal matter," Reacher said.

"Privileged?"

"No, it was about a third party."

"And the third party would be Major Susan Turner, of the 110th MP, currently under investigation by the army on corruption charges?"

"Correct."

"And Major Sullivan witnessed this conversation, is that right?"

"Yes, she was there."

"She says you wanted Colonel Moorcroft to do something, is that correct?"

"Yes, it is."

"You wanted him to appeal Major Turner's pre-trial confinement?"

"Yes, I did."

"But he wouldn't? Is that correct? And in fact he told you to butt out?"

"At one point, yes."

"You argued, in fact. In a heated manner."

"We didn't argue. We discussed a technical matter. It wasn't heated."

"But the bottom line is you wanted Colonel Moorcroft to do something for you, and he refused to do it. Is that a fair summary?"

Reacher said, "What exactly is this about?"

Podolski said, "It's about Colonel Moorcroft getting beaten half to death, late this morning, in southeast D.C. On my streets."

Chapter 15

Podolski took out a notebook and a pen, and he laid them neatly on the table, and he said, "You should have a lawyer here."

Reacher said, "I wasn't in southeast D.C. today. Or any other part. I didn't even cross the river."

"Do you want a lawyer?"

"I already have a lawyer. Two of them, actually. They're not much use to me. In fact one of them in particular seems to be doing me no good at all."

"Major Sullivan, you mean?"

"She left before the conversation was over. Moorcroft was going to file the paperwork. He agreed just after Sullivan was gone."

"That's convenient."

"It's also true. Is Moorcroft saying different?"

"Moorcroft isn't saying anything. He's in a coma."

Reacher said nothing.

"You had a car, didn't you?" Podolski asked. "A blue Chevrolet sedan, borrowed from the 110th HQ."

"So what?"

"You could have grabbed Moorcroft up and driven him across the river."

"Could have, I suppose, but didn't."

"It was a brutal attack."

"If you say so."

"I do say so. There must have been blood everywhere."

Reacher nodded. "Brutal attacks and blood everywhere tend to go hand in hand."

"Tell me about your clothes."

"What clothes?"

"The clothes you're wearing."

Reacher looked down. "They're new. I just bought them."

"Where?"

"At a strip mall two blocks from my motel."

"Why did you buy them?"

She'll be out and about before long.

"It was time," Reacher said.

"Were your old clothes dirty?"

"I suppose."

"Did you get something on them?"

"Like what?"

"Blood, for instance."

"No, there was no blood on them."

"Where are they now?"

Reacher said nothing.

Podolski said, "We talked to the clerk at your motel. He said you made a point of asking for your trash to be emptied."

"I didn't really make a point."

"But still, he emptied your trash. Like you asked him to. Just before the garbage truck came. So now, your old clothes are gone."

"Coincidence."

"That's convenient," Podolski said again. "Isn't it?"

Reacher didn't reply.

Podolski said, "The clerk checked the clothes. He's that kind of guy. They were too big for him, of course, but they might have had some value. But they didn't. Too dirty, he said. And too stained. Including with what looked like blood to him."

"Not Moorcroft's," Reacher said.

"Whose, then?"

"I'd been wearing them a long time. I have a hard life."

"You fight a lot?"

"As little as possible. But sometimes I cut myself shaving."

"You showered, too, didn't you?"

"When?"

"When you trashed the clothes. The motel clerk said you asked him for new towels."

"Yes, I showered."

"Do you normally shower twice a day?"

"Sometimes."

"Was there a particular reason, today?"

She'll be out and about before long.

Reacher said, "No particular reason."

"To rinse the blood, maybe?"

"I wasn't bleeding."

"If we checked the drain, what would we find?"

"Dirty water," Reacher said.

"You sure about that?"

"The whole room is dirty."

"You're facing a homicide charge right now, is that correct? From sixteen years ago? Juan Rodriguez? Some guy you beat up?"

"False accusation."

"I've heard that before. Which is what Colonel Moorcroft said too, isn't it? Major Sullivan told me you mentioned the matter to him. But he wasn't sympathetic. Did that make you angry?"

"It made me a little frustrated."

"Yes, it must get tiring, being so widely misunderstood."

Reacher said, "How bad is Moorcroft?"

"Feeling guilty now?"

"I'm feeling concerned, about him and his client."

"I heard you never even met the woman."

"Should that make a difference?"

"The doctors say Moorcroft might wake up at some point. No one can say when, or what state he'll be in when he does. If he does."

Reacher said, "I was at the 110th HQ part of the morning."

Podolski nodded. "For about twenty minutes total. We checked. What were you doing the rest of the morning?"

"Walking."

"Where?"

"Here and there."

"Anyone see you walking?"

"I don't think so."

"That's convenient," Podolski said, for the third time.

"You're talking to the wrong guy, detective. Last I saw of Moorcroft, he was making his way out of the OC dining room right here, happy as a clam. Whoever attacked him is running around out there, laughing at you, while you're wasting your time with me."

"In other words, some other dude did it?"

"Obviously."

"I've heard that before," Podolski said again.

"You ever been wrong?"

"Doesn't matter. What matters is, am I wrong now? And I don't think I am. I've got a guy with a history of violence, who was seen arguing with the victim right before the time of the crime, and who dumped a full set of clothes right after the time of the crime, and took his second shower of the day, and who had access to a vehicle, and whose movements aren't entirely accounted for. You were a cop, correct? What would you do?"

"I would find the right guy. I'm sure I saw that written down somewhere."

"Suppose the right guy says he's the wrong guy?"

"Happened all the time. You have to use your judgment."

"I am."

"Pity," Reacher said.

"Show me your hands."

Reacher put his hands on the table, flat, palms down. They looked big and tan, and worn and rough.

Both sets of knuckles were very slightly pink, and very slightly swollen. From the night before. The two guys, in the T-shirts. The left hook, and the right uppercut. Big impacts. Not the biggest ever, but solid. Podolski stared for a long time.

"Inconclusive," he said. "Maybe you used a weapon. A blunt instrument of some kind. The doctors will tell me."

Reacher said, "So what next?"

"That's the DA's decision. In the meantime you'll come with me. I want you locked up downtown."

The room went quiet, and then Espin spoke for the first time.

"No," he said. "Unacceptable. He stays here. Our homicide beats your felony assault."

Podolski said, "This morning beats sixteen years ago."

Espin said, "Possession is nine points of the law. We've got him. You don't. Imagine the paperwork."

Podolski didn't answer.

Espin said, "But you can come over and talk to him anytime you want."

"Will he be locked up?" Podolski asked.

"Tighter than a fish's butt."

"Deal," Podolski said. He stood up, and gathered his pen and his notebook, and walked out of the room.

After that it was straight into routine pre-trial confinement. Reacher was searched again, and his boot laces were taken away, and he was half-pushed and half-led along a narrow blank corridor, past two grander interview rooms opposite, and around two corners, all the way to the cell block. Which was a lot more civilized than some Reacher had seen. It was more like the far corner of a chain hotel than a prison. It was a warren of subcorridors and small lobbies, and the cell itself was like a motel room. Hardened, for sure, with bolts and locks, and a steel door that opened outward, and concrete walls, and a barred foot-high slit window near the ceiling, and metal fittings in the bathroom, and a narrow barracks-style cot for a bed, but it was spacious and reasonably comfortable all the same. Better than the place on the three-lane, overall. That was for damn sure. There was even a chair next to the bed. Joint Base Dyer-Helsington House, in all its opulent glory. High-status prisoners on the inside got it better than low-status officers on the outside.

Reacher sat down in the chair.

Espin waited in the doorway.

Hope for the best, plan for the worst.

Reacher said, "I need to see the duty captain, as soon as possible."

Espin said, "He'll stop by anyway. He'll need to tell you the rules."

"I know the rules. I was a duty captain myself, once upon a time. But I still need to see him as soon as possible."

"I'll pass on the message."

And then Espin left.

The door slammed, and the lock turned, and the bolts shot home.

* * *

Twenty minutes later the same sounds happened in reverse. The bolts slammed back, and the lock turned the other way, and the door opened. The beanpole captain ducked his head under the lintel and walked in. He said, "Are we going to have trouble with you?"

Reacher said, "I don't see why you should, as long as you all behave yourselves properly."

The tall guy smiled. "What can I do for you?"

"You can call someone for me. Sergeant Leach at the 110th. Tell her where I am. She might have a message for me. If she does, you can come and tell me what it is."

"You want me to feed your dog and pick up your dry cleaning, too?"

"I don't have dry cleaning. Or a dog. But you can call Major Sullivan, at JAG, if you like. She's my lawyer. Tell her I want to see her, here, by the close of business today. Tell her I need a client conference. Tell her it's extremely important."

"That it?"

"No. Next you can call Captain Edmonds, at HRC. She's my other lawyer. Tell her I want to see her right after Major Sullivan. Tell her I have urgent things to discuss."

"Anything else?"

"How many customers do you have today?"

"Just you and one other."

"Which would be Major Turner, right?"

"Correct."

"Is she nearby?"

"This is the only cell block we got."

"She needs to know her lawyer is out of action. She

needs to get another one. You need to go see her and make sure she does."

"That's a weird thing for you to say."

"What happened to Moorcroft was nothing to do with me. You'll know that soon enough. And the best way of getting the egg off your face is not to get it on in the first place."

"Still a weird thing for you to say. Who died and made you president of the ACLU?"

"I swore an oath to uphold the Constitution. So did you. Major Turner is entitled to competent representation at all times. That's the theory. And a gap will look bad, when the appeals kick in. So tell her she needs to meet with someone new. As soon as possible. This afternoon would be good. Make sure she grasps that."

"Anything else?"

"We're all good now," Reacher said. "Thank you, captain."

"You're welcome," the tall guy said. He turned around and folded himself under the lintel again and stepped out to the corridor. The door slammed, and the lock turned, and the bolts shot home.

Reacher stayed where he was, in the chair.

Fifteen minutes later the door sounds came again. The bolts, the lock, the hinges. This time the duty captain stayed out in the corridor. Less strain on his neck. He said, "Message from Sergeant Leach, over at your HQ. The two guys in Afghanistan were found dead. On a goat trail in the Hindu Kush. Shot in the head.

Nine millimeter, probably. Three days ago, possibly, by the looks of it."

Reacher paused a beat, and then he said, "Thank you, captain."

Hope for the best, plan for the worst.

And the worst had happened.

Chapter 16

Reacher stayed in his chair, thinking hard, flipping an imaginary coin in his head. First time: heads or tails? Fifty-fifty, obviously. Because the coin was imaginary. A real coin flipped by a real human trended closer to 51-49 in favor of whichever side was uppermost at the outset. No one could explain exactly why, but the phenomenon was easily observed in experiments. Something to do with multiple axes of spin, and wobble, and aerodynamics, and the general difference between theory and practice.

But Reacher's coin was imaginary. So, second time: heads or tails? Exactly fifty-fifty again. And the third time, and the fourth time. Each flip was a separate event all its own, with identical odds, statistically independent of anything that came before. Always fifty-fifty, every single time. But that didn't mean the chances of flipping four heads in a row were fifty-fifty. Far from it. The chances of flipping four heads in a row were about ninety-four to six against. Much worse than fifty-fifty. Simple math.

And Reacher needed four heads in a row. As in: Would Susan Turner get a new lawyer that afternoon? Answer: either yes or no. Fifty-fifty. Like heads or tails, like flipping a coin. Then: Would that new lawyer be a white male? Answer: either yes or no. Fifty-fifty. And then: Would first Major Sullivan or subsequently Captain Edmonds be in the building at the same time as Susan Turner's new lawyer? Assuming she got one? Answer: either yes or no. Fifty-fifty. And finally: Would all three lawyers have come in through the same gate as each other? Answer: either yes or no. Fifty-fifty.

Four yes-or-no answers, each one of them a separate event all its own. Each one of them a perfect fifty-fifty chance in its own right. But four correct answers in a row were a six-in-a-hundred improbability.

Hope for the best. Which Reacher did. To some extent justifiably, he felt. Statistics were cold and indifferent. Which the real world wasn't, necessarily. The army was an imperfect institution. Even in noncombatant roles like the JAG Corps, it wasn't perfectly gender-neutral, for instance. Senior ranks favored men. And a senior rank would be seen as necessary for the defense of an MP major on a corruption charge. Therefore the gender of Susan Turner's new lawyer wasn't exactly a fifty-fifty proposition. Probably closer to seventy-thirty, in the desired direction. Moorcroft had been male, after all. And white. Black people were well represented in the military, but in no greater proportion than the population as a whole, which was about one in eight. About eighty-seven to thirteen, right there.

And Reacher could keep at least one of his own lawyers in the building practically indefinitely. All he had to do was keep them talking. One spurious point after another. Some big show of anxiety. He could keep them there forever, until they grew bored or impatient enough to abandon legal propriety and good manners. Therefore the chances of his lawyer and Turner's being present in the building together were better than fifty-fifty, too. Seventy-thirty again, possibly. Maybe even better.

And regular visitors to Dyer might know the north gate was closer to the guardhouse, and therefore they could be relied upon to use it. Maybe. Which put the gate question better than fifty-fifty, too. If Turner's new lawyer was a regular visitor. Which he might not be. Pointy-headed classroom stars didn't necessarily get around much. Call it fifty-five to forty-five. A marginal advantage. Not overwhelming.

Nevertheless, overall, the plan's chances were a little better than six in a hundred.

But not a whole lot better.

If Turner got a new lawyer in the first place, that was.

Hope for the best.

Reacher waited. Relaxed, patient, inert. He counted off the time in his head. Three o'clock in the afternoon. Three-thirty. Four o'clock. The chair was comfortable. The room was warm. And fairly soundproof.

Very little noise was audible from the outside. Just a dull acoustic. Not that the place was remotely like a regular prison. It was a civilized place, for civilized people.

All of which, Reacher hoped, was going to help.

Finally at four-thirty in the afternoon the bolts slammed back, and the lock turned, and the door opened. The beanpole captain said, "Major Sullivan is here to see you."

Showtime.

Chapter 17

The tall guy stood back and let Reacher walk in front of him. The corridor dog-legged left, and then right. Reacher pieced together the geography from what little he had seen. He figured the main office was around three more corners. Still some distance away. Before that would come the small square lobby, with the locked quarantine doors, and the clerk, and the rear door to the outside. Before that would come the interview rooms, on both sides of a short stretch of corridor all its own. The scuffed spaces for cops and suspects would be on the right, and on the left would be the slightly grander spaces he had seen on his way to the cells. There were two of them. His destination, he assumed. Higher quality, for conferences between lawyers and clients. They had windows in their doors, narrow vertical rectangles of wired glass, set off-center above the handles.

He walked straight past the first door, glancing in the window but pretending not to, seeing Sullivan in there, seated on the left side of a table, in her neat Class A uniform, hands folded on top of her closed briefcase, and he kept on walking, to the second door, where he stopped and glanced in the window quite openly.

The second room was empty.

No client, and no lawyer, male or otherwise.

Neither heads nor tails.

Not yet.

Behind him the tall guy said, "Hold up, major. You're in this one back here."

Reacher turned around and tracked back. The door wasn't locked. The tall guy just turned the handle and opened it up. Reacher listened to the sounds it made. A solid metallic click from the handle, a cursive precision grind from the hinges, an air-locked swish from the silicone seals. Not loud, but distinctive. Reacher stepped inside. Sullivan looked up. The tall guy said, "Buzz when you're done, counselor."

Reacher sat down opposite Sullivan, and the tall guy closed the door and walked away. The door was not locked because there was no handle on the inside. Just a flat expanse, with something missing, unexpected, like a face without a nose. There was a doorbell button next to the jamb. *Buzz when you're done.* The room itself was plain and pleasant. No windows, but it was cleaner and crisper than the cop room. The light bulb was brighter.

Sullivan kept her briefcase closed, and her hands clasped on top of it. She said, "I won't represent you in the Moorcroft assault. In fact I really don't want you as a client at all."

Reacher didn't answer. He was checking what he could hear from the corridor. Which wasn't much, but which was maybe enough.

Sullivan said, "Major?"

Reacher said, "I'm what they're giving you, so get used to it."

"Colonel Moorcroft is a friend of mine."

"Your old teacher?"

"One of them."

"Then you know what those guys are like. In their heads they're never out of the classroom. Socratic, or whatever they call it. He was yanking my chain, for the sake of it. He was arguing, for the fun of it, because that's what they do. You left, and then as soon as he finished his toast he said he was going to file the paperwork. He intended to all along. But straight answers aren't his style."

"I don't believe you. No paperwork was filed this morning."

"The last I saw of him he was walking out of the dining room. About two minutes after you."

"So you're denying this one, too?"

"Think about it, counselor. My aim was to get Major Turner out of her cell. How would attacking Moorcroft help me? It would set me back, at least a day, if not two or three."

"Why do you care so much about Major Turner?"

"I liked her voice on the phone."

"Maybe you were angry with Moorcroft."

"Did I look angry?"

"A little."

"You're wrong, major. I didn't look angry at all. Because I wasn't angry. I was sitting there quite patiently. He wasn't the first classroom guy I ever met. I went to school, after all."

"I felt uncomfortable."

"What did you tell Podolski?"

"Just that. There was a dispute, and I felt uncomfortable."

"Did you tell him it was heated?"

"You confronted him. You argued."

"What was I supposed to do? Stand up and salute? He's not exactly the Chief Justice of the Supreme Court."

"The evidence against you appears to be considerable. The clothes, in particular. That's classic."

Reacher didn't answer. He was listening again. He heard footsteps in the corridor. Two people. Both men. Low voices. Short, uncontroversial sentences. A succinct and everyday exchange of information. The footsteps moved on. There were no door sounds. No click, no grind, no swish.

Sullivan said, "Major?"

Reacher said, "Do you have a wallet in your briefcase?"

"What?"

"You heard me."

"Why would I?"

"Because you're not carrying a purse, and if you don't mind me saying so, your uniform is tailored very close to your figure, and there are absolutely no bulges in your pockets."

Sullivan kept her hands on her briefcase and said, "Yes, I have a wallet in here."

"How much money is in it?"

"I don't know. Thirty dollars, maybe."

"How much was your last ATM withdrawal?"

"Two hundred."

"Got a cell phone in there, too?"

"Yes."

"Then there's as much evidence against you as me. Clearly you called an accomplice and offered him a hundred and seventy bucks to kick your old teacher's ass. Maybe because your grades weren't perfect, all those years ago. Maybe you were still angry about it."

"That's ridiculous."

"That's what I'm saying."

Sullivan didn't answer.

Reacher asked, "How were your grades?"

Sullivan said, "Not perfect."

Reacher listened again. Silence in the corridor.

Sullivan said, "Detective Podolski will order a landfill search. He'll find your clothes. It won't be difficult. Last in, first out. Will they stand up to DNA analysis?"

"Easily," Reacher said. "It wasn't me."

Then: more footsteps in the corridor. Soft, quiet, two people. A procession, maybe. One person leading another. A halt, an explanation, a casual, low-toned, ten-beat sentence. Maybe: *This one, colonel. The other one's in use.* And: door sounds. The crisp metallic click of the handle, the slick grind of the hinges, and the suck of the silicone seal.

The arrival of a lawyer. Turner's, for sure. Because she was the only other customer in the place. While

Reacher's lawyer was still in the building. His first lawyer, yet. So far, so good.

Heads and heads.

Score two.

Reacher said, "Tell me about the Rodriguez affidavit."

Sullivan said, "An affidavit is a sworn statement of fact."

"I know that," Reacher said. "Like I told your old pal Moorcroft, this stuff isn't brain surgery. *Affidavit* is Latin for *he has declared upon oath.* But does it really speak from beyond the grave? In a practical sense? Real world?"

For the first time Sullivan took her hands off her briefcase. She rocked them from side to side. Equivocal. All kinds of academic gestures. *Maybe, maybe not.* She said, "In American jurisprudence it's fairly unusual to rely on an unsupported affidavit, especially if the person who swore it out is unavailable for cross examination. But it can be allowed, if the interests of justice demand it. Or the interests of public relations, if you want to be cynical. And the prosecution will argue that Rodriguez's affidavit is not exactly unsupported, anyhow. They have the daily summary from the 110th's files, showing your visit with him, and they have the ER report from immediately afterward, showing the results of it. They'll claim the three things together present a seamless and coherent narrative."

"Can you argue against that?"

"Of course," Sullivan said. "But our argument looks suddenly very weak, dynamically. What they're going to say makes perfect sense, in an everyday way.

This happened, then this happened, then this happened. We'll need to take out the middle *this* and replace it with something that sounds very unlikely on its face. As in, you left, and someone else just happened to show up in the same place at the same time and beat the guy to a pulp."

Reacher didn't answer. He was listening again.

Sullivan said, "Our problem is whether an attempted defense that fails will annoy the court to the point where you get a worse sentence than you would have gotten with the plea bargain. Which is a serious risk. My advice is to play safe and take the deal. Two years is better than five or ten."

Reacher didn't answer. He was still listening. At first, to nothing. Just silence. Then: more footsteps in the corridor. Two people. One following the other.

Sullivan said, "Major?"

Then: door sounds. The same door. The same crisp metallic click of the handle, the same slick grind of the hinges, the same suck of the silicone seal. Then a pause, and the same sounds all over again, in the reverse sequence, as the door closed. And then: one set of footsteps, walking away.

So now Turner was in the next-door room with her lawyer, and the corridor was empty.

Showtime.

Reacher said, "I have a serious problem with my cell, counselor. You really need to come see it."

Chapter 18

Sullivan asked, "What kind of a problem do you have with your cell?" She said it a little wearily, but not impatiently. She wasn't dismissing the matter out of hand. Defense lawyers dealt with all kinds of bull-shit. Suspects were always looking for an edge or an angle. For the inevitable appeal. Any imagined slight or unfairness had to be investigated and evaluated. Reacher knew that. He knew how the game was played.

He said, "I don't want to put something in your mind. I don't want to preempt your honest opinion. I need you to see this for yourself."

"Now?"

"Why not?"

"OK," she said, a little wearily.

She stood up. She stepped over to the door. She pressed the buzzer.

She left her briefcase on the table.

Reacher stood up and waited behind her.

One minute.

Two.

Then the narrow glass window in the door darkened, and the door opened up, and the duty captain said, "All done, counselor?"

Sullivan said, "No, he has a problem with his cell."

The tall guy looked at Reacher, with a quizzical expression on his face, part resigned, part surprised, as if to say, *Really? You? This old shit?*

But he said, "OK, whatever. Let's go take a look."

Like he had to. He knew how the game was played.

Reacher led the way. Sullivan went next. The tall guy brought up the rear. They walked in single file, through the dog-legs, left and then right, to the cell door, which was unlocked and unbolted, because Reacher wasn't in it. Reacher pulled it open and held it for the others. The tall guy smiled and took the door from him and gestured: *after you.* He was dumb, but not brain damaged.

Reacher went in first. Then came Sullivan. Then the tall guy. Reacher stopped and pointed.

"Over there," he said. "In the crack."

Sullivan said, "What crack?"

"In the floor, near the wall. Under the window."

Sullivan stepped forward. The tall guy stopped short of the bed. Sullivan said, "I don't see a crack."

Reacher said, "There's something in it. It's wriggling."

Sullivan froze. The tall guy leaned in. Human nature. Reacher leaned the other way, just a subtle drift, but the tall guy's mass was moving one way, and Reacher's the other. Reacher shoved the guy, below his shoulder, on his upper arm, hard, like a swimmer pushes off the end of the pool, and the guy went down over the bed like he was falling off a pair of stilts. Sullivan spun around and Reacher stepped to the door, and out to the corridor, and he closed the door and bolted it.

Then he ran back, awkward in his laceless boots, past the room with Sullivan's briefcase in it, to the next room. He stood well back and looked in through the narrow rectangular window.

And saw Susan Turner for the very first time.

She was worth the wait, he thought.

Totally worth it.

She was sitting on the right-hand side of the table. She was wearing army combat uniform, with all the hook-and-loop tapes and tags pulled off, and tan combat boots, with no laces. She was an inch or two above average height. She was small-boned and slender, with dark hair pulled back, and tanned skin, and deep brown eyes. Her face was showing mostly fatigue, but there was spirit in it too, and intelligence, and a kind of detached, ironic mischief.

Spectacular, in Reacher's considered opinion.

Totally worth the wait, he thought again.

Her lawyer was on the left side of the table, a full bird colonel in Class A uniform. Gray hair and a lined face. Middle-aged and medium-sized.

A man.

A white man.

Heads.

Score three.

* * *

Reacher moved on, all the way to the quarantine door between himself and the rear lobby. There was no inside handle. Just a buzzer button, like the conference rooms. He kicked off his boots, and then he hit the button, urgently, over and over again. Less than five seconds later the door opened. The lobby clerk stood there, the handle in his hand. His keys were on a squared-off metal screw ring, like a small piece of mountaineering equipment, secured in a belt loop.

Reacher said, breathless, "Your captain is having some kind of a seizure. Or a heart attack. He's thrashing around. You need to check him out. Right now, soldier."

Command presence. Much prized by the military. The guy hesitated less than a second and then stepped into the inner corridor. The door started to swing shut behind him. Reacher nudged his left boot into the gap, and then turned to follow. He ran bootless and quiet behind the guy and then overtook him and wrenched open the first cell door he came to. Unlocked and unbolted, because it was empty.

But not for long.

"In here," he said.

The lobby guy shouldered in, fast and urgent, and Reacher grabbed his keys and tore them right off his pants, belt loop and all, and then he shoved him hard and sent him sprawling, and he closed the door and shot the bolts.

He breathed in, and he breathed out.

Now came the hard part.

Chapter 19

Reacher padded bootless back to the room where Sullivan's briefcase still rested on the table. He pushed the door all the way open and darted in and grabbed the case and then he turned back fast and caught the door again before it slammed shut behind him. He knelt on the floor in the corridor and opened the case. He ignored all the files and all the legal paperwork and rooted around until he found a car key, which he put in his pants pocket. Then he found the wallet. He took out the army ID. Sullivan's first name was Helen. He put the ID in his shirt pocket. He took out her money and put it in his other pants pocket. He found a pen and tore off a small triangle of paper from a Xeroxed form and he wrote *Dear Helen, IOU $30,* and he signed it *Jack Reacher.* He put the slip of paper in the money slot, and he closed the wallet, and he closed the briefcase.

Then he stood up, with the briefcase in his hand.

He breathed in, and breathed out.

Showtime.

He moved on, twelve feet, to the next room, and he glanced in through the narrow window. Susan Turner was talking, patiently, marshaling arguments, using her hands, separating one point from another. Her lawyer was listening, head cocked, writing notes on a yellow legal pad. His briefcase was open on the table, pushed to the side. It was emptier than Sullivan's, but the guy's pockets were fuller. His uniform was not well tailored. It was baggy and generous. The nameplate on the pocket flap said Temple.

Reacher moved on again, all the way to the quarantine door between him and the lobby. He replaced his left boot with Sullivan's car key, so the door stayed unlatched, and he put his boots back on, slack and laceless. Then he headed back to Turner's interview room, and he stopped outside the door.

He breathed in, and he breathed out.

Then he opened the door, fast and easy, and he stepped inside the room. He turned and bent and placed Sullivan's briefcase against the jamb, to stop the door from closing again. He turned back, and saw both Turner and her lawyer looking up at him, nothing much in the lawyer's face, but what looked like dawning recognition in Turner's.

He said, "Colonel, I need to see your ID."

The guy said, "Who are you?"

"Defense Intelligence Agency. Purely routine, sir."

Command presence. Much prized by the military. The guy stalled a second, and then he fished in an inside pocket and came out with his ID. Reacher stepped over and took it from him and looked hard at it. *John*

James Temple. He raised his eyebrows, as if surprised, and he looked again, and then he slipped the ID into his shirt pocket, right next to Sullivan's.

He said, "I'm sorry, colonel, but I need a minute of your time."

He stepped back to the door and held it open. *After you.* The guy looked uncertain for a moment, and then he got up from the table, slowly. Reacher glanced over his shoulder at Turner and said, "You wait here, miss. We'll be right back."

The lawyer paused a beat and then shuffled out ahead of him. Reacher said, "Sir, to your right, please," and followed after him, also shuffling, literally, because of the loose boots. Which were the weak points. Lawyers weren't necessarily the most physically observant of people, but they had brains and they were generally logical. And this phase of the plan was a low-speed proposition. No urgency. No rush, no panic. Practically slow-motion. This guy had time to think.

Which, evidently, he used.

About twenty feet short of the first vacant cell the guy stopped suddenly and turned around and looked down. Straight at Reacher's boots. Instantly Reacher spun him face-front again and put him in the kind of arresting-a-senior-officer grip that any MP learns early in his career, about which there was nothing in the field manual, and which was not taught in any way except by hints and example. Reacher grabbed the guy's right elbow from behind, in his left hand, and simultaneously squeezed it hard and pulled it downward and propelled it forward. As always the guy was left fighting the downward force so hard he forgot all about resisting the forward motion. He just stumbled onward, crabwise, twisted and bent, gasping a little, not really from pain, but from outraged dignity. Which Reacher was happy about. He didn't want to hurt the guy. This was not his fault.

Reacher maneuvered the guy to an open and empty cell, which he guessed might have been Turner's, from the look of it, and he pushed him inside, and he closed the door on him, and he bolted it.

Then he stood in the corridor, just a beat, and he breathed in, and he breathed out.

Good to go.

He shuffled back to the second conference room and stepped inside. Susan Turner was on her feet, between the table and the door. He held out his hand. He said, "I'm Jack Reacher."

"I know you are," she said. "I saw your photo. From your file. And I recognized your voice. From the phone."

And he recognized hers. From the phone. Warm, slightly husky, a little breathy, a little intimate. Just as good as he remembered. Maybe even better, live and in person.

He said, "I'm very pleased to meet you."

She shook his hand. Her touch was warm, not hard, not soft. She said, "I'm very pleased to meet you too. But what exactly are you doing?"

He said, "You know what I'm doing. And why. At least, I hope you do. Because if you don't, you're not worth doing it for."

"I didn't want you to get involved."

"Hence the thing about not visiting?"

"I thought you might show up. Just possibly. If you did, I wanted you to turn tail and get the hell out, immediately. For your own sake."

"Didn't work."

"What are our chances of getting out of here?"

"We've been lucky so far." He fished in his shirt pocket and took out Sullivan's ID. He checked the picture against Turner's face. Same gender. Roughly the same hair color. But that was about all. He gave her the ID. She said, "Who is she?"

"My lawyer. One of my lawyers. I met her this morning."

"Where is she now?"

"In a cell. Probably hammering on the door. We need to get going."

"And you're taking my lawyer's ID?"

Reacher patted his pocket. "I've got it right here."

"But you don't look anything like him."

"That's why you're going to drive."

"Is it dark yet?"

"Heading that way."

"So let's go," she said.

They stepped out to the corridor and walked to the quarantine door. It was still held open an inch by Sullivan's car key. Reacher pulled the door, and Turner scooped up the key, and they stepped into the small square lobby, and the door sucked shut behind them. The exit door was locked, with a small neat mechanism, no doubt expensive and highly secure. Reacher took out the clerk's keys, and started trying them, one after the other. There were eight in total. The first was no good. Neither was the second. Nor the third. Nor the fourth.

But the fifth key did the trick. The lock snicked open. Reacher turned the handle and pulled the door. Cold air came in, from the outside. The afternoon light was fading.

Turner said, "What car are we looking for?"

"Dark green sedan."

"That helps," she said. "On a military base."

Warm, husky, breathy, intimate.

They stepped out together. Reacher closed the door behind them, and locked it. He figured that might buy an extra minute. Ahead of them to the left was a small parking lot, about thirty yards away, across an expanse of blank blacktop. Seventeen cars in it. Mostly POVs. Only two plain sedans, neither one of them green. Beyond the lot a road curved away west. On the right the same road turned a corner and ran out of sight.

"Best guess?" Turner said.

"If in doubt, turn left," Reacher said. "That was always my operating principle."

They turned left, and found another lot hidden beyond the corner of the building. It was small, nothing more than a bumped-out strip with diagonal bays. Six cars in it, all of them nose in. All of them identical dark green sedans.

Turner said, "That's better."

She lined herself up equidistant from the six rear bumpers and pressed the button on the key fob.

Nothing happened.

She tried again. Nothing. She said, "Maybe the battery is out."

"In the car?" Reacher said.

"In the key," she said.

"Then how did Sullivan get here?"

"She stuck the key in the door. Like we used to, back in the day. We'll have to try them one by one."

"We can't do that. We'll look like car thieves."

"We are car thieves."

"Maybe none of these is the right car," Reacher said. "I didn't see the plate. It was dark this morning."

"We can't wander about this base much longer."

"Maybe we should have turned right."

They tracked back, as brisk and unobtrusive as they could be in boots without laces, past the rear door to the guardhouse again, and onward around the corner. It felt good to walk. Freedom, and fresh air. Reacher had always figured the best part of getting out of jail was the first thirty yards. And he liked having Turner next to him. She was nervous as a cat, but she was holding it together. She looked confident. They were just two people walking, like con artists everywhere: *act like you're supposed to be there.*

There was another bumped-out bay around the east corner, six diagonal slots, symmetrical with the one they had already seen to the west. There were three cars in it. Only one of them was a sedan. And it was dark green. Turner hit the key fob button.

Nothing happened.

She stepped up close and tried the key in the door. It didn't fit.

She said, "Where does a lawyer who's visiting the

guardhouse come in? The front entrance, right? Is there a parking lot out front?"

"Bound to be," Reacher said. "But I wish there wasn't. We'll be very exposed out front."

"We can't just hang around here. We're sitting ducks."

They walked on, to the front corner of the building, and stopped short, in the shadows. Reacher sensed open space ahead, and maybe lights, and maybe traffic.

"On three," Turner said. "One, two, three."

They turned the corner. *Act like you're supposed to be there.* They walked fast, like busy people going somewhere. There was a fire lane along the front face of the building, and then a curbed divider, with a long one-row lot beyond it, full of parked cars except for one empty slot. And to the left of the empty slot was a dark green sedan.

"That's it," Reacher said. "I kind of recognize it."

Turner headed straight for it and hit the key fob button, and the car lit up inside and its turn signals flashed once, and its door locks clunked open. Ahead on the left, about a hundred yards away, a car was crawling toward them, at a cautious on-post kind of speed, with its headlights on against the gloom. Reacher and Turner split up, Reacher going right, Turner going left, down the flanks of the green car, Reacher to the passenger's door, Turner to the driver's door. They opened up and climbed in together, no fumbling, no hesitation. The approaching car was getting nearer. They closed their doors, slam, slam, like overworked staffers with minutes between vital appointments, and Turner put the key in the slot and started the engine.

The oncoming car turned in to the lot, and rolled toward them, from the left, its headlight beams lighting them up.

"Go," Reacher said. "Go now."

Turner didn't. She got it in reverse gear and touched the gas, but the car went nowhere. It just reared up against the parking brake. Turner said, "Shit," and fumbled the lever down, but by then it was too late. The oncoming car was right behind them. It stopped there, blocking them in, and then its driver turned the wheel hard and crawled forward again, aiming to park in the empty slot right next to them.

Its driver was Captain Tracy Edmonds. Reacher's lawyer. Working with HRC. Candice Dayton. His second appointment of the afternoon.

Reacher slumped right down in his seat, and cradled his face in his hand, like a man with a headache.

Turner said, "What?"

"That's my other lawyer. Captain Edmonds. I scheduled back to back meetings."

"Why?"

"I wanted to be certain I was out of my cell when your lawyer showed up."

"Don't let her see you."

"That's the least of our problems. The shit will hit the fan about a minute after she goes inside, don't you think?"

"You should have figured one lawyer would be enough."

"Would you have?"

"Probably not."

Alongside them Edmonds jacked back and forth a couple of times until she was all neat and straight in her allotted space. She flicked her lights off and Turner flicked hers on and backed straight out and cut the wheel hard. Edmonds opened her door and climbed out of her car. Reacher swapped hands on his face. Turner rattled the lever into a forward gear and straightened up and took off, slowly. Edmonds waited patiently for her to complete the maneuver. Turner waved a thank-you gesture and hit the gas.

"South gate," Reacher said. "Don't you think? I figure all these guys will have come in from the north."

"Agreed," Turner said. She rolled on south, brisk but not suicidal, all the way through the complex, past buildings large and small, turning here and there, slowing here and there, waiting at stop signs, peering left and right, moving on again, until finally the last of the base fell away behind them, and then they were into the exit road, heading for the first guard shack barrier.

The first of three.

Chapter 20

The first barrier was easy. *Act like you're sup-posed to be there.* Turner collected Reacher's bor-rowed ID from him, and held it with hers, fanned in her hand like a pair of threes, and she slowed to a walk, and buzzed her window down, and popped the trunk as she eased to a stop, the whole performance a natural, flowing sequence, as if she did it every single day of her life.

And the sentry in the shack responded to the per-formance perfectly, like Reacher guessed she hoped he would. He spent less than a second glancing at the fanned IDs, and less than a second glancing into the open trunk, and less than a second slamming it shut for them.

Turner nudged the gas, and rolled forward.

And breathed out.

Reacher said, "Edmonds has to be inside by now."

"Got any bright ideas?"

"Any sign of a problem, just hit the gas. Straight

through the barrier. Busting up a piece of metal with stripes on it can't get us in much more trouble."

"We might run over a sentry."

"He'll jump out the way. Sentries are human, like anyone else."

"We'll dent an army car."

"I already dented an army car. Last night. With two guys' heads."

"You seem to have a thing about denting army property with heads," she said. Warm, husky, breathy, intimate. "Like the desk in my office."

He nodded. He had told her the story on the phone. From South Dakota. An old investigation, and a little resulting frustration. A short story, made long. Just purely to keep her talking. Just to hear more of her voice.

She asked, "Who were the two guys from last night?"

"Complicated," he said. "I'll tell you later."

"I hope you'll be able to," she said.

They rolled toward the second checkpoint. Where blasting through turned out not to be an available option. It was just after five in the afternoon. Rush hour, military style. There was a modest queue of vehicles waiting to get out, and a modest queue waiting to get in. Already two cars were in line in the exit lane, and three in the entrance lane. There were two guys on duty in the shack. One was darting left and right, letting one vehicle in, then letting one vehicle out, back and forth in strict rotation.

The other guy was inside the shack.

On the phone. Listening intently.

Turner eased to a stop, third car in line, in a narrowing lane, with the guard shack ahead on her left, and an unbroken row of concrete dragons' teeth on her right, each one of them a squat, truncated pyramid about three feet tall, each one of them no doubt built on a rebar armature and socketed deep below grade.

The second guy was still on the phone.

In the other lane the barrier went up and a car drove in. The first guy ducked across and checked ID, and checked a trunk, and hit a button, and the exit barrier went up, and a car drove out. Reacher said, "Maybe rush hour is our friend. It's all kind of cursory."

Turner said, "Depends what that phone call is."

Reacher pictured Tracy Edmonds in his mind, walking in the main door of the guardhouse, and stepping into the front office, and finding the duty captain absent. Some clerk would nod and shuffle. How patient would Edmonds be? How patient would the clerk be? Rank would play its part. Edmonds was a captain, too. Same as the duty guy. An officer of equal rank. She would cut the guy some slack. She wouldn't get instantly all up on her high horse, like a major or a colonel would. And certainly the clerk would be slow to intervene.

Inside the guard shack the second guy was still on the phone. Outside the guard shack the first guy was still darting side to side. A second car drove in, and a second car drove out. Turner rolled forward and stopped, now first in line to leave, but also completely boxed in, on the left and the right, with two cars behind her, and the striped metal barrier in front of her. She took a breath, and popped the trunk, and fanned the IDs, and buzzed her window down.

The second guy got off the phone. He put the instrument down and looked straight at the exit lane. He scanned it, front to back, and back to front, starting with Turner and finishing with Turner. He came out of the shack and stepped to her window.

He said, "Sorry for the delay."

He glanced at the fanned IDs, and stepped back and glanced at the trunk, and closed it for them, and hit the button on the side of the shack, and the barrier went up, and Turner rolled forward.

And breathed out.

Reacher said, "One more. And good things come in threes."

"You really believe that?"

"No, not really. The chances of three yes-or-no propositions working out right are about twelve in a hundred."

Up ahead the third guard shack looked to be an exact repeat of the second. The same queue of the same three cars, a matching queue on the entrance side, two guys on duty, one of them outside ducking back and forth, and one of them inside on the phone.

Listening intently.

Turner said, "These phone calls have to be important, right? I mean, these guys have got better things to do right now. There's a whole bunch of senior officers getting delayed here. And some of them must be Marines. They don't like that kind of stuff."

"And we do?"

"Not like the Marines don't. We're not always on standby to save the world."

"My dad was a Marine."

"Did he save the world?"

"He wasn't a very senior officer."

"I wish I knew who was on the phone."

Reacher thought back to when he had been a captain. How long would he have waited for another captain to finish up his business? Not too long, probably. But maybe Edmonds was a nicer person. More patient. Or maybe she felt out of her depth, in a guardhouse environment. Although she was a lawyer. She must have seen plenty of guardhouses. Unless she was mostly a desk person. A paperwork lawyer. Which she might have been. She was assigned to HRC, after all. That had to mean something. How much of HRC's work was done in the cells?

He said, "This is a big base. Those calls aren't necessarily coming from the guardhouse."

"What else would be so important?"

"Maybe they have to clear the way for a general. Or maybe they're ordering pizza delivery. Or telling their girlfriends they'll be home soon."

"Let's hope so," Turner said. "One of the above. Or all of them."

In the opposite lane the barrier went up and a car drove in. The guy on the outside ducked across to the exit lane and checked ID, and checked a trunk, and raised the barrier, and a car drove out. Turner rolled forward one place. The inside guy was still on the phone.

Still listening hard.

Turner said, "They don't even need a phone call. I'm not wearing my tapes or my tags. They were taken away from me. I look exactly like an escaping prisoner."

"Or a Special Forces hardass. Undercover and anonymous. Look on the bright side. Just don't let them see your boots."

Another car drove in, and another car drove out. Turner rolled forward to the head of the line. She popped the trunk, and fanned the IDs, and buzzed her window down. The inside guy was still on the phone. The outside guy was occupied in the other lane. Up ahead beyond the last barrier the dragons' teeth stopped and the exit road widened out and became just a regular Virginia street.

There was an Arlington County police cruiser parked on it.

Turner said, "Still want me to bust out?"

"Only if we have to," Reacher said.

The outside guy finished up checking and raised the entrance barrier. The inside guy finished up listening and put the phone down. He came out and bent down and looked at the IDs in Turner's hand. Not just a glance. His eyes flicked from the photos to the faces. Reacher looked away and stared ahead through the windshield. He stayed low in his seat and tried to look middle-aged and medium-sized. The guy at the window stepped back to the trunk. More than a glance. And then he put his palm on the lid and eased it back down and gently latched it shut.

Then he stepped away to the side of the shack.

And hit the exit button.

The barrier raised up high, and Turner nudged the gas, and the car rolled forward, under the barrier, and past the last of the dragons' teeth, and out into the neat suburban street, all wide and prosperous and tree-lined, and then onward, past the parked Arlington cruiser, and away.

Reacher thought: *Captain Tracy Edmonds must be one hell of a patient woman.*

Chapter 21

Susan Turner seemed to know the local roads. She made a left and a right and skirted the northern edge of the cemetery, and then she turned again and drove partway down its eastern flank. She said, "I assume we're heading for Union Station. To dump the car and make them think we took a train."

"Works for me," Reacher said.

"How do you want to get there?"

"What's the dumbest route?"

"At this time of day?" she said. "Surface streets, I guess. Constitution Avenue, for sure. We'd be slow and visible, all the way."

"Then that's what we'll do. They'll expect something different."

So Turner got in position and lined up to cross the river. Traffic was bad. It was rush hour in the civilian world, too. Nose to tail, like a moving parking lot. She drummed her fingers on the wheel, and watched her mirror, looking to jink from lane to lane, trying to find a tiny advantage.

"Relax," Reacher said. "Rush hour is definitely our friend now. There's no chance of pursuit."

"Unless they use a helicopter."

"Which they won't. Not here. They'd be too worried about crashing and killing a congressman. Which would do their budget no good at all."

They crept onto the bridge, slowly, and they moved out over the water, and they left Arlington County behind. Turner said, "Talking of budgets, I have no money. They took all my stuff and put it in a plastic bag."

"Me too. But I borrowed thirty bucks from my lawyer."

"Why would she lend you money?"

"She doesn't know she did. Not yet. But she'll find out soon enough. I left her an IOU."

"We're going to need more than thirty bucks. I need street clothes, for a start."

"And I need boot laces," Reacher said. "We'll have to find an ATM."

"We don't have cards."

"There's more than one kind of ATM."

They came off the bridge, slowly, stopping and starting, into the District of Columbia itself. Metro PD territory. And immediately Reacher saw two Metro cruisers up ahead. They were parked nose to nose on the curb behind the Lincoln Memorial. Their motors were running, and they had about a dozen radio antennas between them. Each car held one cop, all warm and comfortable. A standard security measure,

Reacher hoped. Turner changed lanes and rolled past them on the blind side of a stalled line of nose-to-tail traffic. They didn't react at all.

They drove onward, through the gathering dark, slow and halting, anonymous among a glacial pack of fifty thousand vehicles crowding the same few miles of streets. They went north on 23rd, the same block Reacher had walked the day before, and then they made the right onto Constitution Avenue, which ran on ahead of them, seemingly forever, straight and long, an unending river of red tail lights.

Turner said, "Tell me about the two guys from last night."

Reacher said, "I came in on the bus and went straight to Rock Creek. I was going to ask you out to dinner. But you weren't there, obviously. And the guy who was sitting in for you told me about some bullshit assault charge lodged against my file. Some gang-banger we had looked at all of sixteen years ago. I wasn't impressed, so he pulled some Title 10 thing and recalled me to service."

"What, you're back in the army?"

"As of yesterday evening."

"Outstanding."

"Doesn't feel that way. Not so far."

"Who is sitting in for me?"

"A light colonel named Morgan. A management guy, by the look of him. He quartered me in a motel north and west of the building, and about five minutes after I checked in, two guys showed up in a car. NCOs for sure, late twenties, full of piss and wind about how I had brought the unit into disrepute, and how I should get out of town, to spare them the embarrassment of a court martial, and how they were going to kick my ass if I didn't. So I banged their heads against the side of their car."

"Who the hell were they? Did you get names? I don't want people like that in my unit."

"They weren't from the 110th. That was totally clear. Their car was warm inside. It had been driven a lot farther than a mile from Rock Creek. Plus their combat skills were severely substandard. They weren't your people. I know that for sure, because I did a kind of unofficial headcount back at the building. I wandered all over, and checked all the rooms. Those guys weren't there."

"So who were they?"

"They were two small parts of a big jigsaw puzzle."

"What's the picture on the box?"

"I don't know, but I saw them again today. Only from a distance. They were at the motel, with reinforcements. Two other guys, for a total of four. I guess they were checking if I was gone yet, or else aiming to speed up my decision."

"If they weren't from the 110th, why would they want you gone?"

"Exactly," Reacher said. "They didn't even know me yet. Usually people don't want me gone until later."

They crept onward, past the Vietnam Wall. There was another Metro car there. Engine running, bristling with antennas. Reacher said, "We should assume the shit has hit the fan by now, right?"

"Unless your Captain Edmonds fell asleep waiting," Turner said.

They crawled past the parked cruiser, close enough for Reacher to see the cop inside. He was a tall black man, thin, like a blade. He could have been the duty captain's brother, from Dyer. Which would have been unfortunate.

Turner asked, "What was the assault charge from sixteen years ago?"

Reacher said, "Some LA gangbanger selling black market ordnance, from the Desert Storm drawdown. A big fat idiot who called himself Dog. I remember talking to him. Hard to forget, actually. He was about the size of a house. He just died, apparently. Leaving behind an affidavit with my name all over it. But I didn't hit him. Not a glove. Hard to see how I could, really. I would have been elbow-deep in lard before I connected with anything solid."

"So what's the story?"

"My guess is some disgruntled customer showed up with a bunch of pals and a rack of baseball bats. And some time later the fat guy started to think about how he could get compensated. You know, something for nothing, in our litigious society. So he went to some ambulance chaser, who saw no point in going after the guys with the bats. But maybe the fat guy mentioned the visit from the army, and the lawyer figured Uncle Sam had plenty of money, so they cooked up a bullshit claim. Of which there must be hundreds of thousands, over the years. Our files must be stiff with them. And quite rightly they're all looked at and laughed at and put away in a drawer and ignored forever. Except this one was hauled out again into the light of day."

"Because?"

"It's another piece of the jigsaw. Morgan told me my file had a flag on it. He said it malfunctioned when you pulled it, but triggered when you sent it back. I don't believe that. Our bureaucrats are better than that. I don't think there was a flag at all. I think there was a whole lot of last-minute scrambling going on. Someone got in a big panic."

"About you?"

Reacher shook his head. "No, about you, initially. You and Afghanistan."

Then he stopped talking, because the car filled with blue and red light. Through the mirrors. A cop car, behind them, forcing its way through. Its siren was going, cycling through all the digital variants it had, fast and urgent. The whooping, the manic cackling, the plaintive two-tone horn. Reacher turned in his seat. The cruiser was about twenty cars back. Ahead of it traffic was diving for the curb, scattering, trying to squeeze an extra lane out of the jammed roadway.

Turner glanced back, too. She said, "Relax. That's a Metro car. The army will hunt us itself. We don't use Metro for anything. The FBI, maybe, but not those clowns."

"Metro wants me for Moorcroft," Reacher said. "Your lawyer. A detective called Podolski thinks I did it."

"Why would he?"

"I was the last guy who talked to him, and I trashed

my old clothes afterward, and I was alone and unaccounted for at the relevant time."

"Why did you trash your clothes?"

"Cheaper than laundry, overall."

"What did you talk to Moorcroft about?"

"I wanted him to get you out of jail."

Now the cop was about ten cars back, shouldering through the jam, pretty fast.

Reacher said, "Take your jacket off."

Turner said, "Normally I want a cocktail and a movie before I remove my clothing."

"I don't want him to see your uniform. If he's looking for me, he's looking for you, too."

"He's got our plate number, surely."

"He might not see the plate. We're nose to tail here."

The cars in front were heading for the gutter. Turner followed after them, steering left-handed, using her right hand on her jacket, tearing open the placket, hauling down the zipper. She leaned forward and shrugged out of the left shoulder, and then the right. She got her left arm out, and she got her right arm out. Reacher hauled the jacket from behind her and tossed it in the rear foot well. She had been wearing a T-shirt under the jacket, olive green, short sleeved. Probably an extra small, Reacher thought, which fit her very well, except it was a little short. It barely met the waistband of her pants. Reacher saw an inch of skin, smooth and firm and tan.

He looked back again. Now the cop was two places behind, still coming, still flashing red and blue, still whooping and cackling and whining.

He said, "Would you have come out to dinner with me, if you'd been in the office yesterday? Or tonight, if Moorcroft had gotten you out?"

She said, with her eyes on the mirror, "You need to know that now?"

They were yards short of 17th Street. Up ahead on the right the Washington Monument was lit up in the gloom.

The cop car came right alongside.

And stayed there.

Chapter 22

It stayed there because the car one place ahead hadn't moved all the way over, and because in the next lane there was a wide pick-up truck with exaggerated bulges over twin rear wheels. The cop had no room to get through. He was a white man with a fat neck. Reacher saw him glance across at Turner, fleeting and completely incurious, and then away again, and then down at his dashboard controls, where evidently his siren switches were located, because right then the note changed to a continuous cackling blast, manic and never ending, and unbelievably loud.

But evidently there was something else down between the seats, and evidently it was a lot more interesting than siren switches. Because the guy's head stayed down. He was staring at something, hard. A laptop screen, Reacher thought. Or some other kind of a modern communications device. He had seen such things before. He had been in civilian cop cars, from time to time. Some of them had slim gray panels, on swan-neck stems, full of instant real-time notes and bulletins and warnings.

He said, "We got trouble."

Turner said, "What kind?"

"I think this guy is on his way to Union Station, too. Or the bus depot. To look for us. I think he's got notes and pictures. Pictures would be easy to get, right? From the army? I think he's got them right in front of him, right now. See how he's making a big point of not looking at us?"

Turner glanced to her left. The cop was still staring down. His right arm was moving. Maybe he was fumbling for his microphone. Up ahead the traffic moved a little. The car in front got out of the way. The pick-up with the wide arches slid over six inches. The cop had room to get through.

But he didn't look up. And his car didn't move.

The siren blasted on. The guy started talking. No way to make out what he was saying. Then he shut up and listened. He was being asked a question. Possibly some stilted radio protocol that meant: *Are you sure?* Because right then the guy turned face-on and ducked his head a little for a good view out his passenger window. He stared at Turner for a second, and then he flicked onward to Reacher.

His lips moved.

A single syllable, brief, inaudible, but definitely a voiced palatal glide morphing into a voiceless alveolar fricative. Therefore almost certainly: *Yes.*

Then he unclipped his seat belt and his right hand moved toward his hip.

Reacher said, "Abandon ship."

He opened his door hard and part rolled and part fell out to the curb. Turner scrambled after him, away from the cop, over the console, over his seat. The car rolled forward and nestled gently against the car in front, like a kiss. Turner came out, all arms and legs, awkward in her loose boots. Reacher hauled her upright by the hand and they hustled together across the width of the sidewalk and onto the Mall. Bare trees and evening gloom closed around them. Behind them there was nothing to hear except the cackling blast of the siren. They looped around toward the near end of the Reflecting Pool. Turner was in her T-shirt, nothing more, and the air was cold. Reacher took off his jacket and handed it to her.

He said, "Put this on. Then we'll split up. Safer that way. Meet me in fifteen minutes at the Vietnam Wall. If I don't arrive, keep on running."

She said, "Likewise if I don't," and then she went one way and he went the other.

Reacher was distinctive in any context, because of his height, so the first thing he looked for was a bench. He forced himself to walk slow and easy, with his hands in his pockets, without a care in the world, because a running man attracted the eye a hundred times faster than a walking man. Another old evolutionary legacy. Predator and prey, motion and stillness. And he didn't look back, either. He made no furtive glances. He kept his gaze straight and level, and he walked toward what he saw. Full dark was coming down fast, but the Mall was still busy. Not like summertime, but there were plenty of winter tourists finishing up their days, and up ahead the Wall had its usual crowd of people, some of them there to mourn, some of them to pay more general respects, and some of them the gaggle of weird folks the place always seemed to attract. He couldn't see Turner anywhere. The siren had stopped, replaced by honking horns. Presumably the cop was out of his car by that point, and presumably his and Sullivan's stationary vehicles were jamming up the traffic flow.

Reacher saw a bench in the gloom twenty yards away, unoccupied, positioned parallel with the still waters of the Pool, and he strolled on toward it, slow and relaxed, and then he paused as if deciding, and he sat down, and leaned forward, with his elbows on his knees. He looked down, like a contemplative man with things on his mind. A long and careful stare would betray him, but at first glance nothing about his pose would say *tall man,* and nothing would say *fugitive,* either. The only notable tell was his lack of a jacket. It wasn't exactly shirtsleeve weather.

Thirty yards behind him the horns were still sounding.

He waited, head down, still and quiet.

And then forty yards away in the corner of his eye he saw the cop with the fat neck, hustling along on foot, with a flashlight in his hand, but no gun. The guy was twitching left and right, nervous and searching hard, presumably in his boss' bad books for getting close and getting beat. Reacher heard two new sirens, both of them far away in the distance, one in the south, maybe all the way down on C Street, and one

in the north, on 15th possibly, or 14th, maybe level
with the White House or the Aquarium.

Reacher waited.

The cop with the fat neck was heading for the Wall,
halfway there, but then he stopped and turned a full
circle. Reacher felt his gaze pass right over him. A guy
sitting still and staring at the water was of no interest
at all, when there were plenty of better prospects all
around, like a crowd of thirty or forty heading for the
base of the Monument, either a tour group or a crowd
of strangers all coincidentally drifting in the same direction at the same time, or a mixture of the two.
Moving targets. Evolution. The cop set off after them.
Not a bad percentage play, Reacher thought. Anyone
would expect motion. Sitting still was tough.

The distant sirens came closer, but not very close.
Some kind of a center of gravity seemed to pull them
east. Which again was a decent percentage play. The
Metro PD knew its own turf, presumably. To the east
were the museums and the galleries, and therefore the
crowds, and then came the Capitol, and beyond that
came the best getaways north and south, by road and
rail.

Reacher waited, not moving at all, not looking
around, just staring ahead at the water. Then when
the stopwatch in his head hit ten minutes exactly, he
eased himself to his feet and ran through as many
un-fugitive-like motions as he could think of. He
yawned, and he put his palms hard on the small of his
back, and he stretched, and he yawned again. Then he
set off west, just strolling, like he had all the time in
the world, with the Pool on his left, in a long leisurely

curve through the bare trees that brought him to the Wall four minutes later. He stood on the edge of the crowd, just one pilgrim among many, and he looked for Susan Turner.

He couldn't see her anywhere.

Chapter 23

Reacher walked above the Wall, following the rise and the fall and the shallow angle, from 1959 to 1975, and then back again at the lower level, from 1975 to 1959, past more than fifty-eight thousand names twice over, without once seeing Susan Turner anywhere. *If I don't arrive, keep on running,* he had said, and she had replied, *Likewise if I don't.* And they were well past their agreed fifteen minutes. But Reacher stayed. He made one more pass, from the lonely early deaths on their low eight-inch panels, past the peak casualties more than ten feet high in 1968 and 1969, and onward to the lonely late deaths, on low eight-inch panels again, looking at every person he saw either straight on or reflected in the black stone, but none of them was Turner. He came out at the end of the war and ahead of him on the sidewalk was the usual huddle of souvenir sellers and memorabilia merchants, some of them veterans and some of them pretending to be, all of them hawking old unit patches and branch insignia and engraved Zippo lighters, and a thousand other things of no value at all, except in the sentimental sense. As always tourists came and chose and paid and went, and as always a static cadre of picturesque and disaffected types hung around, more or less permanently.

Reacher smiled.

Because one of the disaffected types was a thin girl with a curtain of dark hair hanging loose, wearing an oversized coat wrapped twice around her, knee length, with camo pants below, and the tongues hanging out of her boots. Her coat sleeves were rolled to her wrists, and her hands were in her pockets. She was standing huddled, head down, in a daze, rocking just perceptibly from foot to foot, out of it, like a stoner.

Susan Turner, acting the part, fitting in, hiding in plain sight.

Reacher walked up to her and said, "You're really good."

"I needed to be," she said. "A cop walked right by. As close as you are. It was the guy we saw before, in the cruiser that was parked back there."

"Where is he now?"

"He went east. Like a rolling cordon. It passed me by. You, too, I guess."

"I didn't see him."

"He went down the other side of the Pool. You never raised your head."

"You were watching me?"

"I was. And you're pretty good, too."

"Why were you watching me?"

"In case you needed help."

Reacher said, "If they're combing east, we better go west."

"Walking?"

"No, by taxi," Reacher said. "Taxis in this town are as invisible as it gets."

Every significant tourist site along the Mall had a rank of two or three cabs waiting. The Wall was no exception. Behind the last souvenir booth were battered cars with dirty paint and taxi lights on their roofs. Reacher and Turner got in the first in line.

"Arlington Cemetery," Reacher said. "Main gate."

He read the printed notice on the door. The fare was going to be three bucks for the flag drop, plus two dollars and sixteen cents per mile thereafter. Plus tip. They were going to be down about seven bucks, total. Which was going to leave them about twenty-three. Which was better than a poke in the eye with a sharp stick, but which was a long way short of what they were going to need.

They sat low in sagging seats and the cab crashed and bounced like its wheels were square. But it made the trip OK. Around the back of the Lincoln Memorial, and out over the water on the Memorial Bridge, and back into Arlington County. To the bus stop at the cemetery gate. Right where Reacher had started out, almost exactly twenty-four hours previously.

Which was a weird kind of progress.

* * *

The bus stop at the cemetery gate had a small crowd waiting, all small dark Hispanic men, all laborers, all tired, and patient, and resigned. Reacher and Turner took their places among them. Turner blended in fairly well. Reacher didn't. He was more than a head taller and twice as wide as anyone else. And much paler. He looked like a lighthouse on a dark rocky shore. Therefore the wait was tense. And long. But no cop cars rolled past, and eventually the bus came. Reacher paid the fares, and Turner sat at a window, and Reacher sat next to her on the aisle and hunched down as low as he could go. The bus moved off, slow and ponderous, on the same route Reacher had taken the day before, past the stop where he had gotten off at the bottom of the three-lane hill, and onward up the steep incline toward the 110th HQ.

Turner said, "They'll call the FBI, because they'll assume we're going interstate. The only question is who calls first. My money is on the Metro PD. The army will wait until morning, most likely."

"We'll be OK," Reacher said. "The FBI won't use roadblocks. Not here on the East Coast. In fact they probably won't get off their asses at all. They'll just put our IDs and our bank cards on their watch lists, which doesn't matter anyway, because we don't have IDs or bank cards."

"They might tell local PDs to watch their bus depots."

"We'll keep an eye out."

"I still need clothes," Turner said. "Pants and a jacket at least."

"We've got nineteen dollars. You can have one or the other."

"Pants, then. And I'll trade you your jacket back for your shirt."

"My shirt will look like a circus tent on you."

"I've seen women wear men's shirts. Like wraps, all chic and baggy."

"You'll be cold."

"I was born in Montana. I'm never cold."

The bus labored up the hill past the 110th HQ. The old stone building. The gates were open. The sentry was in his hutch. The day guy. Morgan's car was still in the lot. The painted door was closed. Lights were on in all the windows. Turner swiveled all the way around in her seat, to keep the place in sight as long as she could. Until the last possible moment. Then she let it go and faced front again and said, "I hope I get back there."

Reacher said, "You will."

"I worked so hard to get there in the first place. It's a great command. But you know that already."

"Everyone else hates us."

"Only if we do our job properly."

The bus made the turn at the top of the hill, onto the next three-lane, that led to Reacher's motel. There was rain in the air. Just a little, but enough that the bus driver had his wipers going.

Turner said, "Tell me again how this is all my fault. Me and Afghanistan."

The road leveled out and the bus picked up speed. It rattled straight past Reacher's motel. The lot was empty. No car with dented doors.

He said, "It's the only logical explanation. You put a fox in someone's henhouse, and that someone wanted to shut you down. Which was easy enough to do. Because as it happened no one else in the unit knew what it was about. Your duty captain didn't. Neither did Sergeant Leach. Or anyone else. So you were the only one. They set you up with the Cayman Islands bank account scam, and they busted you, which cut your lines of communication. Which stayed cut, when they beat on your lawyer Moorcroft, as soon as he showed the first sign of trying to get you out of jail. Problem solved, right there. You were isolated. You couldn't talk to anyone. So everything was hunky dory. Except the records showed you had spent hours on the phone to South Dakota with some guy. And scuttlebutt around the building said the guy had been a previous 110th CO. Your duty captain knew that for sure, because I told him, first time I called. Maybe lots of people knew. Certainly I got a lot of name recognition when I showed up yesterday. And you and I could be assumed to share some common interests. We might have talked about the front burner. Either just shooting the shit, or maybe you were even asking me for a perspective."

"But I didn't mention Afghanistan to you at all."

"But they didn't know that. The phone log shows duration, not content. They didn't have a recording. So I was a theoretical loose end. Maybe I knew what you knew. Not much of a problem, because I wasn't likely to show up. They seem to have checked me out. They claim to know how I live. But just in case, they made some plans. They had the Big Dog thing standing by, for instance."

"I don't see how that would help them any. You'd have been in the system, with plenty of time to talk."

"I was supposed to run," Reacher said. "I was supposed to disappear and never come near the army again, the whole rest of my life. That was the plan. That was the whole point. They even showed up at the motel to make sure I understood. And the Big Dog thing was a great choice for that. The guy is dead, and there's an affidavit. There's no real way to fight it. Running would have been entirely rational. Sergeant Leach thought if she could find a way of warning me, I'd head for the hills."

"Why didn't you run?"

"I wanted to ask you out to dinner."

"No, really?"

"Not my style. I figured it out when I was about five years old. A person either runs or he fights. It's a binary choice, and I'm a fighter. Plus, they had something else in their back pocket."

"Which was?"

"Something else designed to make me run, which didn't, either."

"Which was?"

Samantha Dayton.

Sam.

Fourteen years old.

I'll get to it.

"I'll tell you later," Reacher said. "It's a complicated story."

* * *

The bus ground onward, all low gears and loud diesel, past the strip mall Reacher knew, with the hardware store, and the pharmacy, and the picture framing shop, and the gun store, and the dentist, and the Greek restaurant. Then it moved out into territory he hadn't seen before. Onward, and away.

He said, "Look on the bright side. Your problem ain't exactly brain surgery. Whatever rabbit you were chasing in Afghanistan is behind all this shit. So we need to work backward from him. We need to find out who his friends are, and we need to find out who did what, and when, and how, and why, and then we need to bring the hammer down."

Turner said, "There's a problem with that."

Reacher nodded.

"I know," he said. "It won't be easy. Not from the outside. It's like we've got one hand tied behind our back. But we'll give it our best shot."

"Unfortunately that's not the problem I'm talking about."

"So what is?"

"Someone thinks I know something I don't. That's the problem."

"What don't you know?"

"I don't know who the rabbit is," Turner said. "Or what the hell he's doing, or where, or why. Or how. In fact I don't know what's happening in Afghanistan at all."

"But you sent two guys there."

"Much earlier. For a completely different reason. In

Kandahar. Pure routine. Entirely unconnected. But along the way they picked up on a whisper from a Pashtun informer, that an American officer had been seen heading north to meet with a tribal leader. The identity of the American was not known, and his purpose was not known, but the feeling was it can't have been anything good. We're drawing down. We're supposed to be heading south, not north, toward Bagram and Kabul, prior to getting the hell out. We're not supposed to be way up in-country, having secret meetings with towelheads. So I sent my guys to chase the rumor. That was all."

"When?"

"The day before I was busted. So I won't even have a name until they report back to me. Which they won't be able to, not until I'm back on the inside."

Reacher said nothing.

Turner said, "What?"

"It's worse than that."

"How can it be?"

"They won't be able to report back ever," Reacher said. "Because they're dead."

Chapter 24

Reacher told Turner about the missed radio checks, and the agitation in the old stone building, and the semi-authorized air search out of Bagram, and the two dead bodies on the goat trail. Turner went still and quiet. She said, "They were good men. Natty Weeks and Duncan Edwards. Weeks was an old hand and Edwards was a good prospect. I shouldn't have let them go. The Hindu Kush is too dangerous for two men on their own."

"It wasn't tribesmen who got them," Reacher said. "They were shot in the head with nine-millimeter rounds. U.S. Army sidearms, most likely. Beretta M9s, almost certainly. The tribesmen would have cut their heads off. Or used AK47s. Different kind of hole altogether."

"So they must have gotten close to the wrong American."

"Without even knowing it," Reacher said. "Don't you think? A handgun to the head is an up-close-and-personal kind of a thing. Which they wouldn't have allowed, surely, if they had the slightest suspicion."

"Very neat," Turner said. "They shut me down, at both ends. Here, and there. Before I got anything at all. As in, right now I have nothing. Not a thing. So I'm totally screwed. I'm going down, Reacher. I don't see a way out of this now."

Reacher said nothing.

They got off the bus in Berryville, Virginia, which was one town short of its ultimate destination. Better that way, they thought. A driver might remember a pair of atypical passengers who stayed on board until the very end of the line. Especially if it came to radio or TV appeals, or routine police interviews, or public enemy photographs in the post office.

The rain had stopped, but the air was still damp and cold. Berryville's downtown area was pleasant enough, but they backtracked on foot, back the way the bus had come, across a railroad track, past a pizza restaurant, to a hardware store they had seen from the window. The store was about to close, which was not ideal, because clerks tend to remember the first and last customers of the day. But they judged yet more time in ACU pants was worse. So they went in and Turner found a pair of canvas work pants similar to Reacher's. The smallest size the store carried was going to be loose in the waist and long in the leg. Not perfect. But Turner figured the discrepancy was going to be a good thing. A feature, not a bug, was how she put it. Because the pant legs would pool down over her army boots, thereby hiding them to some extent, and making them less obvious.

They bought the pants and three pairs of boot laces, one for Reacher's boots, and one for Turner's, and one for her to double up and use as a belt. They conducted their business in as unmemorable a manner as they could. Neither polite nor impolite, neither rushing nor stalling, not really saying much of anything. Turner didn't use the restroom. She wanted to change, but they figured for the last customer of the day to go in wearing ACU pants and come out in a new purchase would likely stick in the clerk's memory.

But the store had a big parking lot on one side, and it was empty and dark, so Turner changed her pants in the shadows and dumped her army issue in a trash container at the rear of the building. Then she came out, and they traded jacket for shirt, and they sat down on a curb together and tied their boots.

Good to go, with four dollars left in Reacher's pocket.

Four bucks was a week's wage in some countries of the world, but it wasn't worth much of a damn in Berryville, Virginia. It wouldn't buy transportation out of the state, and it wouldn't buy a night in a motel, and it wouldn't buy a proper sit-down meal for two, not in any kind of restaurant or diner known to man.

Turner said, "You told me there's more than one kind of ATM."

"There is," Reacher said. "Fifty miles ahead, or fifty miles back. But not here."

"I'm hungry."

"Me, too."

"There's no point in holding on to four dollars."

"I agree," Reacher said. "Let's go crazy."

They walked back toward the railroad track, fast and newly confident in their newly laced boots, to the pizza restaurant they had seen. Not a gourmet place, which was just as well. They bought a single slice each, to go, pepperoni for Reacher, plain cheese for Turner, and a can of soda to share between them. Which left them eighty cents in change. They ate and drank sitting side by side on a rail at the train crossing.

Turner asked, "Did you lose guys when you were CO?"

"Four," Reacher said. "One of them was a woman."

"Did you feel bad?"

"I wasn't turning cartwheels. But it's all part of the game. We all know what we're signing up for."

"I wish I'd gone myself."

Reacher asked, "Have you ever been to the Cayman Islands?"

"No."

"Ever had a foreign bank account?"

"Are you kidding? Why would I? I'm an O4. I make less than some high school teachers."

"Why did you take a day to pass on the name of the Hood guy's contact?"

"What is this, the third degree?"

"I'm thinking," Reacher said. "That's all."

"You know why. I wanted to bust him myself. To make sure it was done properly. I gave myself twenty-four hours. But I couldn't find him. So I told the FBI.

They should think themselves lucky. I could have given myself a week."

"I might have," Reacher said. "Or a month."

They finished their pizza slices, and drained the shared can of soda. Reacher wiped his mouth with the back of his hand, and then wiped the back of his hand on his pants. Turner said, "What are we going to do now?"

"We're going to walk through town and hitch a ride west."

"Tonight?"

"Better than sleeping under a bush."

"How far west?"

"All the way west," Reacher said. "We're going to Los Angeles."

"Why?"

Samantha Dayton.

Sam.

Fourteen years old.

"I'll tell you later," Reacher said. "It's complicated."

They walked through the downtown area, on a street called East Main, which became a street called West Main after a central crossroads. All the store windows were dark. All the doors were shuttered. Berryville was no doubt a fine American town, matter-of-fact and unpretentious, but it was no kind of hub. That was for damn sure. It was all closed up and slumbering, even though it was only the middle of the evening.

They walked on. Turner looked good in the shirt,

even though she could have gotten herself and her sister in it together. But she had rolled the sleeves, and she had shrugged and wriggled like women do, and it had draped and fallen into some kind of a coherent shape. Somehow its hugeness emphasized how slender she was. Her hair was still down. She moved with lithe, elastic energy, a wary, quizzical look never leaving her eyes, but there was no fear there. No tension. Just some kind of an appetite. For what, Reacher wasn't entirely sure.

Totally worth the wait, he thought.

They walked on.

And then on the west edge of town they came to a motel.

And in its lot was the car with the dented doors.

Chapter 25

The motel was a neat and tidy place, entirely in keeping with what they had seen in the rest of the town. It had some red brick, and some white paint, and a flag, and an eagle above the office door. There was a Coke machine, and an ice machine, and probably twenty rooms in two lines, both of them running back from the road and facing each other across a broad courtyard.

The car with the dented doors was parked at an angle in front of the office, carelessly and temporarily, as if someone had ducked inside with a brief inquiry.

"Are you sure?" Turner asked, quietly.

"No question," Reacher said. "That's their car."

"How is that even possible?"

"Whoever is running these guys is deep in the loop, and he's pretty smart. That's how it's possible. There's no other explanation. He heard we broke out, and he heard we took thirty bucks with us, and he heard about that Metro cop finding us on Constitution Avenue. And then he sat down to think. Where can you go with thirty bucks? There are only four possibilities. Either you hole up in town and sleep in a park, or you head for Union Station, or the big bus depot right behind it, and you go to Baltimore or Philly or Richmond, or else you head the other way, west, on the little municipal bus. And whoever is doing the thinking here figured the little municipal bus was the favorite. Because the fare is cheaper, and because Union Station and the big bus depot are far too easy for the cops to watch, as are the stations and the depots at the other end, in Baltimore and Philly and Richmond, and because sleeping in the park really only gets you busted tomorrow instead of today. And on top of all that they claim to know how I live, and I don't spend much time on the East Coast. I was always more likely to head west."

"But you agreed to head for Union Station."

"I was trying to be democratic. Trying not to be set in my ways."

"But how did they know we'd get out of the bus in Berryville?"

"They didn't. I bet they've already checked everywhere from about Leesburg onward. Every visible motel. Hamilton, Purcellville, Berryville, Winchester. If they don't find us here, that's where they're heading next."

"Are they going to find us here?"

"I sincerely hope so," Reacher said.

* * *

The motel office had small windows, for a decorative effect, like an old colonial house, and on the inside they were fitted with sheer drapes of some kind. No way of telling who was in the room. Turner walked to a window, and put her face close to the glass, and looked ahead, and left, and right, and up, and down. She whispered, "No one there. Just the clerk, I think. Or maybe he's the owner. Sitting down, in back."

Reacher checked the car doors. They were locked. As was the trunk. He put his hand on the hood, above the radiator chrome. The metal was hot. The car hadn't been parked there long. He moved left, into the mouth of the courtyard. No one there. No one going from room to room, no one checking doors or looking in windows.

He stepped back and said, "So let's talk to the guy."

Turner pulled the office door, and Reacher went in ahead of her. The room was a lot nicer than the kind of place Reacher was used to. A lot nicer than the place a mile from Rock Creek, for instance. There was quality vinyl on the floor, and wallpaper, and all kinds of framed commendations from tourist authorities. The reception desk was an actual desk, like something Thomas Jefferson might have used to write a letter. Behind it was a red leather chair with a guy in it. The guy was about sixty, tall and gray and impressive. He looked like he should have been running a big corporation, not a small motel.

Turner said, "We're looking for our friends. That's their car outside."

"The four gentlemen?" the guy said, with a tiny and skeptical hesitation before the word *gentlemen*.

"Yes," Turner said.

"I'm afraid you just missed them. They were looking for you about ten minutes ago. At least, I assume it was you they were looking for. A man and a woman, they said. They wondered if you'd checked in already."

"And what did you tell them?" Reacher asked.

"Well, naturally, I told them you hadn't arrived yet."

"OK."

"Are you ready to check in now?" the guy asked, in a tone that suggested it wouldn't break his heart if they didn't.

"We need to find our friends first," Reacher said. "We need to have a discussion. Where did they go?"

"They wondered if perhaps you'd gone to get a bite to eat. I directed them to the Berryville Grill. It's the only restaurant open at this time of the evening."

"The pizza place doesn't count?"

"It's not exactly a restaurant, is it?"

"So where's the Berryville Grill?"

"Two blocks behind us. An easy walk."

"Thank you," Turner said.

There were two ways to walk two blocks behind the motel. On the left-hand cross street, or the right-hand cross street. Covering both at once would involve splitting up, which would risk a potential one-on-four confrontation for one of them. Reacher was happy with those odds, but he wasn't sure about Turner. She was half his size, literally, and she was unarmed. No gun, no knife.

He said, "We should wait here. We should let them come to us."

But they didn't come. Reacher and Turner stood in the shadows, for five long minutes, and nothing happened. Turner moved a little, to let the light play along the flank of the car. She whispered, "Those are pretty good dents."

Reacher said back, "How long does it take to check out a damn restaurant?"

"Maybe they got sent on somewhere else. Maybe there's a bar with hamburgers. Or a couple of them. Which don't count as restaurants, with the motel guy."

"I don't hear any bars."

"How do you hear a bar?"

"Hubbub, glasses, bottles, extractor fans. It's a distinctive sound."

"Could be too far away to hear."

"In which case they'd have come back for their car."

"They have to be somewhere."

"Maybe they're eating at the grill," Reacher said. "Maybe they got a table. A last-minute decision. We were hungry, they could be hungry too."

"I'm still hungry."

"It might be easier to take them inside a restaurant. Crowded quarters, a little inhibition on their part. Plus knives on the tables. Then we could eat their dinners. They must have ordered by now. Steak, ideally."

"The waiter would call the cops."

Reacher checked the cross street on the right. Nothing doing. He checked the cross street on the left. Empty. He walked back to where Turner was waiting. She said, "They're eating. They have to be. What else could they be doing? They could have searched the whole of Berryville by now. Twice over. So they're in the restaurant. They could be another hour. And we can't stay here much longer. We're loitering on private property. And I'm sure Berryville has laws. And a police department. The motel guy could be on the phone two minutes from now."

"OK," Reacher said. "Let's go check it out."

"Left or right?"

"Left," Reacher said.

They were cautious at the corner. But the left-hand cross street was still empty. It was more of an alley than a street. It had the motel's wooden fence on one side, and the blank flank of a brick-built general store on the other. A hundred yards later it was crossed by a wider street that ran parallel with West Main. The second block was shorter and more varied, with some standalone buildings, and some narrow vacant lots, and then up ahead were the rear elevations of the buildings that stood on the next parallel street, including one on the right, which had a tall metal kitchen chimney, which was blowing steam, pretty hard. The Berryville Grill, for sure, doing some serious midevening business.

Turner said, "Back door or front door?"

"Front window," Reacher said. "Reconnaissance is everything."

They turned right out of the cross street and got cautious again. First came a dark storefront that could have been a flower shop. Then came the restaurant, second in line. It was a big place, but deeper than it was wide. It had four front windows, separated into two pairs by a central door. The windows came all the way down to the floor. Maybe they opened up, for the summer. Maybe they put tables on the sidewalk.

Reacher kept close to the wall and moved toward the near edge of the first window. From that angle he could see about a third of the interior space. Which was considerable. And well filled. The tables were small and close together. It was a family-style restaurant. Nothing fancy. The wait staff looked to be all girls, about high school age. The tables were plain wood. About half of them were occupied. By couples, and threesomes, and by family groups. Old people and their adult children, some of them having fun, some of them a little strained and quiet.

But none of the tables was occupied by four men. Not in the part of the restaurant Reacher could see. He backed off. She leapfrogged past him and walked briskly along the restaurant frontage, looking away, and she stopped beyond the last window. He watched the door. No reaction. No one came out. She hugged the wall and crept back and looked inside from the far edge of the last window. Reacher figured from there she could see a symmetrical one-third, the same as he had, but on the other side of the room. Which would leave a central wedge unexamined.

She shook her head. He set off, and she set off, and they met at the door. He pulled it, and she went in first. The central wedge had plenty of tables. But none of them was occupied by four men. There was no maitre d' lectern. No hostess station, either. Just empty floor inside the door. A young woman bustled over. A girl, really. Seventeen, maybe. The designated greeter.

She was wearing black pants, and a black polo shirt with short sleeves and an embroidered Berryville Grill logo on the front. She had a livid red birthmark on her forearm. She said, "Two for dinner?"

Turner said, "We're looking for some people. They might have been asking for us."

The girl went quiet. She looked from Turner to Reacher, suddenly understanding: *a man and a woman.*

"Were they here?" Reacher asked. "Four men, three of them big, and one of them bigger?"

The girl nodded, and rubbed her forearm, subconsciously. Or nervously. Reacher glanced down.

It wasn't a birthmark.

It was changing shape. And changing color.

It was a bruise.

He said, "Did they do that?"

The girl nodded.

"The big one," she said.

"With the shaved head and the small ears?"

"Yes," the girl said. "He squeezed my arm."

"Why?"

"He wanted to know where else you could be. And I couldn't tell him."

It was a big mark. From a big hand. More than six inches across.

The girl said, "He really scared me. He has cruel eyes."

Reacher asked, "When were they here?"

"About ten minutes ago."

"Where did they go?"

"I don't know. I couldn't tell them where to look."

"No bars, no hamburger joints?"

"That's exactly what he asked. But there's nothing like that here."

The girl was close to tears.

Reacher said, "They won't be coming back."

It was all he could think of to say.

They left the girl standing there, rubbing her arm, and they used the cross street they hadn't used before. It was a similar thoroughfare, narrow, unlit, raggedy at first, and then firming up on the second block, with the motel's fence on the right. They took the corner cautiously, and scanned ahead before moving out.

The motel lot was empty.

The car with the dented doors was gone.

Chapter 26

Three hundred yards later Reacher and Turner hit Berryville's city limit, and West Main became plain old State Route 7. Turner said, "If those guys could figure out where we went, we have to assume the army could too. The FBI as well, even."

Which made hitchhiking a nightmare. It was pitch dark. A winter night, in the middle of nowhere. A long straight road. Oncoming headlights would be visible a mile away, but there would be no way of knowing what lay behind those headlights. Who was at the wheel? Civilian or not? Friend or foe?

Too big of a risk to take a gamble.

So they compromised, in a win-some, lose-some kind of way that Reacher felt came out about equal in terms of drawbacks and benefits. They retraced their steps, and Turner waited on the shoulder about fifty yards ahead of the last lit-up town block, and Reacher kept on going, to where he could lean on the corner of a building, half in and half out of a cross street alley, where there was some light spill on the blacktop. A bad idea, in the sense that any car turning west beyond them was a lost opportunity in terms of a potential ride, but a good idea in the sense that Reacher could make a quick and dirty evaluation of the through-town drivers, as and when they appeared. They agreed he should err on the side of caution, but if he felt it was OK, he would step out and signal to Turner, who would then step up to the curb and jam her thumb out.

Which overall, he thought at the beginning, was maybe more win-some than lose-some. Because by accident their improvised system would imitate a very old hitchhiking trick. A pretty girl sticks out her thumb, a driver stops, full of enthusiasm, and then the big ugly boyfriend jogs up and gets in, too.

But thirty minutes later Reacher was seeing it as more lose-some than win-some. Traffic was light, and he was getting no time at all to make a judgment. He would see headlights coming, he would wait, then the car would flash past in a split second, and his brain would process, *sedan, domestic, model year, specification,* and long before he got to a conclusion the car was already well past Turner and speeding onward.

So he switched to a pre-screening approach. He decided to reject all sedans, and all SUVs younger than five years, and to approve all pick-up trucks, and all older SUVs. He had never known the army to hunt in pick-up trucks, and he guessed all army road vehicles would be swapped out before they got to be five years old. Same for the FBI, surely. The remaining risk was off-duty local deputies, joining in the fun in their POVs.

But some risk had to be taken, otherwise they would be there all night long, which would end up the same as sleeping in a D.C. park. They would get busted at first light tomorrow, instead of last light today.

He waited. For a minute he saw nothing, and then he saw headlights, coming in from the east, not real fast, just a good, safe city speed. He leaned out from his corner. He waited. He saw a shape flash past.

A sedan.

Reject.

He settled back against the building.

He waited again. Five minutes. Then seven. Then eight. Then: more headlights. He leaned out. He saw a pick-up truck.

He stepped out to the sidewalk in its wake and jammed his left fist high in the air and fifty yards away Turner jumped to the curb and stuck out her thumb. Total precision. Like a perfect postseason bang-bang double play, fast and crisp and decisive in the cold night air. The pick-up's headlight beams washed over Turner's immobile form like she'd been there all along.

The pick-up didn't stop.

Shit, Reacher thought.

The next viable candidate was an elderly Ford Bronco, and it didn't stop, either. Neither did a middle-aged F150, or a new Dodge Ram. Then the road went quiet again. The clock in Reacher's head ticked around to ten-thirty in the evening. The air grew colder. He had on two T-shirts and his jacket, with its miracle layer. He started to worry about Turner. She had one T-shirt and one regular shirt. And her T-shirt had looked thin from laundering. *I was born in Montana,* she had said. *I'm never cold.* He hoped she was telling the truth.

For five more minutes nothing came in from the east. Then, more headlights, wide-spaced and low, tracking the road's rise and fall with a rubbery, well-damped motion. A sedan, probably. He leaned out just a fraction, already pessimistic.

Then he ducked back in, fast. It was a sedan, swift and sleek, a Ford Crown Victoria, shiny and dark in color, with black windows and antennas on the trunk lid. MPs, possibly, or the FBI, or Federal Marshals, or the Virginia state cops. Or not. Maybe another agency altogether, on an unconnected mission. He leaned out again and watched it go. It missed Turner in the shadows and blasted onward into the distance.

He waited. One more minute. Then two. Nothing but darkness.

Then more headlights, way back, maybe still on East Main, before the downtown crossroads, coming on steadily, now on West Main for sure, getting closer. They were yellow and weak. Old fashioned and faint. Nothing modern. Not halogen. Reacher leaned out from his corner. The headlights kept on coming, slow and steady. They flashed past.

A pick-up truck.

The same double play. His left fist, her thumb.

The pick-up slowed right down.

It stopped.

Turner stepped off the curb and leaned in at its passenger window and started talking, and Reacher started jogging the fifty yards toward her.

* * *

This time Juliet called Romeo, which was unusual. Mostly Romeo had the breaking news. But their labors were divided, and so sometimes Juliet had the new information.

He said, "No sign of them, all the way to Winchester."

Romeo said, "Are they sure?"

"They checked very carefully."

"OK, but keep them in the area. That bus line is our best option."

"Will do."

Reacher arrived a little out of breath, and saw the pick-up was an old Chevrolet, plain and basic, built and bought for utility, not show, and the driver looked to be a wily old boy of about seventy, all skin and bone and sparse white hair. Turner introduced him by saying, "This gentleman is heading for Mineral County in West Virginia. Near a place called Keyser, not too far from the Maryland line."

Which all meant nothing to Reacher, except that West Virginia sounded one step better than regular Virginia. He leaned in at the window next to Turner and said, "Sir, we'd really appreciate the ride."

The old guy said, "Then hop right in and let's go."

There was a bench seat, but the cab was narrow. Turner got in first, and if Reacher pressed hard against the door there was just about room for her between him and the old guy. But the seat was soft and the cab was warm. And the truck motored along OK. It was happy to do sixty. It felt like it could roll down the road forever.

The old guy asked, "So where are you folks headed ultimately?"

"We're looking for work," Reacher said, thinking of the young couple in Ohio, in the red crew-cab Silverado, with the shedding dog. "So pretty much any place will do."

"And what kind of work are you looking for?"

And so began a completely typical hitchhiking conversation, with every party spinning yarns based on half truths and inflated experiences. Reacher had been out of the service for a long time, and when he had to he worked whatever job he could get. He had worked the doors in night clubs, and he had dug swimming pools, and stacked lumber, and demolished buildings, and picked apples, and loaded boxes into trucks, and he made it sound like those kinds of things had been his lifelong occupations. Turner talked about waiting tables, and working in offices, and selling kitchenwares door to door, all of which Reacher guessed was based on her evening and weekend experiences through high school and college. The old guy talked about tobacco farming in the Carolinas, and horses in Kentucky, and hauling coal in West Virginia, in eighteen-wheel trucks.

They drove through Winchester, crossing I-81 twice, and then onward toward the state line, into Appalachian country, on the last northern foothills of Shenandoah Mountain, the road rising and twisting toward Georges Peak, the motor straining, the weak yellow headlights jerking from side to side on the sharp turns. Then at midnight they were in West Virginia, still elevated in wild country, rolling through wooded passes toward the Alleghenies in the far distance.

Then Reacher saw a fire, far ahead in the west, on a wooded hillside a little south of the road. A yellow and orange glow, against the black sky, like a bonfire or a warning beacon. They rolled through a sleeping town called Capon Bridge, and the fire got closer. A mile or more away, but then suddenly less, because the road turned toward it.

Reacher said, "Sir, you could let us out here, if you wouldn't mind."

The old guy said, "Here?"

"It's a good spot."

"For what?"

"I think it will meet our needs."

"Are you sure?"

"We'd appreciate it very much."

The old guy grumbled something, dubious, not understanding at all, but he took his foot off the gas and the truck slowed down. Turner wasn't understanding, either. She was looking at Reacher like he was crazy. The truck came to a halt, on a random stretch of mountain blacktop, woods to the left, woods to the right, nothing ahead, and nothing behind. Reacher opened his door, and unfolded himself out, and Turner slid out beside him, and they thanked the old man very much and waved him away. Then they stood together in the pitch dark and the dead quiet and the cold night air, and Turner said, "You want to tell me exactly why we just got out of a warm truck in the middle of nowhere?"

Reacher pointed, ahead and to the left, at the fire. "See that?" he said. "That's an ATM."

Chapter 27

They walked on, following the curve of the road, west and a little south, getting closer to the fire all the time, until it was level with them, about two hundred yards into the hilly woods. Ten yards later, on the left shoulder, there was the mouth of a stony track. A driveway, of sorts. It ran uphill, between the trees. Turner wrapped Reacher's shirt tight around her and said, "That's just some kind of random brush fire."

"Wrong season," Reacher said. "Wrong place. They don't get brush fires here."

"So what is it?"

"Where are we?"

"West Virginia."

"Correct. Miles from anywhere, in backwoods country. That fire is what we've been waiting for. But be quiet as you can. There could be someone up there."

"Firefighters, probably."

"That's one thing there won't be," Reacher said. "I can guarantee that."

They started up the stony path. It was loose and noisy underfoot. Hard going. Better driven than walked. On both sides the trees crowded in, some of them pines, some of them deciduous and bare. The track snaked right, and then left again, rising all the way, with a final wide curve up ahead, with the fire waiting for them beyond it. They could already feel heat in the air, and they could hear a vague roar, with loud cracks and bangs mixed in.

"Real quiet now," Reacher said.

They rounded the final curve, and found a clearing hacked out of the woods. Dead ahead was a tumble-down old barn-like structure, and to their left was a tumbledown old cabin, both buildings made of wooden boards alternately baked and rotted by a century of weather. To their far right was the fire, raging in and around and above a wide, low rectangular structure with wheels. Yellow and blue and orange flames blazed up and out, and the trees burned and smoldered near them. Thick gray smoke boiled and swirled and eddied, and then caught the updraft and whipped away into the darkness above.

"What is it?" Turner asked again, in a whisper.

"Like that old joke," Reacher whispered back. "How is a fire in a meth lab the same as a redneck divorce?"

"I don't know."

"Someone's gonna lose a trailer."

"This is a meth lab?"

"Was," Reacher said.

"Hence no firefighters," Turner said. "Illegal operation. They couldn't call it in."

"Firefighters wouldn't come anyway," Reacher said.

"If they came to every meth lab that caught on fire, they wouldn't have time for anything else. Meth labs are accidents waiting to happen."

"Where are the people?"

"Probably just one person. Somewhere around."

They moved into the clearing, toward the cabin, away from the fire, staying close to the trees. Smoke drifted and light and shadow danced all around them, pagan and elemental. The fire roared on, fifty yards away, undisturbed. The cabin was a simple one-story affair, with an outhouse in back. Both unoccupied. No one there. The barn was wide enough for two vehicles, and it had two vehicles in it, a big red Dodge pick-up truck with huge tires and acres of bulging chrome, brand-new, and a red convertible sports car, a Chevrolet Corvette, waxed and gleaming, with tail pipes as big as Reacher's fists. Also brand-new, or close to it.

Reacher said, "This country boy is doing well."

"No," Turner said. "Not so well."

She pointed toward the fire.

The skeleton of the trailer was still visible, twisting and dancing in the flames, and there was burning debris all around it, spilled and fallen, but changing the basic rectangular shape was a flat protrusion on the ground in front of it, like a tongue hanging out of a mouth, something low and rounded and very much on fire, with flames of a different color and a different intensity. The kind of flames you see if you leave a lamb chop on the grill too long, but a hundred times bigger.

"I guess he tried to save it," Reacher said. "Which was dumb. Always better to let it burn."

"What are we going to do?" Turner said.

"We're going to make a withdrawal," Reacher said. "From the ATM. It was a decent-sized lab, and he had a couple of nice cars, so my guess is our credit limit is going to be pretty handsome."

"We're going to take a dead man's money?"

"He doesn't need it anymore. And we have eighty cents."

"It's a crime."

"It was already a crime. The guy was a dope dealer. And if we don't take it, the cops will. When they get here tomorrow. Or the day after."

"Where is it?"

"That's the fun part," Reacher said. "Finding it."

"You've done this before, haven't you?"

"Usually while they're still alive. I was planning to take a walk behind Union Station. Think of it like the IRS. We're government employees, after all."

"That's terrible."

"You want to sleep in a bed tonight? You want to eat tomorrow?"

"Jesus," Turner said.

But she searched just as hard as Reacher did. They started in the cabin. The air was stale. There was nothing hidden in the kitchen. No false backs in the cupboards, no fake tins of beans, nothing buried in flour canisters, no voids behind the wall boards. There was nothing in the living room. No trapdoors in the floor, no hollowed out books, nothing in the sofa cushions, nothing up the chimney. There was nothing in the bedroom, either. No slits in the mattress, no locked drawers in the night table, nothing on top of the wardrobe, and no boxes under the bed.

Turner said, "Where next?"

Reacher said, "I should have thought of it before."

"Where?"

"Where did this guy feel real private?"

"This whole place feels real private. It's a million miles from anywhere."

"But where most of all?"

She got it. She nodded. She said, "The outhouse."

It was in the outhouse ceiling. There was a false panel right above the toilet, which Reacher unlatched and handed to Turner. Then he put his arm in the void and felt around and found a plastic tub. He hauled it out. It was the kind of thing he had seen in houseware stores. In it was about four thousand dollars in bricked twenties, and spare keys for the Dodge and the Corvette, and a deed for the property, and a birth certificate for a male child named William Robert Claughton, born in the state of West Virginia forty-seven years previously.

"Billy Bob," Turner said. "Rest in peace."

Reacher bounced the keys in his hand and said, "The truck or the sports car?"

"We're going to steal his car as well?"

"They're already stolen," Reacher said. "No titles in the box. Probably some tweaker, boosting cars, paying off a debt. And the alternative is walking."

Turner was quiet a second more, like it was going

to be a bridge too far, but then she shook her head and shrugged and said, "The sports car, of course."

So they kept the money and the Corvette key and put the rest of the stuff back in the outhouse ceiling. They hiked over to the barn, and dumped the money in the Corvette's load space. On the edge of the clearing the fire was still going strong. Reacher tossed the car key to Turner and climbed in the passenger seat. Turner started the engine, and found the headlight switch, and clipped her belt low and tight.

And a minute later they were back on the road, heading west in the dead of night, fast, warm, comfortable, and rich.

Chapter 28

Turner took a mile to get settled in and then she upped her speed and found a perfect rhythm through the curves. The car felt big and low and hard and brutal. It threw long super-white headlight beams far ahead, and trailed loud V8 burble far behind. She said, "We should turn off soon. We can't stay on this road much longer. One of those cars that came through Berryville was FBI, I think. Did you see it?"

"The Crown Vic?" Reacher said.

"Yes," she said. "So we need to get away from any logical extension of that bus route. Especially because that old guy in the truck could tell them exactly where he let us out. He won't forget that stop in a hurry."

"He won't talk to the cops. He hauled coal in West Virginia."

"He might talk to the guys in the dented car. They might scare him. Or they might give him money."

"OK, go south," Reacher said. "South is always good in the wintertime."

She upped the speed a little more, and the tail pipes got louder. It was a fine car, Reacher thought. Maybe the best in the world for American roads. Which was logical, because it was an American car. He smiled suddenly and said, "Let's turn the heater way up and put the top down."

Turner said, "You're actually enjoying this, aren't you?"

"Why wouldn't I? It's like a rock and roll song on the radio. A fast car, some money in my pocket, and a little company for once."

So Turner put the heater dial all the way in the red, and she slowed to a stop at the side of the road, and they figured out the latches and the switches, and the top folded itself down into a well behind them. The night air flooded in, cold and fresh. They wriggled lower in their seats, and took off again. All the driving sensations were doubled. The speed, the lights, the noise. Reacher smiled and said, "This is the life."

Turner said, "I might get used to it. But I would like a choice."

"You might get one."

"How? There's nothing to work with."

"Not exactly nothing," Reacher said. "We have an apparent anomaly, and we have a definite piece of procedural information. Which together might suggest a preliminary conclusion."

"Like what?"

"Weeks and Edwards were murdered in Afghanistan, but you weren't murdered here, and I wasn't, and Moorcroft wasn't. And he could have been. A drive-by shooting in southeast D.C. would have been just as plausible as a beating. And I could have been, because who was ever going to notice? And you could have been. A training accident, or carelessness handling your weapon. But they chose not to go down that road. Therefore there's a kind of timidity on the D.C. end. Which is suggestive, when you combine it with the other thing."

"Which is what?"

"Would you know how to open a bank account in the Cayman Islands?"

"I could find out."

"Exactly. You'd search on the computer, and you'd make some calls, and you'd get whatever it was you needed, and you'd get it done. But how long would it take?"

"Maybe a week."

"But these guys did it in less than a day. In an hour, probably. Your account was open by ten in the morning. Which has to imply an existing relationship. They told the bank what they wanted, and it was done right away, immediately, with no questions asked. Which makes them premium clients, with a lot of money. But we know that anyway, because they were prepared to burn a hundred grand, just to nail you. Which is a big sum of money, but they didn't care. They went right ahead and dumped it in your account, and there's no guarantee they'll ever get it back. It might be impounded as evidence. And even if it isn't, I don't see how they can turn around afterward and say, oh by the way, that hundred grand was ours all along and we want it returned to us."

"So who are they?" Turner asked.

"They're very correct people, running a scam that generates a lot of money, prepared to order all kinds of mayhem eight thousand miles away in Afghanistan, but wanting things clean and tidy on their own doorstep. On first-name terms with offshore bankers, able to get financial things done in an hour, not a week, able to search and manipulate ancient files in any branch of the service they want, with fairly efficient muscle watching their backs. They're senior staff officers in D.C., almost certainly."

Turner hung a left just after a town called Romney, on a small road that took them south but kept them in the hills. Safer that way, they thought. They didn't want to get close to the I-79 corridor. Too heavily patrolled, even at night. Too many local PDs looking to boost their municipal revenues with speed traps. The only small-road negative was the complete lack of civilized infrastructure. No gas, no coffee. No diners. No motels. And they were hungry and thirsty and tired. And the car had a giant motor, with no kind of good miles-per-gallon figures. A lone road sign at the turn had promised some kind of a town, twenty miles ahead. About half an hour, at small-road speeds.

Turner said, "I'd kill for a shower and a meal."

"You'll probably have to," Reacher said. "It won't be the city that doesn't sleep. More likely the one-horse crossroads that never wakes up."

They never found out. They didn't get there. Because a minute later they ran into another kind of small-road problem.

Chapter 29

Turner took a curve and then had to brake hard, because there was a red road flare spiked in the black-top directly ahead. Beyond it in the distance was another, and beyond that were headlight beams pointing in odd directions, one pair straight up vertically into the nighttime sky, and another horizontal but at right angles to the traffic flow.

Turner threaded left and right between the two spiked flares, and then she coasted to a stop, with the tail pipes popping and burbling behind them. The vertical headlights were from a pick-up truck that had gone off the road ass-first into a ditch. It was standing more or less upright on its tailgate. Its whole underside was visible, all complicated and dirty.

The horizontal headlights were from another pick-up truck, a sturdy half-ton crew-cab, which had turned and backed up until it was parked across the road at a right angle. It had a short and heavy chain hooked up to its tow hitch. The chain was stretched tight at a steep upward angle, and its other end was wrapped around a front suspension member on the vertical truck. Reacher guessed the idea was to pull the vertical truck over, back onto its wheels, like a falling tree, and then to drag it out of the ditch. But the geometry was going to be difficult. The chain had to be short, because the road was narrow. But the shortness of the chain meant that the front of the falling truck would hit the back of the half-ton, unless the half-ton kept on moving just right and inched out of the way. All without driving itself into the opposite ditch. It was going to be an intricate automotive ballet.

There were three men on the scene. One was sitting dazed on the shoulder, with his elbows on his knees, and his head down. He was the driver of the vertical truck, Reacher guessed, stunned by the accident, and maybe still drunk or high, or both. The other two men were his rescuers. One was in the half-ton's cab, looking back, elbow on the door, and the other was walking side to side, getting ready to direct operations.

An everyday story, Reacher figured. Or an everynight story. Too many beers, or too many pipes, or too many of both, and then a dark winding road, and a corner taken too fast, and panicked braking, and locked rear wheels under an empty load bed, maybe some wintertime ice, and a spin, and the ditch. And then the weird climb out of the tipped-up seat, and the long slide down the vertical flank, and the cell phone call, and the wait for the willing friends with the big truck.

No big deal, from anyone's point of view. Practically routine. The locals looked like they knew what they were doing, despite the geometric difficulties. Maybe they had done it before, possibly many times. Reacher and Turner were going to be delayed five minutes. Maybe ten. That was all.

And then that wasn't all.

The dazed guy on the shoulder became slowly aware of the bright new lights, and he raised his head, and he squinted down the road, and he looked away again.

Then he looked back.

He struggled up and got to his feet, and he took a step.

He said, "That's Billy Bob's car."

He took another step, and another, and he glared ahead, at Turner first, then at Reacher, and he stamped his foot and swung his right arm as if batting away immense clouds of flying insects, and he roared, "What are you doing in it?"

Which sounded like *Whut Chew Doon An At,* maybe due to bad teeth, or booze, or befuddlement, or all of the above. Reacher wasn't sure. Then the guy who was ready to direct operations got interested too, and the guy at the wheel of the half-ton crew-cab got out, and all three guys formed up in a raggedy little semicircle about ten feet ahead of the Corvette's front fender. They were all wiry and worn down. They were all in sleeveless plaid work shirts over no-color sweat-shirts, and blue jeans, and boots. They all had woolen watch caps on their heads. The dazed guy was maybe five-eight, and the director of operations was maybe five-ten, and the half-ton driver was about six feet.

Like small, medium, and large, in a country clothing catalog. From the low end of the market.

"Run them over," Reacher said.

Turner didn't.

The guy from the crew-cab said, "That's Billy Bob's car."

The dazed guy roared, "I already said that."

Are Ready Sud At.

Real loud.

Maybe his hearing had been damaged by the wreck.

The guy from the crew-cab said, "Why are you folks driving Billy Bob's car?"

Reacher said, "This is my car."

"No it ain't. I recognize the plate."

Reacher unclipped his seat belt.

Turner unclipped hers.

Reacher said, "Why do you care who's driving Billy Bob's car?"

"Because Billy Bob is our cousin," the guy said.

"Really?"

"You bet," the guy said. "There have been Claughtons in Hampshire County for three hundred years."

"Got a dark suit?"

"Why?"

"Because you're going to a funeral. Billy Bob doesn't need a car anymore. His lab burned up tonight. He didn't get out in time. We were passing by. Nothing we could do for him."

All three guys went quiet for a moment. They shuffled and flinched, and then shuffled some more and spat on the road. The guy from the half-ton said, "Nothing you could do for him but steal his car?"

"Think of it as repurposing."

"Before he was even cold?"

"Couldn't wait that long. It was a hell of a fire. It'll be a day or two before he's cold."

"What's your name, asshole?"

"Reacher," Reacher said. "There have been Reachers in Hampshire County for about five minutes."

"You taking the mickey?"

"Not really taking it. You seem to be giving it up voluntarily."

"Maybe you started the fire."

"We didn't. Old Billy Bob was in a dangerous business. Live by the sword, die by the sword. Same with the car. Ill-gotten gains, ill gotten all over again."

"You can't have it. We should have it."

Reacher opened his door. He jack-knifed his feet to the ground and stood up fast, in a second, all the way from having his butt four inches off the blacktop to his full six feet five. He stepped around the open door and walked forward and stopped, right on the spot where the ragged little semicircle was centered.

He said, "Let's not have a big discussion about inheritance rights."

The guy from the half-ton said, "What about his money?"

"Possession is nine points of the law," Reacher said, like Espin, in the Dyer interview room.

"You took his money, too?"

"As much as we could find."

Whereupon the dazed guy launched forward and swung his right fist in a violent arc. Reacher swayed backward and let the fist fizz past in front of him, harmlessly, and then he flapped his own right arm, back and forth, as if he was batting away more of the invisible insects, and the dazed guy stared at the pantomime, and Reacher cuffed him on the side of the head with his open left palm, just under the rim of his hat, like an old-time cop with a rude boy from the neighborhood, just a tap, nothing more, but still the guy went down like his head had been blown apart by a round from a high-powered rifle. He lay still on the road, not moving at all.

The guy from the half-ton said, "Is that what you do? Pick on the smallest first?"

"I wasn't picking on him," Reacher said. "He was picking on me. Are you going to make the same mistake?"

"Might not be a mistake."

"It would be," Reacher said. Then he glanced beyond the guy, at the vertical pick-up truck. He said, "Shit, that thing's going to fall over."

The guy didn't turn around. Didn't look. His eyes stayed fixed on Reacher's.

He said, "Good try. But I wasn't born yesterday."

Reacher said, "I'm not kidding, you moron." And he wasn't. Maybe the half-ton had a loose transmission. Maybe it had sagged forward six inches when the guy shut it down before he got out. But whatever, there was new tension in the chain. It was rigid. It was practically humming. And the vertical truck was teetering right on the point of balance, an inch away from falling forward like a tree. A breath of wind would have done it.

And then a breath of wind went right ahead and did it.

The branches all around sighed and moved gently, just once, and the vertical truck's tailgate scraped over small stones trapped beneath it, and the chain went slack, and the truck started to topple forward, almost imperceptibly, one degree at a time, and then it hit the point of no return, and then it was falling faster, and faster, and then it was a giant sledgehammer smashing down into the half-ton's load bed, the weight of its iron engine block striking a mighty blow on the corrugated floor, breaking the axle below it, the half-ton's wheels suddenly canting out at the bottom and in at the top, like knock knees, or puppy feet, the smaller truck's wheels folding the other way, on broken steering rods. The chain rattled to the ground, and competing suspensions settled, and the smaller truck came to rest, up at an angle, partly on top of the larger truck, both of them spent and inert and still.

"Looks like they were having sex," Reacher said. "Doesn't it?"

No one answered. The small guy was still on the floor, and the other two were staring at a whole new problem. Neither vehicle was going anywhere soon, not without a big crane and a flatbed truck. Reacher climbed down into the Corvette. The wreckage was blocking the road, from ditch to ditch, so Turner had no choice. She backed up and threaded between the two burning flares, and she headed back the way they had come.

Chapter 30

Turner said, "Those guys will drop a dime, as soon as they hear about us. They'll be on the phone immediately. To their probation officers. They'll be cutting all kinds of deals. They'll use us as a get-out-of-jail card, for their next ten misdemeanors."

Reacher nodded. The road couldn't stay blocked forever. Sooner or later some other passerby would call it in. Or the Claughton cousins would call it in themselves, having exhausted all other alternatives. And then the cops would show up, and their inevitable questions would lead to exculpatory answers, and deals, and trades, and promises, and exchanges.

"Try the next road south," Reacher said. "There's nothing else we can do."

"Still enjoying yourself?"

"Never better."

They made the turn, on the quiet two-lane road they had quit twenty minutes earlier. It was deserted. Trees to the left, trees to the right, nothing ahead, nothing behind. They crossed a river on a bridge. The river was the Potomac, at that location narrow and unremarkable, flowing north, downhill from its distant source, before hooking east and then broadening into the lazy current it was known as at its mouth. There was no traffic on the road. Nothing going their way, nothing going the other way. No lights and no sounds, except their own.

Reacher said, "If this was a movie, right about now the cowboy would scratch his cheek and say it's too quiet."

"Not funny," Turner said. "They could have sealed this road. There could be state police around the next bend."

But there weren't. Not around the next bend, or the next. But the bends kept on coming. One after the other, like separate tense questions.

Turner said, "How do they know how you live?"

"Who?"

"The senior staff officers."

"That's a very good question."

"Do they know how you live?"

They couldn't find you before. They won't find you now. The army doesn't use skip tracers. And no skip tracer could find you anyway.

"They seem to know I didn't buy a split level ranch somewhere in the suburbs. They seem to know I don't coach Little League and grow my own vegetables. They seem to know I didn't develop a second career."

"But how do they know?"

"No idea."

"I read your file. There was a lot of good stuff in it."

"A lot of bad stuff, too."

"But maybe bad is good. In the sense of being inter-esting to someone. In terms of personality. They were tracking you since you were six years old. You exhib-ited unique characteristics."

"Not unique."

"Rare, then. In terms of an aggressive response to danger."

Reacher nodded. At the age of six he had gone to a movie, on a Marine base somewhere in the Pacific. A kids' matinee. A cheap sci-fi potboiler. All of a sudden a monster had popped up out of a slimy lagoon. The youthful audience was being filmed in secret, with a low-light camera. A psy-ops experiment. Most kids had recoiled in terror when the monster appeared. But Reacher hadn't. He had leapt at the screen instead, ready to fight, with his switchblade already open. They said his response time had been three-quarters of a second.

Six years old.

They had taken his switchblade away.

They had made him feel like a psychopath.

Turner said, "And you did well at West Point. And your service years were impressive."

"If you close your eyes and squint. Personally I re-member a lot of friction and shouting. I was on the carpet a lot of the time."

"But maybe bad is good. From some particular per-spective. Suppose there's a desk somewhere, in the Pentagon, maybe. Suppose someone's sole job is to track a certain type of person, who might be useful in the future, under a certain type of circumstance. Like long-range contingency planning, for a new super-secret unit. Deniable, too. Like a list of suitable personnel. As in, when the shit hits the fan, who are you gonna call?"

"Now it sounds like you who's been watching movies."

"Nothing happens in the movies that doesn't happen in real life. That's one thing I've learned. You can't make this stuff up."

"Speculation," Reacher said.

"Is it impossible there's a database somewhere, with a hundred or two hundred or a thousand names in it, of people the military wants to keep track of, just in case?"

"I guess that's not impossible."

"It would be a very secret database. For a number of obvious reasons. Which means that if these guys have seen it, thereby knowing how you live, they're not just senior staff officers. They're very senior staff officers. You said so yourself. They have access to files in any branch of the service they want."

"Speculation," Reacher said again.

"But logical."

"Maybe."

"Very senior staff officers," Turner said again.

Reacher nodded. Like flipping a coin. Fifty-fifty. Either true, or not true.

The first turn they came to was Route 220, which was subtly wider than the road they were on, and flatter, and better surfaced, and straighter, and altogether more important in every way. In comparison it felt like a major artery. Not exactly a highway, but because of their heightened sensitivities it looked like a whole different proposition.

"No," Turner said.

"Agreed," Reacher said. There would be gas and coffee, probably, and diners and motels, but there could be police, too, either state or local. Or federal. Because it was the kind of road that showed up well on a map. Reacher pictured a hasty conference somewhere, with impatient fingers jabbing paper, with urgent voices saying *roadblocks here, and here, and here*.

"We'll take the next one," he said.

Which gave them seven more tense minutes. The road stayed empty. Trees to the left, trees to the right, nothing ahead, nothing behind. No lights, no sound. But nothing happened. And the next turn was better. On a map it would be just an insignificant gray trace, or more likely not there at all. It was a high hill road, very like the one they had already tried, narrow, lumpy, twisting and turning, with ragged shoulders and shallow rainwater ditches on both sides. They took it gratefully, and its darkness swallowed them up. Turner got her small-road rhythm going, keeping her speed appropriate, keeping her movements efficient. Reacher relaxed and watched her. She was leaning back in her seat, her arms straight out, her fingers on the wheel, sensitive to the tiny quivering messages coming up from the road. Her hair was hooked behind her ears, and he could see slim muscles in her thigh, as she worked first one pedal and then the other.

She asked, "How much money did the Big Dog make?"

"Plenty," Reacher said. "But not enough to drop a hundred grand on a defensive scam, if that's what you're thinking."

"But he was right at the end of the chain. He wasn't the top boy. He wasn't a mass wholesaler. He would be seeing only a small part of the profit. And it was sixteen years ago. Things have changed."

"You think this is about stolen ordnance?"

"It could be. The Desert Storm drawdown then, the Afghanistan drawdown now. Similar circumstances. Similar opportunities. But different stuff. What was the Big Dog selling?"

"Eleven crates of SAWs, when we heard about him."

"On the streets of LA? That's bad."

"That was the LAPD's problem, not mine. All I wanted was a name."

"You could sell SAWs to the Taliban."

"But for how much?"

"Drones, then. Or surface-to-air missiles. Extremely high-value items. Or MOABs. Did you have them in your day?"

"You make it sound like we had bows and arrows."

"So you didn't."

"No, but I know what they are. Massive ordnance air burst. The mother of all bombs."

"Thermobaric devices more powerful than anything except nuclear weapons. Plenty of buyers in the Middle East for things like those. No doubt about that. And those buyers have plenty of money. No doubt about that, either."

"They're thirty feet long. Kind of hard to slip in your coat pocket."

"Stranger things have happened."

Then she went quiet, for a whole mile.

Reacher said, "What?"

"Suppose this is government policy. We might be arming one faction against another. We do that all the time."

Reacher said nothing.

Turner said, "You don't see it that way?"

"I can't make it work deep down. The government can do whatever it wants. So why scam you with a hundred grand? Why didn't you just disappear? And me? And Moorcroft? Why aren't we in Guantanamo right now? Or dead? And why were the guys who came to the motel the first night so crap? That was no kind of government wet team. I barely had to break a sweat. And why would it get to that point in the first place? They could have backed you down some other way. They could have ordered you to pull Weeks and Edwards out of there. They could have ordered you to cease and desist."

"Not without automatically raising my suspicions. It would have put a big spotlight on the whole thing. That's a risk they wouldn't want to take."

"Then they'd have found a better way. They would have ordered a whole countrywide strategic pull-back, all the way to the Green Zone. For some made-up political reason. To respect the Afghans' sovereignty, or some such thing. It would have been a tsunami of bullshit. Your guys would have been caught up in it along with everyone else, and you wouldn't have thought twice about it. It would have been just one of those things. Same old shit."

"So you're not convinced."

"This all feels amateur to me," Reacher said. "Correct, uptight, slightly timid people, somewhat out of their depth now, and therefore relying on somewhat undistinguished muscle to cover their collective asses. Which gives us one small problem and one big opportunity. The small problem being, those four guys know they have to get to us first, before the MPs or the FBI, because we're in deep shit now, technically, with the escape and all, so the assumption is we'll say anything to help with our situations. And even if no one believes us, it would all be out there as a possibility or a rumor, and these guys can't afford any kind of extra scrutiny, even if it was half-assed and by the book. So that's the small problem. Those four guys are going to stay hard on our tails. That's for damn sure."

"And what's the big opportunity?"

"Those same four guys," Reacher said. "Their bosses will be lost without them. They'll be cut off at the knees. They'll be helpless and isolated. They'll be ours for the taking."

"So that's the plan?" Turner said. "We're going to let the four guys find us, and we're going to bust them, and then we're going to move on up from there?"

"Except we're not going to bust them," Reacher said. "We're going to do to them what they were going to do to us."

"Which is what?"

"We're going to put them in the ground. And then we're going to listen out for their bosses howling in the void. And then we're going to explain to them carefully why it's a very bad idea to mess with the 110th."

Chapter 31

They crossed the line into Grant County, and the lonely hill road ran on unchanging, mile after mile. The speedometer was drifting between fifty and sixty, up and down, but the gas gauge was moving one way only, and fast. Then a sign on the shoulder announced the Grant County Airport twenty miles ahead, and a town named Petersburg.

Turner said, "A place with an airport has to have a gas station, right? And a motel. And a place with an airport and a gas station and a motel has to have a diner."

Reacher said, "And a police department."

"Hope for the best."

"I always do," Reacher said.

They hit the town before the airport. It was mostly asleep. But not completely. They came out of the hills and merged left onto a state road that became North

Main Street a hundred yards later, with built-up blocks on the left and the right. In the center of town there was a crossroads with Route 220, which was the road they had avoided earlier. After the crossroads North Main Street became South Main Street. The airport lay to the west, not far away. There was no traffic, but some windows had lights behind them.

Turner went south, across the narrow Potomac again, and she took a right, toward the airport, which was a small place for light planes only, and which was all closed up and dark. So she U-turned, curb to curb, and she headed back, across the river again, toward the downtown crossroads.

Reacher said, "Go right on 220. I bet that's where the good stuff is."

East of the crossroads 220 was called Virginia Avenue, and for the first two hundred yards it was close-but-no-cigar. There was a sandwich shop, closed, and a pizza place, also closed. There was an out-of-business Chevron station, and two fast food franchises, both closed for the night. There was an ancient motor court inn, boarded up, falling down, its lot choked with weeds.

"No good stuff yet," Turner said.

"Free market," Reacher said. "Someone put that Chevron out of business. And that motel. All we have to do is find out who."

They drove on, another block, and another, past the city limit, and then they scored a perfect trifecta on the cheaper land beyond. First came a country cafe, open all night, on the left side of the road, behind a wide gravel lot with three trucks in it. Then there was a motel, a hundred yards later, on the right side of the road, a modern two-story place on the edge of a field. And beyond the motel in the far distance was the red glow of an Exxon station.

All good. Except that halfway between the cafe and the motel was a state police barracks.

It was a pale building, long and low, made from glazed tan brick, with dishes and whip antennas on its roof. It had two cruisers parked out front, and lights behind two of its windows. A dispatcher and a desk sergeant, Reacher figured, doing their night duty in warmth and comfort.

Turner said, "Do they know about this car yet?"

Reacher looked at the motel. "Or will they before we wake up in the morning?"

"We have to get gas, at least."

"OK, let's go do that. We'll try to get a feel for the place."

So Turner eased on down the road, as discreet as she could be in a bright red convertible with six hundred brake horsepower, and she pulled in at the Exxon, which was a two-island, four-pump affair, with a pay hut made of crisp, white boards. It looked like a tiny house. Except that it had antennas on its roof, too.

Turner parked near a pump, and Reacher studied the instructions, which said that without a credit card to dip, he was going to have to pre-pay in cash. He asked, "How many gallons?"

Turner said, "I don't know how big the tank is."

"Pretty big, probably."

"Let's say fifteen, then."

Which was going to cost fifty-nine dollars and

eighty-five cents, at the posted rate. Reacher peeled three twenties out of one of Billy Bob's bricks and headed for the hut. Inside was a woman of about forty behind a bulletproof screen. There was a half moon shape at counter height, for passing money through. Coming out of it were the sweet nasal melodies of an AM radio tuned to a country station, and the chatter and noise of a police scanner tuned to the emergency band.

Reacher slid his money through and the woman did something he guessed permitted the pump to serve up sixty bucks of gas, and not a drop more. One country song ended, and another started, separated only by a muted blast of static from the scanner. Reacher glanced at it and tried a weary-traveler expression and asked, "Anything happening tonight?"

"All quiet so far," the woman said.

Reacher glanced the other way, at the AM radio. "Country music not enough for you?"

"My brother owns a tow truck. And that business is all about being first on the scene. He gives me ten dollars for every wreck I get him to."

"So no wrecks tonight?"

"Not a one."

"No excitement at all?"

The woman said, "That's a nice car you're riding in."

"Why do you say that?"

"Because I always wanted a Corvette."

"Did you hear about us on the scanner?"

"Been speeding?"

"Hard not to."

"Then you've been lucky. You got away with it."

Reacher said, "Long may it continue," and he smiled what he hoped was a conspiratorial little smile, and he headed back to the car. Turner was already pumping the gas. She had the nozzle hooked into the filler neck, and she was turned three-quarters away from him, with the back of one thigh against the flank of the car, and the other foot up on the curb of the island. She had her hands behind her, and her back was arched, as if she was easing an ache. Her face was turned up to the night sky. Reacher imagined her shape, like a slender *S* under the big shirt.

Totally worth it.

He said, "The clerk is listening in on a scanner. We're clean so far."

"You asked her? She'll remember us now."

"She will anyway. She always wanted a Corvette."

"We should trade with her. We should take whatever she's got."

"Then she'd remember us forever."

"Maybe those hillbillies won't call it in. Maybe their trucks were stolen, too. Maybe they just vanished into the woods."

"Possible," Reacher said. "I don't see why they would wait so long."

"We could park way in the back of the motel. Right out of sight. I think we should risk it. We really need to eat and sleep."

The pump clicked off, just short of twelve gallons. Either the tank was smaller than they had guessed, or the gauge was pessimistic.

Turner said, "Now she knows it's not our car. We're not familiar with how much gas it takes."

"Will she give us the change?"

"Maybe we should leave it."

"It's twelve bucks. This is West Virginia. We'd stick out like sore thumbs."

"Tell her we're heading south on 220. Tell her we've got a long way to go before daybreak. Then when she hears about us on the scanner she'll call it in wrong."

Reacher collected twelve dollars and fifty-two cents in change, and said something about trying to make it to I-64 before dawn. The AM radio murmured its tunes, and the police scanner stayed quiet. The woman looked out the window and smiled a little sadly, as if it was going to be a long time before she saw a Corvette again.

Turner picked Reacher up at the pay hut door, and they drove back toward town, and pulled in again three hundred yards later, at the motel.

She said, "Check in first, and then hit the cafe?"

Reacher said, "Sure."

She paused a long beat, and looked straight at him. She said, "How many rooms are we going to get?"

He paused a long beat in turn, and said, "Let's eat first. Then check in."

"Why?"

"There's something I have to tell you."

"What?"

Samantha Dayton.

Sam.

Fourteen years old.

"After we order," he said. "It's a long story."

Chapter 32

The cafe was a rural greasy spoon as perfect as anything Reacher had ever seen. It had a black guy in a white undershirt next to a lard-slick griddle three feet deep and six feet wide. It had battered pine tables and mismatched chairs. It smelled of old grease and fresh coffee. It had two ancient white men in seed caps, one of them sitting way to the left of the door, the other way to the right. Maybe they didn't get along. Maybe they were victims of a feud three hundred years old.

Turner chose a table in the middle of the room, and they rattled the chairs out over the board floor, and they sat down. There were no menus. No chalkboards with handwritten lists of daily specials. It wasn't that kind of a place. Ordering was clearly telepathic between the cook and his regular customers. For new customers, it was going to be a matter of asking out loud, plain and simple. Which the cook confirmed, by raising his chin and rotating his head a little, so that his right ear was presented to the room.

"Omelet," Turner said. "Mushrooms, spring onions, and cheddar cheese."

No reaction from the cook.

None at all.

Turner said it again, a little louder.

Still no reaction. No movement. Just total stillness, and a raised chin, and an averted gaze, and a dignified and implacable silence, like a veteran salesman insulted by a counteroffer. Turner looked at Reacher and whispered, "What's with this place?"

"You're a detective," Reacher said. "You see any sign of an omelet pan up there?"

"No, I guess not. All I see is a griddle."

"So probably the best way to get some enthusiasm out of this guy would be to order something griddle-related."

Turner paused a beat.

Then she said, "Two eggs over easy on a fried biscuit with bacon on the side."

The cook said, "Yes, ma'am."

"Same for me," Reacher said. "And coffee."

"Yes, sir." And immediately the guy turned away and got to work with a wedge of new lard and a blade, planing the metal surface, smoothing it, three feet out and three feet back, and six feet side to side. Which made him a griddle man at heart. In Reacher's experience such guys were either griddle men or owners, but never really both. A griddle man's first instinct was to tend the metal, working it until it was glassy down at a molecular level, so slick it would make Teflon feel like sandpaper. Whereas an owner's first instinct would have been to bring the coffee. Because the first cup of coffee seals the deal. A customer isn't committed until he has consumed something. He can still get up and walk away, if he's dissatisfied with the wait, or if he remembers an urgent appointment. But not if he's already started in on his first cup of coffee. Because then he would have to throw some money down, and who really knows what a cup of diner coffee costs? Fifty cents? A dollar? Two dollars?

"OK, we've ordered," Turner said. "So what do you have to tell me?"

"Let's wait for the coffee," Reacher said. "I don't want to be interrupted."

"Then I have a couple of things," she said. "I want to know more about this guy Morgan, for instance. I want to know who's got his hands on my unit."

"My unit, too," Reacher said. "I always assumed I'd be its worst-ever commander, but I guess I'm not. Your guys in Afghanistan missed two consecutive radio checks, and he did nothing about it."

"Do we know where he's from?"

"No idea."

"Is he one of them?"

"Hard to say. Obviously the unit needed a temporary commander. That's not proof of guilt in itself."

"And how would recalling you to service fit their game plan? Surely they would want to get rid of you, not keep you close at hand."

"I think it was all supposed to make me run. Which I could have. I could have gone permanently AWOL. They made a big point of saying no one would come after me. No skip tracers. Like a one-two punch, with the Big Dog affidavit. A charge I can't beat, and a mandate to stick around to face it. I think most guys in my situation would have headed for the hills at that point. I think that was their expectation, strategically. But it didn't work."

"Because when a monster comes up out of the slime, you have to fight it."

"Or it could have been a JAG order, simple as that. There might have been a sidebar on the file, saying that if I didn't cooperate, then I had to be nailed down. Because of some kind of political sensitivity, in the Secretary's office. Certainly it wasn't Morgan's own decision. A light colonel doesn't decide shit like that. It had to come from a higher level."

"From very senior staff officers."

"Agreed, but which ones, exactly?"

Turner didn't answer that. The griddle man brought the coffee, finally. Two large pottery mugs, and a little pink plastic basket full of creamer pots and sugar packets, and two spoons pressed out of metal so thin they felt weightless. Reacher took a mug and sniffed the steam and tried a sip. The mug's rim was cold and thick, but the coffee was adequate. Hot, and not too weak.

He put the mug back down on the table and linked his hands around it, as if he was protecting it, and he looked at Turner, right in the eye, and he said, "So."

She said, "One more thing. And it's going to be tough to say. So I'm sorry."

"What is it?"

"I shouldn't have asked about one room or two."

"I didn't mind."

"But I did. I'm not sure I'm ready for one room yet. I feel like I owe you. For what you've done for me today. I don't think that's a good state of mind to be in, under those circumstances. The one-room type of circumstances, I mean."

"You don't owe me anything. I had purely selfish motivations. I wanted to take you out to dinner. Which I'm right now in the middle of doing, I guess. In a way. Perhaps not as planned. But whatever, I got what I wanted. Anything else is collateral damage. So you don't owe me shit."

Turner said, "I feel unsettled."

"You just got arrested and broke out of jail. And now you're running for your life and stealing cars and money."

"No, it's because of you."

"Why?"

"You make me feel uncomfortable."

"I'm sorry."

"Not your fault," she said. "It's just the way you are."

"And what way is that?"

"I don't want to hurt your feelings."

"You can't," Reacher said. "I'm a military cop. And a man. I have no feelings."

"That's what I mean."

"I was kidding."

"No, you weren't. Not entirely."

She paused a long moment.

Then she said, "You're like something feral."

Reacher said nothing in reply to that. *Feral*, from the Latin adjective *ferus,* wild, via *bestia fera,* wild animal. Generally held to mean having escaped from domestication, and having devolved back to a natural state.

Turner said, "It's like you've been sanded down to nothing but yes and no, and you and them, and black and white, and live or die. It makes me wonder, what does that to a person?"

"Life," Reacher said. "Mine, anyway."

"You're like a predator. Cold, and hard. Like this whole thing. You have it all mapped out. The four guys in the car, and their bosses. You're swimming toward them, right now, and there's going to be blood in the water. Yours or theirs, but there's going to be blood."

"Right now I hope I'm swimming away from them. And I don't even know who they are or where they are."

"But you will. You're thinking about it all the time. I can see you doing it. You're worrying away at it, trying to catch the scent."

"What else should I do? Buy us bus tickets straight to Leavenworth?"

"Is that the only alternative?"

"What do you think?"

She took her first sip of coffee, slow and contemplative. She said, "I agree with you. And that's the problem, right there. That's what's making me uncomfortable. I'm just like you. Except not yet. And that's the point. Looking at you is like looking into the future. You're what I'm going to be one day. When I'm all sanded down, too."

"So I'm too similar? Most women say no because I'm too different."

"You scare me. Or the prospect of becoming you scares me. I'm not sure I'm ready for that. I'm not sure I ever will be."

"Doesn't have to happen. This is a bump in the road. You'll still have a career."

"If we win."

"We will."

"So best case, I step off the path to stay on it. Worst case, I'm off it forever."

"No, worst case is you're dead or locked up. Worst case is the wrong guys win."

"It's always win or lose with you, isn't it?"

"Is there a third option?"

"Does it burn you up to lose?"

"Of course."

"It's a kind of paralyzing arrogance. Normal people don't get all burned up if they lose."

"Maybe they should," Reacher said. "But you're not really like me. You're not looking at yourself when you look at me. That's why I came all this way. You're a better version. That's what I sensed on the phone. You're doing it the way it should be done."

"Doing what?"

"Everything. Your job. Your life. Being a person."

"Doesn't feel that way. Not right now. And don't think of me like a better version. If I can't look at you and see what's going to be, you can't look at me and see what should have been."

Then the griddle man came back, this time with plates full of eggs and bacon and fried biscuits, all of which looked good, and all of which looked perfectly cooked. The eggs had clean, crisp edges. Clearly the guy cared for his metal well. After he was gone again Turner said, "This is all assuming you have a definite preference, that is, one way or the other, about the number of rooms."

Reacher said, "Honest answer?"

"Of course."

"I do have a definite preference."

"For?"

"I have to tell you my thing first."

"Which is?"

"The other item designed to make me run."

"Which was?"

"A paternity suit," Reacher said. "Apparently I have a daughter in Los Angeles. By a woman I can't remember."

Chapter 33

Reacher talked, and Turner ate. He told her the things he had been told. Red Cloud, between Seoul and the DMZ, and Candice Dayton, and her diary, and her home in LA, and her homelessness in LA, and her daughter, and her car, and her visit with a lawyer.

Turner asked, "What's the kid's name?"

"Samantha," Reacher said. "Sam for short, presumably."

"How old is she?"

"Fourteen. Nearly fifteen."

"How do you feel?"

"Bad. If she's mine, I should have been there for her."

"You really don't remember her mother?"

"No, I really don't."

"Is that normal for you?"

"You mean, exactly how feral am I?"

"I suppose."

"I don't think I forget people. I hope I don't. Especially women I sleep with. But if I did, I would be unaware of it, by definition. You can't be aware of forgetting."

"Is this why we're going to Los Angeles?"

"I have to know," Reacher said.

"But it's suicide. They'll all be waiting for you there. It's the one place they can be sure you'll go."

"I have to know," Reacher said again.

Turner said nothing.

Reacher said, "Anyway, that's the story. That's what I had to tell you. In the interests of full disclosure. In case it had a bearing. On the rooms issue, for instance."

Turner didn't answer.

They finished up, and they got their check, which was for a total represented by a scrawled figure circled beneath three scribbled lines. How much was a cup of diner coffee? No one knew, because no one ever found out. Maybe it was free. Maybe it had to be, because the composite total was modest. Reacher had thirteen dollars and thirty-two cents in his pocket, which was Sullivan's surviving eighty cents plus the change he had gotten in the gas station hut, and he left all of it on the table, thereby including a handsome tip. A guy who worked a hot griddle all night deserved no less.

The car was where they had left it, unmolested, not surrounded by searchlights and SWAT teams. Far to their left the state police barracks looked quiet. The cruisers out front had not moved. The warm lights were still showing in the windows.

"Stay or go?" Turner asked.

"Stay," Reacher said. "This place is as good as any.

As weird as that sounds, with the troopers right here. It's not going to get better than this. Not until it's over."

"Not until we win, you mean."

"Same thing."

They eased themselves into the Corvette's low seats, and Turner fired it up and drove back to the motel. She stopped outside the office.

"I'll wait here," she said. "You go do it."

"OK," he said.

He took a fistful of twenties from one of Billy Bob's bricks.

"Two rooms," she said.

The night clerk was asleep in his chair, but it didn't take much to wake him up. The sound of the door did half the job, and a polite tap from Reacher's knuckles on the counter did the rest. The guy was young. Maybe it was a family business. Maybe this was a son or a nephew.

"Got two rooms?" Reacher asked him.

The guy made a big show of checking on a computer screen, like many such guys do, which Reacher thought was dumb. They weren't the worldwide heads of global operations for giant hotel corporations. They were in motels with rooms they could count on their fingers and toes. If they lost track, then surely all they had to do was turn around and check the keys hanging on the hooks behind them.

The guy looked up from the screen and said, "Yes, sir, I can do that."

"How much?"

"Thirty dollars per room per night. With a voucher included, for breakfast at the cafe across the street."

"Deal," Reacher said, and he swapped three of Billy Bob's twenties for two of the young guy's keys. Rooms eleven and twelve. Adjacent. A kindness, on the young guy's part. Easier for the maid in the morning. Less distance to push her heavy cart.

"Thank you," Reacher said.

He went out to the car, and Turner drove around to the rear of the compound, where she found a patch of lumpy winter grass behind the last of the buildings. She eased the car up onto it, and they raised the top, and they locked it up for the night, and they left it there, not visible from the street.

They walked back together and found their rooms, which were on the second floor, up an exterior flight of concrete stairs. Reacher gave Turner the key to eleven, and kept twelve for himself. She said, "What time tomorrow?"

"Noon," he said. "And I'll drive some, if you like."

"We'll see. Sleep well."

"You, too."

He waited until she was safely inside before he opened his door. The room behind it was a concrete box with a popcorn ceiling and vinyl wallpaper. Better than the place a mile from Rock Creek, but only by degrees. The heater was quieter, but far from silent. The carpet was cleaner, but not by much. As was the bedspread. The shower looked reasonable, and the towels were thin but not transparent. The soap and the shampoo were dressed up with a brand name that sounded like a firm of old Boston lawyers. The furniture was made of pale wood, and the television set was a small off-brand flat screen, about the size of a carry-on suitcase. There was no telephone. No mini-bar refrigerator, no free bottle of water, no chocolate on the pillow.

He turned on the television and found CNN and watched the ticker at the bottom of the screen, all the way through a full cycle. There was no mention of two fugitives fleeing an army facility in Virginia. So he headed for the bathroom and started the shower and stood under it, aimlessly, long after the soap he had used was rinsed away. Fragments of the conversation over the scarred cafe table came back to him, unstop-pably. *You're like something feral,* she had said. *You're like a predator. Cold, and hard.*

But in the end the line that stuck was from earlier in the exchange. Turner had asked about Morgan, and he had told her, *Your guys in Afghanistan missed two consecutive radio checks, and he did nothing about it.* He went over and over it, sounding the words in his head, moving his lips, saying it out loud, breaking it down, sputtering each phrase into the beating water, examining each separate clause in detail.

Your guys in Afghanistan.

Missed two consecutive radio checks.

And he did nothing about it.

He shut off the water and got out of the tub and grabbed a towel. Then, still damp, he put his pants back on, and one of his T-shirts, and he stepped out to the upstairs walkway. He padded barefoot through the cold night air, to room eleven's door.

He knocked.

Chapter 34

Reacher waited in the cold, because Turner didn't open up right away. But he knew she was awake. He could see electric light through the spy hole in her door. Then it darkened briefly, as she put her eye to it, to check who was there. Then he was left to wait some more. She was hauling some clothes on, he guessed. She had showered, too, almost certainly.

Then the door opened, and she stood there, with one hand on the handle and the other on the jamb, blocking his way, either consciously or subconsciously. Her hair was slick with water and finger-combed out of her eyes. She was wearing her army T-shirt and her new work pants. Her feet were bare.

Reacher said, "I would have called, but there's no telephone in my room."

"Mine either," she said. "What's up?"

"Something I told you about Morgan. I just realized what it means."

"What did you tell me?"

"I said your guys in Afghanistan missed two consecutive radio checks, and he did nothing about it."

"I was thinking about that, too. I think it's proof he's one of them. He did nothing because he knew there was nothing to do. He knew they were dead. No point in organizing a search."

"Can I come in?" Reacher asked. "It's cold out here."

No answer.

"Or we could use my room," he said. "If you prefer."

"No, come in," she said. She took her hand off the jamb and moved aside. He stepped in, and she closed the door behind him. Her room was the same as his. His shirt was on the back of a chair. Her boots were under the chair, stowed neatly, side by side.

She said, "I guess I could afford some new shoes now."

"New everything, if you want," he said.

"Do you agree?" she said. "It's proof he's one of them?"

"It could be proof he's lazy and incompetent."

"No commander could be that dumb."

"How long have you been in the army?"

She smiled, briefly. "OK, plenty of commanders could be that dumb."

He said, "I don't think the important part is him doing nothing about it."

She sat down on the bed. Left him standing near the window. Her pants were loose, and her shirt was tight. She was wearing nothing underneath it. That was clear. He could see ribs, and slender curves. On the phone from South Dakota he had pictured her as a blonde, with blue eyes, maybe from northern California, all of which had turned out to be completely wrong. She was dark haired and dark eyed, and from Montana. But he had been right about other things. *Five-six or five-seven,* he had guessed out loud, *but thin. Your voice is all in your throat.* She had laughed out loud and asked: *You saying I'm flat-chested?* He had laughed back and said, *34A at best.* She had said, *Damn.*

But the reality was better than the telephone guesses. Live and in person she was something else entirely.

Totally worth it.

She said, "What was the important part of what Morgan said?"

"The two missed radio checks."

"Because?"

"Your guys checked in on the day you were arrested, but then they missed the next day, and the next."

"As did I, because I was in jail. You know that. It was a concerted plan. They shut us down, both ends, over there and over here, simultaneously."

"But it wasn't simultaneous," Reacher said. "That's my point. Afghanistan is nine hours ahead of Rock Creek. That's practically a whole day's worth of daylight in the winter. And no one walks on a goat trail in the Hindu Kush after dark. That would be a bad idea for a huge number of reasons, including falling down and accidentally breaking your leg. So your guys were out there getting shot in the head during daylight hours. That's for damn sure. No question about it. And daylight hours end by about six o'clock local."

"OK."

"Six o'clock in the evening in Afghanistan is nine o'clock in the morning here."

"OK."

"But my lawyer said you opened your bank account in the Cayman Islands at ten o'clock in the morning, and the hundred grand arrived at eleven o'clock in the morning, and you were arrested at noon."

"I remember that last part."

"Which means your guys were dead at least an hour before they started messing with you. Many hours, most likely. Minimum of one, maximum of eight or nine."

"OK, so not exactly simultaneous. Not two things at once, but one thing after the other. Does that make a difference?"

"I think it does," Reacher said. "But first we have to step back a day. You sent Weeks and Edwards into the hills, and the reaction was instantaneous. The whole thing was over by noon the next day. How did they react so fast?"

"Luck?"

"Suppose it was something else."

"You think they have a mole in the 110th?"

"I doubt it. Not with our kind of people. It would have been impossible in my day, and I can only imagine things have gotten better."

"Then how?"

"I think your comms were penetrated."

"A tap on the Rock Creek phones? I don't think that's possible. We have systems in place."

"Not Rock Creek," Reacher said. "It makes no sense to tap the local ends of the network. There are too many of them. Better to concentrate on the center of the web. Where the spider lives. I think they're reading everything that goes in and out of Bagram. Very senior staff officers, with access to anything they want. Which back at that point was everything. Which was exactly what they got. They sifted through all the chatter, and they got the original rumor, and your orders, and your guys' reactions, and the whole back and forth."

"Possible," Turner said.

"Which makes a difference."

"But only as a background detail."

"No, more than that," Reacher said. "They had already stopped Weeks and Edwards, between one and nine hours previously, so why did they still go ahead and come after you?"

"You know why. They thought I knew something I actually didn't."

"But they didn't need to think anything. Or guess, or plan for the worst. Not if they were reading stuff in *and out* of Bagram. No speculation was required. They knew what Weeks and Edwards told you. They knew for sure. They had it in black and white. They knew what you knew, Susan."

"But I knew nothing. Because Weeks and Edwards told me nothing."

"If that's true, then why did they go ahead and come after you? Why would they do that? Why would they go ahead with a very complex and very expensive scam for no reason at all? Why would they risk that hundred grand?"

"So what are you saying?"

"I'm saying Weeks and Edwards *did* tell you something. I'm saying you *do* know something. Maybe it didn't seem like a big deal at the time, and maybe you don't remember it now, but Weeks and Edwards gave you some little nugget, and as a result someone got his panties in a real big wad."

Chapter 35

Turner put her bare feet up on the bed and leaned back on the pillow. She said, "I'm not senile, Reacher. I remember what they told me. We're paying a Pashtun insider, and they met with the guy, and he told them an American officer had been seen heading north to meet with a tribal elder. But at that point the identity of the American officer was definitely not known, and the purpose of the meeting was definitely not known."

Reacher asked, "Was there a description?"

"No, other than American."

"Man or woman?"

"Has to be a man. Pashtun elders don't meet with women."

"Black or white?"

"Didn't say."

"Army? Marines? Air Force?"

"We all look the same to them."

"Rank? Age?"

"No details at all. An American officer. That's all we knew."

"There has to be something else."

"I know what I know, Reacher. And I know what I don't."

"Are you sure?"

"What does that even mean? This is like you and that woman in Korea. No one is aware of forgetting. Except I'm not forgetting. I remember what they said."

"How much back and forth was there?"

"There was what I just told you, about the rumor, and then there were my orders, which were to go chase it. And that was all. One signal out, and one signal back."

"What about their last radio check? Did you see it?"

"It was the last thing I saw, before they came for me. It was pure routine. No progress. Nothing to see here, folks, so move right along. That kind of thing."

"So it was in the original message. About the rumor. You're going to have to try to remember it, word for word."

"An unknown American officer was seen heading north to meet with a tribal elder. For an unspecified reason. That's it, word for word. I already remember it."

"What part of that is worth a hundred thousand dollars? And your future, and mine, and Moorcroft's? And a bruise on a schoolgirl's arm, in Berryville, Virginia?"

"I don't know," Turner said.

* * *

They went quiet after that. No more talking. No more discussion. Turner lay on her bed, staring at the ceiling. Reacher leaned on the window sill, running her summary through his head, fourteen words, a perfect sentence, with a subject and an object and a verb, and a satisfying rhythm, and a pleasing cadence: *An unknown American officer was seen heading north to meet with a tribal elder.* He went over and over it, and then he broke it into thirds, and stared it down, clause by clause.

An unknown American officer.

Was seen heading north.

To meet with a tribal elder.

Twenty-three syllables. Not a haiku. Or, a little less than a haiku-and-a-half.

Meaning?

Uncertain, but he sensed a tiny inconsistency between the start of the sentence and its finish, like a grain of sand in an otherwise perfect mechanism.

An unknown American.

A tribal elder.

Meaning?

He didn't know.

He said, "I'll get going now. We'll come back to it tomorrow. It might creep up on you in the night. That can happen. Something to do with the way the brain reacts to sleep. Memory processing, or a portal to the subconscious, or something like that. I read an article about it once, in a magazine I found on a bus."

"No," she said. "Don't."

"Don't what?"

"Don't get going," she said. "Stay here."

Reacher paused a beat.

He said, "Really?"

"Do you want to?"

"Does the Pope sleep in the woods?"

"Then take your shirt off."

"Really?"

"Take it off, Reacher."

So he did. He hauled the thin stretchy cotton up over his shoulders, and then up over his head, and then he dropped it on the floor.

"Thank you," she said.

And then he waited, like he always did, for her to count his scars.

"I was wrong," she said. "You're not just feral. You're an actual animal."

"We're all animals," he said. "That's what makes things interesting."

"How much do you work out?"

"I don't," he said. "It's genetic." Which it was. Puberty had brought him many things unbidden, including height and weight and an extreme mesomorph physique, with a six-pack like a cobbled city street, and a chest like a suit of NFL armor, and biceps like basketballs, and subcutaneous fat like a Kleenex tissue. He had never messed with any of it. No diets. No weights. No gym time. If it ain't broke, don't fix it, was his attitude.

"Pants now," she said.

"I'm not wearing anything underneath."

She smiled.

"Me either," she said.

He undid his button. He dropped his zip. He pushed the canvas over his hips. He stepped out. One step closer to the bed.

He said, "Your turn now."

She sat up.

She smiled.

She took her shirt off.

She was everything he thought she would be, and she was everything he had ever wanted.

They woke very late the next morning, warm, drowsy, deeply satiated, roused from sleep only by the sound of automobile engines in the lot below their window. They yawned, and stretched, and kissed, long and slow and gentle.

Turner said, "We wasted Billy Bob's money. With the two-room thing. My fault entirely. I'm sorry."

Reacher asked, "What changed your mind?"

"Lust, I suppose. Prison makes you think."

"Seriously."

"It was your T-shirt. I've never seen anything so thin. It was either very expensive or very cheap."

"Seriously."

"It was on my bucket list since we talked on the phone. I liked your voice. And I saw your photograph."

"I don't believe you."

"You mentioned the girl in Berryville. That's what changed my mind. With the arm. That offended you. And you've done nothing but chip away at my problem. You're ignoring your own, with the Big Dog.

Which is just as serious. Therefore you still care for others. Which means you can't really be feral. I imagine caring for others is the first thing to go. And you still know right from wrong. Which all means you're OK. Which all means my future self is OK, too. It's not going to be so bad."

"You're going to be a two-star general, if you want to be."

"Only two stars?"

"More than that is like running for office. No fun at all."

She didn't answer. There was still motor noise in the lot. It sounded like multiple vehicles were driving around and around, in a big circle. Maybe three or four of them, one after the other. Up one side of the building, and down the other. An endless loop.

Turner asked, "What time is it?"

"Nine minutes before noon."

"How do you know?"

"I always know what time it is."

"What time is check out?"

Then they heard footsteps on the walkway outside, and an envelope slid under the door, and the footsteps reversed direction, and faded away.

"Check out time is noon, I guess," Reacher said. "Because I assume that envelope is our copy of the invoice, paid in full."

"That's very formal."

"They have a computer."

The motor noise was still there. Reacher assumed the lizard part of his brain had already screened it for danger. Were they army vehicles? Cop cars? FBI?

And apparently the lizard brain had made no comment. Correctly, in this case, because they were clearly civilian vehicles outside. All gasoline engines, including an out-of-tune V8 with a holed muffler, and at least one weak four-cylinder cheap-finance-special-offer kind of a thing, plus crashing suspensions and rattling panels. Not military or paramilitary sounds at all.

They got louder and faster.

"What is that?" Turner said.

"Take a look," Reacher said.

She padded slender and naked to the window. She made a peephole in the drapes. She looked out, and waited, to catch the whole show.

"Four pick-up trucks," she said. "Various ages, sizes, and states of repair, all of them with two people aboard. They're circling the building, over and over again."

"Why?"

"I have no idea."

"What town are we in?"

"Petersburg, West Virginia."

"Then maybe it's an old West Virginia folk tradition. The rites of spring, or something. Like the running of the bulls in Pamplona. Except they do it in pick-up trucks, in Petersburg."

"But it looks kind of hostile. Like those movies you mentioned, where they say it's too quiet. The parts where the Indians ride in a circle around the wagon with the busted wheel. Faster and faster."

Reacher looked from her to the door.

"Wait," he said.

He slid out of bed and picked up the envelope. The

flap was not gummed down. Inside was a piece of paper. Nothing sinister. As expected. It was a tri-folded invoice showing a zero balance. Which was correct. Room eleven, thirty bucks, less thirty bucks cash up-front.

But.

At the bottom of the invoice was a cheery printed thank-you-for-staying-with-us line, and below that the motel owner's name was printed like a signature, and below that there was a piece of completely gratuitous information.

"Shit," Reacher said.

"What?"

He met her by the bed and showed her.

We surely appreciated you staying with us!

John Claughton, Owner.

There have been Claughtons in Grant County for three hundred years!

Chapter 36

Reacher said, "I guess they're really serious about that Corvette. They must have gotten on some kind of a phone tree last night. A council of war. A call to action. Hampshire County Claughtons, and Grant County Claughtons, and Claughtons from other counties, too, I'm sure. Probably dozens of counties. Probably vast swaths of the entire Mountain State. And if Sleeping Beauty in the office last night was a son or a nephew, then he's also a cousin. And now he's a made man. Because he dimed us out."

"That Corvette is more trouble than it's worth. It was a bad choice."

"But it was fun while it lasted."

"Got any bright ideas?"

"We'll have to reason with them."

"Are you serious?"

"Spread love and understanding," Reacher said. "Use force if necessary."

"Who said that?"

"Leon Trotsky, I think."

"He was stabbed to death with an ice pick. In Mexico."

"That doesn't invalidate his overall position. Not in and of itself."

"What was his overall position?"

"Solid. He also said, if you can't acquaint an opponent with reason, you must acquaint his head with the sidewalk. He was a man of sound instincts. In his private life, I mean. Apart from getting stabbed to death with an ice pick in Mexico, that is."

"What are we going to do?"

"We should start by getting dressed, probably. Except that most of my clothes are in the other room."

"My fault," she said. "I'm sorry."

"Don't make a whole big thing out of it. We'll survive. You get dressed, and we'll both go next door, and I'll get dressed. Safe enough. We'll only be out there a couple of seconds. But take a shower first. There's no rush. They'll wait. They won't come in here. They won't break down Cousin Asshole's door. I'm sure that's part of the Claughton family code."

Turner matched Reacher's habitual shower time exactly, dead on eleven minutes, from the first hand on the faucet to stepping out the door. Which in this instance involved a long pause, spent trying to time it right, to get to the next room unseen by a circling pick-up truck, and then deciding that with four of them each moving at close to thirty miles an hour, remaining unseen was not an available option. So they went

for it, and for ten of the twenty feet they were ahead of
the game, until a truck came around and Reacher
heard a rush under its hood, as the driver reacted in-
stinctively to the sudden appearance of his quarry, by
stamping on the gas. Chasing it, Reacher supposed.
Running it down. An evolutionary mechanism, like so
many things. He unlocked his door and they spilled
inside. He said, "Now they know for sure we're here.
Not that they didn't know already. I'm sure Cyber Boy
has been giving them chapter and verse."

His room was undisturbed. His boots were under
the window, with his socks nearby, and his underwear, and his second T-shirt on a chair, and his jacket
on a hook. He said, "I should take a shower, too. If
they keep on driving circles like that, they'll be dizzy
before we come out."

Reacher was ready in eleven minutes. He sat on
the bed and laced his boots, and he put his coat on
and zipped it up. He said, "I'm happy to do this by
myself, if you like."

Turner said, "What about the troopers across the
street? We can't afford for them to come over."

"I bet the troopers let the Claughtons do whatever
they want. Because I bet the troopers are mostly
Claughtons, too. But I'm sure we'll do it all out of
sight, anyway. That's what usually happens."

"I'll come with you."

"Have you done this before?"

"Yes," she said. "Not too many times."

"They won't all fight. There'll be a congestion prob-

lem, apart from anything else. And we can curb their
enthusiasm by putting the first few down hard. The
key is not to spend too much time on any one individual. The minimum, ideally. Which would be one blow,
and then move on to the next. Elbows are better than
hands, and kicking is better than both."

"OK."

"But I'll talk to them first. It's not like they don't
have a slight point."

They opened the door and stepped out to the walkway and the bright noon light, and as Reacher expected
they saw the four trucks drawn up tight, nose-in at the
bottom of the concrete staircase, like suckerfish. Eight
guys were leaning against their doors and their fenders
and their load beds, patiently, like they had all the time
in the world, which they did, because there was no way
down from the second-floor walkway other than the
concrete staircase. Reacher recognized the three guys
from the night before, on the hill road, small, medium,
and large, the latter two looking more or less the same
as they had before, and the small guy looking much
better, like he was most of the way recovered from
whatever binge had led to his accident. The other five
were similar fellows, all hardscrabble types, the smallest of them a wiry guy all sinew and leathery skin, the
largest somewhat bloated, by beer and fast food, probably. None of them was armed in any way. Reacher
could see all sixteen hands, and all sixteen were empty.
No guns, no knives, no wrenches, no chains.

Amateurs.

Reacher put his hands on the walkway's rail, and he gazed out over the scene below, serenely, like a dictator in an old movie, ready to address a crowd.

He said, "We need to find a way of getting you guys home before you get hurt. You want to work with me on that?"

He had overheard a guy in a suit on a cell phone one time, who kept on asking *You want to work with me on that?* He guessed it was a technique taught at expensive seminars in dowdy hotel ballrooms. Presumably because it mandated a positive response. Because civilized people felt an obligation to *work with* one another, if that option was offered. No one ever said, *No, I don't.*

But the guy from the half-ton did.

He said, "No one is here to work with you, boy. We're here to kick your butt and take our car and our money back."

"OK," Reacher said. "We can go down that road, if you like. But there's no reason why all of you should go to the hospital. You ever heard of Gallup?"

"Who?"

"It's a polling organization. Like at election time. They tell you this guy is going to get fifty-one percent of the vote, and this other guy is going to get forty-nine."

"I've heard of them."

"You know how they do that? They don't call everyone in America. That would take too long. So they sample. They call a handful of people and scale up the scores."

"So?"

"That's what we should do. We should sample. One

of us against one of you. We should let the result stand in for what would have happened if we'd all gone at it together. Like the Gallup organization does."

No answer.

Reacher said, "If your guy wins, you get to trade your worst truck for the Corvette. And you get half of Billy Bob's money."

No answer.

Reacher said, "But if my side wins, we'll trade the Corvette for your best truck. And we'll keep all of Billy Bob's money."

No answer.

Reacher said, "That's the best I can do, guys. This is America. We need wheels and money. I'm sure you understand that."

No answer.

Reacher said, "My friend here is ready and willing. You got a preference? Would you prefer to fight a woman?"

The guy from the half-ton said, "No, that ain't right."

"Then you're stuck with me. But I'll sweeten the deal. You can increase the size of your sample. Me against two of you. Want to work with me on that?"

No answer.

"And I'll fight with both hands behind my back."

"What?"

"You heard me."

"Both hands behind your back?"

"For the terms we just agreed. And they're great terms, guys. I mean, either way you get to keep the Corvette. I'm being reasonable here."

"Two of us, and your hands behind your back?"

"I'd put a bag on my head if I had one."

"OK, we'll take a piece of that."

"Terrific," Reacher said. "Any of you got health in-surance? Because that would be a good way to choose up sides."

Then suddenly next to him Turner whispered, "I just remembered what I forgot. From last night. The thing in the original report."

"Was it the tribal guy?" Reacher whispered back. *An unknown American. A tribal elder.* The grain of sand. The American was defined as unknown, but the tribal elder was not. "They told you his name?"

"Not his name, exactly. Their names are all too complicated to remember. We use reference numbers instead. Assigned as and when they first become known to U.S. authorities. And the guy's number was in the report. Which means he's already in the system. He's known to somebody."

"What was the number?"

"I don't remember. *A.M.* something."

"What does *A.M.* mean?"

"Afghan male."

"That's a start, I guess."

Then from below the guy from the half-ton called up, "OK, we're all set down here."

Reacher glanced down. The small crowd had sepa-rated out, six and two. The two were the guy from the half-ton himself, and the bloated guy, full of McDon-ald's and Miller High Life.

Turner said, "Can you really do this?"

Reacher said, "Only one way to find out," and he started down the stairs.

Chapter 37

The six spectators hung back, and Reacher and the chosen two moved together, into clear space, a tight little triangle of three men in lock step, two walking backward and one forward, all of them watchful, vigilant, and suspicious. Beyond the parked trucks was an expanse of beaten dirt, about as wide as a city street. To the right was the back of the compound, where the Corvette was, behind the last building, and to the left the lot was open to Route 220, but the entrance was narrow, and there was nothing to see but the blacktop itself and a small stand of trees beyond it. The state police barracks was way to the west. No one on the beaten dirt could see it, and therefore the troopers could see no one on the beaten dirt.

Safe enough.

Good to go.

Normally against two dumb opponents Reacher would have cheated from the get-go. Hands behind his back? He would have planted two elbows into two jaws right after stepping off the last stair. But not with six replacements standing by. That would be inefficient. They would all pile in, outraged, up on some peculiar equivalent of a moral high horse, and thereby buzzed beyond their native capabilities. So Reacher let the triangle adjust and rotate and kick the ground until everyone was ready, and then he jammed his hands in his back pockets, with his palms against his ass.

"Play ball," he said.

Whereupon he saw the two guys take up what he assumed were their combat stances, and then he saw them change radically. Tell a guy you're going to fight with your hands behind your back, and he hears just that, and only that. He thinks, *This guy is going to fight with his hands behind his back!* And then he pictures the first few seconds in his mind, and the image is so weird it takes over his attention completely. *No hands! An unprotected torso! Just like the heavy bag at the gym!*

So guys in that situation see nothing but the upper body, the upper body, the upper body, and the head, and the face, like irresistible targets of opportunity, damage just waiting to be done, unanswerable shots just begging to be made, and their stances open wide, and their fists come up high, and their chins jut forward, and their eyes go narrow and wild with glee as they squint in at the gut or the ribs or the nose or wherever it is they plan to land their first joyous blow. They see nothing else at all.

Like the feet.

Reacher stepped forward and kicked the fat guy in the nuts, solid, right foot, as serious as punting a ball the length of the field, and the guy went down so fast and so hard it was like someone had bet him a million bucks he couldn't make a hole in the dirt with his face. There was a noise like a bag hitting a floor, and the guy curled up tight and his blubber settled and went perfectly still.

Reacher stepped back.

"Poor choice," he said. "Clearly that guy would have been better left on the bench. Now it's just you and me."

The guy from the half-ton had stepped back, too. Reacher watched his face. And saw all the guy's previous assumptions being hastily revised. Inevitably. *Yeah, feet,* he was thinking. *I forgot about that.* Which pulled his center of gravity too low. Now it was all feet, feet, feet. Nothing but feet. The guy's hands came down, almost to his pelvis, and he put one thigh in front of the other, and he hunched his shoulders so tight that overall he looked like a little kid with a stomach cramp.

Reacher said, "You can walk away now and we'll call it done. Give us a truck, take the Corvette, and you're out of here."

The guy from the half-ton said, "No."

"I'll ask again," Reacher said. "But I won't ask three times."

The guy said, "No."

"Then bring it, my friend. Show me the good stuff. You got good stuff, right? Or is driving around in circles all you can do?"

Reacher knew what was coming. The guy was obviously right-handed. So it would be an inswinging right, starting low and never really getting high enough, like a sidearm pitcher, like a boxing glove fixed to a door, and the door slamming, with you in the doorway. That's what it was going to be like. When it came. The guy was still shuffling around, still trying to find a launch pad.

And then he found one, and then it came. Like a glove on a door. What are you going to do? Most people are going to duck out of the way. But one six-year-old at the sci-fi movie isn't. He's going to turn sideways, and push forward hard, off bent knees, and he's going to meet the door with his shoulder, nearer the hinge, about halfway across its width, maybe a little more, a solid aggressive shove where the momentum is lower, well inside the arc of the glove.

Which is what Reacher did with the guy from the half-ton. He twisted, and pushed off, and slammed the guy with his shoulder, right in the center of his chest, and the guy's fist flailed all the way around Reacher's back and came at him from the far side, limp, like the guy was trying to cop a feel in the picture house. After which the guy wobbled backward a long pace and got his balance by jabbing his hands out from his body, which left him stock still and wide open, like a starfish, which he seemed to realize immediately, because he glanced down in horror at Reacher's moving feet.

Newsflash, my friend.

It's not the feet.

It's the head.

The feet were moving in a boxer's shuffle, creating aim and momentum, and then the upper body was whipping forward, and the neck was snapping down, and the forehead was crunching into the bridge of the guy's nose, and then snapping back up, job done, Reacher jerking upright, the guy from the half-ton staggering on rubber knees, half a step, and then the other half, and then a vertical collapse, weak and helpless, like a Victorian lady fainting into a crinoline.

Reacher looked up at Turner on the walkway.

He said, "Which truck do you think is the best?"

Chapter 38

The Claughton code of honor was a wonderful thing. That was clear. None of the six spectators interfered or intervened in any way. Either that, or they were worried about what Reacher might do to them, now that his hands were out of his pockets.

In the end Turner liked the fat guy's truck the best. It was a V8, but not the one with the leaky muffler. It had the second-fullest tank of gas. It had good tires. It looked comfortable. She drove it up next to the hidden Corvette, and they transferred Billy Bob's money from the Corvette's load space to the truck's glove compartment, which two receptacles were about the same size, and then they rumbled back past the sullen crowd, and Reacher tossed the Corvette key out his window. Then Turner hit the gas and made the left on 220, past the state troopers, past the cafe with the griddle, and onward to the crossroads in the center of town.

* * *

Thirty minutes later Petersburg was twenty miles behind them. They were heading west, on a small road on the edge of a national forest. The truck had turned out to be a Toyota, not new, but it ran well. It was as quiet as a library, and it had satellite navigation. It was so heavy it smoothed out the bumps in the road. It had pillowy leather seats and plenty of space inside. Turner looked tiny in it. But happy. She had something to work with. She had a whole scenario laid out.

She said, "I can see why these guys are worried. An A.M. number changes everything. The guy is known to us for a reason. Either his activities, or his opinions. And either thing is going to lead us somewhere."

Reacher asked, "How do we access the database?"

"Change of plan. We're going to Pittsburgh."

"Is the database in Pittsburgh?"

"No, but there's a big airport in Pittsburgh."

"I was just in Pittsburgh."

"At the airport?"

"On the road."

"Variety is the spice of life," she said.

Getting to Pittsburgh meant cutting northwest across the state, and hitting I-79 somewhere between Clarksburg and Morgantown. Then it was a straight shot, basically north. Safe enough, Reacher thought. The Toyota was as big as a house and weighed three tons, but it was effectively camouflaged. What's the best place to hide a grain of sand? On a beach. And if the Toyota was a grain of sand, then West Virginia's roads were a beach. Practically every vehicle in sight was a full-size pick-up truck. And Western Pennsylvania would be no different. A visitor from outer space would assume the viability of the United States depended entirely on the ability of the citizenry to carry eight-by-four sheets of board, safely and in vast quantities.

The late start to the day turned out to be a good thing. Or a feature, not a bug, as Turner might have put it. It meant they would be driving the highway in the dark. Better than driving it in the light. On the one hand highways got the heaviest policing, but on the other hand cops can't see what they can't see, and there was nothing less visible than a pair of headlights doing the legal limit on an Interstate highway at night.

Reacher said, "How are we going to get the exact A.M. number?"

Turner said, "We're going to take a deep breath and go way out on a limb. We're going to ask someone to get all snarled up in a criminal conspiracy, aiding and abetting."

"Who?"

"Sergeant Leach, I hope. She's pretty solid, and her heart is in the right place."

"I agree," Reacher said. "I liked her."

"We have records and transcripts in the file room. All she has to do is go take a look at them."

"And then what?"

"Then it gets harder. We'll have a reference number, but not a name or a biography. And a sergeant can't access that database. I'm the only one at Rock Creek who can. Morgan now, I suppose, but we can hardly ask him."

Reacher said, "Leave that part to me."

"You don't have access."

"But I know someone who does."

"Who?"

"The Judge Advocate General."

"You know him?"

"Not personally. But I know his place in the process. He's forcing me to defend a bullshit charge. I'm entitled to cast the net wide in my own defense. I can ask for pretty much anything I want. Major Sullivan can handle it for me."

"No, in that case my lawyer should. It's much more relevant to my bullshit charge than yours."

"Too dangerous for the guy. Moorcroft got beaten half to death for trying to get you out of jail. They're never going to let your counsel get near that information."

"Then it's dangerous for Sullivan, too."

"I don't think they'll be watching her yet. They'll find out afterward for sure, but by then it's too late. There's no point closing the barn door after the horse is out."

"Will she do it for you?"

"She'll have to. She has a legal obligation."

They drove on, quiet and comfortable, staying in West Virginia, tracking around the jagged dip where the end of Maryland's panhandle juts south, then setting course for a town called Grafton. From there the Toyota's electronics showed a road running north-west, which joined I-79 just south of Fairmont.

Turner said, "Were you worried?"

Reacher said, "About what?"

"Those eight guys."

"Not very."

"Then I guess that study from when you were six was right on the money."

"Correct conclusion," Reacher said. "Wrong rea-soning."

"How so?"

"They thought my brain was wired backward. They got all excited about my DNA. Maybe they were plan-ning to breed a new race of warriors. You know what the Pentagon was like back then. But I was too young to take much of an interest. And they were wrong, anyway. When it comes to fear, my DNA is the same as anyone else's. I trained myself, that's all. To turn fear into aggression, automatically."

"At the age of six?"

"No, at four and five. I told you on the phone. I figured it was a choice. Either I cower back, or I get in their faces."

"I've never seen anyone fight with no hands."

"Neither had they. And that was the point."

They stopped for gas and a meal in a place called Macomber, and then they rolled on, ever westward, through Grafton, and then they took the right fork, through a village called McGee, and eventually they came to the I-79 entrance ramp, which the Toyota told them was about an hour south of the Pittsburgh International Airport, which meant they would arrive there at about eight in the evening. The sky was already dark. Night had already closed in, secure, and enveloping, and concealing.

Turner said, "Why do you like to live like this?"

Reacher said, "Because my brain is wired backward. That's what they missed, all those years ago. They looked at the wrong part of me. I don't like what normal people like. A little house with a chimney and a lawn and a picket fence? People love that stuff. They work all their lives, just to pay for it. They take thirty-year mortgages. And good for them. If they're happy, I'm happy. But I'd rather hang myself."

"Why?"

"I have a private theory. Involving DNA. Far too boring to talk about."

"No, tell me."

"Some other time."

"Reacher, we slept together. I didn't even get a cocktail or a movie. The least you can do is tell me your private theories."

"Are you going to tell me one of yours?"

"I might. But you go first."

"OK, think about America, a long time ago. The nineteenth century, really, beginning to end. The westward migration. The risks those people took. As if they were compelled."

"They were," Turner said. "By economics. They needed land and farms and jobs."

"But it was more than that," Reacher said. "For

some of them, at least. Some of them never stopped. And a hundred years before that, think about the British. They went all over the world. They went on sea voyages that lasted five years."

"Economics again. They wanted markets and raw materials."

"But some of them couldn't stop. And way back there were the Vikings. And the Polynesians, just the same. I think it's in the DNA, literally. I think millions of years ago we were all living in small bands. Small groups of people. So there was a danger of inbreeding. So a gene evolved where every generation and every small band had at least one person who had to wander. That way the gene pools would get mixed up a little. Healthier all around."

"And you're that person?"

"I think ninety-nine of us grow up to love the campfire, and one grows up to hate it. Ninety-nine of us grow up to fear the howling wolf, and one grows up to envy it. And I'm that guy."

"Compelled to spread his DNA worldwide. Purely for the good of the species."

"That's the fun part."

"That's probably not an argument to make at your paternity hearing."

They left West Virginia and entered Pennsylvania, and five miles after the line they saw a billboard for a shopping mall. The billboard was lit up bright, so they figured the mall was still open. They pulled off and found a faded place anchored by a local department store. Turner headed to the women's section with a wad of cash. Reacher followed after her, but she told him to go check the men's section instead.

He said, "I don't need anything."

She said, "I think you do."

"Like what?"

"A shirt," she said. "And a V-neck sweater, maybe. At least."

"If you get something you can give me my old shirt back."

"I'm going to junk it. You need something better."

"Why?"

"I want you to look nice."

So he browsed on his own, and he found a shirt. Blue flannel, with white buttons. Fifteen dollars. And a V-neck sweater, cotton, a darker blue. Also fifteen dollars. He changed in the cubicle and trashed his twin T-shirts and checked the mirror. His pants looked OK. As did his coat. The new shirt and sweater looked neat under it. Nice? He wasn't sure. Nicer than before, maybe, but that was as far as he was prepared to go.

Then twenty minutes later Turner came back, head-to-toe different. New black zip boots, new blue jeans, a tight crew-neck sweater, and a cotton warm-up jacket. Nothing in her hands. No shopping bags. She had trashed the old stuff, and she had bought no spares. She saw him noticing, and said, "Surprised?"

"A little," he said.

"I figured we should stay nimble right now."

"And always."

They moved on to the smaller stores in the mall's outlying regions and found an off-brand pharmacy.

They bought folding toothbrushes and a small tube of toothpaste. Then they headed back to the truck.

The Pittsburgh International Airport was way far out from the city, and the Interstate led them straight to it. It was a big, spacious place, with a choice of hotels. Turner picked one and parked in its lot. They split Billy Bob's remaining money nine different ways, and filled every pocket they had. Then they locked up and headed for the lobby. No luggage was no problem. Not at an airport hotel. Airport hotels were full of people with no luggage. Part of the joy of modern-day travel. Breakfast in New York, dinner in Paris, luggage in Istanbul. And so on.

"Your name, ma'am?" the clerk asked.

Turner said, "Helen Sullivan."

"And sir?"

Reacher said, "John Temple."

"May I see photo ID?"

Turner slid the two borrowed army IDs across the desk. The clerk glanced at them long enough to establish that, yes, they were photo IDs, and yes, they had the names Sullivan and Temple on them. He made no attempt to match the photographs with the customers. In Reacher's experience few such people did. Possibly outside their responsibilities, or talents.

The guy said, "May I swipe a credit card?"

Reacher said, "We're paying cash."

Which again was no problem at an airport hotel. Credit cards and travelers' checks go missing, too, because as bad as the baggage handling is, the pickpocketing is good. Reacher peeled off the room rate plus a hundred extra for incidentals, as requested, and the guy was happy to take it. In exchange he gave up two key cards and directions to the elevators.

The room was fine, if not radically different in principle than the cell in the Dyer guardhouse. But in addition to the basics it had a minibar refrigerator, and free bottles of water, and robes, and slippers, and chocolates on the pillows.

And a telephone, which Turner picked up and dialed.

Chapter 39

Reacher heard the purr of a ring tone. Turner had the handset trapped between her shoulder and her neck, and she mouthed, "Leach's cell number." Then her eyes changed focus as the call was answered. She said, "Sergeant, this is Susan Turner. My official advice to you as your commanding officer is to hang up immediately and report this call to Colonel Morgan. Are you going to do that?"

Reacher didn't hear Leach's answer, but it was obviously no, because the conversation continued. Turner said, "Thank you, sergeant. I need you to do two things for me. First, I need the A.M. number in the original signal from Weeks and Edwards. The transcript should be in the file room. Is Colonel Morgan still in the house?"

Reacher didn't hear the answer, but it was obviously yes, because Turner said, "OK, don't risk it now. I'll call back every hour." Then she stayed on the line, ready to ask about the second thing she wanted Leach to do for her, but Reacher didn't hear what it was, because right then there was a knock at the door. He crossed the room and opened up, and standing there was a guy in a suit. He had a walkie-talkie in his hand, and a corporate button in his lapel. A hotel manager of some kind, Reacher thought.

The guy said, "I apologize, sir, but there's been a mistake."

Reacher said, "What kind of a mistake?"

"The incidentals deposit should have been fifty dollars, not a hundred. When paying in cash, I mean. For the phone and the minibar. If you order room service, we ask you to pay the wait staff direct."

"OK," Reacher said.

So the guy dipped in his pocket and came out with fifty dollars, two twenties and a ten, all fanned out, like Reacher had won a prize on a television show, and he said, "Again, I apologize for the overcharge."

Reacher took the money and checked it. U.S. currency. Fifty bucks. He said, "No problem," and the guy walked away. Reacher closed the door. Turner put the phone down and said, "What was that?"

"I guess the clerk at the desk hadn't gotten a memo. We're supposed to lodge fifty with them, not a hundred, because room service is all cash."

"Whatever."

"How was Sergeant Leach?"

"She's a brave woman."

"You know her number by heart? A sergeant you just met in a new command?"

"I know all their numbers by heart."

"You're a good commander."

"Thank you."

"What was the second thing you asked her for?"

"You'll see," Turner said. "I hope."

Romeo dialed, but Juliet was slow to answer. Romeo rubbed his palm on the leather arm of the chair he was sitting in. His palm was dry, and the leather was smooth and lustrous, made that way by fifty years of suited elbows.

Then in his ear Juliet said, "Yes?"

Romeo said, "The names Sullivan and Temple just came up in an airport hotel in Pittsburgh, Pennsylvania. Fortunately for us its register is linked to Homeland Security. Being at an airport."

"Is it them, do you think?"

"We'll have descriptions soon. The hotel is sending a man up to take a look. But I think it has to be them. Because what are the odds? Those two names in combination? As far as we know, those are the only IDs they have."

"But why the airport in Pittsburgh?"

"Doesn't matter why. Where are our boys?"

"On their way to Los Angeles."

"See how fast you can turn them around."

The room was warm, so Reacher took off his miracle coat, and Turner took off her new jacket. She said, "You want to get room service?"

"Sure."

"Before or after?"

"Before or after what?"

"Before or after we have sex again."

Reacher smiled. In his experience the second time was always better. Still new, but a little less so. Still unfamiliar, but a little less so. Always better than the first time, and in Turner's case the first time had been spectacular.

"After," he said.

"Then take your clothes off," she said.

"No, you first this time."

"Why?"

"Because variety is the spice of life."

She smiled. She took her new sweater off. She was wearing nothing under it. No bra. She didn't really need one, and she wasn't about to pretend. He liked her for that. He liked her for everything, basically. Not that he had a big problem with any kind of a topless woman in his room. But she was special. Mentally, and physically. Physically she was flawless. She was lean and strong, but she looked soft and tiny. One curve flowed into another, endlessly, seamlessly, like a single contour, like a Mobius strip, from the cleft of her back, to her shoulder, to her waist, to her hips, to her back, where it started all over again. Her skin was the color of honey. Her smile was wicked, and her laugh was infectious.

Romeo dialed, and this time Juliet picked up immediately. Romeo said, "It's them. A tall, heavy, fair-haired man, and a younger dark-haired woman, much smaller. That's what the hotel manager saw."

"Any indication how long they intend to stay?"

"They paid cash for one night."

"Did they book a wake up call?"

"No. They can't fly. Not with cash, and not with those IDs. Reacher looks nothing like Temple. Even the TSA would notice. I think they're just holed up. Not a bad choice. Airport hotels are always anonymous, and Pittsburgh isn't the center of the known universe. I'd like to know how they got so much money, though."

"Our boys will get there as soon as they can."

"The hotel manager said Turner was on the phone."

"Who to?"

"I'm having it traced now."

Afterward they lay spent and sweaty in tangled sheets, breathing hard, then breathing low. Turner got up on an elbow and stared at Reacher's face, and ran her fingertips over his brow, slow and searching. She said, "It's not even bruised."

"All bone," he said. "All the way through."

Her touch moved down to his nose.

"This wasn't, though," she said. "Not all the way through. And recent, right?"

"Nebraska," Reacher said. "Some guy, all worked up about something."

Her fingertip traced the cuts, all healed up but not long ago, and the thickened bumps of bone, which now gave his nose a slight right turn. Still a surprise to him, but automatically normal to her. She traced around his ear, and his neck, and his chest. She put the tip of her pinkie in his bullet hole. It fit just right.

"A .38," he said. "A weak load."

"Lucky," she said.

"I'm always lucky. Look at me now."

Her touch moved on, to his waist. To the old shrapnel scar.

"Beirut," she said. "I read your file. A Silver Star and a Purple Heart. Not bad, but still, I bet overall you got more metal in your gut than on your chest."

"It was bone," Reacher said. "Fragments of somebody's head, who was standing nearer."

"It said shrapnel in the file."

"How many times did you read that file?"

"Over and over again."

"You know where the word *shrapnel* comes from?"

"Where?"

"An eighteenth-century British guy named Henry Shrapnel."

"Really?"

"He was a captain in their artillery for eight years. Then he invented an exploding shell, and they promoted him to major. The Duke of Wellington used the shell in the Peninsular Wars, and at the Battle of Waterloo."

"Terrific."

"But thanks for reading that file. It means a lot to me."

"Why?"

"Because now I don't have to spend a lot of time telling you a bunch of old stories. You know them already."

"Telling each other old stories has a nice ring to it."

"You haven't told me any."

"But I will," she said. "I'll tell you as many as you want to hear."

Romeo dialed Juliet and said, "She was calling a pre-paid cell phone almost certainly purchased at a Wal-Mart. If it was paid for in cash, it's untraceable. And I bet it was."

Juliet said, "It was worth a try."

"But you know, one big market for pre-paid cell phones is the military. Because some of them don't make enough for a regular monthly contract. Which is shameful, frankly. And because some of them lead necessarily disorganized lives, and pre-paid suits them better."

"That's a leap."

"The phone is showing up on three cell towers north and west of the Pentagon."

"I see."

"Rock Creek is north and west of the Pentagon."

"Yes, it is."

"I think she was calling the mothership. And someone aboard the mothership took her call."

"Our boys are on their way to Pittsburgh."

"Doesn't matter. No one at Rock Creek can help her now."

Chapter 40

Turner took a shower, but Reacher didn't bother. He wrapped up in a robe and lounged in a chair, warm, deeply satisfied, as relaxed as he could ever remember being. Then Turner came out in the other robe and asked, "What time is it?"

"Four minutes," Reacher said. "Until you're due to call Leach again. Does she know I'm with you?"

Turner nodded. "I'm sure the whole world knows by now. And I told her, anyway."

"Was she OK with that?"

"She's a sergeant in the U.S. Army. I don't think she's a prude."

"That's not the point. If you beat your thing, then no one can touch her for helping you. She'll come out smelling of roses. But if I don't beat my thing, then she's still in trouble for helping me. Or vice versa. And so on and so forth. She's doubling her risk and halving her chances."

"She didn't object."

"You should hang on to her."

"I will," Turner said. "If I ever get back."

And then she picked up the phone and dialed.

A little more than fourteen miles away, a phone rang inside the FBI Field Office on East Carson Street, Pittsburgh, which was a little south and east of the downtown area. A duty agent answered, and found himself talking to the Hoover Building in D.C. He was told that the Homeland Security computers were showing the names Sullivan and Temple as guests in an airport hotel nearby. The duty agent spooled back through his bulletins and his BOLOs, and saw that the D.C. Metro cops and the army MPs were looking for two fugitives presumed to be traveling under those names.

The duty agent called his Special Agent in Charge, and asked, "Do you want me to spread the word to D.C. and the army?"

His SAC was quiet for a moment, and then he said, "No need to complicate things."

No need to share the credit, the duty agent thought.

His SAC said, "Send one of our own to check it out."

"Now?"

"Whenever you can. No big rush. We've got until the morning. I'm sure they aren't going anywhere."

Turner had the room phone trapped between her shoulder and her neck again, as before, and Reacher could hear the ring tone. Then he heard Leach answer. He couldn't make out her words, but he could make out her mood. Which was not good. She launched into a long fast monologue, all of it reduced to a rapid plastic quack by the earpiece, but all of it frustrated and angry. Turner said, "Thanks anyway," and hung up, looking very tired, and bitterly disappointed.

Reacher said, "What?"

"Take a guess."

"There was no number after all."

"The transcript is missing. Someone took it out of the file room."

"Morgan?"

"Has to be. No one else would or could."

"So either he's one of them or he's following orders blindly."

Turner nodded. "They're cleaning house. And they're covering all the bases. Because they're better than I thought they were. And therefore I'm screwed. There's no way out for me now. Not without that A.M. number."

"Isn't it still in a computer somewhere?"

"We don't really trust computers. The feeling is we might as well send stuff straight to *The New York Times.* Or China."

"So your physical transcript is your only record?"

She nodded again. "It's the only one I'm aware of. Maybe Bagram keeps a copy. Why? You thinking of asking JAG to issue a subpoena? Good luck with that."

"Could it be misfiled?"

"No, and Leach checked everywhere anyway. She's not dumb."

"There has to be another way around this."

"Wake me up if you think of it," she said. "Because right now I'm all done thinking. I have to get some sleep."

She dropped her robe to the floor and padded naked around the room, straightening the drapes, turning out the lights, and then she climbed under the covers, and rolled over, and sighed a long, sad, exhausted sigh, and then she lay still. Reacher watched her for a moment, and then he went back to his chair, and sat a spell in the dark. He pictured the Rock Creek file room in his mind, upstairs, first on the left, room 201. He pictured the duty captain downstairs in 103, taking the long-distance call from Weeks and Edwards, writing it up, hand-carrying the sheet of precious paper up the old stone stairs, showing it to Turner, getting her reply, transmitting it, copying it out, and heading upstairs again to file both the call and the response in the right drawer, correctly, sequentially, back to back.

And then he pictured Morgan coming out of his office, just two rooms away, and glancing up and down the corridor. The work of a moment. Two pages, burned or torn up or shredded. Or folded into a pocket, and handed over at a later time, to persons unknown, in exchange for tight nods of appreciation, and implied promises of future consideration.

There has to be another way around this. Reacher might have remembered the number. He liked numbers. This one might have had some intrinsic appeal.

Prime, or nearly, or with interesting factors. But he hadn't seen the number. But nothing was impossible. No system was ever perfect, no security was ever a hundred percent foolproof, and there were always unforeseen wrinkles.

There has to be another way around this.

But Reacher couldn't think of one. Not right then. He stood up, and yawned, and stretched, and then he dropped his robe on top of Turner's, and he slid into bed next to her. She was already deeply asleep. Breathing slow. Warm, and soft. Her circuit breakers had tripped. She had shut down, overwhelmed. Like that old movie: *I'll think about that tomorrow.* He stared up at the ceiling, dim and gray above him. Then he closed his eyes, and breathed in, and breathed out, and he fell asleep.

He slept well, for five solid hours.

And then he woke up, at four o'clock in the morning.

Because someone was hammering on the door.

Chapter 41

Turner woke up, too, immediately, but Reacher put his hand on her shoulder. He whispered, "I'll go." He blinked once and slid out of bed and found his robe on the floor. He put it on as he walked. The hammering didn't quit. It was not a polite or an apologetic sound. Not a hotel-in-the-dead-of-night sound. It was full-on urgent and demanding. *Boom, boom.* Arrogant, and intrusive. It was a no-argument sound. It was the sound of law enforcement. Or the sound of someone pretending to be law enforcement.

Reacher didn't use the spy hole. He didn't like spy holes. He never had. Too easy for an assailant to wait until the lens darkened, and then to fire a handgun through the pre-drilled hole. No aim required. Better to ignore the spy hole altogether, and fling the door open real quick and punch them in the throat. Or not. Depending on who they were, and how many they were.

Behind him Turner was out of bed and in her robe,

too. He pointed her toward the bathroom. Nothing to gain by presenting a single unified target. And she had nowhere else to go. There was only one way out of the room, which was the door. They were on a high floor, and the windows didn't open anyway. Legal issues, presumably, because of inquisitive children, and because it was an airport hotel, with noise and jet fumes from early in the morning until late at night.

Turner stepped into the bathroom, and Reacher put his hand on the handle. He took a breath. MPs or federal agents would have weapons drawn. That was for sure. But they wouldn't shoot. Not right away. They had too much training. And too many protocols. And too much potential paperwork. But the four guys from the dented car might shoot right away. They had training, but no protocols and no paperwork.

So, best bet, open the door but stay behind it. Irresistible. A door that sags open seemingly all by itself just begs for a craned neck and a quick glance inside. And in turn a craned neck and a quick glance inside just begs for a straight right to the temple. Then you kick the door shut again instantly, and you've got a hostage on the floor on one side of the threshold, with his pals left outside on the other. You've got the basis for a negotiation.

Reacher turned the handle. Downward, ten degrees. Twenty. Thirty. No reaction. Forty, fifty, sixty. No reaction. So he continued all the way to ninety, fast, and he gave the handle a sharp tug, to pull the door through maybe two-thirds of its travel, and then he made a fist and cocked his arm and waited.

For a long time.

Clearly the door had been trapped open by a boot applied from the other side, while decisions were being considered. Which process was taking considerable time.

Close to a whole minute passed.

Then an object came sailing in.

Reacher didn't look at it. Didn't follow it with his conscious vision. He wasn't born yesterday. But the brief flash he caught in the corner of his eye said *envelope*. A brown letter-size envelope, sealed with a metal closure, he thought, like something out of an office. Lightly loaded, with no thickness to it. And the sound it made when it fluttered to the carpet backed up the first impressions. Papery but stiff, with a faint resonant crackle, where it hit edge-on, and tiny sliding sounds, as if it carried a small number of separate items inside, each one of them thin and light.

Reacher waited.

Then a head came around the door.

With a face.

Sergeant Leach's face.

Leach was in her ACUs. She looked very tired. She stepped into the room, and Turner stepped out of the bathroom, and Reacher closed the door. Turner saw the envelope on the carpet and said, "Is it all there?"

Leach said, "Yes."

"I thought you were going to overnight it."

"I think you're going to need it sooner than FedEx can get it to you."

"So you drove out all this way?"

"Well, I didn't walk or fly."

"How long did it take?"

"About four hours."

"Thank you, sergeant."

"You're welcome."

"What time are you due on post in the morning?"

"Soon enough that I really should leave right about now."

"But?"

"I'm in a position I don't want to be in."

"What position?"

"I'm going to have to criticize a fellow team member, and a senior officer."

"Is that one person or two?"

"One person, ma'am."

"Me?"

"No, ma'am."

"Morgan?"

"No, ma'am. Someone else. But you're the CO and I'm not a snitch."

"Then tell Reacher. He's no one's CO."

Leach paused a beat, and weighed up the artifice. And came out in favor, apparently, because she turned to Reacher and said, "Sir, I have a longstanding concern about the duty captain."

Reacher said, "How longstanding?"

"Permanent."

"Why haven't you done anything about it?"

"I don't know how. He's a captain and I'm a sergeant."

"What's the issue?"

"He's a doodler. He draws and scribbles all the time he's on the phone."

Reacher nodded.

"I've seen the results," he said. "On his desk. An old legal pad."

"Do you know why he does it?"

"Because he's bored."

"But sometimes he's not bored. When big news comes through. He changes. Suddenly he's happy."

"No law against that."

"But the pen is still in his hand. He changes, and the drawings change, too. Sometimes they're not even drawings. Sometimes he jots things down. Key words."

Reacher said nothing.

Leach said, "Don't you see? He deals with classified information, which is supposed to exist in physical form in one place only, which is the Rock Creek file room. For the information or parts of the information to exist in physical form elsewhere is dead against regulations."

Turner said, "Oh please, tell me."

Reacher said, "He wrote the number down?"

"Yes, ma'am," Leach said. "Yes, sir. He wrote the number down."

Leach pulled a crumpled sheet of paper from her pocket. It was a page from the yellow legal pad Reacher had seen. It was curled at the top, wide and generous, from several days of being rolled over. It was practically covered in black ink, from a ballpoint pen. There were shapes and whorls and boxes and machines and spirals, with occasional plaintext times and names and words, some of them heavily underlined, some of them boxed in and shaded over almost to the point of illegibility.

Leach put her fingertip on the first legible word, which was a little less than a third of the way down the page. The word was *Kandahar.* A proper noun. The name of a place. It had a vivid arrow sketched next to it. The arrow was pointing away from the word, emphatically. Leach said, "This is the last signal before the one that's missing. This is Weeks and Edwards moving out of Kandahar, going back to Bagram on standby, as ordered. That all is still in the file room, exactly where it should be."

Then she jumped her fingertip to the bottom third of the page, where two words stood out, separated by a hyphen: *Hood - Days.* The *H* of *Hood* was enhanced after the fact, with baroque curlicues. A man on the phone, bored. Leach said, "This is the next signal after the one that's missing. It's still in the file room, too, immediately after the Kandahar thing. This is our guys checking in from Fort Hood in Texas, reporting that they expect to be all wrapped up in a matter of days."

Then she moved her hand upward again and bracketed her fingers over the middle third of the page. She said, "So this part here is what corresponds to the gap in the record."

The middle third of the page was a mass of bleak doodles, with shapes and whorls repeated endlessly, and boxes and mazes and spirals. But buried right in the center of it all were the letters *A* and *M,* followed by a four-digit number. The whole thing had been first scrawled, and then gone over carefully, with more precise lines, squared up, and sharpened, and underlined, and then abandoned.

A.M. 3435.

Turner smiled and said, "He's technically in the wrong, sergeant, but we're going to overlook it this one time."

A.M. 3435.

Which was a number that Reacher might have remembered pretty well, because it was mildly engaging, in the sense that 3 and 4 and 3 and 5, if raised to the powers of 3 and 4 and 3 and 5 respectively, would collectively add up to exactly 3435. Which was slightly interesting. Such numbers had been much discussed by a guy called Joseph Madachy, who once upon a time had been the owner, publisher, and editor of a magazine called *Journal of Recreational Mathematics*. Reacher had read a stack of back issues, as a kid, in the library on a Marine base in the Pacific. He said, "Sergeant, what's my best way of contacting Major Sullivan at JAG?"

"Directly, sir?"

"Person to person."

"When, sir?"

"Right now."

"In the middle of the night?"

"Right this minute."

Leach pulled another piece of paper from her pocket. Smaller. A sheet from a scratch pad, torn in half. She said, "This is Major Sullivan's personal cell. I'm sure right now it's on her night table."

"How did you know I would need it?"

"I figured that was how you were going to have to do it. Defense motions get pretty wide latitude. But permission to speak freely?"

"Of course."

Leach took a second slip of paper from her pocket. Another sheet from a scratch pad, torn in half, just the same. She said, "This is Captain Edmonds' personal cell. Your other lawyer. I think she's a better prospect. She's more likely to pursue it with vigor. She likes to see the right thing done."

"Even after I busted myself out of jail?"

"I think so."

"So she's an idealist?"

"Get it while you can. It won't last. It didn't with Major Sullivan."

Reacher asked, "Is the FBI involved yet?"

Leach said, "They've been notified."

"Who is organizing the army's efforts?"

"The 75th MP. A team led by Warrant Officer Espin. Who you met. He was the one who brought you to Dyer. People say he's taking it personally. He claims you abused his good nature. He claims he did you a favor, and thereby inadvertently set the whole thing in motion."

"What did he do for me?"

"He kept you at Dyer. Detective Podolski wanted to take you downtown. Espin said no. And then on top of that, you asked him to go get the MP duty captain right away, which he did, which he's counting as another favor exploited."

"The duty captain would have come anyway."

"But not so quickly. And your whole plan depended on getting everything done before late afternoon. So you had to start early. Which Espin feels he accidentally facilitated."

"Is he getting anywhere?"

"Not so far. But not through lack of trying."

"Can you get a message to him?"

"Probably."

"Tell him to get over himself. Ask him what he would have done, in our situation."

"I will, sir. If I can."

"What's your name, sergeant?"

"Sir, it's Leach."

"No, your first name."

"Sir, it's Chris."

"As in Christine or Christina or something?"

"Just Chris, sir. That's what's on my birth certificate."

"Well, Chris, if I was still CO of the 110th, I'd move heaven and earth to keep you there. That unit has had its share of great NCOs, and you're right up there with the best of them."

"Thank you, sir."

"No, thank *you*, sergeant."

Leach left after that, in a hurry, facing a four-hour drive back, followed by a full day at the office. Reacher looked at Turner and said, "You must be a hell of a good commander, to inspire loyalty like that."

"No more than you were," she said. "You had Frances Neagley."

"You been reading her file, too?"

"I've been reading all the files. All the operational histories, too. I wanted to know the 110th inside out."

"Like I said, you're a great commander." Reacher flattened the page from the legal pad against the top of the hotel desk, and he smoothed the torn half of the scratch pad paper next to it. Then he picked up the phone and dialed Captain Tracy Edmonds' private cell number.

Chapter 42

There was a lot of ring tone, but Reacher expected that. Cell networks can take eight seconds to route a call. And very few sleepers jump up like the movies. Most people wake up slow, and then blink and fumble.

But Edmonds answered eventually. She said, "Hello?" Her tone was a little anxious, and the sound of her voice was a little plummy, as if her tongue was thick, or her mouth was full.

Reacher said, "Captain Edmonds?"

"Who is this?"

"Your client, Jack Reacher. Major, United States Army. Recently recommissioned. Currently maneuvering with the 110th MP. Are you alone?"

"What kind of a question is that?"

"We're about to have a privileged conversation, counselor. We have legal matters to discuss."

"You're damn right we do."

"Calm down, captain."

"You broke out of jail."

"That's not allowed anymore?"

"We have to talk."

"We are talking."

"Really talk, I mean."

"Are you alone?"

"Yes, I'm alone. So what?"

"Got a pen?"

She paused a beat. "Now I have."

"Paper?"

"Got it."

"OK, pay attention. To better mount an adequate defense, I need hard copies of everything anyone has on a citizen of Afghanistan known to us only as A.M. 3435."

"That's probably secret."

"I'm entitled to due process. Courts take that shit very seriously."

"Whatever, it's a big ask."

"Fair's fair. They have their bullshit with the affidavit."

"Reacher, I'm representing you in a paternity suit. Not the Juan Rodriguez thing. That's Major Sullivan. And to get hard copies of military intelligence out of Afghanistan would be huge even in a criminal case. You won't get it in a paternity suit. I mean, why would you?"

Reacher said, "You told me the Uniform Code of Military Justice still lists adultery as a crime. What's the penalty?"

"Potentially substantial."

"So it's not just a paternity suit. It's a criminal case, too."

"That's tenuous."

"They can't have it both ways, counselor. They mentioned adultery as a crime. Either that means something or it doesn't."

"Reacher, we have to talk."

"Is this where you tell me coming in from the cold would be the best thing to do?"

"It would be."

"Perhaps. But I've chosen Plan B anyway. So I need that information."

"But how does it relate? Afghanistan hadn't even started when you were in Korea. Or when you saw the Big Dog."

Reacher said nothing.

Edmonds said, "Oh."

"Correct," Reacher said. "You're pretty quick, for a lawyer. This is about Major Turner, not me. Or maybe it's about Major Turner *and* me, because what we've got here is someone laying down a challenge to two COs of the 110th Special Unit. Which means there are going to be winners and losers, and the smart money says you need to be with the winners, because being on the right side of history brings bounty beyond imagining, in this man's army."

"Are you going to be the winners?"

"Count on it. We're going to beat them like rented mules. And we need to, captain. They killed two of our own in Afghanistan. And beat one of your colleagues half to death."

Edmonds said, "I'll see what I can do."

* * *

Turner was still in her robe, and she was showing no signs of going back to bed. Reacher asked her, "What was in the envelope?"

"The other thing I asked Sergeant Leach for."

"Evidently. But what was it?"

"We're going to Los Angeles next."

"Are we?"

She nodded. "You need to take care of the Samantha situation."

"I'll get to it."

"Worst case, we're going to fail here, and they're going to lock us up and throw away the key. I can't let that happen to you. Not before you've met your daughter. You'd think about nothing else, for the rest of your life. So you can put my problem on the back burner for a spell, and you can move yours to the front."

"When did you make this plan?"

"Some time ago. As I was entitled to. You're in my unit, apparently. Therefore I'm your CO. We're going to Los Angeles next."

"What was in the envelope?"

She answered by spilling the contents on the bed.

Two credit cards.

And two driver's licenses.

She paired them up and kept one of each for herself, and she passed the others to Reacher. A New York State driver's license, and a Visa credit card. The license was made out to a guy named Michael Dennis Kehoe, forty-five years old, at a Queens address. Male, blue eyes, height six-six. He was an organ donor. The picture showed a square face and a wide neck. The Visa card was in the same name, Michael D. Kehoe.

Reacher said, "Are they real?"

"Mine are."

"And mine aren't?"

"They're kind of real. They're from the undercover locker."

Reacher nodded. The 110th sent people undercover all the time. They needed documents. The government supplied them, authentic in every way, except for never having been issued to an actual person.

He asked, "Where are yours from?"

"A friend of Leach's. She said she knew someone who looked like me."

"So what's your name now?"

Turner answered by flipping the license into his lap, like a card trick. Illinois, Margaret Vega, five-seven, brown eyes, thirty-one years old. Not an organ donor. The photograph showed a light-skinned Hispanic woman. At first glance a little like Turner, but not a whole lot.

Reacher flipped the license back.

"And Ms. Vega was happy to give up her DL?" he said. "Just like that? And her credit card, too?"

"We have to return them. And we have to pay back any charges we make. Obviously I had to promise. But Billy Bob's money can take care of that."

"That's not the point. Ms. Vega is way out on a limb now."

"I guess Leach can be persuasive."

"Only because she thinks you're worth it."

"She had no friends who looked like you. Not even

close. Which is why we had to use the locker. Probably Mr. Kehoe was the target in a training scenario. He looks like the guy with the chainsaw in a slasher movie."

"Should work fine, then. When are we leaving?"

"As soon as possible," Turner said. "We'll catch an early flight."

They showered and dressed, and then packing was nothing more than jamming their new toothbrushes in their pockets, and putting on their coats. They left the drapes closed and the lights off, and Reacher hung the *Do Not Disturb* card on the outside handle, and then they hustled down the corridor to the elevator. It was just after five in the morning, and Turner figured the long-hauls to the West Coast would start around six. Not an infinite choice of carriers out of Pittsburgh International, but there would be at least several. Worst case, they could connect through San Francisco, or Phoenix, or Las Vegas.

The elevator reached the lobby and they stepped out to a deserted scene. There was no one at the desk. No one anywhere. So Reacher dropped their key cards in the trash, and they headed for the door, where they got straight into a hesitant after-you-no-after-you thing with a lone guy who had chosen that exact moment to come in from the dark sidewalk outside. He was a compact man in a navy suit and a white shirt and a navy tie. He had a fresh haircut, short and conservative, and a pink face, recently shaved. Eventually they worked out a three-way pecking order. The guy held the door for Turner, who stepped out, and then Reacher hung back, and the guy stepped in, and finally Reacher stepped out.

There were no taxis at the curb. But there was a hotel shuttle bus, with its engine running and its door open. No driver at the wheel. Inside, maybe, taking a leak.

Ten yards farther on a Crown Vic was parked in the fire lane. Dark blue, clean and shiny, with antennas on the trunk lid. Reacher turned and looked back at the hotel door. Deep in the lobby the guy who had come in was waiting for service at the desk. Navy suit. White shirt. Navy tie. Short hair, pink face, clean shave.

Reacher said, "FBI."

Turner said, "They were tracking those names. Sullivan and Temple."

"He walked right past us. How long till his brain kicks in?"

"He's FBI, so it won't be instantaneous."

"We could head back to the truck and drive ourselves."

"No, the truck should stay here. We need to keep breaking the chain. Get on the bus. The driver will be back in a minute. Got to be. He left it running."

Reacher said, "We'll be sitting ducks."

"We'll be invisible," Turner said. "Just folks on a bus."

Reacher glanced around. The guy was still at the counter. No one behind it. The shuttle bus was all done up in chrome and a corporate style. It had black windows. Like a movie star's limousine. A touch of glamour, for the everyday traveler.

Black windows. Just folks on a bus. Predator and prey, motion and stillness. An old evolutionary legacy. Reacher said, "OK, we'll get on the bus."

They climbed aboard, and the suspension dipped under their weight, and they shuffled along a low narrow aisle and took seats on the far side, halfway to the back.

And then they sat still and waited.

Not a great feeling.

The view out was not great either, because of the distance and the window tint and the multiple layers of glass, but Reacher could still see the guy. He was getting impatient. He had turned around to face the empty lobby, and he had stepped a yard away from the desk. Claiming the wider space, expressing his resentment, but staying close enough to the help to remain definitively first in line. Not that he had any competition. Nor would he for an hour or so. Red-eye arrivals would start about six, too.

Then the guy suddenly moved forward, a long pace, eager, as if he was about to greet someone. Or accost someone. On the right of the frame a second figure stepped into view. A man, in a black uniform with a short jacket. A bellboy, maybe. The FBI guy asked a question, accompanied by a sweeping gesture with his arm, like *where the hell is everybody,* and the guy in the short jacket paused, uncomfortable, as if obliged to venture outside his accustomed territory, and then he squeezed behind the counter and rapped on a door, with no result, so he opened the door a crack and called through, inquiringly, and fifteen seconds later a young woman came out, running her fingers through her hair. The FBI guy turned back to the desk, and the young woman moved up face to face with him, and the guy in the short black jacket walked out of the lobby.

Not a bellboy.

The bus driver.

He climbed aboard, and saw that he had customers, and he glanced back at the lobby, to see if he was about to get more, and he must have concluded not, because he asked, "Domestic or international?"

Turner said, "Domestic."

So the guy dumped himself down in his seat, and unspooled a long seat belt, and clipped it tight, and the door closed with a wheezing sigh, and the guy put the bus in gear.

And then he waited, because he had to, because an arriving car was maneuvering around the parked Crown Vic, and thereby blocking his exit.

It was the car with the dented doors.

Chapter 43

The car with the dented doors squeezed around the parked Crown Vic, and then it slowed to a walk and prepared to pull up just short of the hotel entrance. The bus moved off into the vacated space, grinding slow and heavy, and it passed the car close by, flank to flank. Reacher got up off his seat and stared out the window. All four guys were in the car. The two he had met on the first night, and the third guy, and the big guy with the tiny ears. The whole crew was there.

"Leave it," Turner said.

"We need to take them off the table."

"But not here, and not now. Later. They're on the back burner, remember?"

"No time like the present."

"In a hotel lobby? In front of an FBI agent?"

Reacher craned around and saw the four guys climb out of the car. They glanced left and right, fast and fluid, and then they headed straight inside, single file, a crisp linear stream, one, two, three, four, like men with an urgent purpose. Turner said, "Stand easy, major. Another time, another place. We're going to LA."

The bus picked up speed and left the hotel behind. Reacher watched for as long as there was something to see, and then he turned back. He said, "Tell me what you know about how the FBI tracked our names."

"The modern world," Turner said. "Homeland Security. It's an information-dependent operation. All kinds of things are linked together. Airlines for sure, and no doubt airport hotels, too. In which case it would be easy enough to set up an alert in case two specific names appeared in the same place at the same time."

"Would the Bureau share that information?"

"Are you kidding?"

"Then we need to revisit what we said about the top boys here. They're not very senior staff officers. They're very, *very* senior staff officers. Don't you think? To be inside Homeland Security's databases, independently, in real time?"

"Maybe not-so-real time. The FBI beat them here, after all."

"From their Pittsburgh field office. Our guys had further to come. They must have set out much earlier. They must have known before the FBI did. They had an alert of their own."

The hotel bus let them out at the terminal, and they ducked inside to check the departure boards. Next out were two flights within a minute of each other, U.S.

Airways to Long Beach, and American Airlines to Orange County.

"Got a preference?" Turner asked.

"Long Beach," Reacher said. "We can rent a car.
Straight shot up the 710. Then the 101. The mother's
affidavit was out of a law office in North Hollywood.
I'm guessing that's where she is."

"How are you going to find her?"

"I'll start in her lawyer's parking lot. That's one
place she won't get moved on."

"Her lawyer's office will be staked out, surely. By
elements of the 75th and the FBI for sure. And our
four unofficial friends will be there about six hours
after they realize we're not in the hotel."

"So we'll have to be very careful."

The U.S. Airways ticket counter was opening up. A
cheerful woman of about fifty spent a minute booting
computers and sorting labels and papers and pens,
and then she turned toward them with a smile. Turner
asked about seats to Long Beach, on the morning
flight. The woman clicked away on her keyboard, flat-
fingered because of her nails, and said she didn't have
many. But two was no problem. So first Turner and
then Reacher handed over driver's licenses and credit
cards, absently and casually, as if they had just pulled
them at random from a full deck of documentation.
The woman lined them up in front of her, in a neat
physical analogue of a window seat and an aisle, and
she typed the names, moving her head back and forth
as she glanced between the licenses and the screen,
and then she swiped the cards, and she hunted and
pecked and clicked some more, and then a machine

kicked in and printed boarding cards. The woman swept them up, and collated them with the right licenses and the right credit cards, and she said, "Ms. Vega, Mr. Kehoe, here you go," and she handed them over, like a little ceremony.

They thanked her and walked away, and Reacher said, "This is why you made me buy a sweater, right?"

"You're going to meet your daughter," Turner said. "And first impressions count."

Juliet called Romeo, because there was a division of labor, and some of the responsibilities were his, and he said, all excited, "Our boys are in the corridor, right now, directly outside their room."

Romeo said, "Corridor?"

"Hotel corridor. Hotel room. Our guys say the room is dark, it is quiet, there is a *Do Not Disturb* notice on the door, and they have not yet checked out."

"So they're in the room?"

"They have to be."

"Then why are our boys in the corridor?"

"There's a problem."

Romeo said, "What kind of a problem?"

"The FBI is there."

"Where?"

"With our boys. Literally. In the corridor. Just kind of standing around. One guy. He can't do anything because he thinks he has four civilian witnesses. We can't do anything because we know we have one FBI witness. We're all just standing around."

"In the corridor?"

"Right outside their room."

"Do we know they're in there? For certain?"

"Where else would they be?"

"Are they both in there?"

"Why do you ask?"

"I did some cutting and pasting."

"Of what?"

"Data. After that call to the mothership. It threw me a little. I thought some precautions might be appropriate. Among the things I put on the alert list was the 110th's undercover locker. For no good reason. Just for the sake of being able to feel I was doing everything I could. But I just got something back. One of the identities just bought a ticket on U.S. Airways, from Pittsburgh to Long Beach, in California."

"For when?"

"First flight this morning. About half an hour from now."

"Only one of them?"

"None of the other identities is showing up as active."

"And which one is?"

"Michael Dennis Kehoe. The man, in other words. They've split up. I guess they had to. All the woman has is the Helen Sullivan ID, and by now they must realize no one named Helen Sullivan is getting on an airplane anytime soon. Not without extensive trials and tribulations beforehand. Which Turner can't afford. Therefore Reacher is heading to California alone. Which makes sense. He needs to be there. She doesn't."

Juliet said, "Maybe Turner is in the room on her own."

"Logical. If Reacher is on his way to California."

"Perfectly logical. If he is."

"But not if he isn't. We need to find out, right now. We need to cut a deal with the FBI. We won't rat them out, and they won't rat us out. Or whatever. But we need to get our boys through that door, right now. Even if the FBI gets in as well."

Turner was the CO, and she wanted to get airside as soon as possible. She thought airport security would be some kind of a barrier. Against the four guys, at least. If they got as far as the airport, that was. Which they might, if they talked to the bus driver. Two passengers? Yes, sir, domestic. But airport security was useless against the FBI or the army. Those guys went to the head of the line, and then in through the side door.

So, not really a barrier. More of a filter.

They had nothing made of metal in their pockets, except small change, which they pooled in a scuffed black bowl. They stepped through the hoop one after the other, just two coatless, shoeless figures among a building crowd. They put their coats back on and laced up their boots and split the change and moved off in search of coffee.

Juliet called Romeo and said, "Our boys got a look inside the hotel room. They claimed they were worried about their friend, and the FBI guy was all over that immediately. It made opening the door look like a public service."

Romeo said, "And?"

"There was no one in the room."

"They're in the airport terminal."

"Both of them?"

"One of the women passengers on the same U.S. Airways flight used a credit card that comes back to a bank in Arlington County. A woman named Margaret Vega."

Juliet said, "And?"

"She was a very late booking. Within the last hour."

"And?"

"She was one of only two passengers who booked at that time. The other being Michael Dennis Kehoe. Their cards were charged within the same minute."

"Where did Turner get a credit card in the name of Margaret Vega?"

"I don't know. Yet."

"Not the undercover locker?"

"No. A real person, possibly. From the mothership, perhaps. I'll check."

"When does the flight leave?"

"They'll start boarding in about fifteen minutes."

"OK, I'm sending our boys straight to the terminal. They can check landside, at least."

"I'm ahead of you," Romeo said. "They can go airside. They can even get on the plane, if they need to. I got them two seats and two standby seats. Which was difficult, by the way. It's shaping up to be a full flight.

Tell them the boarding cards will be at the ticket counter."

The gate area was a wide, spacious lounge, carpeted, painted in soothing pastel colors, but it was far from restful, because it was packed with more than a hundred people. Clearly Pittsburgh to Long Beach was a popular route. Reacher wasn't sure why. Although he had read that Pittsburgh was becoming an in-demand moviemaking town. Because of money. Financial incentives were being offered, and production companies were responding. All kinds of movies had already been shot there, and more were planned. So maybe these were show folk, heading home. The Long Beach airport was no less convenient for Hollywood and Beverly Hills than LAX. Both were the same freeway slog. But whatever, the crowd was large and unruly. And as always Reacher tried to hang back beyond its edge, but Turner was the CO, and she wanted to get on the plane as early as possible. As if the narrow fuselage was sovereign territory, like an embassy on foreign soil, not the same as the city that surrounded it. They had a high row number, which meant their seats would be toward the back, which meant they would board before most of the rest, directly after the halt and the lame, and the families with small children, and the first class cabin, and the frequent fliers. So Turner was all in favor of pushing up close to the desk. She had a small person's deftness. She slid through gaps denied to Reacher's clumsier frame. But he followed her doggedly, and he got to the spot she had staked out about a minute after her.

And then more or less immediately the boarding process began. A woman opened the official door and used a microphone on a curly cord, and the crowd surged, and wheelchairs pushed through, and old guys with walking canes limped after them, and then couples carrying children and fantastically complicated seating equipment went next, and then sleek men and women in suits rushed on, and then Reacher was carried along in the flow, down the jet way, through cold air and kerosene stink, and finally into the cabin. He hunched and ducked and made his way down the aisle to his seat, which was a narrow thing with adequate legroom only if he folded himself into it bolt upright. Next to him Turner looked happier. Hers was the body type the seats had been designed for.

They clipped their belts and waited.

Romeo called Juliet and said, "I'm watching the U.S. Airways system right now."

Juliet said, "And?"

"Bad news, I'm afraid. Kehoe and Vega have already boarded. And we just lost both our standby seats. Two of their frequent fliers showed up and preempted them. They get priority."

"Can't you call U.S. Airways and tell them they don't?"

"I could, but I don't think I will. The airline would make a charge. That's how it works now. Apparently goodwill has monetary value, at least when Uncle

Sam is paying the bill. And a charge would generate paperwork, which we can't afford. So we'll have to live with it. We'll get two of them on, at least."

"Which two?"

"It seems to have been done alphabetically."

"Not ideal," Juliet said.

"Eyes and ears are all we need at this point. A holding operation. I got the other two on American to Orange County. They'll arrive around the same time. They can link up in California."

Reacher stared ahead, down the long aluminum tube, and watched people as they shuffled in, and turned right, and shuffled some more, and peered at their seat numbers, and jammed large suitcases and bulky coats into the overhead lockers. Luggage, baggage, burdens. Not his thing. Some of the approaching faces were happy, but most were glum. He remembered taking flights as a kid, long ago, at the military's expense, on long-forgotten carriers like Braniff and Eastern and Pan American, when jet travel was rare and exotic and people dressed up for it and glowed with excitement and novelty. Suits and ties, and summer dresses, and sometimes even gloves. China plates, and milk jugs, and silver silverware.

Then he saw the guy he had punched in the side of the head.

Chapter 44

There was no mistaking the guy. Reacher remembered him well. At the motel, on the first night, the car showing up, not yet dented, the guy climbing out of the passenger seat and tracking around the hood and starting in with all the verbal chit-chat.

We're not worried about you, old man.

Reacher remembered the long left hook, and the feel of bone, and the sideways snap of the guy's head. And then he had seen him again, from a distance in the motel lot the next day, and for a third time just minutes ago, getting out of the car at the hotel.

It was the guy, no question.

And right behind him was the guy Reacher thought of as the third man. Not the driver from the first night, and not the big guy with the small ears, but the make-weight from the second day. Both guys peered ahead, left and right, close and far, until they located their quarry, and then they looked away fast and acted innocent. Reacher watched the space behind them, but the next passenger was a woman, as was the next after that, who was also the last. The steward came on the PA and said he was about to close the cabin door and everyone should turn off their portable electronic equipment. The two guys kept on shuffling up the aisle, and then they dumped themselves down, in separate lone seats, one on the left and one on the right, three rows and four rows ahead, respectively.

Turner said, "This is crazy."

"That's for damn sure," Reacher said. "How long is this flight?"

Which question was answered immediately, not by Turner, but by the steward on the PA again, with another of his standard announcements. He said the computer was showing a flight time of five hours and forty minutes, because of a headwind.

Reacher said, "This back burner thing isn't working. It isn't working at all. Because they're not letting it work. I mean, what exactly is this? Now they're coming on the plane with us? Why? What are they going to do? In front of a hundred other people in a small metal tube?"

"Could just be close-order surveillance."

"Do they have eyes in the back of their heads?"

"Then it's a warning shot of some kind. We're supposed to feel intimidated."

"Yeah, now I'm really scared. They sent Tweedledum and Tweedledumber."

"And where are the other two?"

"Full flight," Reacher said. "Maybe two seats was all they could get."

"In which case why not send the big guy?"

"The question is not why or why not. It's how. How are they doing this? They started from stone cold and now they're five minutes behind us. And as far as they know we have no ID. Except Sullivan and Temple, and they have to figure we know no one named Sullivan or Temple is getting on a plane today, not without some serious scrutiny. So how did they know we were heading for departures? Why would we, without ID? It was much more likely we'd head for the parking lot and get back on the road."

"The bus driver told them."

"Too quick. He's not even back yet. It's them. There's no information they can't get. They're in this airline's operating system, right now. They saw us buy the tickets, and they watched us board. Which means they're in the 110th's undercover locker, too. Because how else would the name Kehoe mean anything to them? They're watching everything we do. Every move we make. We're in a goldfish bowl."

"In which case they must have matched Vega to Kehoe by now. Because we booked at the same time, and we're sitting together. So they know I'm Vega. Which means the real Vega is in bad trouble. As is Leach, too, for brokering the loan. And for delivering the stuff. We really need to warn them both."

"We can't warn either one of them. We can't do anything. Not for the next five hours and forty minutes."

The plane taxied, earthbound and clumsy, ahead of an American Airlines departure, which Reacher figured was the Orange County flight, due to leave a minute later. The sky was still dark. There was no sign of the morning sun.

Then came the runway, and the plane turned and paused, as if to compose itself, and then its engines roared and it accelerated on its way, rumbling over the concrete sections, relentlessly, and Reacher watched out the window and saw the ground fall away below and the broad aluminum wing dip and flex as it took the weight. The lights of Pittsburgh twinkled in the distance, carved into curves and headlands by broad black rivers.

Three and four rows in front the two guys were staring studiously ahead. Both had middle seats. The least desirable, and therefore the last to sell. On the left of the cabin was the guy from the first night. He had a younger woman next to him at the window, and an older woman next to him on the aisle. On the right of the cabin was the makeweight from the second day. He had an old white-haired guy next to him at the window, one of the early boarders, Reacher thought, with a walking stick. On the aisle was a woman in a suit, who would have looked more at home in first class. Maybe she was on a business trip. Maybe her employer had cut back on benefits.

Turner said, "I wish we knew who they were."

"They're on a plane this time," Reacher said. "Not in a car. Which implies two major certainties. This time they have IDs in their pockets. And no weapons."

"How far up the chain of command would you have to go before you found someone with unfettered twenty-four-seven access to every national security system this country has?"

"I assume everything changed after 9/11. I was gone four years before that. But I would guess an O8 in Intelligence might have that capability. Although not unfettered. They're a paranoid bunch. They have all kinds of checks and balances. To do a little private snooping on an airline's passenger manifest at five o'clock in the morning would be something else entirely."

"So who?"

"Think about it the other way around. How far down the chain of command would you have to go? The president could do it. Or the National Security Advisor. Or anyone who gets in the Situation Room on a regular basis. The Chiefs of Staff, in other words. Except this is a round-the-clock responsibility, and it's been running for more than a dozen years now. So there must be a separate desk. A Deputy Chief of Staff. Some kind of a go-to guy, tasked to be on top of everything, all the time. He could dip in and out any old time he wanted to. No checks and balances for him, because he's the guy the checks and balances get reported to."

"So we're dealing with a Deputy Chief of Staff?"

"The bigger they are, the harder they fall."

"Conspiring with someone in Afghanistan?"

"Those guys all know each other. They're very social. Probably classmates."

"So who are these guys on the plane? They don't look like Pentagon staffers."

Reacher didn't answer. He just watched and waited.

And then ten minutes later his patience was rewarded.

The woman in the fancy business suit got up and headed for the bathroom.

Chapter 45

Reacher waited for the woman in the suit to pass by, and then he unclipped his belt and got up and headed forward, one row, two, three, four. He dropped into the woman's vacated seat, and the makeweight from the second day reared back against the white-haired old guy with the cane, who was fast asleep with his head against the window.

Reacher said, "Let me see your ID."

Which the guy didn't. He just sat there, completely disconcerted, pressed up against his quarry like a sardine in a can. He was wearing some kind of nylon cargo pants, and a black sweatshirt under a black pea coat. He had a Hamilton watch on his left wrist, which meant he was probably right-handed. How long do women take in the bathroom? In Reacher's experience they were not lightning fast. Four minutes, possibly.

Which was about three more than he needed.

He leaned forward, like he was going to head-butt

the seat in front of him, and he rocked to his right, and he leaned back again, all one continuous fluid motion, so the guy ended up half trapped behind his right shoulder and his upper arm, and he reached over with his right hand and grabbed the guy's right wrist, and he dragged the guy's hand over toward him, twisting the wrist so the knuckles came first, with the palm facing away, and with his left hand he grabbed the guy's right index finger, and he said, "Now you've got a choice. You can take it like a man, or you can scream like a little girl."

And he broke the guy's finger, by wrenching it down ninety degrees and snapping the first knuckle, and then he popped the second knuckle with the ball of his thumb. The guy jumped and squirmed and gasped in shock and pain, but he didn't scream. Not like a little girl. Not with a hundred other people there.

Next Reacher broke his middle finger, in the same way, in the same two places, and then the guy started trying to get his trapped left arm free, which Reacher allowed, but only so he could swap hands and attend to the same two fingers on the other side.

Then he said, "ID?"

The guy didn't answer. He couldn't. He was too busy whimpering and grimacing and staring down at his ruined hands. His fingers were all over the place, sticking out at odd angles, bent into L shapes. Reacher patted him down, at close quarters, pushing him and pulling him to get at all his pockets. Nothing exciting in most of them, but he felt a characteristic lump in the right hip pocket. A tri-fold wallet, for sure. He pulled it out and stood up. Across the aisle and one row back the other guy was half on his feet. The woman in the suit was out of the bathroom and coming toward him. She hung back to let him sit, and then she continued on her way.

Reacher dumped the wallet in Turner's lap and re-clipped his belt. She said, "What did you do to him?"

"He won't be pulling any triggers for a week or two. Or hitting anything. Or driving. Or buttoning his pants. He's off the table. Prevention is better than cure. Get your retaliation in first."

Turner didn't answer.

"I know," Reacher said. "Feral. What you see is what you get."

"No, it was good work."

"How did it look?"

"He was hopping around a bit. I knew something was happening."

"What's in the wallet?"

Turner opened it up. It was a fat old item, made of decent leather that had molded itself around its contents. Which were numerous. The back part had cash in two sections, a healthy quarter-inch wad of twenties, but nothing larger, and then a thinner selection of ones and tens and fives. The front part had three pockets sized to carry credit cards. On the top of the deck in the center was a North Carolina driver's license, with the guy's face in the picture, and the name Peter Paul Lozano. Behind the DL was a stack of credit cards, Visa and MasterCard and Discover and

American Express, with more in the slots on the left and the right, all of them current, in-date and unexpired, all of them in the name of Peter P. Lozano.

There was no military ID.

"Is he a civilian?" Turner said. "Or sanitized?"

"I'm guessing sanitized," Reacher said. "But Captain Edmonds can tell us. I'll give her the name. She's working with HRC."

"Are you going to get the other guy's name?"

"Two would triangulate better than one."

"How are you going to do it?"

"I'll think of something."

Four rows ahead the guy named Lozano was hunched over and rocking back and forth in his seat, as if he had his hands clamped up under his arms to manage the pain. A stewardess came by, and he glanced at her, as if he wanted to speak, but then he looked away again. Because what was he going to say? A bad man came by and hurt me? Like a little girl? Like a snitch in the principal's office? Clearly not his style. Not in front of a hundred other people.

"Military," Reacher said. "Don't you think? Boot camp taught him to keep his mouth shut."

Then the other guy squeezed out past the old lady next to him. The guy from the first night, with all the verbal chit-chat. He stepped forward a row and bent down to talk to his buddy. It turned into a regular little conference. There was discussion, there was exhibition of injuries, there were hostile glances over the shoulder. The woman in the business suit looked away, her face blank and frozen.

Turner said, "It won't work twice. Forewarned is forearmed. The guy is getting a damn play by play."

"And hoping his seatmate has a strong bladder."

"Do you really think Edmonds will get us the file on 3435?"

"She either will or she won't. It's about fifty-fifty. Like the toss of a coin."

"And either way is OK with you, right?"

"I'd prefer to have the file."

"But you're not going to be heartbroken if you don't get it. Because just asking for it was enough. Asking for it was like telling them we're one step away. Like our breath on their necks."

"I'd prefer to have the file," Reacher said again.

"Like these guys on the plane. You're sending them back walking wounded. You're sending a message, aren't you?"

Reacher said nothing.

Reacher kept one eye on the guy from the first night, three rows ahead on the left. The woman next to him at the window seemed to be asleep. From behind she looked young, and she was dressed like a homeless person. Definitely no summer frock, and no gloves. But she was clean. A movie person, probably. Junior, to be flying coach. Not an A-lister. Maybe an intern, or an assistant to an assistant. Perhaps she had been scouting locations, or organizing office space. The older woman on the aisle looked like a grandma.

Maybe she was heading out to visit her grandkids. Maybe her ancestors had worked for Carnegie and Frick, in their brutal mills, and then when the city hit hard times maybe her children had joined the rustbelt diaspora and headed for sunnier climes. Maybe they were living the dream, in the warmth of southern California.

Reacher waited.

And in the end it was the guy himself who proved to have a bladder issue. Too much morning coffee, perhaps. Or orange juice. Or water. But whichever, the guy stood up and squeezed out past grandma, and oriented himself in the aisle, and locked eyes with Reacher, and took hesitant steps toward the back of the plane, watching Reacher all the way, one row, two, three, and then as he came alongside he turned and walked backward the rest of the way, his eyes still on Reacher's, exaggerated, as if to say *no way you're getting a jump on me,* and he fumbled behind himself for the door, and he backed ass-first into the bathroom, his eyes still locked on Reacher's until the last possible second, and then the door closed and the bolt shot home.

How long do men take in the bathroom?

Not as long as women, generally.

Reacher unclipped his belt and stood up.

Chapter 46

Reacher waited outside the bathroom, patiently, like a regular passenger, like the next man in line. The door was a standard bi-fold contraption, hinged on the right, cream in color, and a little grimy. No surprises. Then he heard the sudden muted suck of the flush, and then there was a pause, for hand washing, he hoped, and then the red *Occupied* changed to a green *Vacant,* and the center of the door pulled back, and its left-hand edge slid along its track, and as soon as it was three-quarters of the way home Reacher wheeled around and slammed the heel of his left hand through the widening gap and caught the guy in the chest and smashed him back into the bulkhead behind the toilet.

Reacher crammed in after him and closed the door again with a jerk of his hips. The space was tiny. Barely big enough for Reacher on his own. He was jammed hard up against the guy, chest to chest, face to face. He turned half left, so he was hip to hip, so he wouldn't get kneed in the balls, and he jammed his right forearm horizontally into the guy's throat, to pin him against the back wall, and the guy started wriggling and struggling, but uselessly, because he couldn't move more than an inch or two. No swing, no momentum. Reacher leaned in hard and turned his own left hand backward and caught the guy's right wrist, and rotated it like a doorknob, which meant that as the twist in Reacher's arm unwound the exact same twist went into the other guy's arm, more and more, harder and harder, relentlessly, until the guy really needed to do a pirouette or a cartwheel to relieve the agonizing pressure, which obviously he couldn't, due to the complete lack of space. Reacher kept it going until the point of the guy's elbow was facing directly toward him, and then he raised the guy's arm, up and up, still twisting, until it was horizontal, an inch from the side wall, and then he took his forearm out of the guy's throat and smashed his own elbow down through the guy's elbow, shattering it, the guy's arm suddenly folding the way no arm is designed to fold.

The guy screamed, which Reacher hoped would be muffled by the door, or lost in the sound of rushing air, and then the guy collapsed into a sitting position on the commode, and then Reacher broke his other arm, the same way, *twist, twist, smash,* and then he hauled him upright again by the collar and checked his pockets, an inch away, up close and personal, the guy still struggling, his thighs going like he was riding an imaginary bicycle, but generating no force at all because of the extreme proximity, Reacher feeling nothing more than a ripple.

The guy's wallet was in his right hip pocket, the same as the previous guy. Reacher took it and turned to his left and jabbed the guy with his elbow, hard, in the center of his chest, and the guy went back down on the toilet, and Reacher extricated himself from the tangle of flopping limbs, and he shouldered out the door. He closed it behind him as much as he could, and then he walked the short distance back to his seat.

The second wallet was loaded more or less the same as the first. A healthy wad of twenties, and some leathery small bills the guy had gotten in change, and a deck of credit cards, and a North Carolina driver's license with the guy's picture and the name Ronald David Baldacci.

There was no military ID.

Reacher said, "If one is sanitized, they all are."

"Or they're all civilians."

"Suppose they aren't."

"Then they're lifers at Fort Bragg. To have North Carolina DLs."

"Who's at Fort Bragg these days?"

"Nearly forty thousand people. More than two hundred and fifty square miles. It was a city all its own at the last census. There's a lot of airborne, including the 82nd. And Special Forces, and psy-ops, and the Kennedy Special Warfare Center, and the 16th MP, and a lot of sustainment and logistics."

"A lot of people in and out of Afghanistan, in other words."

"Including the logistics people. They brought stuff in, and now they're taking it out again. Or not."

"You still think this is a repeat of the Big Dog scam?"

"Except bigger and better. And I don't think they're selling it here at home. I think they're selling it to the native population."

"We'll find out," Reacher said. "We're one step away, after all."

"Back burner again," Turner said. "You took care of what you had to. Now you're going to meet your daughter."

About five minutes after that the guy came out of the bathroom, pale, sweating, seemingly smaller, much diminished, only his lower body moving, his upper body held rigid, like a robot only half working. He stumbled down the aisle and squeezed past the grandma and dumped himself back in his seat.

Reacher said, "He should ask the stewardess for an aspirin."

Then the flight reverted to normal, and became like most flights Reacher had taken. No food was served. Not in coach. There was stuff to buy, mostly small chemical pellets artfully disguised as various natural products, but neither Reacher nor Turner bought any. They figured they would eat in California. Which would make them hungry, but Reacher didn't mind being hungry. He believed hunger kept him sharp. He believed it stimulated creativity in the brain. Another old evolutionary legacy. If you're hungry, you work out a smarter way to get the next woolly mammoth, today, not tomorrow.

He figured he was owed about three hours' sleep, after being woken by Leach at four in the morning, so he closed his eyes. He wasn't worried about the two guys. What were they going to do? They could spit peanuts at him, he guessed, but that was about all. Beside him he felt Turner arrive at the same conclusion. She rested her head on his shoulder. He slept bolt upright, waking with a start every time his head tipped forward.

Romeo called Juliet and said, "We have a serious problem."

Juliet said, "In what way?"

"Turner must have remembered the number after all. Reacher's lawyer just made an application to see the full bio on A.M. 3435."

"Why Reacher's lawyer?"

"They're trying to slip it by. They assume we're watching her lawyer, but maybe not his. It's not even his main lawyer. It's the newbie doing his paternity case."

"Then we can get it thrown out, surely. It's got nothing to do with his paternity case."

"It's an application, like any other. The process is what it is. We'd have to show good reason. And we can't, because there's nothing demonstrably special about the guy. Except to us. We can't afford that kind of attention. Everyone would think we'd lost our minds.

They'd say, who the hell is redacting that guy? He's just a run-of-the-mill peasant."

"So how long have we got?"

"A day, perhaps."

"Did you cancel their credit cards?"

"I canceled his. Easy enough, because it was the army's to start with. But I can't touch hers without a paper trail. Margaret Vega is a real person."

"What are we going to do?"

"We're going to finish it in California. They'll be on the ground soon, four against two."

Reacher and Turner slept most of three hours, and woke up with the plane on approach into Long Beach, and with the steward on the PA again, talking about seat backs and tray tables and upright positions and portable electronic equipment. None of which interested Reacher, because he hadn't moved his seat back, hadn't used his tray table, and he had no electronic equipment, portable or otherwise. Out the window he could see the brown desert hills. He liked California. He figured he could live there, if he lived anywhere. It was warm, and no one knew him. He could have a dog. *They* could have a dog. He pictured Turner, maybe in a back yard somewhere, pruning a rose or planting a tree.

She said, "We shouldn't use Hertz or Avis. To rent the car, I mean. Or any of the big franchises. Just in case their computers are hooked up with the government."

He said, "You're getting paranoid in your old age."

"Doesn't mean they aren't out to get me."

He smiled.

She said, "What would that leave us with?"

"Local guys. Rent-a-Wrecks, or four-year-old Lamborghinis."

"Will they take cash?"

"We have credit cards."

"They might have canceled them. They seem able to do that kind of thing."

"They can't have. Not yet. They don't even know we've got them."

"They saw us buy these flights."

"They saw Vega and Kehoe buy these flights. But we're not Vega and Kehoe anymore. From now on we're Lozano and Baldacci, at least when it comes to credit cards. We'll use theirs. How's that for a message?"

"They can track credit cards."

"I know."

"You want them to find us, don't you?"

"Easier than us finding them. But I agree with you about Hertz and Avis. We don't want to make it too easy. We need to give them a sense of achievement."

"First we have to make it through the airport. Which could be full of MPs. Because Warrant Officer Espin isn't the dumbest bunny ever born. He must know where you're going. And he's got the personnel. He could have a guy in every airport within a hundred miles of LA. All day and all night. And the FBI could be there, too. Their Pittsburgh people don't need to be geniuses to figure out where we were going."

"We'll keep our eyes open."

* * *

The glide path was long and gentle, and the landing was smooth, and the inward taxi felt fast and nimble. Then a tiny bell sounded and a light went out and about ninety-seven people leapt to their feet. Reacher stayed in his seat, because it was no less comfortable than standing under a six-foot ceiling. And the guys three and four rows ahead stayed sitting, too, because there was no way known to science for an adult male human to get out of an airline seat in coach without using leverage from his hands and his arms.

The plane emptied from the front, with people flowing out in layers, like sand in an hourglass. They grabbed their suitcases and their coats from where they had stowed them, and they funneled away, and the next row slid out to replace them, and the next. The old white-haired guy with the cane and the young movie intern had to struggle out past their immobile center-seat neighbors. Then the next rows cleared, and the two guys were left sitting all alone in a sea of emptied space. Reacher took his turn down the aisle, head bent and hunched, and he paused three rows ahead and hauled the left-hand guy to his feet by the front of his shirt. It seemed the least he could do. He paused again a row later and did the same with the right-hand guy. Then he moved on, down the aisle, through the galley, out the door, through warm air and kerosene stink, and into the Long Beach airport.

Chapter 47

Airports are full of solo loiterers, which makes spotting surveillance almost impossible. Because everyone is a suspect. A guy sitting around doing nothing behind a rumpled newspaper? Rare on the street, but pretty much compulsory in the airport. There could have been fifty undercover MPs and fifty FBI agents inside the first thirty feet alone.

But no one showed any interest in them. No one looked at them, no one approached them, and no one followed them. So they walked away fast, straight to the taxi line, and they got in the back of a beat-up sedan, and they asked the driver for off-airport car rental, but not Hertz, Avis, Enterprise, or anyone else with an illuminated sign. The driver didn't ask supplementary questions. Didn't seek detailed specifications. He just took off, like he knew where he was going. His brother-in-law's, probably, or whichever guy gave him the best finder's fee.

In which case the brother-in-law or the top-dollar

hustler must have been named Al, and he must have been a cool guy, because the cab pulled up in front of a vacant lot filled with about twenty parked cars and backed by a wooden shed, which had *Cool Al's Auto Rental* painted on its roof, inexpertly, by hand, in thin paint, with a wide brush.

"Perfect," Reacher said.

Peter Paul Lozano took care of the cab fare, via a bill peeled off his quarter-inch stack of twenties, and then Reacher and Turner wandered through the lot. Clearly Cool Al had positioned his business in what he must have figured was a sweet spot halfway between the Rent-a-Wreck idea and the four-year-old Lamborghini approach. The lot was filled with vehicles that had started out prestigious, and had probably stayed prestigious for a good long time, but which were now well into a long and sad decline. There were Mercedes-Benzes and Range Rovers and BMWs and Jaguars, all of them last-but-three body styles, all of them scuffed and dented and a little dull.

"Will they work?" Turner asked.

"Don't know," Reacher said. "I'm the last guy to ask about cars. Let's see what Cool Al has to say on the subject."

Which was, translated and paraphrased, "They've lasted this long, so why should they stop now?" Which struck Reacher as both logical and optimistic. Cool Al himself was a guy of about sixty or sixty-five, with a full head of gray hair, and a big belly, and a yellow shirt. He was at a desk that took up half the space in his shed, which was hot, and which smelled of dusty wood and creosote.

He said, "Go on, pick a car, any car."

"A Range Rover," Turner said. "I've never been in one before."

"You'll love it."

"I hope so."

Reacher did the deal, at the giant desk, with licenses from Vega and Baldacci, and a made-up cell number, and one of Baldacci's credit cards, and a scrawled signature that could have been pretty much anything. In return Cool Al handed over a key and waved a wide arm toward the right side of the lot and said, "The black one."

The black one turned out to be sun-hazed down to a steely dark purple, and its window tints were lifting and bubbling, and its seats were cracked and sagging. It was from the 1990s, Turner thought. No longer a premium vehicle. But it started, and it turned right, and it rolled down the road. Turner said, "It's lasted this long. Why should it stop now?"

It stopped a mile later, but on command, for break-fast at the first diner they saw, which was a family-run place on Long Beach Boulevard. It had all the good stuff, including a long-delayed omelet for Turner. She called Sergeant Leach from the payphone and told her to take care. Reacher watched the parking lot, and saw no one. No pursuit, no surveillance, no interest at all. So they got back on the road and headed north and west, looking for a 710 on-ramp, Reacher driving for the first time. The stately old boat suited him well. Its window tints were reassuring. They were nearly opaque. And the mechanical parts seemed up to their task. The car floated along, as if the road surface was just a vague rumor, somewhere far, far away.

Turner said, "What are you going to do if you see them?"

Reacher said, "Who?"

"Your daughter and her mother."

"You mean what am I going to say?"

"No, I mean from a distance, the very first time you lay eyes on them."

"I don't see how I would recognize them."

"Suppose you did."

"Then I'm going to look for the trap."

"Correct," Turner said. "They're bait, until proven otherwise. The MPs and the FBI will be there for sure. It's a known destination. Every single person you see could be undercover. So proceed accordingly."

"Yes, ma'am."

"Between here and North Hollywood the danger doubles with every mile. We're heading straight for the center of the inferno."

"Is this a pre-action briefing?"

"I'm your CO. I'm obliged to give one."

"You're preaching to the choir."

"You might recognize them, you know."

"Daughters don't necessarily resemble their fathers."

"I meant you might remember the mother."

Juliet called Romeo, because some responsibilities were his, and he said, "I have some very bad news."

Romeo said, "Does it relate in any way to Baldacci using his credit card at a car rental called Cool Al's?"

"What kind of Al's?"

"It's a West Coast thing. What happened?"

"Reacher got to them on the plane. He put them out of action and stole their wallets."

"On the plane?"

"He broke Lozano's fingers and Baldacci's arms and no one noticed."

"That's not possible."

"Apparently it is. One against two, on an airplane, with a hundred witnesses. It's a blatant humiliation. And now he's renting cars on our dime? Who does this guy think he is?"

Reacher thought he was a bad driver. At first he had meant it as a safety-first subterfuge, rightly assuming it would remind him to concentrate, but then he had learned it was true. His spatial awareness and his reaction times were all based on a human scale, not a highway scale. They were up close and personal. Animal, not machine. Maybe Turner was right. Maybe he was feral. Not that he was a terrible driver. Just worse than the average driver. But not worse than the average I-710 driver, on that particular morning, on the section known as the Long Beach Freeway. People were eating, and drinking, and shaving, and brushing their hair, and applying makeup, and filing nails, and filing papers, and reading, and texting, and surfing, and holding long conversations on cell phones, some of which were ending in screams, and some of which

were ending in tears. In the midst of it all Reacher
tried to hold his speed and his line, while watching
the drift and the wobble up ahead, and calculating
which way he should swerve if he had to.

He said, "We should stop and call Captain Edmonds. I want to know if she can get what we need."

"Keep it on the back burner," Turner said.

"I would if I could. But they won't let us. Their
other two guys might have been on that flight to Orange County. Or else on the next Long Beach departure. Either way they're only an hour or two behind
us."

"Knowing what Edmonds can or can't get won't
help us with them."

"It's tactically crucial," Reacher said. "Like in the
field manual. We have to assess whether they need to
retain unimpaired cognitive function for future inter-
rogation."

"That's not in the field manual."

"Maybe they cleaned it up."

"You mean if Edmonds has failed, you'll keep the
two guys alive so you can beat it out of them?"

"I wouldn't beat it out of them. I would ask them
nicely, like I did with the Big Dog. But if I know I
don't need to ask them anything, then I can let nature
take its course beforehand."

"What course will that be?"

"The future's not ours to see. But something uncomplicated, probably."

"Reacher, you're on the way to see your daughter."

"And I'd like to live long enough to get there. We
can't do a front burner and a back burner thing. Not

on this. We have to do two front burners. Ma'am. Respectfully submitted."

Turner said, "OK. But we'll buy a phone, so we don't have to keep on stopping. In fact we'll buy two phones. One each. Pre-paid, for cash. And a street map."

Which they did about a mile later, by coming off the freeway into a dense retail strip anchored by a chain pharmacy, which carried pre-paid cell phones, and maps, and whose registers accepted cash along with every other form of payment known to man. They put the map in the car, and stored each other's numbers in their phones, and then Reacher leaned on the Range Rover's warm flank and dialed Edmonds' cell.

She said, "I made the application at start of business today."

"And?"

"So far there have been no motions to deny."

"How soon would you expect them?"

"Instantly. Or sooner."

"So that's good."

"Yes, it is."

"So how long?"

"Later today, or early tomorrow."

"Got a pen?"

"And paper."

"I want you to check Peter Paul Lozano and Ronald David Baldacci with HRC."

"Who are they?"

"I don't know. That's why I want you to check."

"Relevant to anything in particular?"

"To being on the right side of history."

"I heard something you should know."

"As in?"

"Detective Podolski found your clothes in the land-fill. They've been tested."

"And?"

"The blood didn't match."

"Should I hold my breath waiting for an apology from Major Sullivan?"

"She's coming around. She was very touched you left her an IOU."

"Is the Metro PD dropping out now?"

"No. You fled after a lawful police challenge."

"That's not allowed anymore?"

"I'll do my best with Lozano and Baldacci."

"Thank you," Reacher said.

And then they got back on the freeway and headed north, just one of ten thousand moving vehicles winking in the sun.

Romeo called Juliet and said, "I spoke to the gentleman known as Cool Al directly, on a pretext, and he tells us they're in a twenty-year-old black Range Rover."

Juliet said, "That's good to know."

"Not the fastest car on the planet. Not that any would be fast enough. I put our boys on a helicopter. Orange County to Burbank. They'll be in position at least an hour ahead of time."

"Who paid for it?"

"Not the army," Romeo said. "Don't worry."

"Did you cancel Baldacci's credit card? Lozano's, too, I suppose."

"I can't. Those are personal cards. They have to do it themselves, as soon as they get out of the hospital. Until then we'll have to reimburse them, as always."

"This thing is costing us a fortune."

"Little acorns, my friend."

"Not so little."

"Nearly over. Then it's back to business as usual."

Reacher kept on dodging the eaters, and the drinkers, and the shavers, and the hair stylists, and the makeup artists, and the nail filers, and the file filers, and the readers, and the texters, and the surfers, and the screamers, and the criers, and he made it as far as East Los Angeles, where he took the Santa Ana Freeway, up to the 101 in Echo Park. Then it was a long slow grind, northwest through the hills, past names he still found glamorous, like Santa Monica Boulevard, and Sunset Boulevard, and the Hollywood Bowl. And then his telephone rang. He answered it and said, "I'm driving one-handed on the 101 with the Hollywood sign on my right, and I'm talking on my phone. Finally I feel like I belong."

Edmonds said, "Got a pen and paper?"

"No."

"Then listen carefully. Peter Paul Lozano and Ronald David Baldacci are active duty soldiers currently long-term deployed with a logistics battalion out of Fort Bragg, North Carolina. They're assigned to a company trained for the infiltration and exfiltration of sensitive items into and out of Afghanistan, which at the moment, of course, is all exfiltration, because of the drawdown, which is also keeping them very busy. Their fitness reports are currently above average. That's all I know."

Which information Reacher relayed to Turner, after hanging up, and Turner said, "There you go. Stuff that should be making it home isn't."

Reacher said nothing.

"You don't agree?"

He said, "I'm just trying to picture it. All these sensitive items, coming out of caves or wherever, and most of them getting loaded up for Fayetteville, but some of them getting dumped in the back of ratty old pick-up trucks with weird license plates, which then immediately drive off into the mountains. Maybe the trucks were full of cash on the inward journey. Maybe it's a cash-on-delivery business. Is that what you're thinking?"

"More or less."

"Me too. A fishbowl. A lot of stress and uncertainty. And visibility. And risk of betrayal. That's where they learn who to count on. Because everything is against them, even the roads. How sensitive are these things? Are they OK in the back of a ratty old pick-up truck with a weird license plate?"

"What's your point?"

"All the action is in Afghanistan. But our guys are at Fort Bragg."

"Maybe they're just back from Afghanistan."

"I don't think so," Reacher said. "I noticed the first minute I saw the first two. I figured neither one of them had been in the Middle East recently. They had no sunburn, no squint lines, and no stress and strain in their eyes. They're homebodies. But they're also the A team. So why keep your A team in North Carolina when all your action is in Afghanistan?"

"Typically these people have an A team on each end."

"But there is only one end. Stuff comes out of the caves and goes straight into the ratty old pick-up trucks with the weird license plates. It never gets anywhere near Fort Bragg or North Carolina."

"Then maybe I'm wrong. Maybe they're selling it in America, not Afghanistan. That would need an A team at Bragg, to siphon it off."

"But I don't think that's happening either," Reacher said. "Because small arms is all they could sell, realistically. We'd notice anything heavier. And to sell enough small arms to make the money they seem to be making would flood the market. And the market isn't flooded. Or you would have heard about it. Someone would have dropped a dime if there was a torrent of military stuff for sale. Domestic manufacturers, probably, getting squeezed out. The message would have gotten to your desk eventually. That's what the 110th is for."

"So what are they doing?"

"I have no idea."

Reacher remembered all the pertinent data from Candice Dayton's affidavit, including her lawyer's name, and his office address. Turner had found the right block on the street map, and her left thumbnail was resting on it, and her right index finger was tracing their progress, and her two hands were getting very close together. They crossed the Ventura Freeway, and she said, "Keep on going until Victory Boulevard. It should be signposted for the Burbank airport. Then we'll drop down from the north. I imagine most of their focus will be to the south. We'll be on their blind side."

Victory Boulevard turned out to be the next exit. Then they made a right on Lankershim, and tracked back south and east, exactly parallel with the freeway they had left minutes before.

"Now pull over," Turner said. "From here on in we go super-cautious."

Chapter 48

Reacher parked in the mouth of a cross street, and they gazed south together, at the blocks north of the Ventura Freeway, which were a bustling A–Z catalog of American commercial activity, from medium size on down through small and all the way to supertiny, with retail enterprises, and wholesale enterprises, and service enterprises, some of them durable, some of them wildly optimistic, some of them up-and-coming, some of them fading fast, some of them familiar and ubiquitous. A visitor from outer space would conclude that acrylic nails were just as important as eight-by-four boards.

Turner still had the map open, and she said, "He's on Vineland Avenue, two blocks north of the freeway. So make a left on Burbank Boulevard, and then Vineland is a right, and then it's a straight shot. No one knows this car, but we can't afford to drive by more than two times."

So Reacher set off again, and made the turns, and

drove Vineland like anyone else, not slow and peering, not fast and aggressive, just another anonymous vehicle rolling through the sunny morning. Turner said, "He's coming up, on the right side, next block. I see a parking lot out front."

Which Reacher saw, too. But it was a shared lot, not the lawyer's own. Because the right side of the block was all one long low building, with a shake roof and a covered walkway in front, with the exterior walls painted what Reacher thought of as a unique Valley shade of beige, like flesh-colored makeup from the movies. The building was divided along its length, into six separate enterprises, including a wig shop, and a crystal shop, and a geriatric supplier, and a coffee shop, and a Se Habla Espanol tax preparer, with Candice Dayton's lawyer more or less right in the center of the row, between the magic crystals and the electric wheelchairs. The parking lot was about eight slots deep, and it ran the whole width of the building's facade, serving all the stores together. Reacher guessed any customer was entitled to park in any spot.

The lot was about half full, with most of the cars at first glance entirely legitimate, most of them clean and bright under the relentless sun, some of them parked at bad angles, as if their drivers had ducked inside just long enough for a simple errand. Reacher had given much thought to what kind of a car two people could live in, and he had concluded that an old-fashioned wagon or a modern SUV would be the minimum requirement, with a fold-flat rear bench and enough unimpeded length between the front seats and the tailgate to fit a mattress. Black glass to the sides and the rear would be an advantage. An old Buick Road-master or a new Chevy Suburban would fit the bill, except that anyone planning to live in a new Chevy Suburban would surely see an advantage in selling it and buying an old Buick Roadmaster, and keeping the change. So mostly he scanned for old wagons, maybe dusty, maybe on soft tires, settled somehow, as if parked for a long time.

But he saw no such vehicles. Most were entirely normal, and three or four of them were new enough and bland enough to be airport rentals, which is what Espin and the 75th MP would be using, and two or three of them were weird enough to be FBI seizures, reissued for use as unmarked stake-out cars. Shadows and the glare of the sun and window tints made it hard to be sure whether any were occupied, or not.

They drove on, same speed, same trajectory, and they got on the freeway again, because Reacher felt a sudden U-turn or other atypical choice of direction would stand out, and they drove around the same long slow rectangle, and they came down Lankershim for the second time, and they parked in the mouth of the same cross street again, feeling comfortably remote and invisible from the south.

"Want to see it again?" Turner asked.

"Don't need to," Reacher said.

"So what next?"

"They could be anywhere. We don't know what they look like, or what car they've got. So there's no point driving around. We need to get a precise location from the lawyer. If the lawyer even knows, day to day."

"Sure, but how?"

"I could call, or I could get Edmonds to call for me, but the lawyer is going to say all correspondence should come to the office, and all meetings should be held at the office. He can't afford to give her location to a party as involved as I'm supposed to be. He would have to assume any contact I had would end up either creepy or violent. Basic professional responsibility. He could get sued for millions of dollars."

"So what are you going to do?"

"I'm going to do what guys do when they have nothing better going on."

"Which is what?"

"I'm going to call a hooker."

They backed up and headed north again, and they found a hamburger restaurant, where they drank coffee and where Reacher studied certain entries in a Yellow Pages borrowed from the owner, and then they got back on the road again, as far as a motel they saw next to one of the Burbank airport's long-term parking lots. They didn't check in. They stayed in the car, and Reacher dialed a number he had memorized. The call was answered by a woman with a foreign accent. She sounded middle-aged, and sleepy.

Reacher asked her, "Who's your top-rated American girl?"

The foreign woman said, "Emily."

"How much?"

"A thousand an hour."

"Is she available now?"

"Of course."

"Does she take credit cards?"

"Yes, but then she's twelve hundred an hour."

Reacher said nothing.

The foreign woman said, "She can be with you in less than thirty minutes, and she's worth every penny. How would you like her to dress?"

"Like a grade school teacher," Reacher said. "About a year out of college."

"Girl next door? That's always a popular look."

Reacher gave his name as Pete Lozano, and he gave the name and the address of the motel behind him.

"Is that next to the airport parking lot?" the foreign woman asked.

"Yes," Reacher said.

"We use it a lot. Emily will have no trouble finding it."

Reacher clicked off the call, and they got comfortable, and they waited, not talking, doing nothing at all but looking ahead through the windshield.

After ten minutes Turner said, "You OK?"

Reacher said, "Not really."

"Why not?"

"I'm sitting here staring at fourteen-year-old girls. I feel like a pervert."

"Recognize any?"

"Not yet."

Altogether they waited more than thirty-five minutes, and then Reacher's phone rang. Not the foreign woman calling back with an excuse for Emily's late-ness, but Captain Edmonds calling back with what she announced as front-page news. Reacher tilted the phone and Turner put her head close to listen. Edmonds said, "I got the full jacket on A.M. 3435. It came through five minutes ago. Not without a little hustle on my part, I might add."

Reacher said, "And?"

"No, really, you're most welcome, major. Absolutely my pleasure. I don't mind risking my entire career by entering in where JAG captains should fear to tread."

"OK, thank you. I should have said that first. I'm sorry."

"Some things you need to understand. We've been in Afghanistan more than ten years now, and in that context 3435 is a relatively low number. Currently we're well over a hundred thousand. Which means the data on this man were created some time ago. About seven years ago, I think, as far as I can tell. And there have been no significant updates. Nothing beyond the routine minimum. Because this is a fairly ordinary guy. Boring, even. At first glance he's a meaningless peasant."

"What's his name?"

"Emal Gholam Zadran. He's now forty-two years old, and he's the youngest of five Zadran brothers, all of them still alive. He seems to be the black sheep of the family, widely regarded as disreputable. The elder brothers are all fine upstanding poppy growers, working the family farm, like their ancestors did for a thousand years before them, very traditional, small time and modest. But young Emal didn't want to settle for that. He tried his hand at a number of things, and failed at them all. His brothers forgave him, and took him back, and as far as anyone knows he lives near them in the hills, does absolutely nothing productive, and keeps himself to himself."

"What was he written up for seven years ago?"

"One of the things he tried out, and failed at."

"Which was?"

"Nothing was proven, or we'd have shot him."

"What wasn't proven?"

"The story is he set up as an entrepreneur. He was buying hand grenades from the 10th Mountain Division and selling them to the Taliban."

"How much did he get for them?"

"It doesn't say."

"Not proven?"

"They tried their best."

"Why didn't they shoot him anyway?"

"Reacher, you're talking to an army lawyer here. Nothing was proven, and we're the United States of America."

"Suppose I wasn't talking to an army lawyer."

"Then I would say nothing was proven, and right then we were probably kissing Afghan butt and hoping they would set up a civilian government of their own at some point in the not-too-distant future, so we could get the hell out of there, and in that atmosphere shooting indigenous individuals against which nothing had been proven, even by our own hair-trigger military justice system, would have been regarded as severely counterproductive. Otherwise I'm sure they would have shot him anyway."

"You're pretty smart," Reacher said. "For an army lawyer."

And then he clicked off, because he was watching a kid who had gotten out of a cab and was walking into the motel driveway. She was luminous. She was young and blonde, and fresh and energetic, and somehow earnest, as if she was determined to use all the many years ahead doing nothing but good in the world. She looked like a grade school teacher, about a year out of college.

Chapter 49

The kid walked past the motel office, and then she stopped, as if she didn't know where to go. She had a name but no room number. Turner buzzed her window down and called out, "Are you Emily?"

Which was something she and Reacher had rehearsed. No question it was weird to be approached in a motel parking lot by a woman in a car, ahead of what was clearly going to be a bizarre threesome. But a similar approach by a man would have been weirder still. So Turner got to ask the question, which the kid answered by saying, "Yes, I'm Emily."

Turner said, "We're your clients."

"I'm sorry. They didn't tell me. It's more money for couples."

"You've probably heard this before, or not, possibly, but all we want to do is talk. We'll give you two thousand dollars for an hour of your time. Clothes on throughout, all three of us."

The kid came nearer, but not too close, and she

lined herself up with the open window, and she stooped an inch, and she looked in and said, "What exactly is this about?"

Reacher said, "An acting job."

They talked out in the open, to keep it unthreatening, Reacher and Turner leaning on the side of the car, with Emily completing the triangle four feet away, where she was free to turn and run. But she didn't. She ran Lozano's Amex through a slot in her iPhone, and as soon as she saw an authorization number she said, "I don't do porn."

Reacher said, "No porn."

"Then what kind of acting job?"

"Are you an actor?"

"I'm a call girl."

"Were you an actor first?"

"I was an intending actor."

"Do you do role-play?"

"I thought that's what I was doing today. The naive young idealist, prepared very reluctantly to do whatever it takes to get extra funding for her school. Or possibly I want to borrow a lawnmower from one of the PTA dads. But normally it's about interviewing for a job. How can I show I'm really committed to the company?"

"In other words, you're acting."

"All the time. Including now."

"I need you to go see a law firm receptionist and act your way into her good books." Reacher told her what he wanted. She showed no curiosity as to why. He said, "If there's a choice, pick a motherly type. She'll be sympathetic. This is about a struggling mother getting some help. Tell her Ms. Dayton is a friend of your aunt, and she loaned you some money when you were in college, and it got you out of a hole, and now you can repay the favor. And you want to see her again anyway. Something like that. You can write your own script. But the receptionist is not supposed to give up the location. In fact she's prohibited from doing so. So this is your Oscar moment."

"Who gets hurt here?"

"No one gets hurt. The opposite."

"For two thousand dollars? I never heard of that before."

"If she's for real, she gets helped. If she's not for real, I don't get hurt. It's all good."

Emily said, "I don't know if I want to do it."

"You took our money."

"For an hour of my time. I'm happy to stand here and talk. Or we could get in the car. I'll get naked if you like. That's what usually happens."

"How about an extra five hundred in cash? As a tip. When you get back."

"How about seven hundred?"

"Six."

Emily said, "And the Oscar goes to, Emily."

She wouldn't let them drive her. Smart girl. Words were cheap. The long preamble could have been nothing but a hot air fantasy, ahead of her unclothed body being found dead in a ditch three days later. So they gave her the address and twenty bucks and she caught a cab instead. They watched it out of sight, and then they turned back and got in the Range Rover and waited.

Turner said, "Man up, Reacher. A.M. 3435 is Emal Zadran, who has a documented history of buying and selling United States ordnance in the hills of the tribal areas. Whereas Peter Lozano and Ronald Baldacci have a documented history of being part of a company tasked to get that very same United States ordnance in and out of those very same hills. Is that deafening noise I hear the sound of the pieces falling into place?"

"He was buying and selling U.S. ordnance in the hills seven years ago."

"After which he fell off the radar. By getting better at it. He moved right up to the top of the tree. Now he's the top boy and the go-to guy. He's making a fortune for somebody. He has to be. Why else would they go to such lengths to hide him?"

"You're probably right."

"I need your serious input here. Not mindless agreement. You're my executive officer."

"Is that a promotion?"

"Just new orders."

"I mean it, you could be right. The informer called him a tribal elder. Which strikes me as a status-based label. Like an honorific. And a black sheep who sits around all day doing nothing productive wouldn't be thought of as a person of status. More likely the village idiot. Certainly he wouldn't be honored. So old Emal is doing something for somebody. And my only objection was having a team on standby in North Carolina, when all the action is in Afghanistan. But maybe there's a legitimate role for them. Because if what you think is true, then there's a lot of money coming home. Wagonloads, probably. A big, physical quantity. So yes, they need a team in North Carolina. Just not to handle weapons. To handle the money."

Romeo called Juliet and said, "It's getting worse."

Juliet said, "How could it?"

"They just used Lozano's Amex. Two thousand dollars on an entertainer. Do you know what that means?"

"They're bored?"

"There's only one kind of entertainer who carries her own card reader, and that's a prostitute. They're taunting us. They'd be giving it to homeless people, if homeless people had card readers on their phones. Or phones at all, I suppose."

"Which they don't."

"And Reacher's lawyer got Zadran's full jacket, about an hour ago. So it's out there now."

"You worry too much."

"It's an obvious connection. It won't take a genius to work it out."

"Or maybe you worry too soon," Juliet said. "You haven't heard the good news yet."

"Is there any?"

"Our boys just saw them drive past the lawyer's office. In a twenty-year-old Range Rover, black. Hard to be sure, because it had dark windows, but the strong impression was there were two people inside, one large and one small."

"When was this?"

"Less than an hour ago."

"Just once?"

"So far. Reconnaissance, obviously."

"Is there much activity there?"

"It's a strip mall. It's like a Fourth of July parade."

"Where did they go after they cruised by?"

"They took the freeway. Probably looped around. They're probably holed up a few blocks to the north."

"Anything we can do?"

"Yes, I think there is. They were super-cautious around that office. They must know the MPs and the FBI are all over it. And there's nothing to be learned there. Not for them. It would be the worst kind of malpractice. So I don't think they'll go near that office again. In which case guarding it is a waste of personnel. We can't miss them there, because they won't go there. Simple as that. Therefore our boys would be better used elsewhere. Possibly in a more proactive role. Just a suggestion."

"I agree," Romeo said. "Turn them loose."

Reacher and Turner passed the time by trying to figure what kind of ordnance would sell for a lot of money and fit in the back of a pick-up truck. Which was frustrating, because the two categories tended to be mutually exclusive. MOABs were sinister finned pear-shaped cylinders thirty feet long and four feet wide. Drones were worth thirty-seven million dollars a pop, but had a wingspan greater than sixty feet. And without the joystick controls they were just lumps of

dumb metal. And the joystick controls were all in
Texas or Florida. Conversely rifles and handguns and
hand grenades weren't worth much. A Beretta M9
was about six hundred bucks in a store. Maybe four
hundred used, on the street, or in the hills, less overhead and expenses, which meant it would take three
or four hundred sales just to cover the hundred grand
risked in the Cayman Islands. And even the army
would notice if it was losing handguns by the thousand.

They got nowhere.

And then Emily came back.

Chapter 50

Emily got out of a cab, just like the first time, still in character, all radiant and naive, and she hustled over and stood where she had before, about five feet from Turner's window. Turner buzzed the glass down, and Emily said, "I felt bad doing that."

"Why?" Reacher said.

"She was a nice woman. I manipulated her."

"Successfully?"

"I got the location."

"Where is it?"

"You owe me six hundred bucks."

"Not technically. It's a tip, which means it's a gift outside of the main contract. There's no element of owing."

"Are you trying to get out of it now?"

"No, I'm just naturally pedantic."

"Whichever, I still need six hundred bucks."

Which Ronald Baldacci paid, from the plank of twenties in his wallet. Reacher passed it to Turner, who passed it out the window to Emily, who glanced around and said, "This looks like a drug deal."

"What's the location?" Reacher asked.

She gave a street address, complete with a house number.

Reacher said, "What is that? A vacant lot? A business with its own parking?"

"I don't know."

"What was the mood in the office?"

"Very busy. I don't think Ms. Dayton is high on their list of priorities."

"OK, thank you, Emily," Reacher said. "It was nice to meet you. Have a great day."

"That's it?"

"What else is there?"

"Aren't you going to ask what a nice girl like me is doing in a job like this? Aren't you going to give me advice for the future?"

"No," Reacher said. "No one should listen to my advice. And you seem to be doing fine anyway. A thousand bucks an hour ain't bad. I know people who get screwed for twenty."

"Who?"

"People who wear uniforms, mostly."

Turner's map showed the new location to be south of the Ventura Freeway, in a neighborhood without a name. Not really Universal City, not really West Toluca Lake, definitely not Griffith Park, and too far south to be North Hollywood. But Reacher figured it was the right kind of place. It would have a high turnover of people, all coming and going and incurious, and it would have ventures and operations starting up and shutting down. Therefore it would have empty buildings, and it would have staff-only lots in front of failed businesses. Best way to get there was south on Vineland again, past the law office, across the Ventura Freeway, and then the neighborhood lay waiting on the right.

Turner said, "We have to assume the MPs and the FBI have this same information."

"I'm sure they do," Reacher said. "So we'll do it the same way we did the law office."

"One pass."

"Which might be the second pass for some of them, because I'm sure they're rotating back and forth. Between there and the law office, I mean. They can't let either scene get too static."

"What if it's a little alley, or a one-way street?"

"Then we'll abort. We'll find some other way."

"And best case, all we do is eyeball it. No meet and greet. We need a whole lot of long-range surveillance before we even think about that."

"Understood."

"Even if the cutest fourteen-year-old in the world runs out waving a home-made banner that says Welcome Home Daddy. Because it might be the wrong fourteen-year-old, with a different daddy."

"Understood," Reacher said again.

"Say it."

"No meet and greet," Reacher said.

"So let's go."

* * *

They didn't use Vineland Avenue. They figured rolling past the law office again would turn one pass into two, for some of the watchers, for no productive reason at all, and then the two could become three, if the rotation was timed just wrong. And three times was not a charm. Most people picked up on things the third time around. That was Reacher's experience. Even if they didn't know they were noticing. A stumble on a word while talking to a friend? You just saw the same guy for the third time, in the corner of your eye. Or the same car, or the same flower truck, or the same coat or dog or shoes or walk.

So they looped clockwise, east first, and then south, and they crossed the freeway a little to the right of a straight line. Then they pulled over. The target neighborhood was ahead on the right. It was a low-rise warren with concrete curbs and dry grass shoulders, with tarred poles carrying dozens of wires, some of them as thick as Reacher's wrist, and behind them were small buildings, some of them bungalows, some of them garden apartments, some of them stores or bodegas. There was one nail salon and one pick-up truck clearly visible. There were basketball hoops and ice hockey goals and satellite dishes as big as hot tubs, and parked cars everywhere.

"Not good," Turner said.

Reacher nodded, because it wasn't. It was tight-packed and close-quarters, and rolling through would mean stopping and starting and maneuvering around one obstacle after another. Walking speed would be a luxury.

He said, "You're the CO."

She said, "You're the XO."

"I say go for it. But it's your decision."

"Why do you say go for it?"

"The negatives look bad, but they're actually positives. Things could work out in our favor. The MPs and the FBI don't know what we're driving. As far as they're concerned, this is just an old truck with dark windows. They're not looking for it."

"But the two guys from the dented car might be. They're getting good intelligence. Worst case, someone saw the credit card and knows what we're driving."

"Doesn't matter," Reacher said. "They can't do anything to us. Not here. Not in front of government witnesses. They must know the MPs and the FBI are right there with them. It's a perfect Catch-22. They'll just have to sit there and take it."

"They might follow us. The MPs and the FBI wouldn't see anything wrong with that. Just another car leaving the neighborhood."

"I agree. But like I said. That would be things working out in our favor. That would be two birds with one stone. We eyeball the location, and we lure the guys out to a place of our choosing. All in all, I would call that a good day's work. Speaking as an XO, that is. But it's your decision. That's why you get the big bucks. Almost as many as some high school teachers."

Turner said nothing.

Reacher said, "Two front burners, remember."

Turner said, "OK, go for it."

They checked the map and Reacher rehearsed the turns. A right, a left, a right, and that was her street, apparently. Her lot number looked to be about half-way between one end and the other. Turner said, "Remember, eyeballs only. No meet and greet."

"Got it," Reacher said.

"No exceptions."

"Yes, ma'am." He eased off the curb and rolled down to the first turn and swung the wheel, and then he was in the neighborhood. The first street was a mess. Mixed-use zoning, with a bakery truck stopped outside a grocery, and a kid's bike dumped in the gutter, and a car with no wheels up on blocks. The second street was better. It was no wider, but it was straight and less cluttered. The tone of the neighborhood rose through its first fifty yards. There were little houses on the left and the right. Not prosperous, but solid. Some had new roofs, and some had painted stucco, and some had parched plants in concrete tubs. Regular people, doing their best, making ends meet.

Then came the final right turn, and the tone rose some more. But not to dizzying heights. Reacher saw a long straight street, with the 101 plainly visible at the far end, behind hurricane fencing. The street had tract housing on both sides, built for GIs in the late 1940s, and still there more than sixty years later. The houses were all cared for, but to varying degrees, some of them well maintained, some of them refurbished, and some of them extended, but others more marginal. Most had cars on their driveways, and most had extra cars on the curb. Overall so many it was effectively a one-lane road.

Slow, and awkward.

Turner said, "FBI ahead on the right, for sure."

Reacher nodded and said nothing. One of the cars on the curb was a Chevy Malibu, about sixty feet away, plain silver, base specification, with plastic where there should have been chrome, with two stubby antennas glued to the back glass, with a guy behind the wheel wearing a white collared shirt. An unmarked car, but no real attempt at deception. Therefore possibly a supervisor, just stopping by for a moment, to check on morale and spread good cheer. To the guy he was parked right behind, maybe.

Reacher said, "Check out the thing in front of him."

It was a civilian Hummer H2, wide, tall, gigantic, all waxed black paint and chrome accents, with huge wheels and thin tires, like black rubber bands.

"So eight years ago," Turner said. A legal seizure, possibly, because of coke in the door pocket, or because it was charged to a scam business, or it had carried stolen goods in the back, first confiscated and then reissued as an undercover surveillance vehicle, slightly tone-deaf in terms of credibility, like the government usually was.

And sixty feet in front of the Hummer was a small white compact, parked on the other curb, facing toward them, clean and bland, barely used, not personalized in any way. An airport rental, almost certainly. The 75th MP. Some unfortunate guy, coach class to

LAX, and then a bare-bones government account with Hertz or Avis. The worst car on the lot, and no upgrade.

"See it?" Reacher asked.

Turner nodded beside him. "And now we know where the address is. Exactly halfway between the Hummer's front bumper and that thing's, I would say. Subtle, aren't they?"

"As always." Reacher had been checking house numbers, and the lot they were looking for was going to be on the left, about ninety feet ahead, if the government's triangulation was dead-on accurate. He said, "Do you see anyone else?"

"Hard to tell," Turner said. "Any one of these cars could have people in it."

"Let's hope so," Reacher said. "Two people in particular."

He rolled on, slow and careful, giving himself a margin of error. The old truck's steering was a little vague and sloppy. Plus or minus six inches was all it was good for. He passed the silver Malibu, and glanced down to his right. The white collared shirt had a necktie down the front. FBI for sure. Probably the only necktie inside a square mile. Then next up was the Hummer. It had a fair-haired white guy behind the wheel. With a whitewall crew cut, high and tight. Probably the first whitewall crew cut ever seen inside a pimped-out H2. Government. Tone deaf.

Then Reacher glanced to his left, and started tracking the numbers. He wasn't sure what he was expecting. A gap of some kind, basically. Something different from the places before and after. Something boarded up and foreclosed, or burned down and bulldozed, or never built in the first place. With a big old car parked back in the shadow of its neighbors. Maybe a Buick Roadmaster.

But the address Emily had gotten was a house like all the others. Not different from the places before or after, not boarded up by the bank, and not burned and leveled. Just a regular house, on a regular lot. It had a car in its driveway, but it wasn't a Buick Road-master. It was a two-door coupe, imported, sun-faded red, fairly old, and even smaller than the MP's white compact. Therefore not big enough for two people to sleep in. Not even close. The house itself was an old one-story, extended upward, with a ground-floor window on the left, and a ground-floor window on the right, and a new attic window punched out directly above a blue front door.

And coming out the blue front door was a girl.

She could have been fourteen years old. Or fifteen.

She was blonde.

And she was tall.

Chapter 51

Turner said, "Don't stop," but Reacher braked anyway. He couldn't help it. The girl looped around the parked coupe and stepped out to the sidewalk. She was wearing a yellow T-shirt and a blue denim jean jacket, and big black baggy pants, and yellow tennis shoes on her feet, with no socks, and no laces. She was slender and long-limbed, all knees and elbows, and her hair was the color of summer straw. It was parted in the center, and wavy, and it came halfway down her back. Her face was unformed, like teenagers' faces are, but she had blue eyes, and cheekbones, and her mouth was set in a quizzical half-smile, as if her life was full of petty annoyances best tolerated with patience and goodwill.

She set off walking, west, away from them.

Turner said, "Eyes front, Reacher. Hit the gas and pass her and do not stop. Drive to the end of the road, right now. That's an order. If it's her, we'll confirm later, and we'll deal with it."

So Reacher sped up again, from walking pace to jogging, and they passed the girl just as she was passing the MP's white compact. She didn't seem to react to it in any way. Didn't seem to know it was there for her. She hadn't been told, presumably. Because what could they say? *Hi there, miss, we're here to arrest your father. Who you've never met. If he shows up, that is. Having just been told all about you.*

Reacher kept one eye on the mirror and watched her grow smaller. Then he paused at the T, and turned left, and looked at her one more time, and then he drove away, and she was lost to sight.

No one came after them. They pulled over a hundred yards later, but the street behind them stayed empty. Which theoretically was a minor disappointment. Not that Reacher really registered it as such. In his mind right then the two surviving guys from the dented car were on the backest of all back burners, on a stovetop about ten miles deep.

He said, "They told me she was living in a car."

"Maybe her mom got a new job. Or a new boyfriend."

"Did you see any surveillance opportunities?"

"Nothing obvious."

"Maybe we should join the crowd and park on the street. We'd be OK as long as we never got out of the car."

"We can do better than that," Turner said. She checked her map, and looked out through the Range Rover's windows, all around, craning her neck, searching for high ground or elevated vantage points. Of which there were plenty to the south, where the Hollywood Hills rose up in the smog, but they were too distant, and in any case the front of the house would be invisible from the south. In the end she pointed a little north of west, at an off-ramp in the tangle where the 134 met the 101. It was raised up high, and its curve seemed to cradle the whole neighborhood, as it swooped around from one freeway to the next. She said, "We could fake a breakdown, if that ramp has a shoulder. Overheating, or something. This car certainly looks the part. We could stay there for hours. The FBI doesn't do roadside assistance. If the LAPD stops for us, we'll say sure, we're about cooled down now, and we'll get on our way."

"Warrant Officer Espin will have seen it," Reacher said. "He'll have scoped out the terrain, surely. If he sees any kind of a parked vehicle up there, he'll investigate."

"OK, if anything other than a marked LAPD cruiser stops for us, we'll take off immediately, and if it's Espin we'll duke it out in the wilds of Burbank."

"We'll lose him well before Burbank. I bet they gave him a four-cylinder rental."

They wanted a pawn shop next, because they needed a quality item for a short spell of time, and fast, and unmemorably, and they were going to pay for it with a stolen credit card, so overall second hand was the better market. They used surface streets to West Hollywood, and picked one of many establishments, and Reacher said to the guy, "Let me see your best binoculars."

Of which there were many, mostly old. Which made sense. Reacher figured that back in his father's day binoculars were bought simply because binoculars were bought. Every family had a pair. And an encyclopedia. No one used either. Or the clockwork eight-millimeter camera, if the family was a colonel's or better. But they had to be provided. Part of a family man's sacred duty. But now all those family men were dead, and their adult children's houses were of finite capacity. So their stuff found itself stacked between the acoustic guitars and the college rings, still in the velvet-lined leather buckets it came in, and tagged with prices halfway between low and very.

They found a pair they liked, powerful but not too heavy, and adjustable enough to fit both their faces, and Baldacci paid, and they walked back to the car.

Turner said, "I think we should wait for dusk. Nothing will happen before then, anyway. Not if her mom has a new job. And we have a black car. Espin won't even see it in the dark. But the street itself should be lit up enough for binoculars."

"OK," Reacher said. "We should eat first, I guess. This could take hours. How long are you prepared to stay up there?"

"As long as it takes. As many times as it takes."

"Thank you."

"In all of my dating history, I don't know if this is the smartest thing I've ever done, or the dumbest."

* * *

They ate in West Hollywood, well and slowly and expensively, on Peter Paul Lozano's dime, and they let late afternoon turn into early evening, and as soon as the street lights were brighter than the sky they got back in the car and took Sunset Boulevard to the 101. Traffic was bad, as always, but the sky used the wasted minutes to get darker and darker, so that by the time they took the curving off-ramp the day had gone completely.

There was no official shoulder on the ramp, but there was more than a shoulder's width of painted chevrons on the right side, to define the traffic lane through the curve, so they pulled over as if their dashboard was lit up like a Christmas tree. Turner had the new old binoculars out and ready, and they rolled forward until she figured they had as good a view as they were going to get. Reacher shut the motor down. They were about three hundred yards from the blue front door, and about forty feet above it. Just like the field manual. A straight line, with elevation. More than satisfactory. Not bad at all. The house was quiet. The blue door was closed. The old red coupe was still on the driveway. The FBI Malibu had gone from the street, but the Hummer was still there, as was the small white compact sixty feet from it. The rest of the automotive roster had changed a little. Day shift workers were heading home, and night shift workers were heading out.

They took turns with the binoculars. Reacher twisted around in the driver's seat and rested his back on the door, and looked out beyond Turner next to him, through her open window. The optical image was dark and indistinct. No night-vision enhancement. But it was adequate. Behind him cars sped past, just feet away, a steady procession, all of them leaving the 101 and joining the 134. None of them stopped to help. They just rocked the old truck with their slipstreams, and sped onward, oblivious.

Romeo called Juliet and said, "They were just in West Hollywood. They bought something in a pawn shop, on Baldacci's card, and then they ate at a very expensive restaurant, on Lozano's."

Juliet said, "What would they want from a pawn shop?"

"Doesn't matter. The point is they were in West Hollywood, whiling away the hours, apparently aimlessly, which one assumes they wouldn't do if there were things still on their agenda, like determining Ms. Dayton's current location, for instance. So I think we should assume they have it now."

"How did they get it?"

"Doesn't matter how. What matters is what they're going to do next. Possibly they were in West Hollywood just hiding out until dark. In which case they're probably back at the house by now, about to begin a lengthy period of surveillance."

"Our boys aren't there anymore."

"Then get them back. Tell them to look at the neighborhood with a military eye and work out where a skilled team would be watching from. There can't be more than a handful of suitable vantage points. They won't be hunkered down in a neighbor's back yard, for instance. They're probably fairly distant. The field manual calls for a line of sight plus elevation. Upstairs in an empty building, perhaps, or a water tower, or a parking garage. Tell our boys to compile a list of possibilities, and then tell them to split up and investigate. More efficient that way. We need this done tonight."

"You can buy guns in a pawn shop."

"But they didn't. There's a waiting period. California has laws. And they only spent thirty dollars."

"On the credit card. There could have been a side deal in cash. Lozano and Baldacci had plenty with them on the plane."

"An illegal purchase? Then they wouldn't have stuck around to eat. Not in the same neighborhood. They'd have been too nervous. They'd have gone somewhere else. That's my sense. So assume they're still unarmed."

"I hope you're right about that," Juliet said. "It would make things easier."

Turner spent thirty minutes with the binoculars, and then she passed them back to Reacher, blinking and rubbing her eyes. He widened them out to fit, and adjusted the focus, which took a big turn of the wheel. Either he was half blind, or she was.

She said, "I want to call Sergeant Leach again. I want to know she's OK."

He said, "Give her my best." He half listened to Turner's end of the conversation while he watched what was happening three hundred yards away. Which was nothing much. The Hummer stayed where it was, and the small white compact stayed where it was. No one went in or out through the blue front door. Sergeant Leach was apparently OK. As was her cooperative friend Margaret Vega. At that point, at least. So far. The conversation was short. Turner said nothing explicit, but between the lines Leach seemed to be agreeing with her that the die was cast, and the only available options were win big or go home.

The blue door stayed closed. Most of the time Reacher kept the binoculars trained hard on it, but then for maybe four seconds out of every twenty he started a fragmented exploration of the neighborhood. He traced his way back down the street, and out through the elbow where they had come in, with the bakery truck outside the grocery, and the dumped bike, and the car with no wheels. Then came the main drag, which was Vineland Avenue, about as far south of the freeway as the law office was north.

He went back to the blue door, which stayed closed.

And then he traced his way down the street again, but went the other way at the far end, right instead of left, and he found an identical elbow, like a mirror image. The same kind of zoning, and the same kind of issues. And then the main drag again, still Vineland, but a further quarter mile south. Which made the neighborhood not quite a rectangle. It was taller on the right than the left. Like a pennant. Some ways above its top right corner was the freeway, and then the law office, and some ways below its bottom right corner was an old coach diner, all lit up and shiny.

Reacher knew which way he would walk.

He went back to the blue door, which stayed closed.

It stayed closed until a minute before eight o'clock. And then it opened, and she came out again, just the same as before. Same long-limbed stride, almost graceful, same hair, same shirt, same jacket, same shoes. Presumably no socks or laces, and possibly the same wry expression, but it was dark, and the optics had limits.

Just the same as before.

But she turned the other way.

She went east, not west. Away from the freeway interchange. Toward the main drag. No one went with her. No shadow, and no protection. Reacher pointed, and Turner nodded.

He said, "Do you think it's possible they didn't tell either one of them?"

She said, "Obviously they didn't tell the kid. They can't say, we found your daddy but decided to arrest him instead."

"Can they say that to the mother? She's not going to get much child support if they throw away the key."

"What's on your mind?"

"They didn't send anyone with her. Which they should have. If I can't get to her in the house, then I'll try to get to her when she leaves. That's obvious, surely. But no one is with her. The only logical reason is that they haven't told them, and they can't explain away four guys following them everywhere, so they don't follow them everywhere."

"Plus they're cheapskates. If they told them, they'd have to put a woman support officer in the house. Which would cost money."

"OK, so if mother and child are bait but don't know it, and they leave the house, then all Espin or anyone else can do is a long-distance tail, and an occasional pass in a vehicle."

"Agreed."

"But no one is moving and neither vehicle has started its engine."

"Maybe they wait until she's out of sight."

"Let's see if they do."

They didn't. The girl turned right at the far end of the street, and disappeared, but back at her house no one moved, and neither car started.

Turner said, "Maybe there's another team."

"Would you approve that budget?"

"Of course I would."

"Would they? If they won't even put a woman officer in the house?"

"OK, there's only one team and it's not moving. Laziness and complacency. Plus it must be hard to get a parking spot."

"They're not moving because they think I'm dumb enough to walk up the driveway and knock on the door."

Then a car drove in, all the way from the far end of the neighborhood, coming off Vineland, and coming through the elbow they had used before. Its lights swung right and left, and then it came down the street, head-on and blinding, past the Hummer, past the blue door, almost level with the small white compact, and then it stopped, and backed up fast, past the house again, past the Hummer, and all the way back to the last parking spot on the street, which was evidently much farther away than its driver desired. The car parallel-parked neatly and its headlights shut off, and two guys got out, far-off and indistinct, just moving shadows really, one maybe larger than the other.

The lizard brain stirred, and a billion years later Reacher leaned forward an inch.

Chapter 52

The binoculars were marginal at the distance, and the light was very low, so Reacher kept an open mind. On any given day there were nearly forty million people in California, and for two specific individuals to show up while observed by a third was an unlikely event.

But unlikely events happened from time to time, so Reacher kept his field of view tight on the two figures, and he goosed the focus as they walked, for the sharpest image. They walked in the street, not on the sidewalk, straight down the traffic lane, fast, side by side, getting closer all the time, Reacher getting surer all the time. They passed the Hummer again, and they stepped into a pool of light, and then Reacher was certain.

He was looking at the driver from the first night, and next to him was the big guy with the shaved head and the small ears.

They stopped right in front of the house, and they stood still, and then they turned back to face the way they had come, as if they were studying the far horizon, and then they began to rotate in place, slowly, counterclockwise, using small shuffling steps, occasionally pointing, always away from the house and upward.

Reacher said, "They're looking for us."

They continued to rotate, past the midpoint, and then they saw the right-hand end of the off-ramp for the first time. The guy with the ears seemed to understand immediately. His arm came up and he sketched the curve right to left, and then back again left to right, tracking the wide circumference, showing how it cradled the whole neighborhood, and then he pulled his palm back toward his chest, as if to say *it's like the front row of the dress circle up there, and this is the stage, right here,* and then he used the same palm to shade his eyes, and he stared at the ramp in detail, section by section, yard by yard, looking for the best angle, until finally he came to rest, as if staring straight into the binoculars from the wrong end.

Reacher said, "They've found us."

Turner checked the map and said, "They can't get here very quickly. Not with the way the roads go. They'd have to drop down to the Hollywood Bowl, on surface streets, and then come back up again, behind us on the 101. That's a very big square."

"The kid is out on her own."

"It's us they want."

"And it's her we want. They should stick with her. I would."

"They don't know where she went."

"It's not rocket science. Her mom's not home, and

she watched TV shows until the eight o'clock hour, and then she went out to get something to eat."

"They're not going to take her hostage."

"They beat Moorcroft half to death. And they're running out of time."

"So what do you want to do?"

Reacher didn't answer. He just dropped the binoculars in Turner's lap and started the car and jammed it in gear and glanced back over his shoulder. He gunned it off the chevrons and into the traffic lane, and he swooped around the curve, leaving the 101, joining the 134, merging with slow traffic, looking ahead for the first exit, which he figured would be very soon, and which he figured would be Vineland Avenue. And it was, with a choice of north or south. Reacher inched through the congestion, frustrated, and went south, along the taller edge of the neighborhood, past the first mixed-use elbow, past the second, and onward, a hundred yards, until he saw the coach diner ahead, all lit up and shiny.

And crossing Vineland toward it was the girl.

He slowed and let her pass fifty yards in front of him, and then he watched her as she stepped into the diner's lot. There was a gaggle of kids in one corner, maybe eight of them in total, boys and girls, just hanging out in the shadows and the night air, aimlessly, joking around, posturing and preening, the way kids do. The girl headed over toward them. Maybe she wasn't going to eat after all. Maybe she had eaten at home. Something from the freezer, perhaps, microwaved. And maybe this was her after-dinner social life. Maybe she had come out to a regular rendezvous, to join the crowd at their chosen spot, to hang out and have fun, all night long.

Which would be OK. There was safety in numbers.

She stepped up close to the other kids, and there were some deadpan comments, and some high fives, and some laughter, and a little horsing around. Reacher was running out of road, so he took a snap decision and pulled into the lot, and parked in the opposite corner. The girl was still talking. Her body language was relaxed. These were her friends. They liked her. That was clear. There was no awkwardness.

But then minutes later she inched away, her body language saying *I'm going inside now,* and no one moved to follow her, and she didn't look disappointed. Almost the opposite. She looked like she had enjoyed their company for sure, but now she was ready to enjoy her own. Equally for sure. As if it was all the same to her.

Turner said, "She's a loner."

Reacher said, "And tall."

"Doesn't necessarily mean anything."

"I know."

"We can't stay here."

"I want to go inside."

"No meet and greet. Not yet."

"I won't talk to her."

"You'll draw attention to her."

"Only if those guys see this car out front."

Turner said nothing. Reacher watched the girl pull the door and step inside. The diner was built in the traditional style, out of stainless steel, with folds and creases and triple accent lines like an old automobile, and small framed windows like an old railroad car, and neon letters configured in an Art Deco manner. It looked busy inside. The peak period, between the blue plate specials and the late-night coffee drinkers. Reacher knew all about diners. He knew their rhythms. He had spent hundreds of hours in them.

Turner said, "Observation only."

Reacher said, "Agreed."

"No contact."

"Agreed."

"OK, go. I'll hide the car somewhere and wait. Don't get in trouble."

"You either."

"Call me when you're done."

"Thank you," Reacher said. He climbed out and crossed the lot. He heard cars on Vineland, and a plane in the sky. He heard the group of kids, scuffling and talking and laughing. He heard the Range Rover drive away behind him. He paused a beat and took a breath.

Then he pulled the diner door, and he stepped inside.

The interior was built in the traditional style, too, just as much as the outside, with booths to the left and the right, and a full-width counter dead ahead, about six feet from the back wall, which had a pass-through slot to the kitchen, but was otherwise all made of mirror glass. The booths had vinyl benches and the counter had a long line of stools, all chrome and pastel colors, like 1950s convertibles, and the floor was covered with linoleum, and every other horizontal surface was covered with laminate, in pink or blue or pale yellow, with a pattern, like small pencil notations, that given the dated context made Reacher think of endless arcane equations involving the sound barrier, or the hydrogen bomb.

There was a stooped and gray-haired counter man behind the counter, and a blonde waitress about forty years old working the left side of the coach, and a brunette waitress about fifty years old working the right side, and they were all busy, because the place was more than three-quarters full. All the booths on the left were taken, some by people eating at the end of the work day, some by people eating ahead of a night out, one by a quartet of hipsters apparently intent on period authenticity. The right side of the coach had two booths free, and the counter showed nineteen backs and five gaps.

The girl was all the way over on the right, at the counter, on the last stool, owning it, like the place was a bar and she had been a regular patron for the last fifty years. She had silverware and a napkin in front of her, and a glass of water, but no food yet. Next to her was an empty space, and then came a guy hunched over a plate, and another, and another, with the next empty stool nine spots away. Reacher figured he would get a better look at her from one of the empty booths, but diners had an etiquette all their own, and lone customers taking up four-place booths at rush hour was frowned upon.

So Reacher stood in the doorway, unsure, and the blonde waitress from the left side of the coach took pity on him and detoured over, and she tried a welcoming smile, but she was tired and it didn't really work. It came out as a dull and uninterested gaze, nothing there at all, and she said, "Sit anywhere you like, and someone will be right with you." Then she bustled away again, and Reacher figured *anywhere you like* included four-person booths, so he turned to his right and took a step.

The girl was watching him in the mirror.

And she was watching him quite openly. Her eyes were locked on his, in the mirrored wall, via reflections and refractions and angles of incidence and all the other stuff taught in high school physics class. She didn't look away, even when he looked right back at her.

No contact, he had promised.

He moved on into the right side of the coach, and he took an empty booth one away from directly behind her. To see her best he put his shoulder against the window and his back to the rest of the room, which he didn't like, but he had no option. The brunette waitress showed up with a menu and a smile as wan as the blonde's, and she said, "Water?"

He said, "Coffee."

The girl was still looking at him in the mirror.

He wasn't hungry, because the meal Lozano had bought in West Hollywood had been a feast fit for a king. So he slid the menu aside. The brunette was not thrilled with his lack of an order. He got the feeling he wouldn't see her again anytime soon. No free refills for him.

The girl was still watching.

He tried the coffee. It was OK. The counter man brought the girl a plate, and she broke eye contact long enough to say something to him that made him smile. He had an embroidered patch on his uniform, with his name, which was Arthur. He said something back, and the girl smiled, and he moved away again.

Then the girl picked up her silverware and her napkin in one hand, and her plate in the other, and she slid off her stool, and she stepped over to Reacher's booth, and she said, "Why don't I join you?"

Chapter 53

The girl put her silverware down, and her napkin, and her plate, and then she ducked back to the
counter to retrieve her glass of water. She waved to
the guy called Arthur and pointed at the booth, as if
to say *I'm moving,* and then she came back with her
water and put it next to her plate, and she slid along
the vinyl bench, and she ended up directly opposite
Reacher. Up close she looked the same as she did from
a distance, but all the details were clearer. In particular her eyes, which seemed to work well with her
mouth, in terms of getting all quizzical.

He said, "Why would you want to join me?"

She said, "Why wouldn't I?"

"You don't know me."

"Are you dangerous?"

"I could be."

"Arthur keeps a Colt Python under the counter,
about opposite where you're sitting. And another one

at the other end. They're both loaded. With .357 Magnums. Out of eight-inch barrels."

"You eat here a lot?"

"Practically every meal, but the word would be *often*. Not *a lot*. *Lot* refers to quantity, and I prefer small portions."

Reacher said nothing.

"Sorry," she said. "I can't help it. I'm naturally pedantic."

He said, "Why did you want to join me?"

"Why did I see your car three times today?"

"When was the third time?"

"Technically it was the first time. I was at the lawyer's office."

"Why?"

"Curiosity."

"About what?"

"About why we see the same cars three times a day."

"We?"

"Those of us paying attention," she said. "Don't play dumb, mister. There's something going on in the neighborhood, and we would love to know what it is. And you look like you might tell us. If I asked you nicely."

"Why do you think I could tell you?"

"Because you're one of them, cruising around all day, snooping."

Reacher said, "What do you think is happening?"

"We know you're all over the lawyer's office. And we know you're all over my street. So we're guessing someone on my street is the lawyer's client, and they're in some shady business together."

"Who on your street?"

"That's the big question, isn't it? It depends on how much of a head fake you use with your parking places. We think you would want to be close to your target, but not right in front of it, because that would be too obvious. But how close? That's what we don't know. You could be watching a lot of different houses, if you go left and right a little ways, up and down the street."

Reacher said, "What's your name?"

"Remember that Colt Python?"

"Loaded."

"My name is Sam."

"Sam what?"

"Sam Dayton. What's your name?"

"Is that really all you know about the operation on your street?"

"Don't damn us with faint praise. I think we did very well to piece that much together. You're all very tight-lipped about it. Which is a great expression, isn't it? Tight-lipped? But the tell is the way you move your cars between the law office and where I live. I understand why you do it, but it gives away the connection."

"No one has talked to you about it?"

"Why would they?"

"Has your mom said anything?"

"She doesn't pay attention. She's very stressed."

"What about?"

"Everything."

"What about your dad?"

"I don't have one. I mean, obviously I must, biologically, but I've never met him."

"Brothers or sisters?"

"I don't have any."

Reacher said, "Who do you think we are?"

"Federal agents, obviously. Either DEA, ATF, or FBI. This is Los Angeles. It's always drugs or guns or money."

"How old are you?"

"Almost fifteen. You didn't tell me your name yet."

Reacher said, "Reacher," and watched her very carefully. But there was no reaction. No spark. No *aha!* moment. Or no *OMG!!* moment, which Reacher understood to be more likely with kids. His name meant nothing to her. Nothing at all. It hadn't been mentioned in her presence.

She said, "So will you tell me what's going on?"

Reacher said, "Your dinner is getting cold. That's what's going on. You should eat."

"Are you eating?"

"I already ate."

"So why come in?"

"For the decor."

"Arthur is very proud of it. Where are you from?"

"I move around."

"So you are a federal agent." And then she started eating some of her food, which Reacher bet himself was billed on the menu as *Mom's Amazing Meatloaf.* The smell of ground beef and ketchup was unmistakable. He knew all about diners. He had spent hundreds of hours in them, and he had eaten most of what they had to offer.

She said, "So am I right? Is it the lawyer and a client?"

"Partly," Reacher said. "But there's no shady business between them. It's more about a guy who might visit with one of them. Or both of them."

"A third party? With a beef?"

"Kind of."

"So it's going to be an ambush? You're waiting for the guy to show? You're going to bust him on my street? That would be very cool. Unless it happens at the law office. Can you choose? If you can, will you do it on my street? You should think about it anyway. The street would be safer. That little mall is busy. Is the guy dangerous?"

"Have you seen anyone around?"

"Only your own people. They sit in their cars and watch all day. Plus your mobile crews. The guy in the silver Malibu comes by a lot."

"A lot?"

"Frequently, I should say. Or often. And the two guys in the rental. And you two in the Range Rover. But I haven't seen a man on his own, looking dangerous."

"What two guys in a rental?"

"One of them has a funny-shaped head. And cropped ears."

"Cropped?"

"At first from a distance I thought they were just small. But up close you can see they've been cut. Like into tiny hexagons."

"When did you get up close with that guy?"

"This afternoon. He was on the sidewalk outside my house."

"Did he say anything?"

"Not a thing. But why would he? I'm not a lawyer or a client and I don't have a beef with anyone."

Reacher said, "I'm not authorized to tell you much, but those two guys are not with us. They're not ours, OK? In fact they might be a part of the problem. So stay away from them. And tell your friends."

The girl said, "Not so cool."

Then Reacher's phone rang. He was unaccustomed to carrying a phone, and at first he assumed it was someone else's. So he ignored it. But the girl stared at his pocket, until he pulled it out. Turner's stored number was on the screen.

He excused himself, and answered.

Turner was breathing hard.

She said, "I'm heading back, and I need you out front of the diner, right now."

Some kind of tight emotion in her voice.

So Reacher clicked off the call, and left Sam Dayton alone in the booth, and went outside, and hustled through the lot to the street. A minute later he saw headlights way to his left, spaced high and wide, coming toward him fast. The old Range Rover, out of the south, in a big hurry. Then its lights lit him up and it jammed to a hard stop right next to him and he yanked the door and slid inside.

He said, "What's up?"

Turner said, "A situation got a little out of hand."

"How bad?"

"I just shot a guy."

Chapter 54

Turner took the Ventura Freeway going west, and she said, "I figured the law office would be closed for the night by now, and probably the whole strip with it, and therefore I figured the watchers would be gone by now, too, so I went up to take a look around, because there are things we may need to know in the future, including what kind of locks the law office has, and what kind of alarm. Which, by the way, are both fairly basic. You could buy five minutes in there, if you had to. And then I looked at my map and saw how I could get to Mulholland Drive pretty easily, because I've always wanted to drive a car on Mulholland Drive, like a G-man in a movie, and I figured if the kid is in there with you for her dinner, then she's in there for at least thirty minutes more, which gives me time for a personal excursion, so off I went."

"And?" Reacher said, simply to keep her going. Shooting people was stressful, and stress was a complex thing. People reacted to it in all kinds of different ways. Some people bottled it up, and some talked it out. She was a talker, he figured.

She said, "I was followed."

"That was dumb," he said, because she didn't like mindless agreement.

"I spotted him early. There were lights behind him and I could see it was only one guy. A solo driver, and that was all. So I didn't think much of it. And lots of people like Mulholland Drive, so it didn't bother me he was going the same direction."

"So what did?"

"He was also going the same speed. Which is un-natural. Speed is a personal thing. And I'm pretty slow, most of the time. Usually people are bunching up behind me, or I'm getting passed by altogether. But this guy was just there, always. Like I was towing him on a rope. And I knew it wasn't the 75th MP or the FBI, because neither one knows what we're driving, so it had to be our other friends, except there was only one guy in the car, not two, which meant either it was neither one of them, or they've split up now and they're hunting solo, but whatever, it got old real quick, and the movies say Mulholland gets wild real quick, so I figured I better stop at the very first turn-out I saw, like a message, to tell him I had made him, which would then give him a choice, either accept defeat gracefully and keep on rolling down the road, or be a sore loser and stop and harass me in person."

"And he stopped?"

"He sure did. He was the third of the four in the dented car this morning. What you call the driver from the first night. They've split up and they're hunting solo."

"I'm glad it was him, and not the other one."

"He was bad enough."

"How bad?"

"Real bad."

"Bullshit," Reacher said. "He was a waste of food. He was the one I hit second. Which makes him worse than the one who just bought us dinner."

"Busted," Turner said. "It was like taking candy from a baby."

"What kind of taking?"

"He had a gun."

"That would level the playing field a little."

"It did, for about three-quarters of a second, and then he didn't have a gun anymore, which meant I did, and some voice in my head was screaming *threat threat threat center mass bang* and I blinked and found out I had gone and done it, right through the heart. The guy was dead before he hit the ground."

"And you need me right now for what?"

"Are you telling me you don't offer counseling?"

"Not a core strength."

"Fortunately I'm a professional soldier, and won't need counseling."

"Then how may I help you?"

"I need you to move the body. I can't lift it."

Mulholland looked exactly like the movies, but smaller. They drove in as cautious as G-men, prepared to stop if the coast was clear, prepared to keep on going if there were flashing lights and crackling radios already on the scene. But there weren't. So they stopped. Traffic on the road was light. Picturesque, but not practical.

But the nighttime view from the turn-out was spectacular.

Turner said, "Not the point, Reacher."

The dead guy was on the ground near his car's front corner. His knees were folded sideways, but other than that he was flat on his back. There was no doubt about it. It was the driver from the first night. With a hole in his chest.

Reacher said, "What gun was it?"

"Glock 17."

"Which is where right now?"

"Wiped and back in his pocket. For the time being. We have to work out how to play it."

"Only two possible ways," Reacher said. "Either the LAPD finds him sooner, or later. Best bet would be to throw him in the ravine. He could be there a week. He could get eaten up. Or at least chewed, especially the fingers. Putting him in the car is much worse. Doesn't matter if we make it suicide or homicide, because the first thing they'll do is run the fingerprints, and from that moment onward Fort Bragg will go crazy, and this whole thing will unravel from the far end."

"As in, not our end. And you don't want that."

"Do you?"

"I just want it unraveled. I don't care who does it."

"Then you're the least feral person I ever met. They slandered you in the worst possible way. You should cut their heads off with a butter knife."

"No worse than they said about you, with the Big Dog."

"Exactly. I'm about to stop and buy a butter knife. So give me a sporting chance. A few days in the ravine won't hurt anyone. Because even if we don't wrap it up personally, then the LAPD and Fort Bragg will, maybe next week, when they eventually find this guy. Either way it's going to unravel."

"OK."

"And we're keeping the Glock."

Which they did, along with a wallet and a cell phone. Then Reacher bunched the front of the guy's coat in his hands and heaved him off the ground, and staggered with him as close to the edge of the drop as he dared. Most ravine disposals failed. The bodies hung up, six or seven feet down, right there on the slope. Due to a lack of height and distance. So Reacher spun the guy around, like a hammer thrower at the Olympics, two full circles, low on the ground side, high on the air side, and then he let go and hurled him out into the darkness, and he heard the crashing of disturbed trees, and the rattle of stones, and then not much else, apart from the hum of the plain below.

They U-turned off the turn-out and headed back, through Laurel Canyon to the freeway. Reacher drove. Turner stripped the Glock and checked it, and then put it back together and put it in her pocket, with one nine-millimeter in the chamber and fifteen more in the magazine. Then she opened the wallet. It was loaded just like the others. A thick raft of twenties, a handful of smaller bills, a full deck of unexpired and legitimate credit cards, and a North Carolina driver's license with the guy's picture on it. His name had been Jason Kenneth Rickard, and he had finished his earthly sojourn a month shy of his twenty-ninth birthday. He was not an organ donor.

His phone was a cheap item similar to the pair Reacher and Turner had bought at the chain pharmacy. An untraceable mission-specific pre-paid, no doubt. Its directory showed just three numbers, the first two labeled *Pete L* and *Ronnie B,* which were obviously Lozano and Baldacci, and the third was just *Shrago.* The call register showed very little activity. Nothing outgoing, and just three incoming, all from Shrago.

Turner said, "Shrago must be the big guy with the small ears. He seems to have the squad leader's role."

"They're not small," Reacher said. "They're cropped."

"What are?"

"His ears."

"How do you know?"

"The girl told me. She's seen them up close."

"You talked to her?"

"She initiated contact, in the diner."

"Why would she?"

"She thinks we're feds. She's curious about what's happening on her street. She thought we might give her the details."

"Where did she see the guy with the ears?"

"At the end of her driveway."

"She really doesn't know what's happening?"

"Not even about the paternity suit. My name meant nothing to her. Clearly her mother hasn't told her about the affidavit. She doesn't even know her mother is the lawyer's client. She thinks it's one of her neighbors."

"You shouldn't have talked to her."

"I had no choice. She sat herself at my table."

"With a complete stranger?"

"She feels safe in the diner. The counter man seems to look after her."

"What was she like?"

"She's a nice kid."

"Yours?"

"She's the best candidate yet. She's about as weird as me. But I still don't recall a woman in Korea. Not that last time."

Turner said, "Cropped ears?"

"Like little hexagons," Reacher said.

"I never heard of that."

"Me either." Reacher took out his phone and dialed Edmonds. It was nine o'clock on the West Coast, which made it midnight on the East Coast, but he was sure she would answer. She was an idealist. Dial tone sounded seven times, and then she picked up, thick-tongued like before, and Reacher said, "Got a pen?"

Edmonds said, "And paper."

"I need you to check two more names with HRC. Almost certainly from the same logistics company at Fort Bragg, but I need confirmation. The first is Jason Kenneth Rickard, and the second is a guy called

Shrago. I don't know if that's his first or last name. Try to get some background on him. Apparently he has mutilated ears."

"Ears?"

"The things on the side of his head."

"I spoke with Major Sullivan earlier this evening. The office of the Secretary of the Army is pushing for a fast resolution of the Rodriguez issue."

"Dropping the charges would be pretty fast."

"It's not going to happen that way."

"OK, leave it with me," Reacher said. He clicked off the call, and put his phone in his pocket, and went back to driving two-handed. Laurel Canyon Boulevard was a dumb name for the road they were on. It was in Laurel Canyon, for sure, winding its narrow, hilly way through a very desirable and picturesque neighborhood, but it wasn't a boulevard. A boulevard was a wide, straight, ceremonial thoroughfare, often planted with rows of specimen trees or other formal landscaping features. From the old French *boulle-werc*, meaning bulwark, because that was where the idea came from. A boulevard was the landscaped top of a rampart, long, wide, and flat, ideal for strolling.

Then they came out on Ventura Boulevard, which was not the same thing as the Ventura Freeway, but which was at least wide and straight. The Ventura Freeway lay ahead, and Universal City was to the right, and Studio City was to the left.

Reacher said, "Wait."

Turner said, "For what?"

"The Big Dog's lawyer was in Studio City. Right on Ventura Boulevard. I remember from the affidavit."

"And?"

"Maybe his locks and his alarm aren't so great either."

"That's a big step, Reacher. That's a whole bunch of extra crimes right there."

"Let's at least go take a look."

"I'll be an accessory."

"You can have a veto," Reacher said. "Two thumbs on the button, like a nuclear launch."

He turned left, and rolled down the road. Then a phone rang. A loud, electronic trill, like a demented songbird. Not his phone, and not Turner's, but Rickard's, from the back seat, next to his empty wallet.

Chapter 55

Reacher pulled over and squirmed around and picked up the phone. It was trilling loud, and vibrating in his hand. The screen said *Incoming Call,* which was superfluous information, given all the trilling and vibrating, but it also said *Shrago,* which was useful. Reacher opened the phone and held it to his ear and said, "Hello?"

A voice said, "Rickard?"

"No," Reacher said. "Not Rickard."

Silence.

Reacher said, "What were you thinking? A bunch of warehousemen against the 110th MP? We're three for three. It's like batting practice. And you're all that's left. And you're all alone now. And you're next. How does that even feel?"

Silence.

Reacher said, "But they shouldn't have put you in this position. It was unfair. I know that. I know what

Pentagon people are like. I'm not unsympathetic. I can help you out."

Silence.

Reacher said, "Tell me their names, go straight back to Bragg, and I'll leave you alone."

Silence. Then a fast *beep-beep-beep* in the earpiece, and *Call Ended* on the screen. Reacher tossed the phone back on the rear seat and said, "I'll ask twice, but I won't ask three times."

They drove on, and then Studio City came at them, thick and fast. The boulevard was lined with enterprises, some of them in buildings all their own, some of them huddled together in strip malls, like the place in North Hollywood, with some of the buildings and some of the malls approached by shared service roads, and others standing behind parking lots all their own. Numbers were hard to see, because plenty of storefronts were dark. They made two premature turns, in and out of the wrong parking lots. But they found the right place soon enough. It was a lime green mall, five units long. The Big Dog's lawyer was in the center unit.

Except he wasn't.

The center unit was occupied by a tax preparer. Se Habla Espanol, plus about a hundred other languages.

Turner said, "Things change in sixteen years. People retire."

Reacher said nothing.

She said, "Are you sure this is the right address?"

"You think I'm mistaken?"

"You could be forgiven."

"Thank you, but I'm sure." Reacher moved closer, for a better look. The style of the place was not cutting edge. The signage and the messages and the boasts and the promises were all a little dated. The lawyer had not retired recently.

There was a light on in back.

"On a timer," Turner said. "For security. No one is in there."

"It's winter," Reacher said. "Tax time is starting. The guy is in there."

"And?"

"We could talk to him."

"What about? Are you due a refund?"

"He forwards the old guy's mail, at least. Maybe he even knows him. Maybe the old guy is still the landlord."

"Maybe the old guy died ten years ago. Or moved to Wyoming."

"Only one way to find out," Reacher said. He stepped up and rapped hard on the glass. He said, "At this time of night it will work better if you do the talking."

Juliet called Romeo, because some responsibilities were his, and he said, "Shrago tells me Reacher has Rickard's phone. And therefore also his gun, I assume. And he knows they're warehousemen from Fort Bragg."

Romeo said, "Because of Zadran's bio. It was an easy connection to make."

"We're down to the last man. We're nearly defenseless."

"Shrago is worth something."

"Against them? We've lost three men."

"Are you worried?"

"Of course I am. We're losing."

"Do you have a suggestion?"

"It's time," Juliet said. "We know Reacher's target. We should give Shrago permission."

For a spell it looked like Turner was right, and there was no one there, just a light on a security timer, but Reacher kept on knocking, and eventually a guy stepped into view making shooing motions with his arms. To which Reacher replied with beckoning motions of his own, which produced a standoff, the guy miming *I don't do nighttime walk-ins,* and Reacher feeling like the kid in the movie that gets sent to the doctor's house in the middle of the night, all *Come quickly, old Jeb got buried alive in a pile of W9s.* And the guy cracked first. He snorted in exasperation and set off stomping up his store's center aisle. He undid the lock and opened the door. He was a young Asian man. Early thirties, maybe. He was wearing gray pants and a red sweater vest.

He said, "What do you want?"

Turner said, "To apologize."

"For what?"

"Interrupting you. We know your time is valuable. But we need five minutes of it. For which we'd be happy to pay you a hundred dollars."

"Who are you?"

"Technically at the moment we work for the government."

"May I see ID?"

"No."

"But you want to pay me a hundred dollars?"

"Only if you have material information."

"On what subject?"

"The lawyer that had this place before you."

"What about him?"

"Congress requires us to verify certain types of information a minimum of five separate ways, and we've done four of them, so we're hoping you can be number five tonight, so we can all go home."

"What type of information?"

"First of all, we're required to ask, purely as a formality, do you have personal knowledge whether the subject of our inquiry is alive or dead?"

"Yes, I do."

"And which is it?"

"Alive."

"Good," Turner said. "That's just a baseline thing. And all we need now is his full legal name and his current address."

"You should have come to me first, not fifth. I forward his mail."

"No, we tackle the hard ones early. Makes the day go better. Downhill, not up."

"I'll write it down."

"Thank you," Turner said.

"It has to be exact," Reacher said. "You know what

Congress is like. If one guy puts *Avenue* and another guy puts *A-v-e,* it's liable to get thrown out."

"Don't worry," the guy said.

The lawyer's full legal name was Martin Mitchell Ballantyne, and he hadn't moved to Wyoming. His address was still Studio City, Los Angeles, California. Almost walking distance. Turner's map showed it to be close to the Ventura end of Coldwater Canyon Drive. Maybe where the guy had lived all along.

In which case he had been a lousy lawyer. The address was a garden apartment, probably from the 1930s, which was eight decades of decay. It had been dowdy long ago. Now it was desperate. Dark green walls, like slime, and yellow light in the windows.

Turner said, "Don't get your hopes up. He might refuse to see us. It's kind of late to come calling."

Reacher said, "His light is still on."

"And he might not remember a thing about it. It was sixteen years ago."

"Then we're no worse off."

"Unless he calls it tampering with a prosecution witness."

"He should think of it as a deposition."

"Just don't be surprised if he throws us out."

"He's a lonely old guy. Nothing he wants more than a couple of visitors."

Ballantyne neither threw them out nor looked happy to see them. He just stood at his door, rather passively, as if a lot of his life had been spent opening his door late in the LA evening, in response to urgent demands. He looked medium sized and reasonably healthy, and not much over sixty. But he looked tired. And he had a very lugubrious manner. He had the look of a man who had taken on the world, and lost. He had a scar on his lip, which Reacher guessed was not the result of a surgical procedure. And behind him he had what Reacher took to be a wife. She looked just as glum, but less passive and more overtly hostile.

Reacher said, "We'd like to buy fifteen minutes of your time, Mr. Ballantyne. How would a hundred bucks work for you?"

The guy said, "I no longer practice law. I no longer have a license."

"Retired?"

"Disbarred."

"When?"

"Four years ago."

"It's an old case we want to talk about."

"What's your interest in it?"

"We're making a movie."

"How old is the case?"

"Sixteen years."

"For a hundred bucks?"

"It's yours if you want it."

"Come in," the guy said. "We'll see if I want it."

They all four crabbed down a narrow hallway, and into a narrow living room, which had better furniture than Reacher expected, as if the Ballantynes had downsized from a better place. Four years ago, perhaps. Disbarred, maybe fined, maybe sued, maybe bankrupted.

Ballantyne said, "What if I can't remember?"

"You still get the money," Reacher said. "As long as you make an honest effort."

"What was the case?"

"Sixteen years ago you wrote an affidavit for a client named Juan Rodriguez, also known as the Big Dog."

Ballantyne leaned forward, all set to give it a hundred dollars' worth of honest effort, but he got there within about a buck and a quarter.

He sat back again.

He said, "The thing with the army?"

Recognition in his voice. And some kind of misery. As if some bad thing had stirred, and come back from the dead. As if the thing with the army had brought him nothing but trouble.

"Yes," Reacher said. "The thing with the army."

"And your interest in it is what exactly?"

"You used my name, where you had to fill in the blanks."

"You're the guy?" Ballantyne said. "In my house? Haven't I suffered enough?"

And his wife said, "Get the hell out, right now." Which apparently she meant, because she kept on saying it, loud and clear and venomous, over and over again, with heavy emphasis on the *right now.* Which in terms of tone and content Reacher took as clear evidence that consent had been withdrawn, and that trespass had begun, and he had promised Turner two thumbs on the nuclear button, and he was a little mindful of the prosecution witness issue, so he got the hell out, right then, with Turner about a foot behind him. They walked back to the car and leaned on it and Turner said, "So it's all about the filing system."

Reacher nodded.

"Fingers crossed," he said.

"Are you going to use Sullivan?"

"Would you?"

"Definitely. She's senior, and she's right there at JAG, not stuck in HRC."

"Agreed," Reacher said.

He took out his phone and called Edmonds.

Chapter 56

Edmonds picked up, sleepy and a little impatient, and Reacher said, "Earlier tonight you told me Major Sullivan told you the office of the Secretary of the Army is pushing for a fast resolution of the Rodriguez issue."

"And you've woken me up in the middle of the night to give me another witty response?"

"No, I need you to find out exactly who delivered that message to Major Sullivan, or at least which channel it came through."

"Thank you for thinking of me, but shouldn't Major Sullivan handle this direct?"

"She's going to be very busy doing something else. This is very important, captain. And very urgent. I need it done early. So hit up everyone you know, everywhere. As early as you can. While they're still on the treadmill, or whatever it is people do in the morning."

* * *

Reacher patted his pockets and found Sullivan's personal cell number, on the torn-in-half scratch pad page that Leach had given him. He dialed, and counted the ring tones. She picked up after six, which he thought was pretty good. A light sleeper, apparently.

She said, "Hello?"

"This is Jack Reacher," he said. "Remember me?"

"How could I forget? We need to talk."

"We are talking."

"About your situation."

"Later, OK? Right now we have stuff to do."

"Right now? It's the middle of the night."

"Either right now or as soon as possible. Depending on your level of access."

"To what?"

"I just spoke with the lawyer who did the Big Dog's affidavit."

"On the phone?"

"Face to face."

"That was completely inappropriate."

"It was a very short conversation. We left when requested."

"We?"

"Major Turner is with me. An officer of equal rank and equal ability. An independent witness. She heard it, too. Like a second opinion."

"Heard what?"

"Does your legal archive have a computer search function?"

"Of course it does."

"So if I typed *Reacher, complaint against,* what would I get?"

"Exactly what you got, basically. The Big Dog's affidavit, or similar."

"Is the search fast and reliable?"

"Did you really wake me up in the middle of the night to talk about computers?"

"I need information."

"The system is pretty fast. Not a very intuitive search protocol, but it's capable of taking you straight to an individual document."

"I mentioned the case to the lawyer and he remembered it immediately. He called it the thing with the army. Then he asked me what my interest was, and I told him, and he said, haven't I suffered enough?"

"What did he mean by that?"

"You had to be there to hear it. It was all in his tone of voice. The Big Dog affidavit was not just a complaint he mailed in and forgot about. It was not routine. It was a *thing.* It was a whole story, with a beginning, and a middle, and an end. And I'm guessing it was a bad end. That's what we heard. He made it sound like a negative episode in his life. He was looking back on it, with regret."

"Reacher, I'm a lawyer, not a dialog coach. I need facts, not the way people make things sound."

"And I'm an interrogator, and an interrogator learns plenty by listening. He asked me what my interest was, as if he was wondering what possible interest was there left to have? Hadn't all possible interests been exhausted years ago?"

"Reacher, it's the middle of the night. Do you have a point?"

"Hang in there. It's not like you have anything else to do. You won't get back to sleep now. The point is, then he said, haven't I suffered enough? And simultaneously his wife started yelling and screaming and throwing us out the door. They're living in reduced circumstances, and they're very unhappy about it. And the Big Dog was a hot button. Like a defining event, years ago, with ongoing negative consequences. That's the only way to make sense of the language. So now I'm wondering whether this whole thing was actually litigated at the time, all those years ago. And maybe the lawyer got his butt kicked. And maybe he got his first ethics violation. Which might have been the first step on a rocky road that terminated four years ago, when he got disbarred. Such that neither he nor his wife can bear to hear about that case ever again, because it was the start of all their troubles. Haven't I suffered enough? As in, I've had sixteen years of hell because of that case, and now you want to put me through it all again?"

"Reacher, what are you smoking? You didn't remember the case. Therefore you didn't litigate it. Or you'd remember it. And if it was litigated sixteen years ago, to the point where the lawyer got his butt kicked, why are they relitigating it now?"

"Are they relitigating it now?"

"I'm about to hang up."

"What would happen if someone searched *Reacher, complaint against,* and ordered up the Big Dog affidavit, and fed it into the system at unit level? With a bit of smoke and mirrors about how serious it was?"

No answer.

Reacher said, "It would feel exactly like a legal case, wouldn't it? We'd assemble a file, and we'd all start preparing and strategizing, and we'd wait for a conference with the prosecutor, and we'd hope our strategy survived it."

No answer.

Reacher said, "Have you had a conference with the prosecutor?"

Sullivan said, "No."

"Maybe there is no prosecutor. Maybe this is a one-sided illusion. Designed to work for one minute only. As in, I was supposed to see your file and run like hell."

"It can't be an illusion. I'm getting pressure from the Secretary's office."

"Says who? Maybe you're getting messages, but you don't really know where they're coming from. Do you even know the Big Dog is dead? Have you seen a death certificate?"

"This is crazy talk."

"Maybe. But humor me. Suppose it really was litigated sixteen years ago. Without my knowledge. Perhaps one of hundreds, with a specimen case involving some other guy, but I was in the supporting cast. Like class action. Maybe they started some aggressive new policy against ambulance chasers. Which might account for the guy getting his butt kicked so bad. What kind of paperwork would we have seen?"

"If it really was litigated? A lot of paperwork. You don't want to know."

"So if I searched *Reacher, defense against complaint,* what would I find?"

"Eventually you'd find everything they tagged as defense material, I suppose. Hundreds of pages, probably, in a big case."

"Is it like shopping on a web site? Does it link from one thing to another?"

"No, I told you. It's a clunky old thing. It was designed by people over thirty. This is the army, don't forget."

"OK, so if I was worried about a guy called Reacher, and I wanted to scare him away, and I was in a big hurry, I could search the archive for *Reacher, complaint against,* and I could find the Big Dog's affidavit, and I could put it back in circulation, while being completely unaware it was only a small part of a much bigger file. Because of the way the search function works. Is that correct?"

"Hypothetically."

"Which is your job, starting right now. You have to test that hypothesis. See if you can find any trace of a bigger file. Search under all the tags you can think of."

They got in the car and drove east on the freeway, back to Vineland Avenue, and then south, past the girl's neighborhood, to the coach diner. She was gone, inevitably, and so was the blonde waitress, and so were all the other dinnertime customers. Rush hour was definitely over. Late evening had started. There were three men in separate booths, drinking coffee, and there was a woman eating pie. The brunette waitress was talking to the counter man. Reacher and Turner stood at the door, and the waitress broke away and greeted them, and Reacher said, "I'm sorry, but I had to run before. There was an emergency. I didn't pay for my cup of coffee."

The waitress said, "It was taken care of."

"Who by? Not the kid, I hope. That wouldn't be right."

"It was taken care of," the woman said again.

"It's all good," the counter man said. Arthur. He was wiping his counter.

"How much is a cup of coffee?" Reacher asked him.

"Two bucks and a penny," the guy said. "With tax."

"Good to know," Reacher said. He dug out two bills and a lone cent, and he put them on the counter, and he said, "To return the favor, to whoever it was. Very much appreciated. What goes around comes around."

"OK," the guy said. He left the money where it was.

"She told me she came in often."

"Who did?"

"Samantha. The kid."

The guy nodded. "She's pretty much a regular."

"Tell her I was sorry I had to run. I don't want her to think I was rude."

"She's a kid. What do you care?"

"She thinks I work for the government. I don't want to give her a negative impression. She's a bright girl. Public service is something she could think about."

"Who do you work for really?"

"The government," Reacher said. "But not the part she guessed."

"I'll pass on the message."

"How long have you known her?"

"Longer than I've known you. So if there's a choice between her privacy and your questions, I guess I'm going to go with her privacy."

"I understand," Reacher said. "I would expect nothing less. But would you tell her one more thing for me?"

"Which would be what?"

"Tell her to remember what I said about the hexagons."

"The hexagons?"

"The little hexagons," Reacher said. "Tell her it's important."

They got back in the car and they started it up, but they didn't go anywhere. They sat in the diner's lot, their faces lit up pink and blue by the Art Deco neon, and Turner said, "Do you think she's safe?"

Reacher said, "She's got the 75th MP and the FBI staring at her bedroom window all night long, both of them specifically on the alert for an intruder, which they expect to be me, except it won't be, because I'm not going there, and neither is Shrago, in my opinion, because he knows what I know. Neither one of us could get in that house tonight. So yes, I think she's safe. Almost by accident."

"Then we should go find ourselves a place to stay. Got a preference?"

"You're the CO."

"I'd like to go to the Four Seasons. But we should keep radio silence on the credit cards, as far as our overnight location is concerned. So it's cash only, which means motels only, which means we should go back to that hot-sheets place in Burbank, where we met Emily the hooker. All part of the authentic experience."

"Like driving a car on Mulholland Drive."

"Or shooting a man on Mulholland Drive. That's in the movies, too."

"You OK?"

She said, "If I have a problem, you'll be the first to know."

The motel was certainly authentic. It had a wire grille over the reception window, and cash was all it took. The room looked like it should feel cold and damp, but it was in Los Angeles, where nothing was cold and damp. Instead it felt brittle and papery, as if it had been baked too long. But it was functional, and not far from comfortable.

The car was parked five rooms away. No place else to hide it. But safe enough, even if Shrago saw it. He would watch the room in front of it, and then he would break in, and find the wrong people, and assume the car was one step to the side of where it should have been, but left or right was a fifty-fifty chance, which meant if he called it wrong he would have committed three separate burglaries before he even laid eyes on the target, and suppose the car was two steps from where it should have been? How many rooms was that? His head would explode long before he got to five steps. His tiny ears would ping off into the far distance, like shrapnel.

Reacher figured he had about four hours to sleep. He was sure Edmonds was busting a gut in Virginia, on East Coast time, gathering information, so she could call early and wake him up.

Chapter 57

Edmonds' first call came in at two in the morning
local time, which was five o'clock Eastern. Reacher
and Turner both woke up. Reacher put the open phone
between their pillows, and they rolled over forehead
to forehead, so they could both hear. Edmonds said,
"You asked me earlier, about Jason Kenneth Rickard,
and a guy called Shrago. Got a pen?"

Reacher said, "No."

"Then listen carefully. They're the same as the first
two. They're all deployed with the same company at
Fort Bragg. Three teams to a squad, and they're a
team. What that means exactly, I don't know. Possibly
this is skilled work, and they learn to rely on each
other."

"And to keep their mutual secrets," Reacher said.
"Tell me about Shrago."

"Ezra-none-Shrago, staff sergeant and team leader.
Thirty-six years old. Hungarian grandparents. He's
been in the unit since the start of the war. He was in

and out of Afghanistan for five years, and since then he's been based at home, exclusively."

"What's up with his ears?"

"He was captured."

"In North Carolina or Afghanistan?"

"By the Taliban. He was gone three days."

"Why didn't they cut his head off?"

"Probably for the same reason we didn't shoot Emal Zadran. They have politicians, too."

"When was this?"

"Five years ago. They gave him a permanent billet at home after that. And he hasn't been back to Afghanistan since."

Reacher closed the phone, and Turner said, "I don't like that at all. Why would he sell arms to the people who cut his ears off?"

"He doesn't make the deals. He's just a cog in a machine. They don't care what he thinks. They want his muscle, not his opinions."

"We should offer him immunity. We could turn him on a dime."

"He beat Moorcroft half to death."

"I said offer, not give. We could stab him in the back afterward."

"So call him, and make the pitch. He's still on speed dial, in Rickard's phone."

Turner got up and found the right cell, and got back in bed and dialed, but the phone company told her the number she wanted was blocking her calls.

"Efficient," she said. "They're cleaning house as they go, minute by minute. No more Mr. Rickard. Or Baldacci, or Lozano. All consigned to history."

"We'll manage without Shrago's input," Reacher said. "We'll figure it out. Maybe in a dream, about five minutes from now."

She smiled, and said, "OK, goodnight again."

Juliet called Romeo, because some responsibilities were his, and he said, "Shrago has located their car. It's at a motel south of the Burbank airport."

Romeo said, "But?"

"Shrago feels it's likely not in front of the right room, as a basic security measure. He'd have to check ten or a dozen, and he feels he won't get away with that. One or two, maybe, but no more. And there's no point in disabling the car, because they'd only rent another, on one of our own credit cards."

"Can't he get to the girl?"

"Not before she leaves the house again. It's buttoned up tight."

Romeo said, "There's activity in the legal archive. A lone user, with JAG access, searching for something. Which is unusual, at this time of night."

"Captain Edmonds?"

"No, she's in the HRC system. She just took a good look at Rickard and Shrago, about an hour ago. They're closing in."

"On Shrago, perhaps. But not on us. There's no direct link."

"The link is through Zadran. It's like a neon sign. So tell Shrago to get out of Burbank. Tell him to wait on the girl. Tell him we're counting on him, and tell him this mess has to be cleaned up first thing in the morning, whatever it takes."

Edmonds' second call came at five in the morning local time, which was eight in the East. Reacher and Turner did the forehead-to-forehead thing again, and Edmonds said, "OK, here's an update. Treadmill time is over, and office hours are yet to begin, so all I have is rumor and gossip, but in D.C. that's usually more accurate than anything else."

Reacher said, "And?"

"I spoke to eight people either in or associated with the office of the Secretary."

"And?"

"Rodriguez or Juan Rodriguez or Dog or Big Dog is ringing no bells. No one recognizes the name, no one is aware of an active case, no one has passed a message to Major Sullivan, and no one is aware of a senior officer doing so either."

"Interesting."

"But not definitive. Eight people is a small sample, and the feeling is a sixteen-year-old embarrassment wouldn't be given much bandwidth. We'll know more in an hour, when everyone is back in the office."

"Thank you, captain."

"Sleeping well?"

"We're in a motel that rents by the hour. We're getting our money's worth. Was Ezra Shrago offered counseling after the thing with his ears in Afghanistan?"

"Psychiatric notes are eyes-only."

"But I'm sure you read them anyway."

"He was offered counseling, and he accepted, which was considered unusual. Most people seem to do it the army way, which is to bottle it up until they collapse with a nervous breakdown. But Shrago was a willing patient."

"And?"

"As of three years after the incident he still retained strong feelings of anger, resentment, humiliation and hatred. The home deployment was preemptive, just as much as therapeutic. The feeling was he couldn't be trusted among the native population. He was an atrocity waiting to happen. The notes say he hates the Taliban with a passion."

Afterward Turner said, "Now I really don't like it. Why would he sell weapons to people he hates?"

"He's a cog," Reacher said again. "He lives in North Carolina. He hasn't seen a raghead in five years. He gets paid a lot of money."

"But he's participating."

"He's disassociating. Out of sight, out of mind."

Reacher left the phone where it was, between their pillows, and they went back to sleep.

But not for long. Edmonds called for a third time forty minutes later, at a quarter to six in the morning, local time. She said, "Just for fun I went back through the Fort Bragg deployments, because I wanted to see how long they had all served together as a quartet. Shrago was in at the beginning, as I said, and then came Rickard, and then Lozano, and then Baldacci was the last in, which was four years ago, and they've been together ever since. Which makes them the oldest team in the unit, by a big margin. They've had plenty of time to get to know each other."

"OK," Reacher said.

"But that's not the real point. The real point is, four years ago that unit had a temporary commander. The previous guy fell down dead with a heart attack. It was the temporary commander who put Shrago's team together. And guess who he was?"

"Morgan," Reacher said.

"You got it in one. He was a major then. He got his promotion soon after that, for no very obvious reason. His file is pretty thin. You could read it as a cure for insomnia."

"I'll bear that in mind. But right now I sleep fine, apart from getting woken up by the phone."

"Likewise," Edmonds said.

Reacher asked, "Who sent Morgan to Bragg four years ago? Who tells a guy like that where to go?"

"I'm working on that now."

Reacher left the phone where it was, and they went back to sleep.

They got a final half hour, and then the fourth call of the morning came in, at a quarter after six local time, and it came direct from Major Sullivan at JAG. She said, "I just spent three hours in the archive, and I'm afraid your theory is a little off the mark. The Big Dog's claim was not litigated sixteen years ago, nor has it been at any time since."

Reacher paused a beat.

"OK," he said. "Understood. Thanks for trying."

"Now do you want the good news?"

"Is there any?"

"It wasn't litigated, but it was investigated very thoroughly."

"And?"

"It was a fraud, from beginning to end."

Chapter 58

Sullivan said, "Someone really went to bat for you. You must have been very well respected, major. It wasn't a class action thing. There was no new policy regarding ambulance chasers. This was all about you. Someone wanted to clear your name."

"Who?"

"The hard work was done by a captain from the 135th MP, name of Granger."

"Man or woman?"

"A man, based on the West Coast. Don Granger."

"Never heard of him."

"All his notes were copied to an MP two-star, name of Garber."

"Leon Garber," Reacher said. "He was my rabbi, more or less. I owe him a lot. Even more than I thought, clearly."

"I guess so. He must have driven the whole thing. And you must have been his blue-eyed boy, because this was one hell of a full court press. But you owe

Granger, too. He worked his butt off for you, and he saw something everyone else missed."

"What was the story?"

"You guys generate a lot of complaints. Your branch's standard operating procedure is play dumb and hope they go away, which they often do, but if they don't, then they're defended, with historically mixed results. That's how it went for many years. Then the ones that went away started to cause a problem, ironically. You all had old unproven allegations on file. Most of them were obvious bullshit, quite rightly ignored, but some were marginal. And promotions boards saw them. And they started wondering about smoke without fire, and people weren't getting ahead, and it became an issue. And the Big Dog's complaint was worse than most. I guess General Garber felt it was too toxic to ignore, even if it might have gone away by itself. He didn't want to leave it sitting there on the record. It was way too smoky."

"He could have asked me about it direct."

"Granger asked him why he didn't."

"And what was the answer?"

"Garber thought you might have done it. But he didn't want to hear it direct."

"Really?"

"He thought you might have gotten upset at the thought of SAWs on the streets of Los Angeles."

"That was the LAPD's problem, not mine. All I wanted was a name."

"Which you got, and he didn't really see how else you could have gotten it."

"He didn't talk to me afterward, either."

"He was afraid you'd stop by and put a bullet in the lawyer's head."

"I might have."

"Then Garber was a wise man. His strategy was immaculate. He put Granger on it, and the first thing Granger didn't like was the Big Dog, and the second thing he didn't like was the lawyer. But there were no cracks anywhere, and he knew you had been with the guy moments before he was beaten, and the affidavit was what it was, so he was stuck. He came up with the same thing you did, which was some other dude did it, or dudes, maybe a delegation sent over by a disgruntled customer, which in that context meant a gang, either Latino like Rodriguez or black, but he didn't make any progress on his own. So next he went to the LAPD, but the cops had nothing to offer, either. Which Granger didn't necessarily regard as definitive, because at the relevant time the cops had been up to their eyes in racial sensitivity issues, like the LAPD often was back then, and they were nervous about discussing gangs with a stranger, in case the stranger was really a journalist who believed gang issues were code words for racial insensitivity. So Granger went back to the gang idea on his own, and he checked the record for who had been armed and dangerous at the time, as a kind of starting point, and he found no one had been armed and dangerous at the time. There was a seventy-two hour period without a single gang crime reported anywhere. So initially Granger concluded gangs were on the wane in LA, and he better look elsewhere, but he had no luck, and Garber was ready to pull him out. Then Granger saw what he was missing."

From her pillow Turner said, "The seventy-two hour hiatus was because the LAPD trashed all the gang crime reports. Probably on the advice of their PR people. Not because nothing was happening."

"Correct, major," Sullivan said. "But the patrolmen's notebooks still had all the details. Granger got some lieutenant backed up in a corner, and the true story came out, which was bizarre. About twenty minutes after Reacher left, five black guys from El Segundo showed up and started beating the Big Dog in his own front yard. A neighbor called it in, and the LAPD showed up, and they witnessed about a minute of the beating, and then they got themselves in gear and arrested the guys from El Segundo, and it was the patrolmen themselves who took the Big Dog to the hospital. But there had been a degree of excessive force in the arrests, and a number of serious injuries, so the report was reviewed, and then word came down to bury anything that wasn't totally kosher, and the precinct captains erred on the side of caution, and they buried everything. Or maybe it wasn't caution. Maybe there was nothing kosher."

Reacher said, "So I'm in an affidavit for a beating, but the LAPD actually saw someone else doing it?"

"Granger got photocopies of their notebooks. They're all in our archives."

"That's some ballsy lawyer the Big Dog found."

"Worse than you think. Plan A was jump on the bandwagon and sue the LAPD itself. Why not? Everyone else was. Granger was snooping the lawyer's office one night, on Ventura Boulevard, and he found a draft affidavit identical to yours, except it had the LAPD all over it, instead of you. But ironically that couldn't fly, because the LAPD could prove for a fact it hadn't been in the neighborhood that day, because all its records were doctored, so as soon as that little wrinkle sunk in, the lawyer switched to Plan B, which was the army. Which is of course fraudulent and criminal, but the reasoning was very solid. Ever afterward the LAPD could never admit they trashed crime reports for political convenience, so the lawyer was guaranteed absolute silence from that direction. And the Big Dog wanted a big payday, and the guys from El Segundo had no traceable assets, so Uncle Sam was the next best thing."

"How did Granger wrap it up?"

"He had to thread the needle, because he didn't want to embarrass the LAPD in public. But he knew a JAG guy who knew a guy in the Bar Association, and between them they put some professional hurt on the lawyer. Granger made him write out another affidavit, swearing the first one was fraudulent, which he personally witnessed, and which, by the way, is still in the archive one slot away from where the phony one was. And then Granger split the lawyer's lip."

"He put that in the archive, too?"

"Apparently he was defending himself against an unprovoked attack."

"That can happen. How is Colonel Moorcroft doing?"

"He's out of danger, but not good."

"Give him my best, if you get the chance. And thanks for your efforts tonight."

Sullivan said, "I owe you an apology, major."

Reacher said, "No, you don't."

"Thank you. But you still owe me thirty dollars."

Reacher pictured Turner in his mind, in Berryville, Virginia, after the hardware store, in her new pants, with his shirt ballooning around her, its tail touching the backs of her knees. He said, "They were the best thirty dollars I ever had."

They celebrated the best way they knew how, and then it was too late to go back to sleep, so they got up and showered, and Turner said, "How does it feel?"

"No different," Reacher said.

"Why not?"

"I knew I didn't do it, so it contributed no new information, and it brought no relief, because I wasn't upset to begin with, because I don't care what people think."

"Even me?"

"You knew I didn't do it. Like I knew you didn't take a hundred grand."

"I'm glad she apologized. It was very courteous of you to say she didn't need to."

"It wasn't courtesy," Reacher said. "It was a statement of fact. She really didn't need to apologize. Because her initial prejudice was correct. And I shouldn't have said I didn't do it, because I almost did. I was a minute away from making every word of that affidavit true. Not because of SAWs on the streets of Los Angeles. I wasn't worried about them. It takes a lot of strength and training to use one right. And maintenance. The squad machine gun goes to your best guy, not your worst, and are there guys like that on the streets of Los Angeles? I didn't think so. I figured the SAWs would fire once and end up as boat anchors. Nothing to get upset about there. It was the other stuff that upset me. Claymore mines, and hand grenades. No expertise required. But lots of collateral damage, in an urban situation. Innocent passersby, and children. And that sneering tub of lard was making a fortune, and spending it all on dope and hookers and twenty Big Macs a day."

Turner said, "Let's go get breakfast. And let's not come back here. Authenticity is losing its charm."

They put their toothbrushes in their pockets, and they put on their coats, and they headed out to the lot. The street lights were still brighter than the sky. The car was where they had left it, five rooms away.

There was something written on it.

It was written in the grime on the front passenger's window. Someone had used a broad fingertip and traced three words, a total of thirteen letters, all of them block capitals, neatly, with the punctuation all present and correct: WHERE'S THE GIRL?

Chapter 59

Samantha Dayton woke early, like she often did, and she came down the narrow attic stair and checked the view from the living room window. The Hummer was gone. In the middle of the night, probably, due on station at the law office. In its place was the purple Dodge Charger, looking way too cool for a cop car. But a cop car it was, nevertheless. Generically speaking, at least. Technically it was a federal agent's car, she supposed. DEA, or ATF, or FBI. She recognized the driver. She was getting a handle on the rotation. Further on down the street the small white compact was where it always was. And it was the real mystery. Because it was not a cop car. It was a rental, most likely. Hertz or Avis, from LAX, she thought. But the DEA and the ATF and the FBI all had field offices in Los Angeles, with big staffs and cars of their own. Therefore the guy in the small white compact was from an organization important enough to participate, but too small and too specialized to have its own local office. Therefore the guy had flown in, from somewhere else. From D.C., probably, where all the secrets were.

She took her shower, and dressed, in her favorite black pants and her favorite jean jacket, but with a fresh blue T-shirt, and therefore blue shoes. She combed her hair out, and checked the view again. It was coming up to what she called zero hour. Twice a day the small white compact moved, for meals, she guessed, or bathroom breaks, and about four times a day the Hummer and the Charger swapped positions, but there was apparently no coordination between the agencies, because once a day in the early morning everyone was missing at the same time, for about twenty minutes. Zero agents, zero hour. The street went back to its normal self. Some kind of logic issue, she supposed, or simple math, like in class, with x number of cars, and y number of locations, and z number of hours to cover. Something had to give.

She looked out and saw that the small white compact was already gone, and then the Charger moved out as she watched. It started up, and eased away from the curb, and drove away. The street went quiet. Back to its normal self. Zero hour.

Reacher ran through his earlier reasoning one more time: the 75th MP and the FBI were watching her house, and they were specifically on the alert for an intruder. *I'm not going there, and neither is Shrago, because neither one of us could get in.*

He said, "It's a bluff. He's trying to get in our heads.

He's trying to draw us out. That's all. He can't get anywhere near the girl."

Turner said, "Are you absolutely sure about that?"

"No."

"We can't go there. You're still on the shit list, until Sullivan makes it official. And I'm still on the shit list, probably forever."

"We can go there once."

"We can't. They already saw the car once yesterday. Maybe twice. And getting arrested won't help her or us."

"We can get another car. At the Burbank airport. Shrago will know about it inside an hour, but we can use that hour."

Breakfast was always a problem. There was never anything in the house, and anyway her mother slept late in the morning, all tired and stressed, and she wouldn't appreciate a lot of crashing and banging in the kitchen. So breakfast was an expedition, which was a word she really liked, in her opinion based on old Latin, *ex* for out, and *ped* for foot, like pedal or pedicure or pedestrian, so all put together it meant going out on foot, which is exactly what she usually did, because obviously she couldn't drive yet, being only fourteen years old, albeit nearly fifteen.

She was looking forward to driving. Driving would be a big advantage, because it would widen her scope. In a car she could go to Burbank or Glendale or Pasadena for breakfast, or even Beverly Hills. Whereas out on foot her choice was limited to the coach diner, south on Vineland, or alternatively the coffee shop near the law office, north on Vineland, and that was about it, because everything else was tacos or quesadillas or Vietnamese, and none of those places was open for breakfast. Which was frustrating.

Normally.

But not such a big deal on that particular morning, because the federal agents would face the same limited choice, which would make them easier to find. Fifty-fifty, basically, like tossing a coin, and she hoped she tossed it right, because the big one named Reacher seemed willing to talk, about stuff worth listening to, because he was obviously right in the middle of it all, some kind of a senior guy, rushing off after urgent phone calls, and spilling the beans on the man with the ears.

So, heads or tails?

She pulled the blue door shut behind her, and she started walking.

They put the old Range Rover on a curb in a tow zone outside the rental lot, and they lined up at the desk behind a white-haired couple just in from Phoenix. When their turn came they used Baldacci's license and credit card and picked out a mid-size sedan, and after a whole lot of signing and initialing they were given a key. The car in question was a white Ford, dripping wet from washing, parked under a roof, and it was bland and anonymous and therefore adequate in every way, except that its window tints were green and subtle and modern, nothing like the opaque plastic sheets that had been stuck to the Range Rover's glass. Driving the Ford was going to feel very different. Inward visibility was going to be restricted only by sunshine and reflections. Or not.

Turner had brought her book of maps, and she plotted a route that stayed away from Vineland Avenue until the last possible block. The day dawned bright and fresh in front of them, and traffic stayed quiet. It was still very early. They came out of Burbank on small streets, mostly through office parks, and they rolled through North Hollywood, and they crossed the freeway east of Vineland, and they headed for the neighborhood at an angle, feeling exposed and naked behind the thin green glass.

"One pass," Turner said. "Slow constant speed to the end of the street, no stopping under any circumstances, all the time anticipating normality and the presence of law enforcement vehicles, and if it turns out any different we'll continue to the end of the street anyway, and we'll work it out from there. We must not get trapped in front of the house. OK?"

"Agreed," Reacher said.

They turned into the first elbow, and they drove past the grocery, and past the car with no wheels, and they turned left, and then right, and then they were in her street, which stretched ahead long and straight and normal, a narrow metallic lane through nose-to-tail cars, both sides, all parked, all winking in the morning sun.

Turner said, "FBI ahead on the right. Purple Dodge Charger."

"Got it," Reacher said.

"Plus the last car on the lot ahead on the left. The MP special."

"Got it," Reacher said again.

"The house looks normal."

Which it did. It looked solid and settled, and still, as if there were sleeping people inside. The front door was closed, and all the windows were closed. The old red coupe had not moved.

They rolled on.

Turner said, "So far every other vehicle is empty. No sign of Shrago. It was a head fake."

They kept on going, at a slow and constant speed, all the way to the end of the street, and they saw nothing at all to worry about.

"Let's go get breakfast," Reacher said.

Romeo called Juliet and said, "They rented another car. A white Ford, at the Burbank airport."

Juliet said, "Why? Surely they know they can't hide from us."

"They're hiding from the FBI and the MPs. Changing cars is a sound tactic."

"A white Ford? I'll tell Shrago immediately."

"Is he making progress?"

"I haven't heard from him."

Romeo said, "Hold on a minute."

"What's up?"

"More activity on Baldacci's card. The gentleman in Long Beach just took a second day's rental on the Range Rover. Which means they haven't changed cars. What they've done is added a car. Which means they've split up, and they're moving separately. Which is smart. They're two against one. They're pressing their advantage. Make sure Shrago knows."

They looped south of the neighborhood and came back north on Vineland as far as the coach diner. The white Ford was doing its job. It was turning no heads. It was unremarkable and anonymous and invisible, like a hole in the air. Ideal, except for its transparent windows.

The diner was doing good business, at that time of the morning all of it serious and no-nonsense, with early workers fueling up ahead of long days of labor. There were no ironic hipsters present. The girl wasn't there, either. Which wasn't a surprise, because even though she was pretty much a regular, who ate practically every meal there, it was still very early. Reacher knew almost nothing about fourteen-year-old girls, but he imagined early rising was not among their top ten lifestyle preferences. The guy named Arthur was behind his counter, and the brunette waitress was rushing around. A swing shift, maybe, late night and early morning. The blonde wasn't there. Maybe she worked peak hours only, starting just before lunch, and finishing just after dinner.

They took the last booth on the right, directly behind the girl's empty stool. A busboy gave them water, and the brunette gave them coffee. Turner ordered an omelet, and Reacher ordered pancakes. They ate, and enjoyed it, and lingered, and waited. The girl didn't show. The rest of the clientele changed with the passage of time, office workers and retail workers replacing the laborers, their orders a little more delicate and a little less calorific, their table manners a little less like throwing coal in a furnace. Reacher got four refills of coffee. Turner got toast. The girl didn't show.

Reacher got up and stepped over and sat down again on the girl's empty stool. The guy named Arthur tracked the move, like a good counter man should, and he nodded, as if to say *I'll be right with you.* Reacher waited, and Arthur served coffee, and orange juice, and he bussed a plate, and he took an order, and then he came over. Reacher asked him, "Does Samantha get breakfast here?"

The guy said, "Most days."

"What time does she come in?"

The guy asked, "Would I be wrong if I said you'll never see forty again?"

"Generous, not wrong."

"Some people say it's the times we live in, but I think it's never been any different, which is that when a man in his forties starts asking an unhealthy amount of questions about a girl of fourteen, then most people are going to notice, and some of them might even do something, such as ask questions back."

"As they should," Reacher said. "But who died and made you chairman of the board?"

"It was me you asked."

"I enjoyed talking to her, and I'd like to talk to her again."

"Not reassuring."

"She's curious about a law enforcement situation, which is not a good combination."

"The thing on her street?"

"I thought I might trade her some facts for a promise to stay out of the way."

"Are you law enforcement?"

"No, I'm here on vacation. It was this or Tahiti."

"She's not old enough for facts."

"I think she is."

"Are you authorized?"

"Am I breathing?"

"She's an early riser. She would have been in and out by now. Long ago. I guess she's not coming today."

Chapter 60

Reacher paid the check with Baldacci's cash, and they got back in the Ford, and Turner said, "Either she ate at home today, or she skipped breakfast altogether. She's a teenage girl. Don't expect consistency."

"She said she ate practically every meal here."

"Which is not the same as every meal, period."

"The guy said most days."

"Which is not the same as every day."

"But why would she skip today? She's curious, and she thinks I'm a source."

"Why would she expect you to be here?"

"Law enforcement has to eat, too."

"Then the coffee shop would be just as logical, near the lawyer's office. She knows there are two locations."

"We should go take a look."

"Too difficult. We wouldn't see anything from the street, and we can't go in on foot. Plus she's an early riser. She'll have been and gone."

"We should cruise her house again."

"That wouldn't tell us anything. The door is shut. We don't have X-ray vision."

"Shrago is out there somewhere."

Turner said, "Let's go back to the off-ramp."

Reacher said, "In a white car in daylight?"

"Just for ten minutes. To put our minds at rest."

In bright daylight the old binoculars were superb. The magnified image was crisp and hyper-vivid. Reacher could see every detail, of the street, of the white compact, of the purple Dodge, of the blue front door. But nothing was happening. Everything looked quiet. Just another sunny day, and just another endless stake-out, boring and uneventful, like most stake-outs are. There was no sign of Shrago. Some of the parked cars had heavy tints or blinding reflections, but they weren't plain enough to be rentals. And those plain enough to be rentals were empty.

"He's not there," Turner said.

"I wish we knew for sure she was," Reacher said back.

Then his phone rang. Captain Edmonds, in Virginia. She said, "I found another file on Shrago, from five years ago. The decision to keep him out of the Middle East was controversial. We were fighting two wars, we were hurting for numbers, hundreds of people were getting re-upped involuntarily, the National Guard was gone for years at a time, and the idea of paying a loose cannon who couldn't go to Iraq or Afghanistan was seen as absurd. First choice was involuntary separation, but he was making his case on compassionate grounds, so he had to be heard, and eventually the argument went all the way up the HRC chain of command, to an Assistant Deputy Chief of Staff for personnel, who ruled in Shrago's favor."

"And?" Reacher said.

"That same Assistant Deputy was also in charge of temporary commands. He was the guy who moved Morgan to Fort Bragg a year later."

"Interesting."

"I thought so. Which is why I called. Shrago owed him, and Morgan was his chess piece."

"What was his name?"

"Crew Scully."

"What kind of a name is that?"

"New England blue blood."

"Where is he now?"

"He got promoted. Now he's a Deputy Chief of Staff in his own right."

"Responsible for what?"

"Personnel," Edmonds said. "HRC oversight. Technically he's my boss."

"Who moved Morgan to the 110th, this week?"

"Scully's second-in-command, I assume. Unless things have changed."

"Will you check that for me? And will you check whether Scully has access to Homeland Security intelligence systems?"

"I don't think he would have."

"I don't think so either," Reacher said. He clicked off the call, and went back to staring at the street.

* * *

Juliet called Romeo, because some responsibilities were his, and he said, "Shrago tells me they're not traveling separately. He decided to check the rental depot, and he got there just in time to see the Range Rover getting towed."

"More fool them. Using one car limits them. Which is to our advantage."

"That's not the point. The Range Rover is on Baldacci's credit card. We'll have to pay the tow fee and the daily rental. It's another slap in the face."

"What else did Shrago see?"

"He's close. She's out of the house. Just walking around. There's no one within a mile of her. He's going to pick his spot."

"And get the message to them how?"

"At the diner. They've been there twice. There's a gentleman named Arthur who seems willing to pass the word."

Turner's ten minutes had turned into almost forty, but nothing had happened, either on the off-ramp behind them, or on the street in front of them. She said, "We have to go."

Reacher said, "Where?"

"Just drive. Randomly. Within a mile of her door, because if she's out, she's walking. Surface streets only, also because she's walking. Shrago will be thinking the same."

So they fired up the Ford and merged onto the 134,

and got off again immediately, and started the search on Vineland, block by block, randomly, except for her own street, which they decided not to risk. Most blocks were about a thousand feet long and two hundred feet deep, which meant there were about a hundred and twenty in a square mile, which meant there were nearly four hundred inside a circle with a two-mile diameter, which meant there were close to ninety miles of road to cover. But not quite, because some blocks were double-wide, and the highway shoulders and the ramps ate up space, and some tracts had never been built. About sixty miles, probably. Three hours' worth, at a safe speed of twenty. Not that moving around increased the chances of a random encounter. Space and time didn't work that way. But moving around felt better.

They saw nothing in the first hour, except the background blur of sidewalks and poles and trees and houses and stores, and parked cars in their hundreds. They saw not more than a handful of people, and they paid close attention to all of them, but none of them was the girl, and none of them was Shrago. They saw no cars crawling slow like their own. Most were heading from here to there innocently and normally, at a normal speed, and sometimes more. Which caused the only excitement in the whole of the second hour, when a dull black BMW ran a light about a hundred yards ahead, and was T-boned by an old Porsche on the cross street. Steam came up and a small crowd gathered, and then Reacher turned left and saw no more, until another random turn brought him back in line, by which time a cop car was there, with its light bar flashing, and after three more turns there was a second cop car, and an ambulance.

But apart from that, there was nothing. Nothing at all. Thirty minutes later Turner said, "Let's take an early lunch. Because she might, if she had an early breakfast. Or no breakfast at all."

"The diner?" Reacher said.

"I think so. Practically every meal means she might skip one, but not two."

So they worked their way back through the maze, and they joined Vineland just north of the neighborhood, and they rolled south until they saw the old coach diner dead ahead on the left, all gleaming and shining in the sun.

And crossing Vineland toward it was the girl.

Chapter 61

Juliet called Romeo, and he said, "I'm afraid it fell apart. We had a piece of bad luck. He needed to grab her near his car, obviously. Right next to it, ideally. He couldn't drag her down the street screaming, not for any appreciable distance. So he leapfrogged ahead and parked the car, and then he looped around on foot and came out again behind her, and it was all going fine, and he was all set to pass her right alongside the car, and they had about twenty yards left to go, and then some idiot ran a light and got into a fender bender, and suddenly there was a crowd of people, and a cop car, and then another cop car, and obviously Shrago couldn't do anything in front of a crowd of people or the LAPD, so the girl watched the fun for a minute and then walked on, and Shrago had to let her go, because at first he couldn't get his car out from the middle of all the mess, and then when he finally got going, he'd lost her and he couldn't find her again."

Romeo said, "So what next?"

"He's starting over. All her known haunts. Her house, the law office, the diner. He'll pick her up again somewhere."

"This has to be finished in California. We can't afford for them to come home."

Reacher slowed, and let the girl cross fifty yards ahead of him, and then he swung the wheel and followed her into the diner's lot. She went straight in through the door, and he parked the car, and Turner said, "Should I come in with you?"

Reacher said, "Yes, I want you to."

So they went in, and they waited just inside the door, where they had waited before. The diner looked exactly the same as the previous evening, with the blonde waitress back on duty in the left side of the coach, and the long-suffering brunette working the right side, and Arthur behind his counter, and the girl on her stool, way at the end. The blonde waitress came by, like before, with the same blank smile, and Reacher pointed to a booth on the right, one away from directly behind the girl, and the blonde gave them up to the brunette with no marked reluctance at all. They walked in and sat down, Reacher with his back to the room again, Turner facing him across the atomic laminate, the girl with her back to them both, about six feet away.

But she was watching them in the mirror.

Reacher waved at her reflection, partly as a greeting, partly as a *join us* gesture, and the kid lit up like

Christmas was coming and slid off her stool, and caught Arthur's eye and jerked her thumb at the booth behind her, as if to say *I'm moving again,* and then she stepped across, and Turner scooted over and the kid sat down next to her on the bench, the three of them all together in a tight little triangle.

Reacher said, "Samantha Dayton, Susan Turner, Susan Turner, Samantha Dayton."

The kid twisted around on the vinyl and shook hands with Turner and said, "Are you his assistant?"

Turner said, "No, I'm his commanding officer."

"Way cool. What agency?"

"Military police."

"Awesome. Who are all the others?"

"There's only us and the FBI."

"Are you leading or are they leading?"

"We are, of course."

"So it's your guy in the white car?"

"Yes, he's ours."

"Parachuted in from where?"

"I could tell you, but then I'd have to kill you."

The kid laughed, and looked happy as a clam. The inside scoop, and a woman CO, and jokes. She said, "So the guy due to show up is a military guy? Like an AWOL soldier saying goodbye to his family before disappearing forever? But why would his family have a lawyer? Or is it his lawyer? Is he a spy, or something? Like a very senior officer, all old and distinguished, but tragically disillusioned? Is he selling secrets?"

Reacher said, "Have you seen anyone today?"

"The same people as yesterday."

"No men on their own?"

"The man with the cropped ears is on his own today. In the rental. Maybe his partner is out sick."

"Where did you see him?"

"He came down Vineland in his car. I was in the coffee shop for breakfast. Near the lawyer's office. Although we'll need to rethink that involvement. This thing is a triangle, isn't it? And we don't know which one the lawyer is working for. Could be the neighbor, could be the soldier. Could be both of them, I suppose, although I don't see how. Or why, actually."

Reacher asked, "What time did you eat breakfast?"

"It was early. Just after the agents left."

"They left?"

"Just for twenty minutes. That seems to be the pattern. You should coordinate better. Everyone moves at the same time, which leaves a gap."

"That's bad."

"It's OK with me. It means I can get out without them knowing. Then when I come back they're all surprised, because they thought I was still in there."

"Is that what you did this morning?"

"It's what I'm going to do every morning."

"Did the man with the ears see you leave?"

"I don't think so."

"Did he see you anyplace else?"

"I don't think so. I was trying to blend in. Because of your people, not him. I didn't see him. But I saw his car again later. It was parked where there was a fender bender."

Reacher said, "You need to stay away from that guy."

"I know. You told me that yesterday. But I can't stay in the house all day."

Turner paused a beat, and asked, "How long have you lived in that house?"

"Always, I think. I don't remember any other houses. I'm pretty sure I was born in that house. That's what people say, isn't it? Even when they weren't, exactly. Which I wasn't, either. I was born in the hospital. But I went home to that house. Which is what the phrase means these days, I suppose, now that the whole parturition business has been institutionalized."

Turner said, "Have you ever lived in a car?"

"That's a weird question."

"You can tell us. We know people who would love to get that high on the food chain."

"Who?"

"Lots of people. What I mean is, we don't judge."

"Am I in trouble?"

Reacher said, "No, you're not in trouble. We're just checking a couple of things. What's your mom's name?"

"Is she in trouble?"

"No one's in trouble. Not on your street, anyway. This is about the other guy."

"Does he know my mom? Oh my God, is it *us* you're watching? You're waiting for him to come see my mom?"

"One step at a time," Reacher said. "What's your mom's name? And yes, I know about the Colt Python."

"My mom's name is Candice Dayton."

"In that case I would like to meet her."

"Why? Is she a suspect?"

"No, this would be personal."

"How could it be?"

"I'm the guy they're looking for. They think I know your mother."

"You?"

"Yes, me."

"You don't know my mother."

"They think face to face I might recognize her, or she might recognize me."

"She wouldn't. And you wouldn't."

"It's hard to say for sure, without actually trying it."

"Trust me."

"I would like to."

"Mister, I can tell you quite categorically you don't know my mom and she doesn't know you."

"Because you never saw me before? We're talking a number of years here, maybe back before you were born."

"How well are you supposed to have known her?"

"Well enough that we might recognize each other."

"Then you didn't know her."

"What do you mean?"

"Why do you think I always eat in here?"

"Because you like it?"

"Because I get it for free. Because my mom works here. She's right over there. She's the blonde. You walked past her two times already and you didn't bat an eye. And neither did she. You two never knew each other."

Chapter 62

Reacher slid along the bench and craned around and took a look. The blonde waitress was busy, moving left, moving right, blowing an errant strand of hair out of an eye, wiping a palm on a hip, smiling, taking an order.

He didn't know her.

He said, "Has she ever been to Korea?"

The kid said, "That's another weird question."

"How is it weird?"

"It is if you know her."

"How so?"

"Her whole stressed-out martyr shtick is based around how she's never been out of Los Angeles County but one time in her life, when a boyfriend took her to Vegas but couldn't pay for the hotel. She doesn't even have a passport."

"Are you certain about that?"

"That's why she dyes her hair. This is southern California. She has no papers."

"She doesn't need papers."

"She's an undocumented citizen. It takes a long time to explain."

"Is she doing OK?"

"This isn't the life she planned."

"Are you doing OK?"

"I'm fine," the kid said. "Don't worry about me."

Reacher said nothing, and Arthur came out of the blind spot behind his shoulder, and bent down and whispered in the kid's ear, quietly, but his hard consonants made it clear what he was saying, which was: *This lady and gentleman need to have a conference with another gentleman.* Whereupon the kid jumped up, all aglow, perfectly happy to be displaced by a yet-more-senior agent even closer to the heart of the drama. Arthur moved back out of sight, and the kid hustled after him, and smooth as silk her vacated spot on the bench was immediately filled by a small solid figure sliding into place, neatly, elbows already on the table, and triumph in his face.

Warrant Officer Pete Espin.

Reacher looked at Turner, and Turner shook her head, which meant Espin had men in the coach, at least two, probably armed, and probably close by. Espin got comfortable on the bench, and then he cupped his hands, like he was reassembling a shuffled deck, and he said, "You're not her daddy."

Reacher said, "Apparently."

"I checked, just for the fun of it. The State Department said Ms. Dayton never had a passport. The DoD said she never entered Korea on any other kind of document. So I checked some more, and it turns out the lawyer is selling stuff on the internet. Any kind of document, saying anything you want it to say. At one of two price levels, either paper only, or plausible. In this type of case plausible means real women, real children, and a real Xerox of a real birth certificate. And this guy is not the only one. This is a thriving business. There's a lot of inventory. You want a kid born on a certain date, you can take your pick."

"Who bought the affidavit?"

"He gave his name as Romeo, but his money was good. Out of the Cayman Islands."

"When did Romeo buy it?"

"The same morning Major Turner was arrested. It's an instant service. You tell them the names and the places and the dates and they doctor the boilerplate. You can even upload text, if you want. The documents are done in a computer and they come by e-mail, and they look like photocopies. Candice Dayton was chosen because of her kid's birthdate. The lawyer knew her as a waitress, from eating in here. She got a hundred bucks for signing her name. But the birthdate was dumb. Did you notice that? It was exactly halfway through your time at Red Cloud. As in, exactly. Which sounds like a guy looking at a calendar, not natural biology."

"Good point," Reacher said.

"So you're off the hook."

"But why was I ever on the hook? That's the big question. You got an answer for me? Why did Romeo buy that affidavit?"

Espin said nothing.

"And who is Romeo really?" Reacher asked.

No answer.

Turner said, "What happens next?"

Espin said, "You're under arrest."

"Is Reacher, too?"

"Affirmative."

"You need to call Major Sullivan at JAG."

"She called me first. The Big Dog thing is dead in the water, but between stepping into that cell at Dyer and this moment now, Reacher has committed about a hundred crimes we know about, and maybe more beyond that, from unlawful incarceration of a person in furtherance of a separate felony, to credit card fraud."

Reacher said, "Did you get a message from us through Sergeant Leach?"

"Apparently you want me to get over myself."

"I asked what you would have done differently."

"I would have placed my trust in the system."

"Bullshit."

"Especially if I was innocent."

"Was I innocent?"

Espin said, "Initially."

Reacher said, "You didn't answer my question. Why did Romeo buy that affidavit?"

"I don't know."

"And could it have been Romeo who let the Dog out again?"

"Possibly."

"Why would he do that? And the other thing? The

two phony affidavits. What was their purpose? What was their only possible purpose?"

"I don't know."

"Yes, you do. You're a smart guy."

"Romeo wanted you to run."

"Why did Romeo want me to run?"

"Because you were in Major Turner's business."

"And what does that say about Major Turner's business? If she's guilty, Romeo should want me as a witness. He should want me on the stand, confirming all the grisly details for the jury."

Espin paused a beat. Then he said, "I have orders to bring you back, majors. Both of you. The rest of it is above my pay grade."

"You know it's a frame," Reacher said. "You just told me Romeo has money in the Cayman Islands. He created Major Turner's account himself. This is not brain surgery. You've seen better scams than this. This is the idiots' guide. Therefore it's certain to fall apart. Most likely real soon. Because Turner and I are not morons. We're going to burn their house down. Which gives you a choice. Either you're the drone who brings us home in handcuffs mere days before our greatest triumph, or you engage your brain and you start figuring out where you want to be when the dust settles."

"Which would be where?"

"Not here."

Espin shook his head. "You know how it is. I have to come home with something."

"We can give you something."

"What kind of something?"

"An arrest of your own, a medalworthy determination to leave no stone unturned, and the icing on a very large cake. And the icing is always the sweetest and most visible part of a very large cake."

"I'm going to need more than the sales brochure."

"Someone beat Colonel Moorcroft half to death, and I think you've all concluded it wasn't me. So who was it? You'll be bringing in a long-time member of a very big deal, and you'll be tying a bow on it for the political class, by tilting the spotlight."

"Where would I find this long-time member?"

"You would look for someone who was off-post for an unexplained period of time."

"And?"

"You would figure someone tailed Moorcroft out of the breakfast room and either forced him or enticed him into a car. You would figure there was no other way to work it. And you would figure it wasn't an NCO. Because the breakfast room was in the Officers' Club. So you would go looking for an officer."

"Got a name?"

"Morgan. He set Moorcroft up for the beating. He delivered him. Check his laundry basket. I doubt he participated, but I bet he stood close enough to get a real good look."

"Was he off-post at the time?"

"He claims to have been in the Pentagon. His absence was well documented. It was a source of great concern. And the Pentagon keeps records. A lot of work, but a buck gets ten you'll prove he wasn't there."

"Is this solid?"

"Morgan is a part of a small and diverse group,

containing as far as we know at one end four NCOs from a logistics company at Fort Bragg, and at the other end two Deputy Chiefs of Staff."

"That's hard time if you're wrong."

"I know it."

"Two of them?"

"One of them is in Homeland Security, and one of them isn't."

"That's very hard time if you're wrong."

"But am I?"

Espin didn't answer.

Reacher said, "It's always fifty-fifty, Pete. Like tossing a coin. Either I'm wrong, or I'm right, either you bring us back, or you don't, either Deputy Chiefs are what they say they are, or they're not. Always fifty-fifty. One thing or the other is always true."

"And you're an unbiased judge?"

"No, I'm not unbiased. I'm going to rip their faces off while they sleep. But just because I'm mad about it doesn't mean they didn't do it."

"Got names?"

"One so far. Crew Scully."

"What kind of name is that?"

"New England blue blood, apparently."

"I bet he's a West Pointer."

"I'm a West Pointer, and I don't have a stupid name."

"I bet he's rich."

"Plenty of rich people in prison."

"Who's the other one?"

"We don't know."

"Crew Scully's best bud from prep school, probably. Those guys stick together."

Reacher said, "Maybe."

Espin said, "I get Morgan, and Major Turner gets those guys?"

"You'll be the human interest story."

"What is it they're supposed to be doing?"

So Turner ran through it all, starting with cash money obtained on the secondary markets, and ratty old pick-up trucks with weird license plates, with the cash in the trucks, and then the cash in army containers, and the contents of the army containers in the trucks, which then drive off into the mountains, while the cash is secretly loaded, ready to be secretly unloaded again by the four guys in North Carolina. All enabled by an Afghan native with a documented history of arms sales, and all coordinated by, and presumably enriching, the two Deputy Chiefs, who may or may not also be operating a rogue strategic initiative.

Espin said, "I thought you were being serious."

Chapter 63

Espin said, "What you describe just ain't happening. The United States military learned its lessons, major. Long ago. We count the paperclips now. Everything has a barcode. Everything is in a bombproof computer. We have companies of MPs at every significant site. We have more checks than a dog has fleas. We're not losing stuff anymore. Believe me. That old-style chaos is way out of date now. If there's a sock with a hole in it, that sucker comes home. If a single bullet got lost, there would be a shitstorm so bad we'd see the sky turn brown from here. It just ain't happening, ma'am."

Turner said nothing.

Reacher said, "But something is happening. You know that."

"I'm listening. Tell me what's happening."

"Talk to Detective Podolski at Metro. Morgan was off-post at the critical time."

"Morgan is still what you're giving me?"

"He's worth having. All I got was two fake law-suits."

"Seems like Morgan's value just went down, as part of a credible conspiracy."

"Something is happening," Reacher said again. "Fake bank accounts, fake legal documents, beatings, four guys chasing us all over. It's all going to look plenty credible when it's done. It always does. Hindsight is a wonderful thing. And the smart guys get their hindsight in first."

"Hell of a gamble," Espin said.

"It's always fifty-fifty, Pete. Like tossing a coin. Either Morgan is high value or he's low, and either something is happening or it isn't, and either you're a boring drone or you're the guy who was way ahead of the curve, getting ready to put another ribbon on his chest."

Espin said nothing.

Reacher said, "It's time to flip that coin, Pete. Heads or tails."

"Do you have a plan?"

"We're going back to D.C. You don't need to bring us home. We're going anyway."

"When?"

"Now."

"That's where Morgan is."

"That's where they all are."

Espin said, "Suppose you agree we fly together?"

Reacher said, "Works for us. But only you. No one else."

"Why?"

"I want you to leave your guys here another day.

The last of the four from Fort Bragg is hanging around. He thinks the girl still works as bait. So I want her protected. She might not be mine, but she's a sweet kid. Maybe because she's not mine."

"I guess my guys could spare a day."

"I want close personal protection, but unobtrusive. Don't scare her. Treat it like an exercise. Because it's likely nothing more than theoretical, anyway. It's us he wants. And he'll know what plane we're on, because Romeo will tell him. So he'll be right behind us. He might even be on the same flight."

Espin said nothing.

Reacher said, "Make your mind up, soldier."

Espin said, "I don't need to make my mind up. What you're proposing gives me six hours to make my mind up."

"But you need to make a decision."

"Delta at LAX ninety minutes from now," Espin said. He backed down the guys Reacher couldn't see, with standard infantry hand signals, and then he slid out to the aisle, and he stood up, and he walked away.

Reacher and Turner followed him out a minute later. The girl was in her mother's half of the coach, sitting on a stool, saying something to Arthur that was making him smile. Reacher watched her as he walked. All legs and arms, all knees and elbows, the jean jacket, the pants, the new blue T-shirt, the matching shoes, no socks, no laces, the hair like summer straw, halfway down her back, the eyes, and the smile. Fatherhood. Always unlikely. Like winning the Nobel Prize, or playing in the World Series. Not for him.

In the car Turner said, "How do you feel?"

"No different," he said. "I didn't have a kid before, and I don't have one now."

"What would you have done?"

"Doesn't matter now."

"You OK?"

"I guess I was getting used to the idea. And I liked her. We might have had things in common. Which is weird. I guess people can be the same, the world over. Even if they're not related."

"Do you think she's going to fear the howling wolf?"

"I think she envies it already."

"Then maybe you are related. From way back in time."

Reacher took one last look at her, through the diner's small framed window, and then Turner drove away, south on Vineland, and she was lost to sight.

LAX was going to be the 101 to the 110, with a final sideways hop on El Segundo Boulevard, and it was going to take most of the ninety minutes Espin had given them, because the freeways were rolling slow. Edmonds called again from Virginia while they were still north of the Hollywood Bowl, and she said, "Crew Scully moved Morgan to the 110th personally. He didn't delegate on that occasion. And he normally does, with temporary commands. And he has no access to Homeland Security intelligence systems."

Reacher said, "Check if he has a friend who does."

"I'm already on it."

"Let me know."

"Are we still on the right side of history?"

"Count on it," Reacher said, and hung up.

The traffic rolled on, but strangely, always moving but very slowly, as if every driver was a movie guy shooting a scene in slow motion. Turner said, "This could be like we arrested ourselves, you know. We could walk off that plane, and Espin could cuff us right there in the D.C. terminal."

"We'll think of something," Reacher said. "Six hours is a long time."

"Got any ideas?"

"Not yet."

"These are professional weapons handlers. That's all they do."

"Fifty-fifty, Susan. Either it's all they do or it isn't."

"What else could they do?"

"We have six hours to figure that out."

"Suppose we don't figure it out?"

Reacher said, "Espin heard the name Crew Scully and figured the guy was rich. Suppose he is? Suppose they both are?"

"We know they're rich."

"But we're making an assumption about how they got rich. Suppose they were rich before. Suppose they were always rich. Suppose they're old-money East Coast aristocrats."

"OK, I'll watch out for old men in faded pink pants."

"It might alter the equation. We're assuming a powerful profit motive here. We might need to downgrade that. They could smooth out their own bumps. That hundred grand might have been their own money."

"This is not a hobby, Reacher. Not with fake bank accounts, and fake legal papers, and old men getting beat up, and four guys coming after us."

"I agree, this is way more than a hobby."

"Then what is it?"

"I don't know. I'm just thinking out loud. I'm trying to get a jump on the six hours."

They left the white Ford in a covered lot at the Delta terminal, and they dropped the key in a trash can, which they figured would cost Romeo plenty in rental and recovery fees. Turner stripped Rickard's Glock and put the separated parts in four more trash cans. Then they walked inside through the wrong door and took the long way around. They came up on the ticket counters from behind. Espin was already there. He must have taken the 405. And he must have taken it alone. There was no one with him. No one next to him, and no one in the shadows. He was standing still, facing the main terminal doors. They walked up behind him, and he spun around, and Reacher bought three first class seats with Baldacci's credit card.

Chapter 64

They were at the gate twenty minutes before boarding started, in seats with a wide field of view, and they didn't see Shrago. Not that Reacher expected to. LA was a big place, hard to get around, and first the bank charge would have to be spotted, and then Shrago would have to get himself to the airport, and there simply wasn't enough time. So Reacher drank coffee and relaxed, and then boarding started, and then his phone rang, so he took his seat while talking, which was what pretty much everyone else was doing.

It was Edmonds on the phone, from Virginia. She said, "The 75th MP just informed me about the Candice Dayton situation."

"I told you I didn't remember her."

"I apologize. I should have been less skeptical."

"Don't worry about it. I almost believed it myself."

"I asked around about Crew Scully's friends."

"And?"

"He had a West Point classmate he stayed close to.

They came up together like bottle rockets. I asked five separate people, and this is the guy I got from all of them."

"What is he?"

"Currently the army's Deputy Chief of Staff for intelligence."

"That would do it."

"They share similar backgrounds, they live near each other in Georgetown, and they're members of all the same clubs, including some very exclusive ones."

"Are they rich?"

"Not like some people are rich. But they're comfortable, in an old-fashioned way. You know how it is with those people. Comfortable takes a few million."

"What's the guy's name?"

"Gabriel Montague."

"You were right about the similar backgrounds. Gabe and Crew. Sounds like a bar near Harvard. Or a store where you buy torn jeans for three hundred dollars."

"These are huge targets, Reacher. These are giants walking the earth. And you have precisely zero evidence of anything."

"You think like a lawyer. One of which I need right now, by the way. I'm an innocent man. I don't want any smoke and mirrors about what happened after they locked me up for two things I didn't do. If I broke out, it was because I was entitled to."

"Major Sullivan is working on that. She wants everything dismissed. The fruits of a poisoned tree."

"Tell her to be quick. We're heading back right now, with a semi-official escort. I don't want any fun and games at Reagan National. She's got about six hours."

"I'll tell her."

Then the steward came on the PA and said the cabin door was closing, and all devices should be in the off position. So for the first time in his life Reacher complied with the crew member's instruction, and he dropped the phone in his pocket, and the plane pushed back and started to taxi. It took off over the ocean, and then it pulled a wide right-hand 180, so it was facing east again, and it recrossed the coast above Santa Monica, and it climbed as it flew inland, so that North Hollywood and the Ventura Freeway and Vineland Avenue and the coach diner and the little house with the blue door were all off the port side, far away and far below, barely visible at all.

A three-way conversation in first class was not easy. The chairs were wide, which put the window seat on one side pretty far from the aisle seat on the other. And the crew members were always back and forth from the galley, with endless free food and drink. Which all helped Reacher see why being rich was called being comfortable, but which made talking difficult. In the end Espin got up and perched on the arm of Turner's chair, and Turner leaned over nearer Reacher in the window, and they got it to where everyone could see and hear everyone else, and Espin said, "If I need any kind of warrant for Morgan, obviously they're going to ask me about the nature of this alleged conspiracy. So you better have a story for me by the time we get off this plane. Or you're giving me nothing. In which case we'd need to rethink your special status."

Reacher said, "It's not going to work that way, Pete. This is not an audition. We're not trying to break into the movies. And you have no vote here. We're going our separate ways at Reagan National, whether or not we have a story, and whether or not you like it, and you're going to wave us goodbye with a cheery smile on your face, either standing up by the door or sitting down in a wheelchair with a broken leg. Those are the ground rules. Are we clear?"

Espin said, "But we share what information we have?"

"Absolutely. As in, Captain Edmonds just told me Crew Scully has a close personal friend named Gabriel Montague."

"He would. Did they go to prep school together?"

"More or less. West Point, anyway."

"Who is he?"

"The army's Deputy Chief of Staff for intelligence."

"That's about as high as it gets."

"Almost."

"Do you have evidence?"

"My lawyer assessed it as precisely zero. In the interests of full disclosure."

"But you think those are the two?"

"I do now."

"Why now?"

"William Shakespeare. He wrote a play called *Romeo and Juliet*. Two households, both alike in dignity. A pair of star-crossed lovers, because Juliet was a Capulet and Romeo was a Montague. Like the Sharks and the Jets in *West Side Story.* You could rent the movie."

"You think Montague goes by Romeo? Would he be that dumb?"

"He probably thinks it's cute. Like faded pink pants. He probably thinks people like us never heard of William Shakespeare."

"Your lawyer was right. Precisely zero."

"She's a lawyer. You're not. You're the guy with the coin. Either Montague is Romeo or he's not. It's exactly fifty-fifty."

"That's like going to Vegas and betting the mortgage on red."

"An even chance is a wonderful thing."

"These are Deputy Chiefs of Staff, Reacher. You'd want to be very sure. You'd have to shoot to kill."

Romeo called Juliet and said, "They're on the way home. Three tickets in first class. Which is another slap in the face. The third ticket is Espin, from the 75th MP. At first I thought he had made the arrest, but then why would Reacher buy the tickets? They've turned our flank. That's what they've done. Espin has gone native."

Juliet said, "Shrago is at least an hour from the airport."

"Tell him to hustle. He's on American, the next flight out."

"How far behind Reacher will he be?"

"Two hours."

"That's a long time. We have one man left, and he isn't even here. I think we're beaten."

"It was always a possible outcome. We knew what kind of business we were getting into. We knew what we might have to do."

"We survived a good long time."

"And we'll survive a two-hour gap. Nothing will happen. Major Turner will need to shower. Traveling with women is inefficient. And after that it will get easier for Shrago. They'll have to come looking for us. We won't have to look for them."

Espin came and went, back and forth across the aisle, based on the forensic value of the conversation, and his comfort level. Perching on an arm was not the kind of ride Baldacci had paid for. Most of the time he sat and pondered on his own. As did Turner, and as did Reacher. Without notable success. Then Turner called Espin back, and when he was settled she said, "We have one fixed point, which is the logistics chain. It's a two-way conveyor belt, and it never stops. Right now it's sending empty boxes in and bringing full boxes out. And those full boxes are full of all the right stuff. Barcoded socks with holes in them. I accept that. So nothing's happening. Except we know something's happening. So what if those empty boxes aren't empty? We know the tribesmen aren't buying the stuff with the barcodes, but what if they're buying stuff sent over exclusively for them? Almost like mail order. Which is why the four guys at Fort Bragg were important. They packed the crates that should have been empty."

Espin said, "There are systems in place at both ends."

"Equally paranoid?"

"I don't think that's possible."

"So it could be happening?"

"It could be."

"But Reacher thinks the profit motive might not be front and center. Which might make this a personal project. Maybe they're playing favorites. Maybe they're arming one faction over another. Maybe they think they're big experts on Afghanistan. Those old New England guys always think they're half British. Maybe they remember the old days on the Northwest Frontier. Maybe they think they have unique expertise."

"Possible."

"But the conveyor belt is two way. We must never forget that. They might be bringing stuff out, not in, concealed among the returning ordnance. Which also makes the guys at Bragg important. They'd have to unpack it in secret, and move it along."

"What kind of stuff?"

"If profit isn't front and center, then it could be some kind of personal enthusiasm. Art, maybe, like statues or sculptures. The stuff the Taliban trashes. If you're a refined gentleman, that kind of thing might appeal to you. Except their reaction has been way over the top for art. No one gets beat up over an old statue."

"So what kind of stuff?"

"We've got two old gentlemen with personal enthusiasms that have to be kept very secret. Because the

enthusiasms are criminal, and also shameful somehow. But also lucrative, in a gentlemanly way. That's
the feeling I'm getting."

"Young girls? Young boys? Orphans?"

"Look at it from Emal Zadran's point of view. He
was a screw-up and a failure, but he rehabilitated himself. He earned some respect in his community. How?
Someone gave him a role, that's how. As an entrepreneur again, most likely. Someone wanted to buy or
sell, and Zadran became the go-to guy. Because he
knew the right people. He had connections already in
place. Maybe crucial relationships, maybe just by
chance."

Espin said, "Buy or sell what?"

Reacher said, "We'll figure that out in D.C. Right
after you wave us goodbye, either standing up or sitting down."

They slept the rest of the way. The cabin was warm,
and the chairs were comfortable, and the motion was
soothing. Reacher dreamed about the girl, at a much
younger age, maybe three, chubby not bony, dressed
in the same outfit but miniaturized, with tiny laceless
tennis shoes. They were walking on a street somewhere, her small hand soft and warm in his giant paw,
her little legs going like crazy, trying to keep up, and
he was glancing over his shoulder all the time, anxious about something, worried about how she was
going to run if she had to, in her laceless shoes, and
then realizing he could just scoop her up in his arms,
and run for her, maybe forever, her fragrant weight-

less body no burden at all, and relief flooded through him, and the dream faded away, as if its job was done.

Then the air pressure changed and the steward started up with the stuff about seat backs and tray tables and upright positions. Espin glanced across the aisle, and Reacher and Turner glanced back at him. The coin was in the air, right then. The guy was deciding. Was he a drone, or was he ahead of the curve? Fifty-fifty, Reacher thought, like everything else in the world.

Then they were on approach, the big plane suddenly heavy and ponderous again, and as soon as the crew members had taken their seats everyone turned on their phones, and Reacher saw he had a voice mail message from Major Sullivan, an hour old. He called it up and heard some static, and then, "Confirming no action will be taken against you for any matters arising out of either of the phony affidavits. So you're in the clear, as of now. But Major Turner is still considered a legitimate fugitive. Her situation is the same as it always was. So the clock will start ticking all over again, the moment you touch down. You'll be seen as aiding and abetting. You'll be an accessory to a very serious felony. Unless you walk away from her in the airport. Which I strongly suggest you do, speaking as your lawyer."

He deleted the message, and dialed Edmonds. She answered, and he asked, "Where were Scully and Montague seven years ago?"

She said, "I'll try to find out."

And then the plane touched down, and the clock started ticking.

Chapter 65

First on meant first off, too, and the official door at the end of the jet bridge was still closed when they got there. Time zones meant it was very late on the East Coast. Reacher pushed the door and scanned ahead. There was a thin crowd at the gate. Not as bad as Long Beach. Maybe only ten undercover MPs and ten FBI agents inside the first thirty feet alone. Reacher held the door and let Espin go first, and he watched him very carefully. But Espin looked for no one in particular, and he made no eye contact with anyone, and he made no furtive signs or gestures. He just moved through the crowd like a regular person. Reacher and Turner followed after him, and a minute later they all regrouped in a yard of clear space, in the corridor under the baggage claim sign, and Reacher said, "You go on ahead. We're going to stay here."

Espin said, "Why?"

"In case you put your guys the other side of security."

"There are no guys."

"We'll stay here anyway."

"Why?"

"Tactical considerations."

"I'll give you twenty-four hours."

"You'll never find us."

"I found you in LA. And there's bait here, too. I'll know where to look."

"You should concentrate on Morgan."

"Twenty-four hours," Espin said, and then he walked away. Reacher and Turner watched him go, and Reacher said, "Let's get coffee."

Turner said, "Are we staying here?"

Reacher looked at the arrivals board, and said, "It would make some kind of sense. Next in is American, in about two hours. Shrago's bound to be on it. And from the airplane door to the other side of security, he's bound to be unarmed. So this would be the place to hit him."

"Are we going to?"

"No, but I wanted to put the idea in Espin's head. In case he gets cold feet an hour from now. He'll assume we're still here. But we won't be. We'll get the coffee to go. We'll be right behind him."

In Reacher's experience every successful venture in Washington, D.C., had one indispensable thing in common, which was a sound base of operations. But such a place could not be bought with cash. Any kind of a decent hotel was going to need a credit card. Which meant either Margaret Vega was going to pay, or they were going to tell Gabriel Montague where they were staying. Turner was in favor of telling him, so Shrago would show up, so they could deal with him. Reacher disagreed.

She said, "Why?"

"If they send Shrago to our location, and he disappears, they're going to know what happened to him."

"Obviously."

"I don't want them to know what happened to him. I want them uncertain. For as long as humanly possible. I want them not knowing. I want them staring into the void, hoping for a sign."

"This is why we need more women officers. For us it's enough to win. For you, the other guy has to know he lost."

"I want them to keep their cell phones switched on. That's all. It might be the only way we prove this for sure. It might be the only way we find them in the first place. Shrago needs to disappear somewhere unknown, and we have to get the numbers out of his phone, and then Sergeant Leach needs to hit up a whole different bunch of friends, and we need to find those phones before they finally give up on Shrago and switch them off."

So Margaret Vega paid for a night on the twelfth floor of a very nice hotel with a view of the White House, in a room that had everything they needed, and plenty they didn't. Turner wanted to get clothes, but it was midnight and nothing was open. So they showered long and slow and wrapped up in robes about two inches thick, and then they sat and ticked away the time until they figured it was twenty minutes before Shrago's plane would go wheels-down across the river. At which point they got dressed again, and went out.

Romeo called Juliet and said, "I kept a flag on the Margaret Vega card, just in case Turner went shopping on her own, and it just bought a night in a hotel here in town."

Juliet said, "Shrago's phone will be on again about two minutes from now."

"Tell him not to take a cab straight there."

They saw Shrago come out of the terminal. They were in a cab, twenty yards away. The cab was sixteen feet long and six feet wide, but it was invisible. It was a cab at an airport. Shrago didn't see it. He just waited in line behind one other person, and got in a cab of his own.

"That's the guy," Reacher said.

"I see him," the driver said. The meter was still running from the ride from the hotel. Plus a hundred dollar tip. Plus another hundred for the fun of it. That was the deal. It wasn't their money.

The driver eased off the curb and stayed about fifty yards behind Shrago's cab. Which headed for the heart of town, over the bridge and straight onto 14th Street, and across the Mall and through the Federal Triangle. Then it crossed New York Avenue and stopped.

Shrago got out.

The cab drove away.

They were about level with Lafayette Square, which was right in front of the White House, but they were two blocks east, still on 14th Street. Turner said, "What's here?"

"Nothing, apparently," Reacher said, because Shrago had started walking, north on 14th, to the corner with H Street.

He turned left.

Reacher paid the driver with Billy Bob's money, three hundred keep-the-change dollars, and they got out and hustled up to the same corner. Shrago was already into his second block. He was moving fast. He was about to pass the corner of Lafayette Square, which would give him nothing to look at on his left. Not in the dark. And only one thing to look at on his right, basically.

"He's going to our hotel," Turner said. "An approach on foot, so the cab driver doesn't remember. Montague has the Vega card, too."

"From the first flight. Smart guy. He kept on tracking it."

"This derails your strategy a little."

"No plan ever survives first contact with the enemy."

They hung back, but Shrago didn't. He went straight in the hotel door, full speed. Like a busy man with important issues to resolve. Getting himself into the role.

Turner said, "Got a new plan?"

Reacher said, "We're not in there. He'll figure that out eventually. Then he'll come out again."

"And?"

"Did you like the first plan, with the cell phones?"

"It was pretty good."

"Shrago might rescue it for us. Soon as he figures out we're not in there, he might call his boss immediately. Like a real time update. Maybe his boss demands it. In which case what happens after that is nothing to do with you and me. We weren't there. He just told them that. They're back in the unknown."

"If he calls."

"Fifty-fifty. Either he does, or he doesn't."

"If we know that he's called."

"He might be on the phone as he walks out."

"He might have called from our empty room."

"Fifty-fifty. Either we see it, or we don't. Either we know, or we guess."

They hung back in the park's outer shadows, and waited. It was almost two o'clock in the morning. The weather had not changed. It was cold and damp. Reacher thought about the girl's laceless sneakers. Not fifty-state shoes. Then he thought about hotel security, the night watch, checking a bogus ID, opening the register, placing a call to the room, heading upstairs with a pass key. Ten minutes, maybe.

It was nine minutes.

Shrago came back out through the door.

There was no phone in his hand.

Turner said, "Heads or tails, Reacher."

Reacher stepped out of the shadows and said, "Sergeant Shrago, I need you over here. I have some urgent news."

Chapter 66

Shrago didn't move. He stood still, right there on the H Street sidewalk. Reacher was directly opposite, on the other sidewalk. It was quiet. Two o'clock in the morning. A company town. Reacher said, "Sergeant Shrago, the news is that as of this very moment you fit a demographic otherwise known as shit out of luck. Because now you can't win. We're too close. Unless you take us both out, right here and right now. On this street. Which you won't. Because you can't. Because you're not good enough. So you're not going home with a prize tonight. What you need is damage control. Which you can get. All you need to do is write everything down."

Shrago didn't answer.

Reacher said, "Or you could speak it out loud into a tape recorder, if writing isn't your thing. But one way or the other they'll make you tell the story. This is going to be a big scandal. Not just the army asking questions. We'll have Senate committees. You need to be the first one in. They always let the first one go. Like you're a hero. You need to be that guy, Shrago."

Shrago said nothing.

"You can say you don't know the top boys. Less stress that way. They'll believe you. Concentrate on Morgan instead. About how he delivered Moorcroft for the beating. They'll eat that up with a spoon."

No response.

"There are only two choices, sergeant. You can run away, or you can cross the street. And running away buys you nothing. If we don't get you tonight, we'll get you tomorrow. So crossing the street is the better option. Which you have to do anyway, whether you want to shake our hands, or take us out."

Shrago crossed the street. He stepped off his curb, and walked, across lanes that could feel small in a car, but which looked pretty wide on foot. Reacher watched him all the way, his eyes and his shoulders and his hands, and he saw a kind of off-Broadway performance, a man seeing the light, a man finally understanding where his duty lay, and it was a pretty good act, but showing through all the time was a plan to get past Reacher long enough to put Turner out of action, which would level the contest at one on one. Reacher could see it in his eyes, which were manic, and in his shoulders, which were tensed and driven forward by adrenaline, and in his hands, which were open but which were clenching and unclenching, just a quarter inch either way, like the guy couldn't wait to set things in motion.

He stepped up on Reacher's curb.

Reacher said nothing. He didn't push it. He didn't

need to. Either way Shrago was going to talk to Espin. After getting out of a car, or after getting out of a coma. The choice was his. He had been born free.

But not smart. He passed on the car, and opted for the coma. Which Reacher understood. Immediate action was always the best bet. Shrago lined himself up, with Reacher to his right, and Turner beyond Reacher's far shoulder. Reacher figured the guy was planning a left elbow backhand to his throat, which he would use to claw his way onward, as if propelled by an oar, so he could get to Turner instantly, with a free right hand and time for a single decisive blow, which would have to be hard, and which would have to be to the center of her face. Busted nose, maybe cheekbones, maybe orbital sockets, unconsciousness, concussion. Maybe even a cracked skull, or a broken neck.

Which wasn't going to happen.

"Ground rules," Reacher said. "No ear biting."

Up close the guy looked extraordinary. His head was gleaming in the street lights, and his eyes were socketed way back, and the bones in his face looked hard and sharp, like a person could break his hand just by hitting them. The waistband of his pants was cinched in tight with a belt, and below it his thighs ballooned outward, and above it his chest swelled wide. He was maybe fifteen years younger than Reacher, a young bull, hard as a rock, with aggression coming off him like a smell. His ears had the center whorls intact like any other guy, but the flatter parts around them had been cut away, probably with scissors, very tight in, so that what was left looked like pasta, like uncooked tortellini florets, shiny, the color of a white man's flesh. Not exactly hexagons. A hexagon was a regular shape, with six equal sides, and Shrago's stubs had been trimmed for extreme closeness, not geometric regularity. They were irregular polygons, more accurately. Reacher figured if the kid had been his, he would have had a discussion. No point in being a pedant, unless you got it exactly right.

He said, "Last chance, sergeant. Time to make the big decision. We know all about Scully, and Montague, and Morgan. The only way to save yourself is to start talking. A soldier's best weapon is his brain. Time to start using yours. But either way I'm going to break your arm. Full disclosure. Because you hurt the girl in the Berryville Grill. Which was uncalled for. Do you have a problem with women? Was it women who cut your ears off?"

Shrago planted his feet and twisted from the waist, violently, to his right, and downward a little, so fast that his left arm was flung way beyond him, so far that his bent back showed in the light. Next up would have been the same twist back again, even faster, even more violent, with the left arm carefully marshaled this time, with the elbow aiming for the far side of Reacher's throat, with extension, so the blow would both do its job and serve as a kind of foothold, to lever himself onward to Turner.

Would have been.

Reacher knew it was coming, so he was moving a hair-trigger split second after Shrago was, matching Shrago's twist with a twist of his own, like two dancers almost coordinated, with Reacher's giant right fist hooking low to exactly where Shrago's exposed kidney was about to arrive, because of his big turn, with Reacher all the time trying to parse the emotion, trying to judge how much of it was about the ears, and how much of it was about Scully and Montague, because the degree of passion in a cause's defense was an indicator of its depth, and in the end he figured a lot of it was the ears, but some of it was defense, of something sweet and cozy and lucrative.

Then Shrago reached his point of equilibrium, all wound up like a spring, and he started to unwind the violent twist in the opposite direction, with his elbow coming up on target, but before he got even an inch into it Reacher's right fist landed, a perfect hit, a paralyzing blow to the kidney, a sick, stunning, spreading pain, and Shrago staggered, his coordination lost, his stance opening wide, and Reacher was left to unwind his own twist, all by himself in his own good time, which he did, with his left fist coming up low to high and finding the side of Shrago's neck, below the corner of his jaw, a fast and heavy double tap, one, two, right, left, the kidney, the neck, which rocked Shrago the other way, leaving him upright but good for an eight count, which he didn't get, because fighting in the dark on the edge of Lafayette Square was not a civilized sport with rules. Instead Reacher looked him over in the dim light and figured only one part of his body was harder than the bones of Shrago's face, so he skipped in and head-butted him, right on the bridge of his nose, like a bowling ball swung fast, like there was a head on the floor at the end of the maple lane, right there at the point of release. Reacher danced back and Shrago stayed on his feet for a long second, and then his knees got the message that the lights were out upstairs, and he went down in a vertical heap, like he had jumped off a wall. Reacher rolled him on his front, with the sole of his boot, and then he bent down and got hold of a wrist, and twisted it until the arm was rigid and backward, and then he broke the elbow with the same boot sole. He went through the pockets, and found a wallet and a phone, but no gun, because the guy had come straight from the airport.

Then he stood up and breathed out and looked at Turner and said, "Call Espin and tell him to come pick this guy up. Tell him he'll get what he needs for his warrant."

They waited in the shadows at the far corner of the park. Shrago's phone was the same cheap instrument as Rickard's, a mission-specific pre-paid throwaway, and it was set up the same way, but with four numbers in the contacts list, not three, the first being Lozano, Baldacci, and Rickard, and the fourth entered simply as *Home.*

And the call register showed Shrago had phoned home two minutes before stepping out of the hotel.

"From our empty room," Turner said. "You guessed right. Your plan survived contact with the enemy."

Reacher nodded. He said, "They probably sent him searching elsewhere. In which case they won't expect a call from him, not until he has news. And they won't call him before morning, probably. Which we won't

answer anyway. Which will leave them a little con-
fused and anxious. We might get twelve hours, before
they quit on him."

"We better tell Espin to keep it under the radar. Or
Montague will see the arrest. He's certain to be mon-
itoring the 75th." So Turner did that, with a second
call to Espin, and then she dialed Sergeant Leach's
cell. She started out with the same good-conscience
preamble she had used the first time, advising Leach
to hang up and report the call to Morgan, but for the
second time Leach didn't, so Turner gave her the
number Shrago had been calling, and she asked her to
hit up anyone she knew who was capable of a little
freelance signals intelligence. From Turner's tone it
was clear Leach was offering a cautiously optimistic
outlook. Reacher smiled in the dark. U.S. Army sergeants. There was nothing they couldn't do.

Then a car stopped at the other end of the park, a
battered sedan like the thing that had dumped Reacher
at the motel on the first night, and two big guys got
out, in boots and ACUs, and they hauled Shrago out
of the bushes and laid him on the rear seat. Not without a little difficulty. Shrago was no lightweight.

Then the guys got back in their car and drove away.
Reacher and Turner paused a decent interval, like a
funeral, and then they crossed the street again, and
stepped in through the hotel door, and rode up to
their room in the elevator.

Chapter 67

They showered again, purely as a piece of cleansing symbolism, and to use some more towels, of which there were about forty in the bathroom, most of them big enough and thick enough to sleep under. Then they waited for Leach to call back, which they figured would happen either soon or never, because either her network had the right kind of people in it, or it didn't. But the first phone to ring was Reacher's, with information from Edmonds. She said, "Seven years ago Crew Scully had just made Assistant Deputy Chief of Staff, for personnel. He hasn't changed his billet since. Back then he was based in Alexandria. Now all of HRC is at Fort Knox, in Kentucky. Except for the Deputy Chief's office, which stayed in the Pentagon. Which is why Scully is still able to live in Georgetown."

Reacher said, "He sounds like a very boring guy."

"But Montague doesn't. Seven years ago Montague

was in Afghanistan. He commanded our in-country intelligence effort. All of it. Not just the army's."

"Big job."

"You bet."

"And?"

"I can't prove anything. There's no surviving paperwork."

"But?"

"He must have signed off on Zadran. That's the way the protocol works. No way did a suspected grenade smuggler go home to the mountains without a say-so from Intelligence. So that question you asked before, about why didn't they just shoot him anyway? Basically because Montague told them not to, that's why. So Zadran owed Montague, big time."

"Or Zadran had something on Montague, big time."

"Whichever, we can trace the relationship back at least seven years."

Reacher said, "I should have asked you to look at Morgan seven years ago."

Edmonds said, "I was surprised you didn't. So I used my own initiative. Morgan has been in and out of everywhere, basically. He's the go-to guy for filling a gap. But we live in a random universe, and he's been in more logistics battalions than randomness alone would predict. None of them supplying Iraq, and all of them supplying Afghanistan. Which is not entirely random either."

"Was it always Scully who moved him?"

"Every single time."

"Thank you, captain."

"What side of history are we on right now?"

But Reacher hung up without answering, because another phone was ringing. Not Turner's, but Shrago's. Like Rickard's had, with the crazy birdsong. The same kind of phone. Shrago's was on the hotel dresser, loud and piercing, grinding away like a mechanical toy. The window on the front said: *Incoming Call.* Which was superfluous information. But then directly below it said: *Home.*

The phone rang eight times, and then it stopped.

Reacher said nothing.

Turner said, "That was anxiety. Simple as that. We haven't spent any more money, so we haven't generated any new leads. So they've got nothing to tell him."

"I wonder how long they'll stay anxious. Before they get real."

"Denial is a wonderful thing." Turner walked over to the window, and peered out between the drapes. She said, "When I get back I'm going to have my office steam cleaned. I don't want any trace of Morgan left behind."

"Why did Montague let Zadran go home to the mountains?"

"You would want to say either political reasons or legal reasons."

"Both of which are possible. But what if it was something else?"

"I can't see what else. The guy was in his middle thirties at the time, and the youngest of five, which was two strikes against in a very hierarchical culture, and he was a screw-up and a failure, which was strike three, so the guy had no status and no value, and clearly no real talent either. So he was nobody's number-one draft pick. This was not about recruiting an asset, either for the day job or the personal enthusiasm."

Then Shrago's phone rang again. Same birdsong, same grinding, same words on the screen. It rang eight times, and then it stopped.

Juliet came back into the room, and sat down on a daybed. From a second daybed six feet away Romeo said, "Well?"

Juliet said, "I tried twice."

"Gut feeling?"

"He might have been busy. If he gets within a hundred feet of them he's going to turn his phone off. I think that's pretty obvious."

"How long would he remain in close proximity to them?"

"Could be hours, theoretically."

"So we just wait for his call?"

"I think we have to."

"Suppose it doesn't come?"

"Then we're finished."

Romeo breathed out, long and slow. He said, "Win or lose, it's been a good ride."

Turner's phone rang a minute after Shrago's stopped for the second time. She put it on speaker and Leach said, "It's a pre-paid burner probably bought at a Wal-Mart. If it was bought for cash it's about as traceable as my sister's ex-husband."

Turner said, "Any details at all?"

"Plenty. The only thing we don't know is who owns it. We can see everything else. That phone has called only two numbers in its life, and it's been called by only two numbers in its life, both of which are the same two numbers."

"Equally divided?"

"Very lopsided."

"In favor of?"

Leach read out a number, and it wasn't Shrago's.

"That's got to be Romeo," Reacher said. "Sergeant, we need you to check that number next."

"I already took that liberty, major. It's the same deal. A pre-paid burner from Wal-Mart, but this one is even more lonely. The only number it ever called, and the only number that ever called it, is its mate. This is a very compartmentalized communications network. Their tradecraft and their discipline look exemplary to me. You're dealing with very smart people. Permission to speak freely?"

Turner said, "Of course."

"You should proceed with extreme caution, majors. And you could start by tightening up a little."

"In what way?"

"The other number the first guy called belongs to a phone currently immobile two blocks north of the White House. My guess is you're in that fancy hotel, and either a bad guy is watching the building, or you already took the phone away from him, and it's in your room. In which case you need to bear in mind, if I can see it, they can see it, too. Until you switch it off, that is. Which you should think about doing."

"You can see it?"

"Technology is a wonderful thing."

"Can you see the other two phones?"

"Absolutely. I'm looking at them right now."

"Where are they?"

"They're together at an address in Georgetown."

"Now? Is this real time?"

"As it's happening. Refreshed every fifteen seconds."

"It's the middle of the night. Most folks are fast asleep."

"Indeed."

"Scully's place, or Montague's?"

"Neither one. I don't know what the building is."

Chapter 68

Leach said there was a lot of argument about triangulation and wifi and GPS and margins of error, and no one was talking left coat pocket or right pants pocket, but most would agree you could say with reasonable certainty which individual building a cell phone was in. And the bigger the building, the greater the certainty became, and Leach was fixed on a fairly large building. She had been able to isolate the address, and she had found it on the computer, and she said the street view showed it to be a fairly grand townhouse. She relayed the visuals, which included an antique brick facing, and four stories, and twin sash windows either side of a fancy front door, which was painted shiny black and had a brass lantern above it. There was a letter slot and a street number on the door, and a small brass plaque that seemed to say *Dove Cottage*.

Turner stayed on the line with Leach, and Reacher called Edmonds from his own phone. He gave her the address in question, and he asked her to search wherever she could, like tax records or title data or zoning applications. She said she would, and they hung up, and Turner hung up with Leach, and Turner said, "We don't have a car."

Reacher said, "We don't need one. We'll do what Shrago did. We'll take a cab, and we'll approach on foot."

"Didn't work out so well for Shrago."

"We're not Shrago. And they're defenseless now. Deputy Chiefs live in a bubble. It's a very long time since they did anything for themselves."

"Are you going to cut their heads off with a butter knife?"

"I didn't get one yet. Maybe I could ask room service."

"Am I still CO?"

"What's on your mind?"

"I want a clean arrest. I want them in the cells at Dyer, and I want a full-dress court martial. I want it textbook, Reacher. I want to be exonerated in public. I want the jury to hear every word, and I want a ruling from the bench."

Reacher said, "A clean arrest needs probable cause."

"So should cutting their heads off with a butter knife."

"Why did Montague let Zadran go home to the mountains?"

"Because of his history."

"I wish we knew more about him."

"We know all we're going to know."

Reacher nodded. *A meaningless peasant, forty-two*

years old, the youngest of five, the black sheep of the family, disreputable, tried his hand at a number of things, and failed at them all. He said, "The butter knife would be easier."

Then his phone rang. It was Edmonds. He said, "That was quick."

She said, "I figured I might get an hour's sleep tonight if I was quick."

"Don't count on it. What have you got?"

"Dove Cottage is a private members' club. It opened four years ago. Membership roll is confidential."

"Four years ago?"

"We have no evidence."

"Four years ago we have Morgan at Bragg, building a team around Shrago."

"We can't prove a connection."

"Are Scully and Montague members?"

"Which part of confidential didn't you get?"

"Any rumors?"

"The membership is said to be all male. Including politicians, but it's not a political salon, and military, and media, and business, but no deals seem to get done. Guys go there to enjoy themselves, that's all. Sometimes they stay all night."

"Doing what?"

"No one knows."

"How do you get to be a member?"

"I don't, if it's all male."

"How would I?"

"Invitation only, I guess. You'd have to know a guy who knows a guy."

"And no one knows what they do in there?"

"There are hundreds of private clubs in D.C. There's no way of keeping track."

Reacher said, "Thank you, counselor. For everything. You've done a fine job."

"That sounds like goodbye."

"It might be. Or not. Like flipping a coin."

The latitude and the season meant they had about ninety minutes before the sun came up. So they took what they needed and rode down to the street, where a man in a hat got them a cab. The cab went way north on 16th, to Scott Circle, where it took Mass Ave to Dupont, where it took P Street across the park and into Georgetown. They went as far as the corner with Wisconsin Avenue, where they got out. The cab drove away, and they walked two blocks, back the way they had come, and they made a left, and they headed for their target, which was another two blocks north, on the right, in what looked like the most expensive neighborhood since money was invented. To the left were the landscaped grounds of some immense mansion. On the right were townhouses, gleaming in the dark, lustrous, burnished, each one substantial in its own right, each one proudly taking its place in line.

Their target fit right in.

"Some cottage," Turner said.

It was a tall, handsome house, strictly symmetrical, restrained and discreet and unshowy in every way, but still gleaming with burnished luster nonetheless. The brass plaque was small. There were lights on in some of the windows, most of which still had old wavy glass, which made the light look soft, like a candle. The door had been repainted about every election year, starting with James Madison. It was a big door, solidly made, and properly fitted. It was the kind of door that didn't open, except voluntarily.

No obvious way in.

But they hadn't been expecting miracles, and they had been expecting to watch and wait. Which was helped a little by the landscaped grounds of the immense mansion. The grounds had an iron fence set in a stone knee-wall, which was just wide enough for a small person to sit on, and Turner was a small person, and Reacher was used to being uncomfortable. Overhead was a tight lattice of bare branches. No leaves, and therefore no kind of total concealment, but maybe some kind of camouflage. The branches were tight enough to break up the street light. Like the new digital patterns, on the pajamas.

They waited, half hidden, and Turner said, "We don't even know what they look like. They could come out and walk right past us." So she called Leach again, and asked for an alert if the phones moved. Which they hadn't yet. They were still showing up on a bunch of towers, triangulated ruler-straight on the house in front of them. Reacher watched the windows, and the door. *Guys go there to enjoy themselves. Sometimes they stay all night.* In which case they would start leaving soon. Politicians and military and media and businessmen all had jobs to do. They would come staggering out, ready to head home and clean up ahead of their day.

But the first guy out didn't stagger. The door opened

about an hour before dawn, and a man in a suit stepped out, sleek, showered, hair brushed, shoes gleaming as deep as the door, and he turned left and set off down the sidewalk, not fast, not slow, relaxed, seemingly very serene and very satisfied and very content with his life. He was older than middle age. He headed for P Street, and after fifty yards he was lost in the dark.

Reacher guessed subconsciously he had been expecting debauchery and disarray, with mussed hair and red eyes and undone ties, and lipstick on collars, and maybe bottles clutched by the neck below open shirt cuffs. But the guy had looked the exact opposite. Maybe the place was a spa. Maybe the guy had gotten an all-night hot stone massage, or some other kind of deep-tissue physical therapy. In which case it had worked very well. The guy had looked rubbery with well-being and satisfaction.

"Weird," Turner said. "Not what I was expecting."

"Maybe it's a literary society," Reacher said. "Maybe it's a poetry club. The original Dove Cottage was where William Wordsworth lived. The English poet. I wandered lonely as a cloud, and a host of golden daffodils, and all that shit. A little lime-washed house, in England. In the English Lake District, which is a beautiful spot."

Turner said, "Who stays up all night reading poetry?"

"Lots of people. Usually younger than that guy, I admit."

"To enjoy themselves?"

"Poetry can be deeply satisfying. It was for the daffodil guy, anyway. He was talking about laying back and spacing out and remembering something good you saw."

Turner said nothing.

"Better than Tennyson," Reacher said. "You have to give me that."

They watched and waited, another twenty minutes. The sky behind the house was lightening. Just a little. Another dawn, another day. Then a second guy came out. Similar to the first. Old, sleek, pink, besuited, serene, deeply satisfied. No sign of stress, no sign of rush. No angst, no embarrassment. He turned the same way as the first guy, toward P Street, and he walked with easy, relaxed strides, head up, half smiling, deep inside a bubble of contentment, like the master of a universe in which all was well.

Reacher said, "Wait."

Turner said, "What?"

Reacher said, "Montague."

"That was him? Leach didn't call."

"No, this is Montague's club. He owns it. Or he and Scully own it together."

"How do you know?"

"Because of the name. Dove Cottage is like Romeo. Deep down this guy is a poor intelligence officer. He's way too clever by half. He just can't resist."

"Resist what?"

"Why did he let Zadran go home to the mountains?"

"Because of his history."

"No, despite his history. Because of who he was. Because of who his brothers were. His brothers forgave him and took him back. Zadran didn't rehabilitate himself and find a role. His brothers rehabilitated him and gave him a role. Part of their deal with Montague. It was a two-way street."

"What deal?"

"People remember that William Wordsworth lived with his sister Dorothy, but they forget that both of them lived with his wife and his sister-in-law and a passel of kids. Three in four years, I think."

"When was this?"

"More than two hundred years ago."

"So why are we even talking about it?"

"The original Dove Cottage was a little lime-washed house. Too small, for seven people. They moved out. It got a new tenant."

"Who?"

"A guy named Thomas De Quincey. Another writer. It was wall to wall writers up there, at the time. They were all friends. But Wordsworth had stayed only eight years. De Quincey stayed for eleven. Which makes Dove Cottage his, more than Wordsworth's, in terms of how much time they spent there. Even though Wordsworth is the one people remember. Probably because he was the better poet."

"And?"

"Wait," Reacher said. "Watch this."

The door was opening again, and a third guy was coming out. Gray hair, but thick and beautifully styled. A pink face, washed and shaved. A three-thousand-dollar suit, and a shirt as fresh as new snow. A silk tie, beautifully knotted. A politician, probably. The guy stood for a second and took a deep breath of the morning air, and then he started walking, just like the first two, relaxed, unconcerned, serenity coming off him in waves. He headed the same way, toward P Street, and eventually he was lost to sight.

Reacher said, "Conclusions?"

Turner said, "Like we already figured before. It's a sanctuary for refined older gentlemen with personal enthusiasms."

"What's coming home in the ordnance shipments?"

"I don't know."

"What did Zadran's brothers do for a living?"

"They worked the family farm."

"Growing what?"

Turner said, "Poppies."

"Exactly. And they gave Zadran a role. As their salesman. Because he had connections already in place. Like you said. What did Thomas De Quincey write?"

"Poetry?"

"His most famous work was an autobiographical book called *Confessions of an English Opium-Eater.* That's what he did in Dove Cottage, for eleven straight years. He eased away the tensions of the day. Then he wrote a memoir about it."

Turner said, "I wish we could get in there."

Reacher had been in the original Dove Cottage, in England. On a visit. He had paid his entrance money at the door, and he had ducked under the low lintel. Easy as that. Getting into the new Dove Cottage was going to be much harder. Penetrating a house was something Delta Force and Navy SEALs trained for all their careers. It was not a simple task.

Reacher said, "Do you see cameras?"

Turner said, "I don't, but there have to be some, surely."

"Is there a doorbell?"

"There's no button. Just a knocker. Which is more authentic, of course. Maybe there are zoning laws."

"Then there must be cameras. A place like this can't fling its door open every time there's a knock. Not without knowing who it is."

"Which implies an operations room, with screens, and some kind of remote unlock function. One guy could run it. Will there be security?"

"There have to be servants. Discreet little guys in dark suits. Like butlers or stewards. Who are also security. I guess the cameras are small. Maybe just fiber-optic lenses, poking out through the wall. There could be dozens of them. Which would make sense. Someone has to keep an eye open for what could go on, in a place like this."

"We need to see someone go in, not out. We need to see how the system works."

But they didn't. No one went in. No one came out. The house just sat there, looking smug. The same lights stayed on. The first smears of morning came up over the roof.

Turner said, "We've never met them."

Reacher said, "They've seen our photographs."

"Have they shown our photographs to their operations guy?"

"I sincerely hope so. Because we're talking about

the top boy in charge of intelligence for the United States Army."

"Then the door will stay locked," Turner said. "That's all. Costs us nothing."

"Does it alert them? Or are they alert already?"

"You know they're alert. They're staring into the void."

"Maybe they don't let women in."

"They would have to send someone down to explain that. If they don't recognize us, then we could be anybody. City officials, or whatever. They'd have to talk to us."

"OK," Reacher said. "Knocking on the door is an option. How far up the list do you want to put it?"

"In the middle," Turner said.

Five minutes later Reacher asked, "Below what?"

"I think we should call the DEA. Or Espin, at the 75th. Or the Metro PD. Or all of the above. The FBI, too, probably. They can start work on the financial stuff."

"You're the CO."

"I want a legal arrest."

"So do I."

"Really?"

"Because you do."

"Is that the only reason?"

"I like a legal arrest wherever possible. Every time. I'm not a barbarian."

"We can't stay here anyway. It's getting light."

And it was. The sun was on the far horizon, shooting level rays, backlighting the house, casting impossibly long shadows. A cone of sky was already blue. It was going to be a fine day.

"Make the call," Reacher said.

"Who first?"

"Leach," Reacher said. "Better if she coordinates. Otherwise it will be like the Keystone Cops."

Turner emptied her pockets of phones, of which there were two, hers and Shrago's. She checked she had the right one, and she opened it, and she turned away from the street, ready to dial. She was lit up from the back, warm and gold in the new dawn sun.

And then Shrago's phone rang. On the stone knee-wall, on the ledge below the fence. The crazy birdsong was switched off, but the grinding wasn't. It was happening big time. The phone was squirming around, like it was trying to choose a direction. The screen was lit up as before, with *Incoming Call,* and *Home.*

The phone buzzed eight times, and then it stopped.

"Dawn," Turner said. "Some kind of deadline. Either prearranged, or in their own minds. They must be getting plenty anxious by now. They're going to give up on him soon."

They watched the house a minute more, and as they turned away an upstairs window lit up bright, just a brief yellow flash, like an old-fashioned camera, and they heard two muffled gunshots, almost simultaneous but not quite, a little ragged, too quick for a double tap from a single weapon, but just right for two old guys counting to three and pulling their triggers.

Chapter 69

Nothing happened for a long, eerie minute.
Then the black door was hauled open fast and a whole
stream of guys started pouring out, in various states
of readiness, some clean and dressed and ready to go,
some almost, some still rumpled and creased, all of
them white and old, maybe eight or nine of them in
total, and mixed in with them were half a dozen
younger men in uniform, like hotel pages, and a
younger man in a black turtleneck sweater, who
Turner thought could be the operations guy. They all
slowed down on the sidewalk, and they composed
themselves, and then they sauntered away, like nothing was anything to do with them. One guy in a suit
walked right past Reacher, with a look on his face that
said, *Who, me?*

Then Reacher and Turner started moving against
the fleeing tide, toward the house, toward the black
door, and they were buffeted by a couple of late strag-
glers, and then they were inside, in a wide, cool hall-

way, done in a Colonial style, all pale yellow, and brass candlesticks, and clocks, and dark mahogany wood, and an oil portrait of George Washington.

They went up the stairs, which were wide and thickly carpeted, and they checked an empty room, which had two elegant daybeds in it, next to two elegant coffee tables. The coffee tables held fine examples of the opium smoker's needs. Lamps and bowls and long, long pipes, the heights all arranged so that a man lying relaxed on his side would find the pipe exactly where he wanted it. There were pillows here and there, and a warm, dull weight in the air.

They found Scully and Montague in the next room along. They were both around sixty years old, both gray, both trim, but not iron-hard like the kind of general who wants people to know he came from the infantry. These two were happy for folk to know they came from the back rooms. They were wearing dark pants and satin smoking jackets. Their pipes were made of silver and bone. They both had holes in both temples, through and through with jacketed bullets. Nine-millimeters, from the service Berettas that had fallen to the floor. The entry wounds were on the right. Reacher pictured them, the dawn call, as agreed, but no answer, so maybe a handshake, and then muzzles against skin, and elbows out, and one, two, three.

And then the street was suddenly howling with sirens, and about a hundred people jumped out of cars.

A guy from the DEA told them the story, in a front room off the wide, cool hallway. It turned out Shrago had spilled to Espin inside about a second and a half, which meant Morgan was in custody thirty minutes later, and Morgan had spilled inside a second and a half, too, whereupon Espin had called three different agencies, and a raid had been planned. And executed. But five minutes late.

"You weren't late," Reacher said. "You could have come yesterday, and they would have done the same thing. It didn't matter who was coming up the stairs. You or us or anybody, they were going down like gentlemen."

The guy said there were opium dens like Dove Cottage everywhere, all over the world, for the kind of civilized man who prefers fine wine over beer. Opium was the authentic product, heated to a vapor, the vapor inhaled, a gentleman's relish, as sweet as organic honey. The real thing. The source. Not cut or altered or extracted or converted. Not in any way. Not sordid, not street, and unchanged for thousands of years. Archeologists would tell you Stone Age had a double meaning.

And like fine wine, all kinds of bullshit crept in. Terrain was held to be important. The best was held to be Afghan. Individual hillsides were examined. Like vineyards. Montague did a deal with the Zadran brothers. Their stuff was high grade. They branded it Z and talked it up, and pretty soon Dove Cottage was getting enormous membership fees. It all worked fine for four years. Then their in-country guy was seen heading north for the ritual pow-wow, and the whole thing unraveled, despite their best efforts. Espin came by and said their best efforts had been considerable.

He said he was halfway through the financial stuff, and already he could see the hundred grand had come straight out of Montague's own account.

Then eventually the crowd in the house included Colonel John James Temple, who was still Turner's attorney of record, and both Major Helen Sullivan and Captain Tracy Edmonds, who were still Reacher's. Temple had gotten a permanent stay on Turner's confinement order. She was basically free to go, pending formal dismissal of charges. Sullivan and Edmonds had bigger problems. Given Morgan's current status, it was impossible to say whether Reacher was or was not still in the army. It was likely a question that would run all the way to the Deputy Chief for personnel, who was dead upstairs.

Turner begged a ride for them both, with Colonel Temple, who had been little placated when Reacher returned his ID. The atmosphere was tense. But Reacher was keen to get Turner back to the hotel, and Colonel Temple's sedan was better than walking. Except they didn't go back to the hotel. Evidently Turner had given Rock Creek as their destination, because Temple drove over the water into Virginia. The old stone building. Her command. Her base. Her home base. Her home. *When I get back I'm going to have my office steam cleaned. I don't want any trace of Morgan left behind.*

Which was when he had known for sure. She loved the campfire. As had he, once upon a time, but only briefly, and only that special fire inside the 110th Special Unit. Which was now hers.

It was well into the morning when they arrived, and everyone was there. The night watch had stayed. Espin had kept them in the loop, and they had followed the play by play. The day watch had gotten in to find it a done deal, all bar the shouting. Sergeant Leach was there, and the duty captain. Reacher wondered if Turner would ever mention the doodling. Probably not. More likely promote him sideways.

Her first hour was largely ceremonial, with a lot of fist bumps, and shooting the shit, and slaps on the back, and then somehow she ended the tour in her office, and she stayed there, starting where she had left off, reviewing every piece of information, and checking every disposition. Reacher hung out with Leach for a spell, and then he went down the old stone steps and took a long walk, a random figure-eight around bland three-lane blocks. He got back and found her still occupied, so he hung out with Leach some more, and then it went dark, and then she came down the stairs, with a car key in her hand.

She said, "Ride with me."

The little red sports car had been down a few days, but it started fine, and it ran steady, if a little loud and throaty, but Reacher figured that might have been dialed in on purpose by the guy who designed the muffler. Turner put the heater dials in the red and unlatched the top, and dropped it down behind the seats.

"Like a rock and roll song on the radio," she said.

She backed out of her slot, and she drove out through the gate, and she turned left, and she followed the bus route, past the motel and onward to the mall, where she pulled up in front of the big stucco place with the Greek style of menu.

"Buy you dinner?" she said.

There were all kinds of people in the restaurant. Couples, and families, and children. Some of the children were girls, and some of them might have been fourteen. Turner chose a booth at the front window, and they watched a bus go by, and Reacher said, "I'm a detective, and I know what you're going to say."

She said, "Do you?"

"It was always fifty-fifty. Like flipping a coin."

"That easy?"

"You have no obligation even to think about it. This was my thing, not yours. I came here. You didn't come to South Dakota."

"That's true. That's how it started. I wasn't sure. But it changed. For a time. Starting in that cell, in the Dyer guardhouse. You were taking Temple away, and you looked over your shoulder at me and told me to wait there. And I did."

"You had no choice. You were in the guardhouse."

"And now I'm not."

"I understand," Reacher said. "The 110th is better."

"And I got it back. I can't just walk away."

"I understand," Reacher said again. "And I can't stay. Not here. Not anywhere. So it's not just you. We're both saying no."

"The 110th was your creation. If that makes you feel better."

"I wanted to meet you," Reacher said. "That was all. And I did. Mission accomplished."

They ate, and paid, and they emptied their pockets on the table. Turner took the wallets, and the credit cards, and Shrago's phone, for processing, and Reacher took the cash money, for the upcoming weeks, less thirty dollars, which Turner promised to return to Sullivan. Then they walked out to the lot. The air was cold, and a little damp. The middle of the evening, in the middle of winter, in the northeastern corner of Virginia. The lazy Potomac was not far away. Beyond it in the east D.C.'s glow lit up the clouds. The nation's capital, where all kinds of things were going on. They kissed for the last time, and hugged, and wished each other luck, and then Turner got in her little red car and drove away. Reacher watched her until she was lost to sight. Then he dropped his cell phone in the trash, and he crossed the street, and he walked until he found a bus bench. North, not south. Out, not in. Onward, and away. He sat down, alone.

No one knows suspense like
#1 *New York Times* bestselling author
Lee Child.
And there's no bigger name in suspense
than Jack Reacher.

If you enjoyed *Never Go Back,*
please keep reading for the
Jack Reacher short story

"High Heat"

and then for an exciting preview of

Personal

A Jack Reacher Novel

Coming in hardcover and eBook
from Delacorte Press

Fall 2014

High Heat

The man was over thirty, Reacher thought, and solid, and hot, obviously. He had sweated through his suit. The woman face to face with him could have been younger, but not by much. She was hot too, and scared. Or tense, at least. That was clear. The man was too close to her. She didn't like that. It was nearly half past eight in the evening, and going dark. But not cooling off. A hundred degrees, someone had said. A real heat wave. Wednesday, July 13th, 1977, New York City. Reacher would always remember the date. It was his second solo visit.

The man put the palm of his hand flat on the woman's chest, pressing damp cotton against her skin, the ball of his thumb down in her cleavage. Not a tender gesture. But not an aggressive gesture, either. Neutral, like a doctor. The woman didn't back off. She just froze in place and glanced around. Without seeing much. New York City, half past eight in the evening, but the street was deserted. It was too hot. Waverly Place, between Sixth Avenue and Washington Square. People would come out later, if at all.

Then the man took his hand off the woman's chest, and he flicked it downward like he wanted to knock a bee off her hip, and then he whipped it back up in a big roundhouse swing and slapped her full in the face, hard, with enough power for a real *crack,* but his hand and her face were too damp for pistol-shot acoustics, so the sound came out exactly like the word: *slap.* The woman's head was knocked sideways. The sound echoed off the scalding brick.

Reacher said, "Hey."

The man turned around. He was dark haired, dark eyed, maybe five-ten, maybe two hundred pounds. His shirt was transparent with sweat.

He said, "Get lost, kid."

On that night Reacher was three months and sixteen days shy of his seventeenth birthday, but physically he was pretty much all grown up. He was as tall as he was ever going to get, and no sane person would have called him skinny. He was six-five, two-twenty, all muscle. The finished article, more or less. But finished very recently. Brand-new. His teeth were white and even, his eyes were a shade close to navy, his hair had wave and body, his skin was smooth and clear. The scars and the lines and the calluses were yet to come.

The man said, "Right now, kid."

Reacher said, "Ma'am, you should step away from this guy."

Which the woman did, backward, one step, two, out of range. The man said, "Do you know who I am?"

Reacher said, "What difference would it make?"

"You're pissing off the wrong people."

"People?" Reacher said. "That's a plural word. Are there more than one of you?"

"You'll find out."

Reacher looked around. The street was still deserted.

"When will I find out?" he said. "Not right away, apparently."

"What kind of smart guy do you think you are?"

Reacher said, "Ma'am, I'm happy to be here alone, if you want to take off running."

The woman didn't move. Reacher looked at her.

He said, "Am I misunderstanding something?"

The man said, "Get lost, kid."

The woman said, "You shouldn't get involved."

"I'm not getting involved," Reacher said. "I'm just standing here in the street."

The man said, "Go stand in some other street."

Reacher turned back and looked at him and said, "Who died and made you mayor?"

"That's some mouth, kid. You don't know who you're talking to. You're going to regret that."

"When the other people get here? Is that what you mean? Because right now it's just you and me. And I don't foresee a whole lot of regret in that, not for me, anyway, not unless you've got no money."

"Money?"

"For me to take."

"What, now you think you're going to mug me?"

"Not mug you," Reacher said. "More of a historical thing. An old principle. Like a tradition. You lose a war, you give up your treasure."

"Are we at war, you and me? Because if we are, you're going to lose, kid. I don't care how big of a corn-fed country boy you are. I'm going to kick your ass. I'm going to kick it bad."

The woman was still six feet away. Still not moving. Reacher looked at her again and said, "Ma'am, is this gentleman married to you, or related to you in some other way, or known to you either socially or professionally?"

She said, "I don't want you to get involved." She was younger than the guy, for sure. But not by much. Still way up there. Twenty-nine, maybe. A pale-colored blonde. Apart from the vivid red print from the slap she was plenty good looking, in an older-woman kind of a way. But she was thin and nervous. Maybe she had a lot of stress in her life. She was wearing a loose summer dress that ended above her knee. She had a purse hooked over her shoulder.

Reacher said, "At least tell me what it is you don't want me to get involved in. Is this some random guy hassling you on the street? Or not?"

"What else would it be?"

"Domestic quarrel, maybe. I heard of a guy who busted one up, and then the wife got real mad with him afterward, for hurting her husband."

"I'm not married to this man."

"Do you have any interest in him at all?"

"In his welfare?"

"I suppose that's what we're talking about."

"None at all. But you can't get involved. So walk away. I'll deal with it."

"Suppose we walk away together?"

"How old are you, anyway?"

"Old enough," Reacher said. "For walking, at least."

"I don't want the responsibility. You're just a kid. You're an innocent bystander."

"Is this guy dangerous?"

"Very."

"He doesn't look it."

"Looks can be deceptive."

"Is he armed?"

"Not in the city. He can't afford to be."

"So what's he going to do? Sweat on me?"

Which did the trick. The guy hit boiling point, aggrieved at being talked about like he wasn't there, aggrieved at being called sweaty, even though he manifestly was, and he came in at a charge, his jacket flapping, his tie flailing, his shirt sticking to his skin. Reacher feinted one way and moved another, and the guy stumbled past, and Reacher tapped his ankles, and the guy tripped and fell. He got up again fast enough, but by then Reacher had backed off and turned around and was ready for the second maneuver. Which looked like it was going to be an exact repeat of the first, except Reacher helped it along a little by replacing the ankle tap with an elbow to the side of the head. Which was very well delivered. At nearly seventeen Reacher was like a brand-new machine, still gleaming and dewy with oil, flexible, supple, perfectly coordinated, like something developed by NASA and IBM on behalf of the Pentagon.

The guy stayed down on his knees a little longer than the first time. The heat kept him there. Reacher figured the hundred degrees he had heard about must have been somewhere open. Central Park, maybe. Some little weather station. In the narrow brick canyons of the West Village, close to the huge stone sidewalk slabs, it must have been more like a hundred and twenty. And humid. Reacher was wearing old khakis and a blue T-shirt, and both items looked like he had fallen in a river.

The guy stood up, panting and unsteady. He put his hands on his knees.

Reacher said, "Let it go, old man. Find someone else to hit."

No answer. The guy looked like he was conducting an internal debate. It was a long one. Clearly there were points to consider on both sides of the argument. Pros, and cons, and plusses, and minuses, and costs and benefits. Finally the guy said, "Can you count to three and a half?"

Reacher said, "I suppose."

"That's how many hours you got to get out of town. After midnight you're a dead man. And before that too, if I see you again." And then the guy straightened up and walked away, back toward Sixth Avenue, fast, like his mind was made up, his heels ringing on the hot stone, like a brisk, purposeful person on a just-remembered errand. Reacher watched until he was lost to sight, and then he turned back to the woman and said, "Which way are you headed?"

She pointed in the opposite direction, toward Washington Square, and Reacher said, "Then you should be OK."

"You have three and a half hours to get out of town."

"I don't think he was serious. He was hauling ass, trying to save face."

"He was serious, believe me. You hit him in the head. I mean, Jesus."

"Who is he?"

"Who are you?"

"Just a guy passing through."

"From where?"

"Pohang, at the moment."

"Where the hell is that?"

"South Korea. Camp Mujuk. The Marine Corps."

"You're a Marine?"

"Son of a Marine. We go where we're posted. But school's out, so I'm traveling."

"On your own? How old are you?"

"Seventeen in the fall. Don't worry about me. I'm not the one getting slapped in the street."

The woman said nothing.

Reacher said, "Who was that guy?"

"How did you get here?"

"Bus to Seoul, plane to Tokyo, plane to Hawaii, plane to LA, plane to JFK, bus to the Port Authority. Then I walked." The Yankees were out of town, in Boston, which had been a major disappointment. Reacher had a feeling it was going to be a special year. Reggie Jackson was making a difference. The long drought might be nearly over. But no luck. The Stadium was dark. The alternative was Shea, the Cubs at the Mets. In principle Reacher had no objection to Mets baseball, such as it was, but in the end the pull of downtown music had proven stronger. He had figured he would swing through Washington Square and check out the girls from NYU's summer school. One of them might be willing to go with him. Or not. It was worth the detour. He was an optimist, and his plans were flexible.

The woman said, "How long are you traveling?"

"In theory I'm free until September."

"Where are you staying?"

"I just got here. I haven't figured that out yet."

"Your parents are OK with this?"

"My mother is worried. She read about the Son of Sam in the newspaper."

"She should be worried. He's killing people."

"Couples sitting in cars, mostly. That's what the papers say. Statistically unlikely to be me. I don't have a car, and so far I'm on my own."

"This city has other problems too."

"I know. I'm supposed to visit with my brother."

"Here in the city?"

"Couple hours out."

"You should go there right now."

Reacher nodded. "I'm supposed to take the late bus."

"Before midnight?"

"Who was that guy?"

The woman didn't answer. The heat wasn't letting up. The air was thick and heavy. There was thunder coming. Reacher could feel it, in the north and the west. Maybe they were going to get a real Hudson Valley thunderstorm, rolling and clattering over the slow water, between the high cliffs, like he had read about in books. The light was fading all the way to purple, as if the weather was getting ready for something big.

The woman said, "Go see your brother. Thanks for helping out."

The red handprint on her face was fading.

Reacher said, "Are you going to be OK?"

"I'll be fine."

"What's your name?"

"Jill."

"Jill what?"

"Hemingway."

"Any relation?"

"To who?"

"Ernest Hemingway. The writer."

"I don't think so."

"You free tonight?"

"No."

"My name is Reacher. I'm pleased to meet you." He stuck out his hand, and they shook. Her hand felt hot and slick, like she had a fever. Not that his didn't. A hundred degrees, maybe more, no breeze, no evaporation. Summer in the city. Far away to the north the sky flickered. Heat lightning. No rain.

He said, "How long have you been with the FBI?"

"Who says I am?"

"That guy was a mobster, right? Organized crime? All that shit about his people, and getting out of town or else. All those threats. And you were meeting with him. He was checking for a wire, when he put his hand on you. And I guess he found one."

"You're a smart kid."

"Where's your backup? There should be a van, with people listening in."

"It's a budget thing."

"I don't believe you. The city, maybe, but the feds are never broke."

"Go see your brother. This isn't your business."

"Why wear a wire with no one listening?"

The woman put her hands behind her back, low

down, and she fiddled and jiggled, as if she was working something loose from the waistband of her underwear. A black plastic box fell out below the hem of her dress. A small cassette recorder, swinging knee-high, suspended on a wire. She put one hand down the front of her dress, and she pulled on the wire behind her knees with her other hand, and she squirmed and she wriggled, and the recorder lowered itself to the sidewalk, followed by a thin black cable with a little bud microphone on the end.

She said, "The tape was listening."

The little black box was dewed with perspiration, from the small of her back.

Reacher said, "Did I screw it up?"

"I don't know how it would have gone."

"He assaulted a federal agent. That's a crime right there. I'm a witness."

The woman said nothing. She picked up the cassette recorder and wound the cord around it. She slid her purse off her shoulder and put the recorder in it. The temperature felt hotter than ever, and steamy, like a hot wet towel over Reacher's mouth and nose. There was more lightning in the north, winking slow, dulled by the thick air. No rain. No break.

Reacher said, "Are you going to let him get away with that?"

The woman said, "This really isn't your business."

"I'm happy to say what I saw."

"It wouldn't come to trial for a year. You'd have to come all the way back. You want to take four planes and two buses for a slap?"

"A year from now I'll be somewhere else. Maybe nearer."

"Or further away."

"The sound might be on the tape."

"I need more than a slap. Defense lawyers would laugh at me."

Reacher shrugged. Too hot to argue. He said, "OK, have a pleasant evening, ma'am."

She said, "Where are you going now?"

"Bleecker Street, I think."

"You can't. That's in his territory."

"Or nearby. Or the Bowery. There's music all over, right?"

"Same thing. All his territory."

"Who is he?"

"His name is Croselli. Everything north of Houston and south of 14th is his. And you hit him in the head."

"He's one guy. He won't find me."

"He's a made man. He has soldiers."

"How many?"

"A dozen, maybe."

"Not enough. Too big of an area."

"He'll put the word out. All the clubs and all the bars."

"Really? He'll tell people he's frightened of a sixteen-year-old? I don't think so."

"He doesn't need to give a reason. And people will bust a gut to help. They all want brownie points in the bank. You wouldn't last five minutes. Go see your brother. I'm serious."

"Free country," Reacher said. "That's what you're

working for, right? I'll go where I want. I came a long way."

The woman stayed quiet for a long moment.

"Well, I warned you," she said. "I can't do more than that."

And she walked away, toward Washington Square. Reacher waited where he was, all alone on Waverly, head up, head down, searching for a breath of air, and then he followed after her, about two minutes behind, and he saw her drive away in a car that had been parked in a tow zone. A 1975 Ford Granada, he thought, mid-blue, vinyl roof, a big toothy grille. It took a corner like a land yacht and drove out of sight.

Washington Square was much emptier than Reacher had expected. Because of the heat. There were a couple of unexplained black guys hanging around, probably dealers, and not much else. No chess players, no dog walkers. But way over on the eastern edge of the square he saw three girls go into a coffee shop. Coeds for sure, long hair, tan, lithe, maybe two or three years older than him. He headed in their direction, and looked for a payphone on the way. He found a working instrument on his fourth try. He used a hot damp coin from his pocket and dialed the number he had memorized for West Point's main switchboard.

A sing-song male voice said, "United States Military Academy, how may I direct your call?"

"Cadet Joe Reacher, please."

"Hold the line," the voice said, which Reacher thought was appropriate. West Point was in the business of holding the line, against all kinds of things, including enemies foreign and domestic, and progress, sometimes. West Point was Army, which was an unusual choice for the elder son of a Marine, but Joe's heart had been set on it. And he claimed to be enjoying it so far. Reacher himself had no idea where he would go. NYU, possibly, with women. The three in the coffee shop had looked pretty good. But he didn't make plans. Sixteen years in the Corps had cured him of that.

The phone clicked and buzzed as the call was transferred from station to station. Reacher took another hot wet coin from his pocket and held it ready. It was a quarter to nine, and dark, and getting hotter, if such a thing was possible. Fifth Avenue was a long narrow canyon running north ahead of him. There were flashes of light in the sky, low down on the horizon, way far in the distance.

A different voice said, "Cadet Reacher is currently unavailable. Do you have a message?"

Reacher said, "Please tell him his brother is delayed twenty-four hours. I'm spending the night in the city. I'll see him tomorrow evening."

"Roger that," the new voice said, with no interest at all, and the line went dead. Reacher put the second coin back in his pocket, and he hung up the phone, and he headed for the coffee shop on the eastern edge of the square.

An air conditioner over the coffee shop's door was running so hard it was trembling and rattling, but it wasn't making much difference to the temperature of the air. The girls were together in a booth for four, with tall soda glasses full of Coke and melting ice. Two of them were blondes and one was a brunette. All of them had long smooth limbs and perfect white teeth. The brunette was in short shorts and a sleeveless button-front shirt, and the blondes were in short summer dresses. They all looked quick and intelligent and full of energy. Storybook Americans, literally. Reacher had seen girls just like them in greasy old out-of-date copies of *Time* and *Life* and *Newsweek*, at Mujuk and every other base he had lived on. They were the future, the stories had said. He had admired them from afar.

Now he stood at the door under the roaring air conditioner and admired them from a whole lot closer. But he had no idea what to do next. Life as a Corps kid taught a guy plenty, but absolutely nothing about bridging a fifteen-foot door-to-table distance in a New York City coffee shop. Up to that point his few conquests had not really been conquests at all, but mutual experiments with Corps girls just as isolated as himself, and just as willing and enthusiastic and desperate. Their only negatives had been their fathers, who were all trained killers with fairly traditional views. The three students in front of him were a whole different can of worms. Much easier from the parental point of view, presumably, but much harder in every other way.

He paused.

Nothing ventured, nothing gained.

He moved on, fifteen feet, and he approached their table, and he said, "Do you mind if I join you?"

They all looked up. They all looked surprised. They were all too polite to tell him to get lost. They were all too smart to tell him to sit down. New York City, in the summer of 1977. The Bronx, burning. Hundreds of homicides. The Son of Sam. Irrational panic everywhere.

He said, "I'm new here. I was wondering if you could tell me where to go, to hear some good music."

No answer. Two pairs of blue eyes, one pair of brown, looking up at him.

He said, "Are you headed somewhere this evening?"

The brunette was the first to speak.

She said, "Maybe."

"Where to?"

"Don't know yet."

A waitress came by, barely older than the coeds themselves, and Reacher maneuvered himself into a spot where her approach gave him no choice but to sit down. As if he had been swept along. The brunette scooted over and left an inch between her thigh and his. The vinyl bench was sticky with heat. He ordered a Coke. It was way too hot for coffee.

There was an awkward silence. The waitress brought Reacher's Coke. He took a sip. The blonde directly opposite asked him, "Are you at NYU?"

"I'm still in high school," he said.

She softened a little, as if he was a rare curiosity.

"Where?" she asked.

"South Korea," he said. "Military family."

"Fascist," she said. "Get lost."

"What does your dad do for a living?"

"He's a lawyer."

"Get lost yourself."

The brunette laughed. She was an inch shorter than the others, and her skin was a shade darker. She was slender. Elfin, almost. Reacher had heard the word. Not that it meant much to him. He had never seen an elf.

The brunette said, "The Ramones might be at CBGB. Or Blondie."

Reacher said, "I'll go if you go."

"It's a rough area."

"Compared to what? Iwo Jima?"

"Where's that?"

"It's an island in the Pacific."

"Sounds nice. Does it have beaches?"

"Lots of them. What's your name?"

"Chrissie."

"Pleased to meet you, Chrissie. My name is Reacher."

"First or last?"

"Only."

"You have only one name?"

"That anyone uses."

"So if I go to CBGB with you, do you promise to stick close by?"

Which was pretty much a do-bears-sleep-in-the-woods type of a question, in Reacher's opinion. Is the Pope a Catholic? He said, "Sure, count on it."

The blondes on the opposite side of the table started fidgeting with dubious body language, and immediately Reacher knew they wouldn't come too. Which was dead-on A-OK with him. Like a big green light. A one-on-one excursion. Like a real date. Nine o'clock in the evening, Wednesday, July 13th, New York City, and his first civilian conquest was almost upon him, like a runaway train. He could feel it coming, like an earthquake. He wondered where Chrissie's dorm was. Close by, he guessed.

He sipped his Coke.

Chrissie said, "So let's go, Reacher."

Reacher left money on the table for four Cokes, which he guessed was the gentlemanly thing to do. He followed Chrissie out through the door, and the night heat hit him like a hammer. Chrissie, too. She held her hair away from her shoulders with the backs of her hands and he saw a damp sheen on her neck. She said, "How far is it?"

He said, "You've never been?"

"It's a bad area."

"I think we have to go east about five blocks. Past Broadway and Lafayette to the Bowery. Then about three blocks south to the corner with Bleecker."

"It's so hot."

"That's for sure."

"Maybe we should take my car. For the AC."

"You have a car?"

"Sure."

"Here in the city?"

"Right there." And she pointed, to a small hatchback car on the curb about fifty feet away. A Chevrolet Chevette, Reacher thought, maybe a year old, maybe baby blue, although it was hard to tell under the yellow street lights.

He said, "Doesn't it cost a lot to keep a car in the city?"

She said, "Parking is free after six o'clock."

"But what do you do with it in the daytime?"

She paused a beat, as if unraveling the layers of his question, and she said, "No, I don't live here."

"I thought you did. Sorry. My mistake. I figured you were at NYU."

She shook her head and said, "Sarah Lawrence."

"Who's she?"

"It's a college. Where we go. In Yonkers. North of here. Sometimes we drive down and see what's going on. Sometimes there are NYU boys in that coffee shop."

"So we're both out-of-towners."

"Not tonight," Chrissie said.

"What are your friends going to do?"

"About what?"

"About getting home tonight."

"I'm going to drive them," Chrissie said. "Like always."

Reacher said nothing.

"But they'll wait," Chrissie said. "That's part of the deal."

The Chevette's air conditioner was about as lousy as the coffee shop's, but something was better than nothing. There were a few people on Broadway, like ghosts in a ghost town, moving slow, and a few on Lafayette, slower still, and homeless people on the Bowery, waiting for the shelters to open. Chrissie parked two blocks north of the venue, on Great Jones Street, between a car with its front window broken and a car with its back window broken. But it was under a working street light, which looked to be about as good as it got, short of employing a team of armed guards, or a pack of vicious dogs, or both. And the car would have been no safer left on Washington Square, anyway. So they got out into the heat and walked to the corner through air thick enough to eat. The sky was as hot and hard as an iron roof at noontime, and it was still flickering in the north, with the kind of restless energy that promised plenty and delivered nothing.

There was no line at the door of the club, which Chrissie felt was a good thing, because it meant there would be spots to be had at the front near the stage, just in case it really was the Ramones or Blondie that night. A guy inside took their money, and they moved past him into the heat and the noise and the dark, toward the bar, which was a long low space with dim light and sweating walls and red diner stools. There were about thirty people in there, twenty-eight of them kids no older than Chrissie, plus one person Reacher already knew, and another person he was pretty sure he was going to get to know, pretty well and pretty soon. The one he knew was Jill Hemingway, still thin and blonde and nervous, still in her short summer dress. The one he felt he would get to know looked a lot like Croselli. A cousin, maybe. He was the same kind of size and shape and age, and he was wearing the same kind of clothes, which were a sweated-through suit and a shirt plastered tight against a wet and hairy belly.

Jill Hemingway saw Reacher first. But only by a second. She moved off her stool and took a step and immediately the guy in the suit started snapping his fingers and gesturing for the phone. The barkeep dumped the instrument in front of him and the guy started dialing. Hemingway pushed her way through the thin crowd and came up to Reacher face to face and said, "You idiot."

Reacher said, "Jill, this is my friend Chrissie. Chrissie, this is Jill, who I met earlier this evening. She's an FBI agent."

Beside him Chrissie said, "Hi, Jill."

Hemingway looked temporarily nonplussed and said, "Hi, Chrissie."

Reacher said, "Are you here for the music?"

Hemingway said, "I'm here because this is one of the few places Croselli doesn't get total cooperation. Therefore this is one of the few places I knew he would have to put a guy. So I'm here to make sure nothing happens to you."

"How did you know I would come here?"

"You live in South Korea. What else have you heard of?"

Chrissie said, "What exactly are we talking about?"

Croselli's guy was still on the phone.

Reacher said, "Let's sit down."

Hemingway said, "Let's not. Let's get you the hell out of here."

Chrissie said, "What the hell is going on?"

There were tiny cafe tables near the deserted stage. Reacher pushed through the crowd, left shoulder, right shoulder, and sat down, his back to a corner, most of the room in front of him. Chrissie sat down next to him, hesitant, and Hemingway paced for a second, and then she gave it up and joined them. Chrissie said, "This is really freaking me out, guys. Will someone please tell me what's going on?"

Reacher said, "I was walking down the street and I saw a guy slap Agent Hemingway in the face."

"And?"

"I hoped my presence would discourage him from doing it again. He took offense. Turns out he's a mobster. Jill thinks they're measuring me for concrete shoes."

"And you don't?"

"Seems oversensitive to me."

Chrissie said, "Reacher, there are whole movies about this stuff."

Hemingway said, "She's right. You should listen to her. You don't know these people. You don't understand their culture. They won't let an outsider disrespect them. It's a matter of pride. It's how they do business. They won't rest until they fix it."

Reacher said, "In other words they're exactly the same as the Marine Corps. I know how to deal with people like that. I've been doing it all my life."

"How do you plan to deal with them?"

"By making the likely cost too high. Which it already is, frankly. They can't do anything in here, because they'd be arrested, either by you or the NYPD. Which is too high of a cost. It would mean lawyers and bribes and favors, which they won't spend on me. I'm not worth it. I'm nobody. Croselli will get over it."

"You can't stay in here all night."

"He already tried it on the street, and he didn't get very far."

"Ten minutes from now he'll have six guys out front."

"Then I'll go out the back."

"He'll have six guys there too."

Chrissie said, "You know when I asked you to stick close by me?"

Reacher said, "Sure."

"You can forget that part now, OK?"

Reacher said, "This is nuts."

Hemingway said, "You hit a made man in the head. What part of that don't you understand? That just doesn't happen. Get used to it, kid. And right now you're in the same room as one of his goons. Who just got off the phone."

"I'm sitting next to an FBI agent."

Hemingway said nothing in reply to that. Reacher thought: *NYU. Sarah Lawrence.* Hemingway had never confirmed it either way. He had asked her: How long have you been with the FBI? She had answered: Who says I am?

He said, "Are you or are you not?"

She said nothing.

"It's not real hard. It's a yes or no answer."

"No," she said. "It really isn't."

"What does that mean?"

"It's yes and no. Not yes or no."

Reacher paused a beat.

"What, you're freelancing here?" he said. "Is that it? This isn't really your case? Which is why there was no back-up van? Which is why you were using your little sister's tape player?"

"It was my tape player. I'm suspended."

"You're what?"

"Medical grounds. But that's what they always say. What it means is they took my badge, pending review."

"Of what?"

"Like you said. The lawyers and the bribes and the favors. They're weighing me in the balance. Me against all the good stuff."

"This was Croselli?"

Hemingway nodded. "Right now he's fireproof. He had the investigation shut down. I figured I might get him to boast about it, on the tape. I might have gotten something I could use. To make them take me back."

"Why wasn't Croselli armed in the city?"

"Part of the deal. They all can do what they want in every other way, but the homicide figure has to come down. Give and take. Everyone's a winner."

"Does Croselli know you're suspended?"

"Of course he does. He made them do it."

"So in fact the goon in the same room as me knows it too, right? Is that what we're saying here? He knows you're not about to pull a badge. Or a gun. He knows you're just a member of the public. Legally, I mean. In terms of your powers of arrest, and so on. And less than that, in terms of your credibility. As a witness against Croselli's people, I mean."

"I told you to go see your brother."

"Don't get all defensive. I'm not blaming you. I need to make a new plan, that's all. I need to understand the parameters."

Chrissie said, "You shouldn't have gotten involved in the first place."

"Why not?"

"At Sarah Lawrence we would say it was uncomfortably gender normative behavior. It was patriarchal. It spoke to the paternalistic shape of our society."

"You know what they would say in the Marine Corps?"

"What?"

"They would point out you asked me to stick close by, because you think the Bowery is dangerous."

"It is dangerous. Twelve guys are about to show up and kick your butt."

Reacher nodded. "We should go, probably."

"You can't," Hemingway said. "The goon won't let you. Not until the others get here."

"Is he armed?"

"No. Like I said."

"You sure?"

"Hundred percent."

"Do we agree one opponent is better than twelve?"

"What are you talking about?"

"Wait here," Reacher said.

Reacher walked across the dim room, as graceful as a bulked-up greyhound, with all the dumb confidence a guy gets from being six-five and two-twenty and sixteen years old. He moved on through the bar, toward the restroom corridor. He had been in relatively few bars in his life, but enough to know they were superbly weapons-rich environments. Some had pool cues, all neatly lined up in racks, and some had martini glasses, all delicate and breakable, with stems like stilettos, and some had champagne bottles, as heavy as clubs. But the CBGB bar had no pool table, and its customers were apparently indifferent to martinis and champagne. The most numerous local resource was long-neck beer bottles, of which there were plenty. Reacher collected one as he walked, and out of the corner of his eye he saw Croselli's guy get up and follow him, no doubt worried about rear exits or bathroom windows. There was in fact a rear exit, at the end of the restroom corridor, but Reacher ignored it. Instead he stepped into the men's room.

Which was perhaps the single most bizarre place he had ever seen, outside of a military installation. The walls were bare brick covered in dense graffiti, and there were three wall-hung urinals and a lone sit-down toilet all exposed up on a step like a throne. There was a two-hole metal sink, and unspooled toilet rolls everywhere. No windows.

Reacher filled his empty beer bottle with water from the faucet, for extra weight, and he wiped his palm on his T-shirt, which neither dried his hand nor made his shirt appreciably wetter. But he got a decent grip on the long glass neck, and he held the bottle low down by his leg and he waited. Croselli's guy came in seconds later. He glanced around, first amazed by the decor, then reassured by the lack of windows, which told Reacher all he really needed to know, but at sixteen he still played it by the book, so he asked anyway. He said, "Do we have a problem, you and me?"

The guy said, "We're waiting for Mr. Croselli. He'll be here in a minute. Which won't be a problem for me. But it will be for you."

So Reacher swung the bottle, the water kept in by centrifugal force, and it caught the guy high on the cheekbone and rocked him back, whereupon Reacher whipped the bottle down again and smashed it on the lip of a urinal, glass and water flying everywhere, and he jabbed the jagged broken circle into the guy's thigh, to bring his hands down, and then again into his face, with a twist, flesh tearing and blood flowing, and then he dropped the bottle and shoved the guy in the chest, to bounce him off the wall, and as he came back toward him he dropped a solid head butt straight to the guy's nose. Which was game over, right there, helped a little by the way the guy's head bounced off the urinal on his way to the floor, which all made a conclusive little head-injury trifecta, bone, porcelain, tile, good night and good luck.

Reacher breathed in, and breathed out, and then he checked the view in the busted mirror above the sink. He had diluted smears of the guy's blood on his forehead. He rinsed them off with lukewarm water and shook like a dog and headed back through the bar into the main room. Jill Hemingway and Chrissie were on their feet in the middle of the dance floor. He nodded them toward the exit. They set off toward him and he waited to fall into step. Hemingway said, "Where's the goon?"

Reacher said, "He had an accident."

"Jesus."

They hustled on, through the bar one more time, into the lobby corridor, fast and hot.

Too late.

They got within ten feet of the street door, and then it opened wide and four big guys in sweated-through suits stepped in, followed by Croselli himself. All five of them stopped, and Reacher stopped, and behind him Chrissie and Jill Hemingway stopped, eight people all in a strung-out, single-file standoff, in a hot narrow corridor with perspiration running down the bare brick walls.

From the far end of the line Croselli said, "We meet again, kid."

Then the lights went out.

Reacher couldn't tell if his eyes were open or closed. The darkness was total and profound, like the next stop after nothing. And the darkness was completely silent, way down at some deep primeval level, all the low subliminal hum of modern life suddenly gone, leaving nothing in its place except blind human shufflings and a kind of whispered eerie keening that seemed to come up from ageless rocks below. From the twentieth century to the Stone Age, at the flick of a switch.

From behind him Reacher heard Chrissie's voice say, "Reacher?"

"Stand still," he said.

"OK."

"Now turn around."

"OK."

He heard her feet on the floor, shuffling. He searched his last retained visual memory for where the first of Croselli's guys had stopped. *The middle of the corridor, facing dead ahead, maybe five feet away.* He planted his left foot and kicked out with his right, hard, blindly, aiming groin-high into the pitch-black emptiness ahead. But he hit something lower, making contact a jarring split second before he expected. A kneecap, maybe. Which was fine. Either way the first of Croselli's guys was about to fall down, and the other three were about to trip over him.

Reacher spun around and felt for Chrissie's back, and he put his right arm around her shoulders, and with his left hand he found Hemingway, and he half pulled and half pushed them back the way they had come, to the bar, where a feeble battery-powered safety light had clicked on. Which meant it hadn't been the flick of a switch. The whole building had lost power.

He found the restroom corridor and pushed Chrissie ahead of him and pulled Hemingway behind him, to the rear door, and they barged through it, out to the street.

Which was way too dark.

They hustled onward anyway, fast, out in the heat again, muscle memory and instinct compelling them to put some distance between the door and themselves, compelling them to seek the shadows, but it was all shadows. The Bowery was a pitch-dark and sullen ditch, long and straight both ways, bordered by pitch-dark and sullen buildings, uniformly massive and gloomy, their unlit bulk for once darker than the night sky. The skyline sentinels forty blocks north and south weren't there at all, except in a negative sense, because at the bottom of the sky there were dead fingers where inert buildings were blocking the glow of starlight behind thin cloud.

"The whole city is out," Hemingway said.

"Listen," Reacher said.

"To what?"

"Exactly. The sound of a billion electric motors not running. And a billion electric circuits switched off."

Chrissie said, "This is unbelievable."

Hemingway said, "There's going to be trouble. Give it an hour or so, and there's going to be rioting, and arson, and a whole lot of looting. So you two, right now, head north as far and as fast as you can. Do not go east or west. Do not use the tunnels. Do not stop until you're north of 14th Street."

Reacher said, "What are you going to do?"

"I'm going to work."

"You're suspended."

"I can't stand by and do nothing. And you have to get your friend back where you found her. I think those are our basic obligations." And then she ran, south toward Houston Street, and was lost in the dark within seconds.

The street light on Great Jones was no longer working, but the blue Chevette was still under it, gray and formless in the dark, as yet unmolested. Chrissie opened it up, and they got in, and she started the motor and put it in gear. She didn't turn on the lights, which Reacher understood. Disturbing the massive darkness didn't seem right. Or possible, even. The great city felt stunned and passive, an immense organism laid low, implacable and indifferent to tiny scurrying humans. Of which there was a growing number within view. Windows were opening, and folks on lower floors were walking downstairs and coming out, standing near their doors and peering about, full of wonder and apprehension. The heat was still way up there. It wasn't cooling down at all. A hundred degrees, maybe more, clamping down and now smug and settled and supreme, unchallenged by fans or air conditioning or any other kind of manmade mediation.

Great Jones Street was one-way west, and they crossed Lafayette and Broadway, and continued on West Third, Chrissie driving slow and tentative, not much faster than walking pace, a dark car in the dark, one of very few about. Maybe drivers had felt compelled to pull over, as part of the general paralysis. The traffic lights were all out. Each new block was newly weird, still and silent, blank and gray, absolutely unlit. They turned north on LaGuardia Place, and went counterclockwise around the bottom right-hand corner of Washington Square, back to the coffee shop. Chrissie parked where she had before, and they got out into the soupy air and the silence.

The coffee shop was dark, obviously, with nothing to see behind its dusty glass window. The air conditioner above the door was silent. And the door was locked. Reacher and Chrissie cupped their hands and pressed them to the glass and peered through, and saw nothing except vague black shapes in the dark. No staff. No customers. Maybe a health board thing. If the refrigerators went out, maybe they had to abandon ship.

Reacher said, "Where will your friends have gone?"

Chrissie said, "No idea."

"You said there was a plan."

"If one of us gets lucky, we meet back here at midnight."

"I'm sorry you didn't get luckier."

"I feel OK now."

"We're still south of 14th Street."

"They won't find you in the dark, surely."

"Will we find your friends in the dark?"

"Why would we want to? They'll get back by midnight. Until then we should hang out and experience this. Don't you think? This is pretty amazing."

And it was. There was a hugeness to it. Not just a room or a building or a block, but the entire city, slumped inert and defeated all around them, as if it was ruined, as if it was dead, like a relic from the past. And maybe it was more than just the city. There was no glow on any horizon. Nothing from across either river, nothing from the south, nothing from the north. Maybe the whole Northeast was out. Maybe all of America. Or the whole world. People were always talking about secret weapons. Maybe someone had pulled a trigger.

Chrissie said, "Let's go look at the Empire State Building. We may never see it like this again."

Reacher said, "OK."

"In the car."

"OK."

They went up University, and used Ninth Street across to Sixth Avenue, where they turned north. Sixth Avenue was nothing at all. Just a long black hole, and then a small rectangle of night sky where it ended at Central Park. There were a few cars on it. All were moving slow. Most had their lights off. Like the Chevette. Instinctive, somehow. A shared assumption. Crowd behavior. Reacher caught a sudden whiff of fear. *Hide in the dark. Don't stand out. Don't be seen.*

Herald Square had people in it. Where Broadway cut across, at 34th Street. Most of them were out in the middle of the triangle, away from the buildings, trying to see the sky. Some of them were formed up in moving bunches, like sports fans leaving the stadium after a win, with the same kind of boisterous energy. But Macy's windows were all intact. So far.

They kept going all the way to West 38th, crawling past the dead traffic lights and the cross streets, unsure every time whether they should yield or keep on going, but it turned out there was no real danger of either fender benders or confrontation, because everyone was moving slow and acting deferential, all *after you, no, after you.* Clearly the spirit so far was cooperation. On the roads, at least. Reacher wondered how long it would last.

They went east on 38th and turned on Fifth four blocks north of the Empire State. Nothing to see. Just a broad dark base, like both sides of every other block, and then nothing above. Just spectral darkness. They parked on the Fifth Avenue curb, on the block north of 34th Street, and got out for a closer look. Thirty-fourth was a double-wide street, with a clear view east and west, dark all the way, except for an orange glow in the far distance above what must have been Brooklyn. Fires were burning there.

"It's starting," Reacher said.

They heard a cop car coming north on Madison, and they saw it cross the six-lane width of 34th Street one block over. Its lights looked amazingly bright. It drove on out of sight, and the night went quiet again. Chrissie said, "Why did the power go out?"

"Don't know," Reacher said. "Overload from all the AC, or a lightning strike somewhere. Or the electromagnetic pulse from a nuclear explosion. Or maybe someone didn't pay the bill."

"Nuclear explosion?"

"It's a known side effect. But I don't think it happened. We'd have seen the flash. And depending where it was, we'd have been burned to a crisp."

"What kind of military are you?"

"No kind at all. My dad's a Marine, and my brother is going to be an army officer, but that's them, not me."

"What are you going to be?"

"I have no idea. Probably not a lawyer."

"Do you think your FBI friend was right about riots and looting?"

"Maybe not so much in Manhattan."

"Are we going to be OK?"

Reacher said, "We're going to be fine. If all else fails, we'll do what they did in the olden days. We'll wait for morning."

* * *

They turned onto 34th Street and drove over as close as they could get to the East River. They stopped on a trash-strewn triangle half under the FDR Drive, and they stared through the windshield over the water to the dark lands beyond. Queens dead ahead, Brooklyn to the right, the Bronx way far to the left. The fires in Brooklyn looked pretty big already. There were fires in Queens, too. And the Bronx, but Reacher had been told there were always fires in the Bronx. Nothing behind them, in Manhattan. Not yet. But there were plenty of sirens. The darkness was getting angry. Maybe because of the heat. Reacher wondered how Macy's windows were doing.

Chrissie kept the engine running, for the AC. The gas was about half full. The tails of her shirt hid her shorts completely. She looked like she was wearing nothing else. Just the shirt. Which looked great. She was very pretty. He asked, "How old are you?"

She said, "Nineteen."

"Where are you from?"

"California."

"You like it here?"

"So far. We get seasons. Heat and cold."

"Especially heat."

She asked, "How old are you?"

"I'm legal," he said. "That's really all you need to know."

"Is it?"

"I hope so."

She smiled, and turned off the engine. She locked her door, and leaned over to lock his. She smelled of hot clean girl. She said, "It's going to get warm in here."

"I hope so," he said again. He put his arm around her shoulders and pulled her close and kissed her. He knew how to do it. He had more than three years of practice. He put his free hand on the curve of her hip. She was a great kisser. Warm, wet, plenty of tongue. Closed eyes. He pushed her shirt up a little and ducked his hand under it. She was lean and firm. Hot, and a little damp. She brought her spare hand over and put it under his shirt. She smoothed it up over his side, over his chest, and down to his waist. She put the tips of her fingers under his waistband, which he took to be an encouraging sign.

They came up for air, and then they started again. He moved his free hand to her knee, and slid it up the wondrous smooth skin of her thigh, on the outside, with his thumb on the inside, to the hem of her shorts, and back again, to the other knee, and up her other leg, just as smooth and luscious, his fingers on the inside this time, his thumb on the outside, all the time trying to imagine anything more splendid than the feel of a warm girl's skin, and failing. And this time he went a little further, until his leading finger was jammed against the hard seam between her legs, at the bottom of her zip. She clamped hard on his hand, which at first he took as an admonition, but then he realized she had another purpose in mind, so he kept his hand there, pushing hard as she ground away, almost lifting her off the seat. Then she sighed and gasped and went all rubbery, and they came up for air again, and he moved his crushed hand to the buttons on her shirt, and he tried to make his fingers work. Which they did, reasonably well, one button, two, three, all the way down until her shirt fell open.

They kissed again, the third marathon, and his free hand went to work in a different area, first outside a silky bra, and then inside, from below, until it was all pushed up and her small damp breasts were his. He moved his mouth to her neck, and then to her nipples, and he put his hand back where it had been before, and she started grinding again, long and slow, long and slow, breathing hard, until for a second time she sighed and gasped and fell against him, as if she had no bones in her body.

Then she put a hand on his chest and pushed him away, back toward his window, which again he took as a reproach, until she smiled like she knew something he didn't, and unbuttoned his pants. Slim brown fingers took care of his zip, at which exact point for the first time in his life he truly understood the phrase *died and gone to heaven.* Her head went down into his lap, and he felt cool lips and a tongue, and he closed his eyes, and then he opened them again and stared about, determined to remember every last detail of his situation, the where and the when, and the how, and the who and the why, especially the why, because his conscious mind could find no logical path between the Port Authority bus terminal and what had to be some kind of enchanted kingdom. *New York, New York. It's a wonderful town.* That was for damn sure. So he stared around, locking it all in, the river, the formless boroughs beyond, the distant fires, the wire fences, the bleak concrete pillars holding up the road above.

He saw a man standing thirty yards away in the dark, silhouetted against the glow coming off the water. Mid-twenties, maybe, judging by his posture, medium height, thick in the upper body, a geeky shape to his head, because of uncooperative hair. He had the kind of hair that should have been cut much shorter, but it was 1977. He was holding something in his right hand.

Chrissie was still busy. She was unquestionably the best ever. No comparison. None at all. He wondered if Sarah Lawrence was coed. He could go there. Just as good as NYU. Not that they were likely to get married or anything. But maybe she had friends. Or a sister. In fact he knew she had friends. The two blondes. *They'll wait. That's part of the deal.* They had two hours until midnight, which suddenly seemed like nothing at all.

The guy moved in the dark. He rolled around a pillar, light on his feet, staying covered, checking the blind spot at ninety degrees, checking the other direction, and then moving forward, fast and straight to the next pillar.

Toward the Chevette.

The guy eased around the new pillar, just to check his new blind spot, and then he pulled back and merged with the concrete, barely visible again, all the time being very careful with the thing in his hand, as if it was valuable or especially fragile.

Chrissie was still busy. And she was doing a fine, fine job. Died and gone to heaven wasn't even close. It was an underestimate of the most serious kind. Egregious, even. It was the kind of faint praise that could cause a diplomatic incident.

The guy moved again. He went through the same routine, reflexively, glance, glance, move, to the next pillar, closer still to the Chevette, and he blended in, bringing his right arm to rest last, solicitous of the thing he was holding, taking care not to bring it into contact with the concrete.

Thereby bringing it separately through the river's glow, all by itself.

Reacher knew what it was.

It was an upside down revolver, swinging by the trigger guard on the guy's right-hand index finger. A squat shape, thick in the upper body like the guy himself, rounded in the grips, a two-and-a-half-inch barrel, smooth, with few projections. Could have been a Charter Arms Bulldog, a five-shooter, sturdy, most often chambered for the .44 Special. Double action. Easy to service. Not a target shooter's gun. But good close up.

Chrissie was still busy. The guy moved again. Closer still to the Chevette. He stared right at it. Before he had gotten on the bus in Pohang Reacher's mother had made him read her newspapers. New York City. A killing spree. The Son of Sam. Named from his crazy letters. But before the letters came he had been called something else. He had been called the .44 Caliber Killer. Because he used .44 caliber bullets. From a revolver.

Specifically, the NYPD said, from a Charter Arms Bulldog.

Chrissie was still busy. And this was no kind of a time to stop. No kind of a time at all. In fact stopping was not a possibility. Physically, mentally, every other way. It was absolutely not on the agenda. It was in a whole different hemisphere than the agenda. Maybe a whole different universe. It was a biological fact. It was not going to happen. The guy stared. Reacher stared back. *He's killing people. Couples sitting in cars.* Way to go, Reacher thought. Do it now. I'll go out on a high note. The highest possible note in the whole history of high notes. *Jack Reacher, RIP. He died young, but he had a smile on his face.*

The guy made no move. He just stared.

Reacher stared back.

The guy made no move.

Couples sitting in cars.

But they weren't. Not from an exterior perspective. Chrissie's head was in his lap. Reacher was alone in the car. Just a driver, off the road in the emergency, waiting in the passenger seat, for the extra legroom. The guy stared. Reacher stared back. Chrissie was still busy. The guy moved on. To the next pillar, and the next, and then he was lost to sight.

And then Chrissie's work was done.

Afterward they repaired the damage as well as they could, straightening and zipping and buttoning and combing. Chrissie said, "Better than Blondie?"

Reacher said, "How could I tell?"

"Better than Blondie live on stage at CBGB, I mean."

"A lot better. No real comparison."

"You like Blondie, right?"

"Best ever. Well, top five. Or ten."

"Shut up." She started the engine again and put the air on max. She slid down in her seat and lifted her shirt tails so the vents blew straight up against her skin.

Reacher said, "I saw someone."

"When?"

"Just now."

"Doing what?"

"Peering into this car."

"Who?"

"Some guy."

"For real? That's kind of creepy."

Reacher said, "I know. And I'm real sorry, but I have to go find Jill Hemingway. I should tell her first. She needs some favors."

"Tell her what?"

"What I saw."

"What did you see?"

"Something she should know about."

"Was it one of Croselli's guys?"

"No."

"So how is it important?"

"She might be able to use it."

"Where is she?"

"I have no idea. Let me out in Washington Square and I'll walk. I bet she's north of Houston."

"You would be going right back in there, where we got chased out before."

"Let's call that phase our reconnaissance."

"What would you do this time?"

"Fastest way to find Hemingway is to look for Croselli."

"I'm not going to let you."

"How could you stop me?"

"I would tell you not to. I'm your girlfriend. At least until midnight."

"Is this what they teach you at Sarah Lawrence?"

"Pretty much."

"Works for me," Reacher said. "We'll just hang out, see if she comes by."

"Really?"

"I mean it."

"Why?"

"Laws of physics. A random encounter doesn't get more likely just because both parties are moving."

"OK, where?"

"Let's say the corner of Bleecker and Broadway. That might make the encounter less random."

"That's way down there."

"It's a block from Houston. We can break out south if we need to."

"We?"

"Was it you who wanted me to stick close by?"

"This is a whole different type of crazy."

Reacher nodded.

"I understand," he said. "I really do. It's your choice. You can let me out in Washington Square. That would be fine. Don't think I'll ever forget you."

"Really?"

"If I'm done before midnight, I'll come say good-bye."

"I mean, really, you won't forget me? That's very sweet."

"Also very true. As long as I live."

Chrissie said, "Tell me more about the guy you saw."

Reacher said, "I think it was the Son of Sam."

"You *are* crazy."

"I'm serious."

"And you just sat there?"

"Seemed like the best thing to do."

"How close did he get?"

"About twenty feet. He had a good look, and he walked away."

"The Son of Sam was twenty feet from me?"

"He didn't see you. I think that's why he walked away."

She glanced all around in the dark and put the car in gear. She said, "The Son of Sam is an NYPD case, not the FBI."

Reacher said, "Whoever passes on a tip gets a brownie point. I imagine that's how it works."

"What's the tip?"

"The way he moved."

There were more sirens behind them. First Avenue, Second Avenue, uptown, downtown, crosstown, there were plenty of cops on the streets. The mood was changing. Reacher could taste it on the air.

"I'll come with you," Chrissie said. "For the experience. These are the big things we'll always remember."

* * *

They used 34th Street again, back toward the center of the island, back toward the heart of darkness. The city was still pitch black, still dead, like a giant creature fallen on its back. There were broken windows. There were people roaming in groups, carrying stuff. There were police cars and fire trucks speeding through the streets, all lit up and whooping and barking, but their lights didn't make much impression on the blackness, and their sirens didn't seem to worry the roaming people. They merely scuttled into doorways as the cars and trucks passed. The people reminded Reacher of tiny nighttime organisms working on a corpse, penetrating its skin, exploring it, disassembling it, feeding off it, recovering its nutrients, recycling its components, like a dead whale feeds a million sea creatures on the ocean bed.

They turned south on Fifth Avenue at the Empire State Building and drove slowly in the middle lane, passing knots of people in the roadway, two of whom were carrying a rolled-up carpet, three of whom were loading the trunk of a big battered car with something in boxes. They veered left onto Broadway at 23rd Street, past the ghostly Flatiron Building, and they continued south, around Union Square, across 14th Street, into enemy territory, and onward. The mayhem got a little worse the further south they went. Broadway looked narrow, like a dark trench through a dark landscape, and there were busted windows, and people everywhere, moving in groups, fast and furtive and silent, barely visible at all, except for the glow of cigarettes. They passed 4th Street, and 3rd, where they had been before, and Chrissie started to slow the car, and Reacher said, "Change of plan. I think Sixth Avenue and Bleecker might be better."

Chrissie said, "Why?"

"What is Croselli worried about right now?"

"Getting his stuff ripped off. Like anyone. If he has stuff."

"I think he does. I mean, how does he earn money between Houston and 14th? Maybe protection rackets and hookers and so on, but dope for sure. He must have a stash somewhere. But where? Not in an ancestral home in Little Italy, because that's way south of Houston."

"You know the geography pretty well."

"I've studied it from afar. And he walked west from Waverly. After the slapping incident. Toward Sixth Avenue. Obviously he was heading back to make his phone calls. About me. So his HQ must be west of Waverly."

"You think Hemingway knows where it is?"

"I'm sure she does. And I'm sure she's watching it, right now. I'm assuming no one gave her an actual role tonight, because she's suspended. So she's still freelancing. I bet she's hoping some bunch of guys busts down Croselli's door, so she can get a record of what's inside. Maybe she'll even get Croselli defending it, which would be pretty much a slam dunk, wouldn't it? Doesn't matter what kind of deal he made. Some things can't be ignored."

"It will be more than just Croselli defending it. He's got twelve guys."

"Ten now," Reacher said. "Two of them are in the

hospital. Or trying to get there. But we'll keep out of their way. It's Hemingway we want."

"Hard to find one woman in the dark."

"All we can do is try."

So they rolled onward, toward Houston Street, past a big stereo store with two busted windows and not much left inside, and they made the right and crept west, past the dark wasteland streets of Soho coming in from the left, Mercer, and Greene, and Wooster, and West Broadway, and Thompson, and Sullivan, and MacDougal. Then they turned right on Sixth, and headed north a block to where Bleecker and Downing and Minetta all met in an untidy little six-way split. Retail was down-market and scruffy in that location, some of it too scruffy even for looters, some of it already busted wide open and stripped. Looking north, Sixth was the same long black hole it had been before, with the same slim upright rectangle of night sky at the end of it.

Chrissie said, "Should I park here?"

Reacher said, "Let's cruise a few blocks."

"You said we would hang out and let her come to us."

"Mission creep. Occupational hazard. Like the Navy transporting the Marines."

"I'm an English major."

"Just five minutes, OK?"

"OK," she said.

But they didn't need five minutes. They were done in barely sixty seconds. They made the tight left onto Downing, and a right on Bedford, and a right on Carmine, back toward Bleecker again, and in a doorway on the right side of the street Reacher caught a flash of pale skin and blonde hair, and he pointed, and Chrissie jammed to a stop, and Jill Hemingway stepped out of the dark and bent down to Reacher's window, like a Seoul streetwalker talking to an enlisted man.

Reacher expected Hemingway to be mad at his reappearance, but she wasn't. He figured she felt exposed. Or caught out in her own obsession. Which she was, basically. And she looked a little sheepish about it.

He asked, "Is his place near here?"

She pointed through the car at a pair of large blank doors across the street. They were tall and wide. Like a wagon entrance, from long ago, big enough for a cart and a team of horses. In the daylight the paint might have looked dark green. Set into the right-hand door was a judas gate, big enough for a person. Presumably the doors would lead to an interior ground-floor yard. It was a two-story building. Offices above, possibly. Or storerooms. Behind the building was a bigger building, blank and dark and massive. A brick church of some kind, maybe.

Reacher asked, "Is he in there?"

Hemingway nodded.

Reacher asked, "With how many others?"

"He's alone."

"Really?"

"He runs protection rackets. Among other things. So now he has to deliver. His guys are all out, watching over his clients."

"I didn't know protection rackets worked that way. I thought they were just extortion, plain and simple."

"They are, basically. But he needs to maintain some kind of credibility. And he needs to keep his best cash cows in business. There's a lot of damage being done tonight. Plenty of places are going to go under. No more payoffs from them. And a wise man keeps an eye on his cash flow."

Reacher turned and looked at the doors. "You hoping someone will break in?"

"I don't know what's taking them so long. That's the problem with junkies. No get-up-and-go."

"What has he got in there?"

"A little of everything. He keeps his inventory low because he's got the New Jersey Turnpike and the Holland Tunnel for rapid resupply, which is apparently what they teach you in business school now, but still, I bet there's a week's worth in there."

"Are we in the way? Should we go park somewhere else?"

"You should go home. This isn't your business."

"I need to talk to you."

"About what?"

"The Son of Sam."

"Croselli isn't enough for you?"

"I saw him."

"Who?"

"I saw a man carrying a Charter Arms Bulldog and peering into cars."

"Are you serious?"

"It was our car he peered into."

"Where?"

"The East River, at 34th Street."

Hemingway said, "You know guns, right? Being a Marine and all?"

"Son of a Marine," Reacher said. "It was the right gun."

"It's pitch dark."

"The moon and the stars and the water."

Hemingway ducked down another inch and looked across Reacher at Chrissie. "Did you see it too?"

Chrissie said, "No."

"How come?"

"I wasn't looking."

Hemingway said, "I don't know what to do. OK, let's say we have a confirmed sighting, but so what? We already know the Son of Sam is in New York. That's the point of the guy. It adds no new information. You'd need something more. You'd need to know who he is. Do you?"

"No," Reacher said. "But I know what he used to be."

They parked on Bleecker, intending to walk back and join Hemingway in her doorway hideout, but suddenly Bleecker had people on it, some of them in groups, some of them in pairs, some of those groups and pairs carrying stuff too heavy for comfort, and therefore consequently looking for alternative modes of transportation, such as small hatchback cars, each one apparently ideal for hauling a large television. Reacher and Chrissie were a yard out of the Chevette, with the doors closed but not locked, when the staring match started. Two guys, staggering under an enormous box, with Sony written on it upside down. They came in a straight line, eyeballing the Chevette all the way, and Reacher said, "Keep walking, guys."

The guy on the left was a shadowy grunting figure, and he said, "Suppose we don't?"

"Then I'll kick your butt and steal your television."

"Suppose you drive us?"

"Just keep walking," Reacher said.

They didn't. They eased the box carefully to the ground and stood up again, breathing deep, two dark figures in the dark. Even from six feet away it was hard to make out detail, but their hands hadn't gone to their pockets yet, which was a good sign. It meant any upcoming combat was likely to be unarmed, which was reassuring. Reacher had grown up in a culture of extreme violence, it being hard to describe the U.S. Marine Corps any other way, and he had taken its lessons on board, with the result that he hadn't lost a fight in more than ten years, against Corps kids from the same culture, and against rivalrous local youth all around the world, who liked to think the U.S. military was nothing special, and who liked to try to prove it by proxy, usually unsuccessfully. Two punks on a blacked-out New York City street were unlikely to prove an unprecedented problem, unless they had knives or guns, which was unknowable at that point.

The guy on the right said, "Maybe we'll take the girl with us. Maybe we'll have ourselves some fun."

The guy on the left said, "Just give us the keys and no one gets hurt."

Which was the moment of decision. Surprise was

always good. Delay was always fatal. Guys who let a situation unfold in its own good time were just stock-piling problems for themselves. Reacher ran at the left-hand guy, two choppy steps, like an infielder charging a grounder, and he didn't slow down. He ran right through the guy, leading with his forearm held horizontal, jerking his elbow into the guy's face, and as soon as he felt the guy's nose burst open he stamped down and reversed direction around the box and went after the second guy, who flinched away and took Reacher's charging weight flat in the back. The guy pitched forward like he had been hit by a truck, and Reacher kicked him in the head, and the guy lay still.

Reacher checked their pockets. No knives, no guns, which was usually the case. But it had been their choice. They could have kept on walking. He hauled the right-hand guy next to the left-hand guy, close to-gether, shoulder to shoulder, and he picked up the heavy box like a strongman in the circus, struggling and tottering, and he took two short steps and dropped it on their heads from waist height.

Chrissie said, "Why did you do that?"

"Rules," Reacher said. "Winning ain't enough. The other guy has to know he lost."

"Is that what they teach you in the Marine Corps?"

"More or less."

"They'll wreck the car when they wake up."

"They won't. They'll throw up and crawl home. By which time you'll be long gone anyway."

So Chrissie locked up, and they walked back through the heat to where Hemingway was waiting on Carmine. Reacher said, "No progress?"

Hemingway said, "Not yet."

"Maybe we should go recruit someone. There are plenty of people on Bleecker."

"That would be suborning a felony."

"Means to an end."

"Tell me what you meant about the guy with the Bulldog."

"Can you use it?"

"Depends what it is."

"It was dark," Reacher said. "Obviously."

"But?"

"He was in his mid-twenties, I would say, medium height, heavy in the chest and shoulders, quite pale, with wavy hair that wouldn't lie down."

"Carrying a .44 Bulldog?"

"Most Bulldogs are .44s. But I don't have X-ray vision."

"How far away was he?"

"Twenty feet, at one point."

"How long were you eyeballing him?"

"Twenty seconds, maybe."

"Twenty seconds at twenty feet," Hemingway said. "In a blackout? That's a tough sell. I bet there have been a thousand reports tonight. People freak out in the dark."

"He was a trained man," Reacher said.

"Trained how?"

"The way he moved through the available cover. He's ex-military. He's had infantry training."

"So have lots of guys. You ever heard of Vietnam?"

"He's too young. This guy was of age six or seven years ago. The draft was winding down. You had to be pretty unlucky. And I don't think he was ever in combat. I've seen lots of people back from Vietnam. They're different. This guy was all theory and training. Second nature, for sure, pretty slick, but he had never lived or died by it. I can guarantee that. And I don't think he was a Marine. They're different too. I think he was army. And I think he's been in Korea. It was like a fingerprint. I think he did basic, and infantry, with the urban specialization, and I think he served in Seoul. Like a particular combination. That's how he looked. I see it all the time. You ever been there? Seoul teaches you to move a certain way. But he's been out at least two years, because of the hair, and he's had time to get a bit heavy. I think he volunteered at eighteen or nineteen, and I think he served a three-year hitch. That was my impression, anyway."

"That's one hell of a detailed impression."

"You could offer it as a filter. They could see if any persons of interest match up."

"It was twenty seconds in the pitch dark."

"What else have they got?"

"Maybe I could."

"Suppose it worked? Suppose they get the guy? Would that be good for you?"

"Of course it would."

"So what's the downside?"

"Sounding desperate and pathetic."

"Your call."

"You should try it," Chrissie said. "Someone needs to catch the guy."

Hemingway said nothing.

* * *

They waited, all crammed together in the doorway opposite Croselli's place, with absolutely nothing happening. They heard sirens, and snatches of conversation from people passing by on Bleecker. Like headline news. It was now only ninety degrees. The lights had gone out at Shea in the bottom of the sixth, with the Mets trailing the Cubs by two to one. Subway riders had spent scary hours trapped underground, but were slowly making their way back to the surface. Cars were using chains and ropes to tear the shutters off stores. Even Brooks Brothers on Madison had been looted. Crown Heights and Bushwick were on fire. Cops had been hurt and arrests had been made.

Then the last of the passersby moved on and Carmine went quiet again and the clock in Reacher's head ticked around toward midnight. He said to Chrissie, "I'll walk you back to your car. Your friends will be waiting."

She said, "Are you staying here?"

"Might as well. I already missed my bus."

"Do you think the roads are open?"

"Wide open. They want people to leave."

"Why?"

"Fewer mouths to feed here."

"Makes sense," Chrissie said. They walked together to the corner, and around it, where the Chevette waited undisturbed. The two guys were still laid out in the roadway, under the box. Like a cartoon accident. They were still breathing.

Reacher said, "Want me to ride with you?"

"No," Chrissie said. "We go back alone. That's part of the deal."

"You know how to go?"

"Up on Sixth and across on 4th. And then it's right there."

"Roger that."

"Take care, OK?"

"I will," Reacher said. "You too. I'll never forget you."

"You will."

"Check back next year, see if I have."

"OK. Let's see who remembers. Same night, same place. Deal?"

"I'll be there," Reacher said.

She got into the car, and she eased away from the tangle of limbs behind her, and she made the left on Sixth, and she waved through her open window. And then she was gone.

Hemingway said, "I'm going to put it in the system. Your impression, I mean. That's the smart play here. They'll ignore it, of course, but it will be in the record. I can say told you so, afterward. If you're right. That's always worth a point or two. Sometimes more. Being right afterward can be a wonderful thing."

"It's a filter," Reacher said. "That's all. It's about efficiency."

"But I still need Croselli."

"The Son of Sam wouldn't get you out of jail?"

"I need Croselli."

"Why?"

"Because he burns me up."

"You ever read a book called *Moby-Dick*?"

"OK, I get it. And I admit it. Croselli is my great white whale. I'm obsessed. But what can I do about it? What could anyone, with a whale pressing on her head?"

"Is that how you feel? Like you have a whale pressing on your head?"

"That's exactly how I feel."

"Then let's trade," Reacher said.

"What for what?"

"I need a ride out of town."

"When?"

"As soon as possible. I'm sure my brother is worrying about me. Which I'm sure is hard on the old guy. I need to put him out of his misery."

"I'm not a taxi dispatcher."

"You have a car."

"I'm not a chauffeur, either."

"You could lend it to me."

"How would I get it back?"

"I don't know."

"Do you even have a license?"

"Not exactly."

"No deal," she said.

"OK," Reacher said.

"What were you going to do for me?"

"Suppose an unknown suspect broke into Croselli's place, and you got a look inside. Then the unknown suspect fled, but you were too busy securing the scene to chase him."

"I've been waiting two hours for that to happen. But it hasn't."

"I could do it."

"You're sixteen years old."

"How is that relevant?"

"Entrapment is bad enough. Entrapment with minors is probably worse."

"Who would ever know, apart from you and me?"

"I have no way of getting you a ride out of town."

Reacher paused a beat, and said, "Maybe we should refine the plan."

"What plan?" Hemingway said. "We don't have a plan."

"Probably better if it's not you who makes the discovery. It could look like a personal vendetta. It could give Croselli's lawyers something to work with. Probably better if it's not even the FBI at all. Better if it's the NYPD. Don't you think? An independent agency, with no ax to grind. If they discover a dope dealer and his stash in their city, then it's out there. It can't be denied. It is what it is. Your people will have to hush up their deal, and they'll have to admit you were right all along, and you can turn your review procedure into a medal ceremony."

"The NYPD is busy tonight."

"They have a narcotics division, surely. Make the call ahead of time. Get a sense of how long they're going to be, and we'll try to time it exactly right. I'll bust in, you hang back and keep an eye on things for a minute until the cops show up, and then we'll both slip away, and you can drive me north. Meanwhile the NYPD will be building your case for you, and by the time you're back in town your bosses will be rolling out the red carpet."

"How far north do you want to go?"

"West Point. It's up the river a ways."

"I know where it is."

"So do we have a deal?"

Hemingway didn't answer.

Hemingway finally agreed about thirty minutes later, close to one o'clock in the morning. But the plan went wrong immediately. First they couldn't find a working phone. They searched up and down Carmine, and they tried the corner of Seventh Avenue, and the corner of Bleecker, and Sixth Avenue, and every payphone they found was silent. They didn't know if it was the result of the blackout, or just the general abject state of the city. Reacher figured the phone company had its own electricity, in its own wires, so he was all in favor of carrying on the search, but Hemingway was reluctant to foray further, in case she missed something over at Croselli's place. So she walked back to the doorway on Carmine and Reacher went on alone, across Sixth, and on the corner between Minetta Street and Minetta Lane he found a phone with a dial tone.

It was too dark to see the numbers, so he dialed by feel, zero for the operator, and he waited a long time before she answered. He asked for the NYPD's Sixth Precinct, and waited again, even longer, before the call was picked up and a voice barked, "Yes?"

Reacher said, "I want to report illegal narcotics in the West Village."

The voice said, "What?"

"There's a storeroom full of drugs on Carmine just been bust open."

"Any dead bodies?"

"No."

"Anyone currently in the act of getting killed?"

"No."

"Fire?"

"No."

The voice said, "Then stop wasting my time," and the phone went dead. Reacher hung up and hustled back, sweating, ninety degrees at one in the morning, and he relayed the news to Hemingway, who nodded in the dark and said, "We should have seen that coming. I guess they're all hands on deck right now."

"We might have to use your own people."

"Forget it. They wouldn't take my call."

Reacher said, "Still got your little sister's cassette recorder?"

"It's my cassette recorder."

"Still got it?"

"Why?"

"Maybe I can get him to boast on the tape."

"You?"

"Same principle. You can't let this look like a vendetta."

"I can't let you. You and him, face to face? I have a conscience."

"What's he going to do to me?"

"Beat you to death."

"He's a made man," Reacher said. "He has soldiers. Which means he tells other people to do the heavy lifting. Which means he's out of practice. He's all hat and no cattle. He's got nothing. We already saw that on Waverly. Any twelve-year-old in the Philippines could eat his lunch."

"Is this a Marine Corps thing?"

"I'm not a Marine."

"How would you get in?"

"I assume the church behind him is locked."

"Tonight for sure. If not every night."

"I'll figure something out."

"How would the military do it?"

"Marines or army?"

"Army."

"They'd call in artillery support. Or air-to-ground."

"Marines?"

"They'd start a fire, probably. That usually brings them out real fast."

"You can't do that."

"I'm not a Marine," Reacher said again. He looked across the street. The second-story windows were dark, obviously. Which meant Croselli could be right there, watching. But without seeing much. A man in a dark room watching a lit street had an advantage. A man in a dark room watching a dark street might as well have saved himself the eyestrain.

Reacher crossed the dark street, to the double doors. He put his fingertips on them. They felt like sandpaper. Fifty-year-old paint, plus fifty years of smoke and grime and dust. He tapped, first with his fingernails, then gently with his knuckles. The wood felt old and thick and solid, like it had been shipped a hundred years before, from some ancient forest out west. He slid his palms across the surface, until he found the judas gate. Same paint, same grime, same wood. He felt for the hinges, and didn't find any. He felt for the lock, and rubbed it with his thumb. It seemed to be a small round Yale, worn brass, probably as old as the paint.

He headed back to Hemingway. He said, "The doors are probably two or three inches thick, and the judas gate is all of a piece. All quality lumber, probably hard as a rock by now."

"Then maybe the army way is the only way."

"Maybe not. The judas gate opens inward. The lock is an old Yale, put in maybe fifty years ago. I'm guessing they didn't chase out a void in the door. Not in wood that hard. Not back then. People weren't so uptight about security. I bet the lock is surface-mounted on the back. Like an old house. The tongue is in a little surface-mounted box. Two screws, is all."

"There will be another door. Out of the yard, into the building. Might have a newer lock."

"Then I'll knock and rely on charm."

"I can't let you do this."

"It's the least I can do. I screwed you up before. You might have gotten something. You were going to take that slap and keep him talking."

"He had already found the wire."

"But he's arrogant. He's got an ego. He might have carried on regardless, just to taunt you."

"That's what I was hoping."

"Then let me put it right."

* * *

Reacher turned around and lifted his shirt and bared his back to Hemingway. He felt hot fingers scrabbling at his waistband, gapping it out, fitting the plastic box behind the elastic on his shorts. Then he felt the scrape of a wire, and her hand burrowed up his back, under his shirt, to his shoulder blade, and then on over the top, a curious vertical embrace, her breath on his neck, and then she turned him around again to face her, and her other hand went up the front of his shirt, to find the microphone, to pass it from hand to hand, and to pull it down into place. She stopped with it trapped against his chest, and she kept her hand there, flat, nothing between her palm and his skin except the small pebble of technology.

She said, "I put it in my bra. But you don't have one."

"Imagine that," Reacher said.

"There's nothing to keep it in place."

Reacher felt an immediate film of sweat between his chest and her hand. He said, "Got a Band-Aid in your purse?"

"You're a smart kid," she said, and she went into a one-hand-two-elbows contortion to root through her bag, and as she craned her neck to look downward into it her forehead touched his lips, just briefly, like a kiss. Her hair was limp, but it smelled like strawberries.

She jerked her bag back up on her shoulder and held up something that crackled slightly. A Band-Aid, he assumed, still in its hygienic wrapper. He took it from her and peeled it open in the space between their faces. Then in turn she took it back from him one-handed and used it to tape the microphone in the trench between his chest muscles. She smoothed the adhesive, once, twice, and then she took her hands out from under his shirt and pulled it down into place.

She put her palm on his chest, like Croselli had put his on hers, pressing hard on the damp cotton, and she said, "He'll find it."

"Don't worry," Reacher said. "If he puts his hands on me, I'll beat him to death."

Hemingway said nothing.

Reacher said, "That's a Marine Corps thing."

The darkness didn't help. It didn't help at all. Reacher lined up on the opposite curb, like a sprinter at the start of a race, but he couldn't exactly see where he was heading. Adjustments were going to be necessary as he ran. He took off, slow and clumsy, partly because of the dark, partly because he was a terrible runner, with long lumbering strides, and three paces out he saw the doors, and two paces out he saw the judas gate, and with one pace to go he saw its lock, and he launched his leading foot in a scything kick, slightly across his body, and he smashed his heel as close to the small Yale circle as he could get, with all his two hundred and twenty pounds behind it, multiplied significantly by the final acceleration of his foot, and by the fact that his whole bulk was moving briskly, if not exactly fast.

But it was enough. The judas gate exploded inward,

with what felt like no resistance at all, and Reacher hurtled through the resulting blank rectangle into a space so dark he could make out nothing at all. There was the feel of cobblestones under his feet, and the sour smell of garbage, and sheer dark walls rising on his left and his right and ahead.

He felt his way along the right-hand wall to the back corner of the yard, where he found a door. Ridged glass above, a panel below, a smooth steel handle, and a lock that felt newer. The glass was probably tempered and reinforced with wire. The lock was probably chased into the door and the jamb. A whole different proposition.

He waited, to see if Croselli would come down and open it himself. Which he might. He must have heard the crash of the judas gate. But he didn't come down. Reacher waited three minutes, breathing hard, stretching his eyes wide open, willing them to see something. But they didn't. He stepped up to the door again and traced its shape with his hands. The panel below the glass would be the weak spot. Plywood, probably, maybe three-eighths thick, painted, retained in the frame by quarter-round moldings. Reacher was wearing shoes he had bought in the London airport two deployments ago, stout British things with welts and toecaps as hard as steel. They had busted heads and kneecaps already that night. Plywood wasn't going to be a major problem.

He stepped back and poked forward with his toe to fix his target in his mind. Then he kicked out, *bang, bang,* concentrating on the corners of the panel, viciously and noisily, until the wood splintered and the moldings came loose.

Then he stopped and listened.

No sound from inside the building.

Which was a bitch. Reacher would have preferred to meet Croselli face to face on the ground floor. He didn't relish heading up a flight of stairs toward an alert opponent at the top.

He waited some more.

No sound.

He squatted down with his back against the door-frame and punched out the panel with his elbow, until it folded inward, like a miniature door itself, hinged on a few surviving nails. Then he twisted around and put his arm and his shoulder through the hole and reached up and scrabbled for the knob. Which he found easily enough. He had arms like a gorilla. Every childhood photograph of him featured six inches of bare wrist, at the end of every sleeve.

The door opened and he struggled upright and backed off a yard, just in case. But there was no sound inside. Croselli didn't come out. There was nothing to see. Just darkness. The inside air smelled hot and stale.

Reacher stepped in, to what felt like a narrow lobby with a tiled floor. He slid his feet ahead, one after the other, and he felt a bottom stair. There was a handrail on the left. The opposite wall was less than three feet away. It was painted, and it was damp with condensation.

Reacher went up the stairs, his right hand out in front of him, his left holding the handrail. There was a yard-wide half landing, and then the stairs dog-legged and continued upward. At the top was dusty superheated air and a six-by-three upstairs lobby with a sticky carpet and a door at each end. A front room, and a back room.

Under the back room door was a bar of faint warm light.

Reacher stared at it, like a thirsty man in the desert might stare at a cold drink. It was a candle, probably. It was the first manmade light he had seen in more than three hours.

He put his hand under his shirt at the back and pushed the button Hemingway had shown him. *It's red,* she had said, which hadn't helped, because he didn't have eyes in the back of his head, and it was pitch dark anyway. So he had learned it by feel. He tapped his chest, so that a thump could mark the start of the recording. Then he put his hand on the door-knob.

Reacher twisted the knob and pushed the door, one, two, fast and hard, and he stepped into a room lit by a guttering candle. The flame danced in the rush of air. The room was a twenty-by-twenty space with a dark window in the back wall, and a row of old-fashioned safes on the left, like something out of a black-and-white Western movie about bank robbers, and on the right there was a row of file cabinets and a desk, and sitting at the desk in a leather reclining chair was Croselli. The chair was pushed out and turned sideways, so that he was sitting face-on to the door.

He had a gun in his hand.

It was a Colt M1911, a .45 automatic, standard military issue for sixty-six years, hence the model number. It looked a little scratched and battered. It was all lit up by the candle, which was on the desk, welded to a china plate by a pool of its own wax. A standard household item, a few cents at the hardware store, but it felt as bright as the sun.

Croselli said, "You."

Reacher said nothing.

Croselli had shed his jacket and pulled down his tie, but his shirt was still wet. He said, "I was expecting Hemingway. What are you tonight, her knight in shining armor? Is she sending a boy to do a man's job?"

Is he armed? Reacher had asked. *Not in the city*, Hemingway had said. *He can't afford to be.* Not applicable inside his own premises, apparently. Which was a bitch. Reacher looked at the row of safes. There were six of them, shoulder to shoulder, each one about a yard wide and six feet tall. They had keyholes, not combination locks. The door on the far end was wide open, and the void behind it was empty. Their armory, Reacher guessed. For dire emergencies. Like that very night. Clearly Croselli's soldiers were all armed, all out on the street, all ensuring protection.

"You have a gun," Reacher said, for the tape.

"I'm defending my property," Croselli said.

"This is your place?"

"I'm not a common burglar."

Reacher took a step. The Colt's muzzle rose a degree, to track him. Reacher asked, "Is your name on the title?"

"I'm not that stupid."

"Then this isn't your place."

"Only technically. Believe me, kid, everything you see here is mine."

"What's in the safes?"

"Inventory."

"Yours?"

"I already told you."

"I need to hear it in short simple words."

"Why?"

"We could do business."

"Business?"

"That's what I said."

"You and me?"

"If you're smart," Reacher said.

"You broke down my door."

"Would you have let me in, if I had knocked?"

"What kind of business could we do, you and I?"

"You're using the New Jersey Turnpike and the Holland Tunnel. Which means you're getting supplied out of Miami, all the way up I-95. Which means you're paying over the odds, and you're losing some to unreliable mules, and you're losing some to routine New Jersey State Police patrols. I could help you with all of that."

"How?"

"I bring stuff in direct from the Far East. On military planes. No scrutiny. My dad's a Marine officer."

"What kind of stuff?"

"Anything you want."

"What kind of price, kid?"

"Show me what you've got and tell me what you paid. Then I'll break your heart."

"You hurt two of my men."

Reacher said, "I hope so. I need you to understand. You do not mess with me." He took another step. The Colt's muzzle rose another degree. Reacher said, "Are you buying from Martinez?"

"I never heard of Martinez."

"Then you're way over the odds already. Who are you buying from?"

"The Medellin boys."

"I could save you forty percent."

Croselli said, "I think you're full of shit. I think this is a Hemingway stunt."

"You shut her down."

"For which I paid good money. For which I expected a durable result. Anything else is liable to make me angry."

"This has nothing to do with Hemingway."

"Pull up your shirt."

"Why?"

"I want to see the wire. Before I shoot you."

Reacher thought: *unregistered guns, a deceptive real estate title, a straight-up reference to the Medellin cartel out of Colombia, and a straight-up reference to bribery.* The tape had enough. He took a deep, deep breath and put his hands on the hem of his T-shirt. Then he jerked forward from the waist and blew out the candle.

* * *

The room went from softly glowing to blacker than the Earl of Hell's winter coat all in a split second, and Reacher blundered straight ahead, forcing passage between Croselli's chair and the desk, and Croselli whipped the Colt around in the same general direction and fired. But he missed by a mile, and the muzzle flash backlit him perfectly, like a photographer's strobe, so Reacher picked his spot and slammed a straight right into the back of his neck, right where soft turns to hard, and Croselli pitched head first out of the chair and landed on his knees. Reacher groped for the chair and lifted it high by the armrests and slammed it down on Croselli's back. He heard the sound of steel on linoleum as the Colt skittered away, and he brushed the chair aside and groped and patted blindly until he found the collar of Croselli's shirt, which he bunched in his left hand while he pounded away with his right, short roundhouse punches to the side of Croselli's head, his ear, his jaw, *one, two, three, four,* vicious clubbing blows, until he felt the steam go out of the guy, whereupon he reached forward and grabbed the guy's wrists and yanked them up behind his back, high and painful, and he clamped them together in his left hand, human handcuffs, a party trick perfected years before, enabled by the freakish strength in his fingers, from which no one had ever escaped, not even his brother, who was of equal size, or his father, who was smaller but stronger. He hauled Croselli to his feet and slapped at his pants pockets until he heard the jingle of keys. Croselli got his second wind and started struggling hard, so Reacher turned him a little sideways and quieted him down again with a pile-driver jab to the kidney.

Then he fished out the keys and held them in his right hand, and he asked, "Where's your book of matches?"

Croselli said, "You're going to die, kid."

"Obviously," Reacher said. "No one lives forever."

"I mean tonight, kid."

Reacher separated a key by feel and pressed the point high on Croselli's cheek. He said, "If so, you won't see it happen. I'll take your eyes out first."

"Matches in the desk drawer," Croselli said.

Reacher turned him again and slammed a short right to his stomach, to fold him over and keep him preoccupied, and he walked him bent over and puking to the desk, and he used his free hand to rattle open the drawers, and to root around, all by feel. There was all kinds of stuff in the drawers. Staplers, pens, rolls of Scotch tape, some in dispensers, pencils, paper clips. And a book of matches, a little limp and damp.

Using a matchbook one-handed was practically impossible, so Reacher turned Croselli toward the window wall, let go of his wrists, and shoved him hard, and used the resulting few undisturbed seconds to detach a match and strike it, all fizzing and flaring in the dark, and to light the candle with it once again, by which time Croselli was shaping up for a charge, so Reacher stepped toward him and dropped him with a right to the solar plexus, just as the room bloomed back to its former cozy glow.

A solar plexus was worth at least a minute, Reacher

thought, and he used that minute to cross the room and pick up the Colt, and to dump its magazine, and to eject the shell from its chamber, and to pick up the chair, and to set it back on its casters, and to turn it just so, and to find the Scotch tape, and to pick the guy up, and to dump him in the chair, and to start taping his wrists to the frame.

Scotch tape was weaker than duct tape, but Reacher made up for it with length, around and around, right hand, left hand, until the guy looked like he had two broken wrists, in casts made of some kind of new see-through yellowish plaster. Then came his ankles. In all Reacher used six whole rolls of tape, and after that there was no way the guy was moving.

Then Hemingway came in the door.

She looked at the candle first, and then at Croselli.

Reacher said, "He admits on tape everything here is his."

She said, "I heard a gunshot."

"He missed. It was about twenty degrees off on the port side."

"I was worried."

"It's the godfather who should worry. This is a made man."

"What did he say on the tape?"

"Take it out of my pants and listen for yourself."

Which she did. Reacher felt the hot quick fingers again, and the weird embrace, under his shirt, as the microphone was passed from hand to hand. Then she clicked and waited and clicked again, and a thin tinny version of Croselli's voice filled the room, taking responsibility for everything in it, admitting to the

Medellin connection, admitting to the bribe, and hinting at the size of it.

She said, "You have his keys?"

Reacher said, "Right here in my hand."

"Open the safe doors."

Which he did, starting next to the empty armory, working away from the window, until all of the safes stood open. All of them were full of smooth-packed plastic-wrapped bricks, some brown or green in color, most white or yellow.

She said, "Can you get his keys back in his pocket?"

He did, and said, "What next?"

"Does his phone work?"

He tried it, and said, "Yes."

She gave him a number and said, "It's our internal credible threat hotline."

He called it in, the exact address, without giving his name, and then the call ended, and she said, "Their response time will be more than five minutes but less than ten."

She put her plastic cassette recorder on the floor near Croselli's feet. She said, "We should go. My car is not close."

Reacher said, "Is this enough?"

She said, "More than enough. Medellin is toxic. And the evidence is right here. It's a photograph, Reacher. This is a photogenic prosecution. It doesn't matter who he bribed. No one is ever going to say a word against this one. It's a tidal wave."

"One last thing," Reacher said, and he turned back to Croselli, and he said, "Slapping women is not permitted. You're supposed to be a man, not a pussy."

Croselli said nothing.

Reacher raised his hand. "How would you like it?"

Croselli said, "You wouldn't hit a guy tied to a chair."

Reacher said, "Watch me," and slapped the guy in the face, hard, a real *crack*, wet or not, and the chair went up on its side legs, and balanced, and balanced, and tottered, and then thumped down on its side, with its casters spinning and Croselli's head bouncing around like a pinball.

Then they hit the bricks, and Hemingway's prediction of five-to-ten came true, in that they saw hurrying cars about six minutes out, and then a pair of heavy trucks. A lot of firepower. And why not, for a credible threat?

Hemingway's car was four blocks away, on Sullivan. It was the mid-blue Granada Reacher had seen before, with the vinyl roof and the toothy grille. He said, "You sure this gets you off the hook?"

She said, "Count on it, kid. Being right afterward is a wonderful thing."

"Then give me a ride out of town."

"I should stay."

"Give them time to grieve. Give them time to figure out how it's really their own idea. I've seen this shit before. All organizations are the same. You need to lay low for a day. You need to be out of the spotlight."

"West Point?"

"Take the Thruway and the Tappan Zee."

"How long will I be gone?"

"They're going to roll out the red carpet, Jill. Just give them time to find it first."

They drove a long, long time in the dark, and then they hit neighborhoods with power, with traffic lights and street lights and the occasional lit room. Billboards were bright, and the familiar nighttime background of orange diamonds on black velvet lay all around.

Hemingway said, "I have to stop and call."

Reacher said, "Call who?"

"The office."

"Why?"

"I have to know whether it worked."

"I'm sure it did."

"I have to know."

"So stop. We could get a cup of coffee."

"It's a hundred degrees."

"Got to be less than ninety now."

"Still too hot for coffee." She pulled over to the right-hand lane, and then she took an exit road to what Reacher imagined was a superpower version of the standard type of highway facility, with multiple restrooms, and gas big enough for trucks, and motel rooms for weary drivers, and not just something to eat, but a restaurant big enough to feed Syracuse. And payphones. There was a long line, right outside the restaurant's extensive and brightly-lit windows. Hemingway used one, and hung up smiling, and said, "It's working. Croselli has been arrested."

He asked, "How's the whale?"

She said, "The whale is gone."

She looked dazed for a second, and then she got a big smile on her face, and they hugged, with some kind of relief and ecstasy in her tight embrace. Reacher felt bony ribs, and the flutter of her heart. It was beating fast.

Then she moved to another phone and dialed another number, and she gave her name, and she dictated a long report about a confirmed sighting of the Son of Sam, made by what she called a confidential informant, who had what she called extensive military experience.

Then she hung up again and said, "This will sound crazy, but I really want to rent a room just to take a shower."

Reacher said, "Doesn't sound crazy to me."

"Does it matter what time you get there?"

"Not within a shower or two."

"So let's do it."

"Both of us?"

"It's a mutual benefit."

"Who goes first?"

"I go first."

"OK," Reacher said.

She paid at the motel office, a visible wad of bills, what Reacher figured must be the whole-night rate, and she came back with a key, to room 15, which was located way in back, the last cabin before the woods. Reacher said, "Do you want me to wait in the car?"

Hemingway said, "You can wait in the room."

So they went in together, and found a hot stale space, with the usual features. Hemingway checked the bathroom, and came out with a bunch of towels, and said, "These are yours," and then she went back in and closed the door.

Reacher waited on the bed until she came out again much later, all hot and pink and wrapped in towels. She said, "Your turn," and she crossed the room, a little unsteady on her feet, as if overcome by steam, or exhaustion.

He said, "You OK?"

She said, "I'm fine."

He paused a beat, and then he went in the bathroom, which was as steamy as a sauna, with the mirror all fogged up, showing the swipes and arcs where the maid had cleaned it. He stripped and hung his limp clothes on a hook, and he started the shower and set it warm, and he stepped into the tub and pulled the curtain. He soaped up and used the shampoo, and he scrubbed and rinsed, and he stood under the warm stream for an extra minute, and then he got out.

Getting dry was not really an option, given the temperature and the humidity. He moved the moisture around his skin with a towel, and he put his old clothes back on, damp and snagging, and he combed his hair with his fingers. Then he stepped out in a billow of moisture.

Jill Hemingway was flat on her back on the bed. At first he thought she was sleeping. Then he saw her eyes were open. He took her wrist and felt her pulse.

Nothing there.

He tried her neck.

Nothing there.

Her eyes stared up at him, blank and sightless.

Medical reasons. Her heart, he thought. No doubt a cause of concern. He had felt it racing and fluttering. He had seen her stagger. He crossed the room and stared out the window. Still the dead of night. Through the trees he could see lights from cars on the highway. He could hear their sound, faint and constant. He crossed back to the bed and checked again, wrist, neck, nothing.

He stepped out to the lot and closed the door behind him, and hiked over to the line of payphones outside the restaurant. He chose one at random and dialed the number she had given him, for the internal hotline. He reported her death, said it looked natural, and gave the location.

He didn't give his name.

Jill Hemingway, RIP. She died young, but she had a smile on her face.

He walked on, to the gas plaza, past the car pumps, past the truck pumps, to the exit road. He kept one foot in the traffic lane, and rested the other on the curb, and he stuck out his thumb. The second car to pass by picked him up. It was a Chevrolet Chevette, baby blue, but it wasn't Chrissie's. It was a whole different car altogether, driven by a guy in his twenties who was heading for Albany. He let Reacher out at an early exit, and a dairyman in a pick-up truck took him onward, and then he walked a mile to the turn that led up to the Academy. He ate in a roadhouse, and he walked another mile, and he saw West Point's lights up ahead, far in the distance. He figured no one would reveille before 0600, which was still two hours away, so he found a bus bench and lay down to sleep.

* * *

The day after the blackout power was restored in part of Queens at seven in the morning, followed by part of Manhattan shortly afterward. By lunchtime half the city was back. By eleven in the evening the whole city was back. The outage had been caused by a maintenance error. A lightning strike in Buchanan, New York—part of the long summer storm Reacher had seen in the distance—had tripped a circuit breaker, but a loose locking nut had prevented the breaker from closing again immediately, as it was designed to do. As a consequence, a cascade of trips and overloads had rolled south over the next hour, until the whole city was out. By morning, more than sixteen hundred stores had been looted, more than a thousand fires had been set, more than five hundred cops had been injured, and more than four thousand people had been arrested. All because of a loose nut.

Twenty-eight days after the blackout the Son of Sam was captured outside his home on Pine Street, Yonkers, New York, less than four miles from Sarah Lawrence College. His year-long killing spree was over. His name was David Berkowitz, and he was twenty-four years old. He was carrying his Charter Arms Bulldog in a paper sack. He confessed to his crimes immediately. And he confirmed he had volunteered for the U.S. Army at age eighteen, and had served three years, partly inside the continental U.S., but mostly in South Korea.

Personal

Chapter 1

Eight days ago my life was an up-and-down affair. Some of it good. Some of it not so good. Most of it uneventful. Long slow periods of nothing much, with occasional bursts of something. Like the army itself. Which is how they found me. You can leave the army, but the army doesn't leave you. Not always. Not completely.

They started looking two days after some guy took a shot at the president of France. I saw it in the paper. A long-range attempt with a rifle. In Paris. Nothing to do with me. I was six thousand miles away, in California, with a girl I met on a bus. She wanted to be an actor. I didn't. So after forty-eight hours in LA she went one way and I went the other. Back on the bus, first to San Francisco for a couple of days, and then to Portland, Oregon, for three more, and then onward to Seattle. Which took me close to Fort Lewis, where two women in uniform got out of the bus. They left an

Army Times behind, one day old, right there on the seat across the aisle.

The *Army Times* is a strange old paper. It started up before World War II and is still going strong, every week, full of yesterday's news and sundry how-to articles, like the headline staring up at me right then: *New Rules! Changes for Badges and Insignia! Plus Four More Uniform Changes On The Way!* Legend has it the news is yesterday's because it's copied secondhand from old AP summaries, but if you read the words sideways you sometimes hear a real sardonic tone between the lines. The editorials are occasionally brave. The obituaries are occasionally interesting.

Which was my sole reason for picking up the paper. Sometimes people die and you're happy about it. Or not. Either way you need to know. But I never found out. Because right next to the obituaries are the personal ads. Which as always were mostly veterans looking for other veterans. Dozens of ads, all the same.

Including one with my name in it.

Right there, center of the page, a boxed column inch, five words printed bold: *Jack Reacher call Rick Shoemaker.*

Which had to be Tom O'Day's work. Which later on made me feel a little lame. Not that O'Day wasn't a smart guy. He had to be. He had survived a long time. A very long time. He had been around forever. Twenty years ago he already looked a hundred. A tall, thin, gaunt, cadaverous man, who moved like he might collapse at any moment, like a broken stepladder. He was no one's idea of an army general. More like a professor. Or an anthropologist. Certainly his thinking had been sound. *Reacher stays under the radar, which means buses and trains and waiting rooms and diners, which, coincidentally or not, is the natural economic habitat for enlisted men and women, who buy the* Army Times *ahead of any other publication in the PX, and who can be relied upon to spread the paper around, like birds spread seeds from berries.*

And he could rely on me to pick up the paper. Somewhere. Sooner or later. Eventually. Because I needed to know. You can leave the army, but the army doesn't leave you. Not completely. As a means of communication, as a way of making contact, from what he knew, and from what he could guess, then maybe he would think ten or twelve consecutive weeks of personal ads might generate a small but realistic chance of success.

But it worked the first time out. One day after the paper was printed. Which is why I felt lame later on.

I was predictable.

Rick Shoemaker was Tom O'Day's boy. Probably his second in command by now. Easy enough to ignore. But I owed Shoemaker a favor. Which O'Day knew about, obviously. Which was why he put Shoemaker's name in his ad.

And which was why I would have to answer it.

Predictable.

Seattle was dry when I got out of the bus. And warm. And wired, in the sense that coffee was being consumed in prodigious quantities, which made it my kind of town, and in the sense that wifi hotspots and handheld devices were everywhere, which didn't, and which made old-fashioned street-corner payphones hard to find. But there was one down by the fish market, so I stood in the salty breeze and the smell of the sea, and I dialed a toll-free number at the Pentagon. Not a number you'll find in the phone book. A number learned by heart long ago. A special line, for emergencies only. You don't always have a quarter in your pocket.

The operator answered and I asked for Shoemaker and I got transferred, maybe elsewhere in the building, or the country, or the world, and after a bunch of clicks and hisses and some long minutes of dead air Shoemaker came on the line and said, "Yes?"

"This is Jack Reacher," I said.

"Where are you?"

"Don't you have all kinds of automatic machines to tell you that?"

"Yes," he said. "You're in Seattle, on a payphone down by the fish market. But we prefer it when people volunteer the information themselves. We find that makes the subsequent conversation go better. Because they're already cooperating. They're invested."

"In what?"

"In the conversation."

"Are we having a conversation?"

"Not really. What do you see directly ahead?"

I looked.

"A street," I said.

"Left?"

"Places to buy fish."

"Right?"

"A coffee shop across the light."

"Name?"

I told him.

He said, "Go in there and wait."

"For what?"

"For about thirty minutes," he said, and hung up.

No one really knows why coffee is such a big deal in Seattle. It's a port, so maybe it made sense to roast it close to where it was landed, and then to sell it close to where it was roasted, which created a market, which brought other operators in, the same way the automakers all ended up in Detroit. Or maybe the water is right. Or the elevation, or the temperature, or the humidity. But whatever, the result is a coffee shop on every block, and a four-figure annual tab for a serious enthusiast. The shop across the light from the payphone was representative. It had maroon paint and exposed brick and scarred wood, and a chalkboard menu about ninety percent full of things that don't really belong in coffee, like dairy products of various types and temperatures, and weird nut-based flavorings, and many other assorted pollutants. I got a plain house blend, black, no sugar, in the middle-sized go-cup, not the enormous *grande* bucket some folks like, and a slab of lemon pound cake to go with it, and I sat alone on a hard wooden chair at a table for two.

The cake lasted five minutes and the coffee another five, and eighteen minutes after that Shoemaker's guy showed up. Which made him Navy, because twenty-eight minutes was pretty fast, and the Navy is right there in Seattle. And his car was dark blue. It was a low-spec domestic sedan, not very desirable, but polished to a high shine. The guy himself was nearer forty than twenty, and hard as a nail. He was in civilian clothes. A blue blazer over a blue polo shirt, and khaki chino pants. The blazer was worn thin and the shirt and the pants had been washed a thousand times. A Senior Chief Petty Officer, probably. Special Forces, almost certainly, a SEAL, no doubt part of some shadowy joint operation watched over by Tom O'Day.

He stepped into the coffee shop with a blank-eyed all-in-one scan of the room, like he had a fifth of a second to identify friend or foe before he started shooting. Obviously his briefing must have been basic and verbal, straight out of some old personnel file, but he had me at *six-five two-fifty*. Everyone else in the shop was Asian, mostly women and very petite. The guy walked straight toward me and said, "Major Reacher?"

I said, "Not anymore."

He said, "Mr. Reacher, then?"

I said, "Yes."

"Sir, General Shoemaker requests that you come with me."

I said, "Where to?"

"Not far."

"How many stars?"

"Sir, I don't follow."

"Does General Shoemaker have?"

"One, sir. Brigadier General Richard Shoemaker, sir."

"When?"

"When what, sir?"

"Did he get his promotion?"

"Two years ago."

"Do you find that as extraordinary as I do?"

The guy paused a beat and said, "Sir, I have no opinion."

"And how is General O'Day?"

The guy paused another beat and said, "Sir, I know of no one named O'Day."

The blue car was a Chevrolet Impala with police hubs and cloth seats. The polish was the freshest thing on it. The guy in the blazer drove me through the downtown streets and got on I-5 heading south. The same way the bus had come in. We drove back past Boeing Field once again, and past the Sea-Tac airport once again, and onward toward Tacoma. The guy in the blazer didn't talk. Neither did I. We both sat there mute, like we were in a no-talking competition and serious about winning. I watched out the window. All green, hills and sea and trees alike.

We passed Tacoma, and slowed ahead of where the women in uniform had gotten out of the bus, leaving their *Army Times* behind. We took the same exit. The signs showed nothing ahead except three very small towns and one very large military base. Chances were therefore good we were heading for Fort Lewis. But it turned out we weren't. Or we were, technically, but we wouldn't have been back in the day. We were heading for what used to be McChord Air Force Base, and was now the aluminum half of Joint Base Lewis-McChord. Reforms. Politicians will do anything to save a buck.

I was expecting a little back-and-forth at the gate, because the gate belonged jointly to the army and the Air Force, and the car and the driver were both Navy, and I was absolutely nobody. Only the Marine Corps and the United Nations were missing. But such was the power of O'Day we barely had to slow the car. We swept in, and hooked a left, and hooked a right, and were waved through a second gate, and then the car was right out there on the tarmac, dwarfed by huge C-17 transport planes, like a mouse in a forest. We drove under a giant gray wing and headed out over open blacktop straight for a small white airplane standing alone. A corporate thing. A business jet. A Lear, or a Gulfstream, or whatever rich people buy these days. The paint winked in the sun. There was no writing on it, apart from a tail number. No name, no logo. Just white paint. Its engines were turning slowly, and its stairs were down.

The guy in the blazer drove a well-judged part-circle and came to a stop with my door about a yard from the bottom of the airplane steps. Which I took as a hint. I climbed out and stood a moment in the sun. Spring had sprung and the weather was pleasant. Beside me the car drove away. A steward appeared above me, in the little oval mouth of the cabin. He was wearing a uniform. He said, "Sir, please step up."

The stairs dipped a little under my weight. I ducked into the cabin. The steward backed off to my right, and on my left another guy in uniform squeezed out of the cockpit and said, "Welcome aboard, sir. You have an all–Air Force crew today, and we'll get you there in no time at all."

I said, "Get me where?"

"To your destination." The guy crammed himself back in his seat next to his co-pilot and they both got busy checking dials. I followed the steward and found a cabin full of butterscotch leather and walnut veneer. I was the only passenger. I picked an armchair at random. The steward hauled the steps up and sealed the door and sat down on a jump seat behind the pilots' shoulders. Thirty seconds later we were in the air, climbing hard.

Chapter 2

I figured we turned east out of McChord. Not that there was much choice. West was Russia and Japan and China, and I doubted such a small plane had that kind of range. I asked the steward where we were going, and he said he hadn't seen the flight plan. Which was obvious bullshit. But I didn't push it. He turned out to be a chatty guy on every other subject. He told me the plane was a Gulfstream IV, confiscated from a bent hedge fund during a federal proceeding, and reissued to the Air Force for VIP transportation. In which case Air Force VIPs were lucky. The plane was terrific. It was quiet and solid, and the armchairs were sensational. They adjusted every which way. And there was coffee in the galley. A proper drip machine. I told the guy to keep it going, but that I would go back and forth myself, for refills. He appreciated that. I think he took it as a mark of respect. He wasn't really a steward, obviously. He was some kind of a security escort, tough enough to get the job, and proud I knew it.

I watched out the window, first at the Rockies, which had dark green trees low down and blinding white snow high up. Then came the tawny agricultural plains, in tiny mosaic fragments, plowed and sowed and harvested, over and over again, and not rained on much. By the look of the land I figured we clipped the corner of South Dakota and saw a bit of Nebraska before setting out over Iowa. Which because of the geometric complexities of high altitude flight meant we were likely aiming some ways south. A Great Circle route. Weird on a flat paper map, but just right for a spherical planet. We were going to Kentucky, or Tennessee, or the Carolinas. Georgia, even.

We droned on, hour after hour, two full pots of coffee, and then the ground got a little closer. At first I thought it was Virginia, but then I figured it was North Carolina. I saw two towns that could only be Winston-Salem and Greensboro. They were on the left, and receding a little. Which meant we were heading southeast. No towns until Fayetteville. But just before that came Fort Bragg. Which was where Special Forces HQ was located. Which was Tom O'Day's natural economic habitat.

Wrong again. Or right, technically, but in name only. We landed in the evening dark at what used to be Pope Air Force Base, which had since been given away to the army. Now it was just Pope Field, just a small corner of an ever-bigger Fort Bragg. Reforms. Politicians will do anything to save a buck.

We taxied a long time, tiny on tarmac big enough for airlift squadrons. Eventually we stopped near a small administrative building. I saw a sign that said 47TH LOGISTICS, TACTICAL SUPPORT COMMAND. The engines shut down and the steward opened the hatch and lowered the steps.

"Which door?" I said.

"The red one," he said.

I went down the steps and walked ahead through the dark. There was only one red door. Not old and dusty, but freshly painted. Still shiny. It opened when I was six feet from it. A young woman in a black skirt suit came out. Dark nylons. Good shoes. A very young woman. She had to be still in her twenties. She had blonde hair and green eyes and a heart-shaped face. Which had a big warm welcoming smile on it.

She said, "I'm Casey Nice."

I said, "Casey what?"

"Nice."

"I'm Jack Reacher."

"I know. I work for the State Department."

"In D.C.?"

"No, here," she said.

Which made some kind of sense. Special Forces were the armed wing of the CIA, which was the hands-on wing of the State Department, and some decisions would require all three fingers in the same pie all at once. Hence her presence on the base, young as she was. Maybe she was a policy genius. Some kind of a prodigy. I said, "Is Shoemaker here?"

She said, "Let's go inside."

She led me to a small room with a wired-glass window. It had three armchairs in it, none of them matching, all of them a little sad and abandoned. She said, "Let's sit down."

I said, "Why am I here?"

She said, "First you must understand everything you hear from this point onward is a classified secret. There will be a severe penalty for a breach of security."

"Why would you trust me with secrets? You never met me before. You know nothing about me."

"Your file has been circulated. You had a security clearance. It was never revoked. You're still bound by it."

"Am I free to leave?"

"We'd prefer you to stay."

"Why?"

"We want to talk to you."

"The State Department?"

"Did you agree to the part about classified secrets?"

I nodded. "What does the State Department want with me?"

"We have certain obligations."

"In what respect?"

"Someone took a shot at the president of France."

"In Paris."

"The French have appealed for international cooperation. To find the perpetrator."

"It wasn't me. I was in LA."

"We know it wasn't you. You're not on the list."

"There's a list?"

She didn't answer that, except to reach high up between her jacket and her blouse and pull out a folded sheet of paper, which she handed to me. It was warm from her body, and slightly curved. But it wasn't a list. It was a summary report from our embassy in Paris. From the CIA Head of Station, presumably. The nuts and bolts of the thing.

The range had been exceptional. An apartment balcony fourteen hundred yards away had been identified as the rifleman's hide. Fourteen hundred yards is more than three-quarters of a mile. The French president had been at an open-air podium behind wings of thick bulletproof glass. Some kind of improved material. No one had seen the shot except the president himself. He had seen an impossibly distant muzzle flash, small and high and far to his left, and then more than three whole perceptible seconds later a tiny white star had appeared on the glass, like a pale insect alighting. A long, long shot. But the glass had held, and the sound of the bullet's impact against it had triggered an instant reaction, and the president had been buried under a scrum of security people. Later enough bullet fragments had been found to guess at a .50 caliber armor-piercing round.

I said, "I'm not on the list because I'm not good enough. Fourteen hundred yards is a very long way, against a head-sized target. Three whole seconds. Like dropping a stone down a well."

Casey Nice nodded and said, "The list is very short. Which is why the French are worried."

They hadn't been worried immediately. That was clear. According to the summary report they had spent the first twenty-four hours congratulating themselves on having enforced such a distant perimeter, and on the quality of their bulletproof glass. Then reality had set in, and they had lit up the long-distance phones. Who knew a sniper that good?

"Bullshit," I said.

Casey Nice said, "What part?"

"You don't care about the French. Not this much. Maybe you would make some appropriate noises and get a couple of interns to write a term paper. But this thing crossed Tom O'Day's desk. For five seconds, at least. Which makes it important. And then you had a SEAL on my ass inside twenty-eight minutes, and then you flew me across the continent in a private jet. Obviously both the SEAL and the jet were standing by, and obviously you had no idea where I was or when I would call, so you must have had a whole bunch of SEALs and a whole bunch of jets standing by, here, there and everywhere, all over the country, day and night. Just in case. And if it's me, it's others too. This is a full-court press."

"It would complicate things if it was an American shooter."

"Why would it be?"

"We hope it isn't."

"What can I do for you that's worth a private jet?"

Her phone rang in her pocket. She answered and listened and put it back. She said, "General O'Day will explain. He's ready to see you now."